THE BONES OF PARADISE

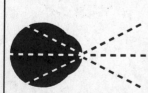

THE BONES OF PARADISE

JONIS AGEE

THORNDIKE PRESS
A part of Gale, Cengage Learning

GALE
CENGAGE Learning·

Farmington Hills, Mich • San Francisco • New York • Waterville, Maine
Meriden, Conn • Mason, Ohio • Chicago

GALE
CENGAGE Learning°

LIBRARY OF CONGRESS CATALOGING-IN-PUBLICATION DATA

Names: Agee, Jonis, author.
Title: The bones of paradise / by Jonis Agee.
Description: Large print edition. | Waterville, Maine : Thorndike Press, 2016. |
  Series: Thorndike Press large print western
Identifiers: LCCN 2016040092| ISBN 9781410495488 (hardcover) | ISBN 1410495485
  (hardcover)
Subjects: LCSH: Large type books. | GSAFD: Western stories.
Classification: LCC PS3551.G4 B66 2016b | DDC 813/.54—dc23
LC record available at https://lccn.loc.gov/2016040092

Published in 2016 by arrangement with William Morrow, an imprint of HarperCollins Publishers

Printed in Mexico
1 2 3 4 5 6 7 20 19 18 17 16

For Ross Agee

One realizes that human relationships are the tragic necessity of human life.

— WILLA CATHER

ACKNOWLEDGMENTS

My gratitude goes to Brent Spencer, my husband, for offering a home for my imagination and my heart; to my daughter, Brenda, for coming home when it mattered most; to Nora for bringing joy and laughter to our family when we needed it; to my sisters, Jackie and Cindy B. and Cindy A.; to my nephews and nieces, who hold the future, Talbot, Travis, Mike, Ross, Blythe, Tara, Ashton, and Laura; to my friends Mollie and Terry Foster, Gillian Howell, Leslie Adrienne Miller, Tom Redshaw, Elizabeth Redshaw, Lon Otto, Jim Cihlar and Bill Reichard, Diana Hopkins, Greg Hewett and Tony Hainault, Tim Schaffert and Rodney Rahl, Dave Madden and Neal Nuttbrock, Gwen Foster and Wheeler Dixon, Carla and Randy Stout, and Sharon and Teddy Warner; to Rebecca Rotert and Bud Shaw, neighbors and writers par excellence; to Noah Ballard for encouragement; to Mad

Jack Hill and Ian Rogers, who dug me out from the hailstorm so I could write; to Micah Hansen, who keeps me riding right; to Joni, whose bright smile lightens the day; and to Alexandra Kafka, who does it all at my house. A special thanks to my students over the years, who continue to inspire me with their extraordinary talent and generous spirits. Thanks to Laura Cherkas for her meticulous copyediting. Thanks to Heid Erdrich for her careful reading. I am especially grateful to my agent, Emma Sweeney, who is the best friend a writer and animal lover could have! You believed in this book. And finally, I thank my editor, Jessica Williams, for her vision and support in seeing this novel to its completion. You made it happen!

■ ■ ■ ■

PART ONE:
WHERE BRIGHT
ANGELS HAVE TROD

■ ■ ■ ■

CHAPTER ONE

It was midmorning in early May when J. B. Bennett crested the hill, stopped, and surveyed the little Sand Hills meadow where the windmill was slowly clanking in a wobbly circle. The metal rubbing on metal in an uneven cadence made him reach for the small tin of grease in his saddlebag, the one he already knew he'd pulled out yesterday and left sitting on the window ledge in the toolshed when he'd repacked his saddlebags for the trip to his father's ranch this morning. It was getting to be harder to keep track of every little detail. He wasn't that old, he reasoned, but then he had the boy and the twenty thousand acres and the men and the cattle. He lifted his hand and let it drop back to the saddle horn. It was the other thing that drove his mind these days.

He reached in his shirt pocket and pulled out the photograph he'd recovered from his son's dresser drawer a few hours ago. God

13

only knew where Hayward had disappeared to. The picture showed his wife, Dulcinea, as she'd been in 1880 when she came to Nebraska: fresh-faced and fiercely happy, her long auburn hair barely contained by a ribbon, her hand shading her eyes as if she could see as far down the years as it would take to find him again and punish him for what he'd done. The wind was blowing so hard that day, he remembered praying that she wouldn't notice the fine grit from the Sand Hills that found its way into every crevice and seasoned your food. That night as they lay out in their bedrolls she teased him about the sand between his toes after they'd made love. It wasn't their first time. That had happened when they agreed to marry at her parents' home in Chicago. By the time they bedded their first night on their new ranch in a new land, her initial shyness was replaced by a light teasing he found delightful. He grimaced now. When had he ever used that word, but that was her effect on him: she brought a new language with her and made it his.

He wondered if Hayward would miss the picture of his mother. This one had been lovingly preserved, wrapped in a pale blue silk scarf that must have been hers, and bedded carefully in a stack of his old baby clothes, hand-me-downs from his older brother, Cullen.

J.B. couldn't even think Cullen's name without wincing, while the staggering whine-clank of the windmill seemed to grate harder on his ears. Today he was determined to find Cullen and bring him home, Drum be damned. He gathered the reins in his fist and the young chestnut horse lifted its head and pawed, impatient with the rider who paused too long.

"Goddamn you, Drum." J.B. cursed his father as part of the chain of thoughts that had become his burden of late. For years he'd managed to work himself to such exhaustion he couldn't begin to think, moving from dark to dark in a state of rigid sleeplessness and pain. When Hayward cried, he was comforted by a woman J.B. hired from town, or lately the wife of his foreman. It wasn't enough, of course. Dulcinea was the shadow beside him every minute of the day. So often as not he ended up in a place like this meadow this morning, the site of the picnic where she'd told him she was pregnant with their first child and they'd made love on a blanket slowly and carefully though she said there was no worry. His only experience the animals he'd cared for, which made his inquiries awkward and ridiculous. He blushed at the thought of how it made her laugh when he asked if she had been in heat of late. She was so happy then. They both were. He brushed the picture with his lips and tucked it safely in his pocket.

He gazed at the hills covered with the mint green of bluestem and grama grass among last year's taller dried stalks that would gradually collapse and disappear as spring progressed. DROUGHT OVER! the *Omaha Herald* proclaimed after a winter of snow and spring rains. PROSPERITY ON 1900 HORIZON! A new patch of low-lying prickly pear cactus had sprung up beyond the windmill and water tank. He'd have the men dig it out. It was a constant battle to hang on to the grass, the only thing to support the cattle that made his living. A person had to keep his eye on the smallest detail while the vast emptiness constantly tugged at his vision. You can get lost in a heartbeat out here, he'd told his wife. It took him most of his life to realize the significance of his own words. For some reason this morning every little thought was like a handful of nettles, stinging and chiding him as he tried to drop it and move past.

Better to make a list of chores, keep a running tally. He took a deep breath. To the left of the tank the ragged edge of grass gave way to the pale sand beneath, where a small herd of his cattle had sheltered in the late spring snowstorm last week. Trapped by the drifts, they had eaten the grass down to its roots and churned up the sand so thoroughly nothing would grow there again unless he could anchor it.

The sun felt good on his face, warm, not burning yet, and the wind wasn't pushing against his skull so hard he could barely think either. He shifted in the saddle, lifted his hand again, and shook his head. Couldn't keep his mind on business at all this morning. The horse reached around and nudged his boot toe with its nose as if to say, come on. Still he didn't move. Something held him back, as if once he went down that hill, everything in his life would be different and he couldn't say why, and it wasn't only the business with Cullen. He had this feeling a lot lately, and it was beginning to worry him. Maybe it was just age, but he thought of his father, Drum, who seemed sharper, more driven as he grew older. Meaner. Old bastard. That's what the men called him when they didn't think J.B. was listening. J.B. called him worse than that when he didn't think they were listening.

It was twenty years almost to the day since J.B. married and took ownership of this land. He looked across the hills in the direction of the main house nestled in a valley and accessible by wagon from the main north-south road only during good weather; otherwise it was a long trip by horseback to go around the gumbo mudflats and low spots that made small lakes out of the road soon as any kind of weather arrived. J.B. had chosen the place with a purpose in mind — to be as far from Drum as possible when he managed to bargain the twenty thousand acres off him. The one part of the bargain he hadn't told his wife the day he met her at the train in North Platte proved to be their undoing. When she stepped off the train, a young woman of eighteen looking for a western adventure on a real cattle ranch and willing to marry an unlikely candidate in the Nebraska Sand Hills, he decided to wait. But as soon as he held his first baby boy, he knew he'd made a terrible mistake.

He and Dulcinea were always together in the beginning, overseeing the building of their brick house made from their own clay deposit on the river that ran through their land. It took more time, but they were terrified of the prairie fires that could sweep down on them with no warning. They'd lived in a rotted timber lean-to that first summer, using dried dung or kerosene toted from town in fifty-gallon drums to cook on the large stove that would eventually become the central feature of their kitchen. Maybe if he had a good year now, cattle prices held, he could offer to buy one of those premade houses out of the Sears, Roebuck catalogue. Maybe she'd see that as a peace offering. A brand-new house. He rubbed his chin, the stubble already starting though he carefully shaved each morning in case she changed her mind and showed up again. First she'd moved to Babylon, then on to Cody, Rushville, and Chadron, towns along the east-west road across the top of the Sand Hills, then she'd come back to Babylon, gone to Chicago visiting her people, then up to Rosebud to teach. Would she stay away for good this time, furious that he refused to send Hayward to live with her in town for school as the other ranch families were starting to do?

Once in a while, when he got the sense she might be near, he shaved of an evening, too, and would catch the reflection of his son Hayward watching him in the shadow of the doorway, face expressionless. That was another thing he had to do. Get that boy to talk to him. Two years ago when the Trans-Mississippi Exposition opened in Omaha, Hayward begged to go, but J.B. had to say no. He hadn't the heart or nerve to admit how close to losing the ranch they were, so he said no and that was final. The boy hadn't spoken more than ten words a year since. But boys his age — what was he now? Fifteen? Sixteen? Seventeen? Was there a birthday J.B. forgot? Had his mother written or arranged to meet?

Dulcinea would know. She kept track of details like that. To her credit, she braved the heat, loneliness, moody men, and sudden storms as well as anyone raised in the hills. J.B. spent that first summer grateful, relieved, and genuinely happy for the first time in his life. That last feeling had left him puzzled more often than not, wondering about the weight that seemed lifted. The iron hand that usually rode gripping the back of his neck simply disappeared. His own mother died when he was a boy, and he had little recollection or understanding of what being around a female meant. His father never remarried, preferred to become the old bastard he remained the rest of his life, convinced that women, the female influence, destroyed a man's character if he wasn't careful, and almost no man could be

20

that careful. Better to do without, he preached to his only child, wait as long as you can before succumbing to the flesh.

J.B. told his new wife about his father on those long nights when they lay in their bed under the stars, unable to sleep for the sheer closeness of the moon, the brightness making their naked bodies glow, and J.B. came to understand how wrong his father could be. Having a woman was the most wonderful thing he ever experienced. He didn't dare use that other word, *love,* didn't even recognize it, and could not say it when his new wife turned to him and whispered the words. His face shone with shyness and joy, which she might have mistaken for satisfaction and pride, he could not be sure. At that moment, he hoped she trusted the shyness, confident that she could teach him the language that would make such a difference in the coming years. When she turned to him, eyes expectant and happy, he thought she was simply satisfied with his lovemaking or the position of the bed away from the prying eyes of the men in the crude bunkhouse beyond the cottonwood trees.

"I love you," she said, her lips parted, forming the words for him to repeat if he could or would. He stared at her in wonder, and heard the distant voice of his own mother, a figure he could only imagine in shadow, a voice so thin and whispery it might be the wind through the hills. Women said these words, it came to him, and they filled a man, made him more than he was before. His father was right about the power of women, but he was wrong about what it did to a person. J.B. pulled Dulcinea close until he felt her chin nestle in the curve of his shoulder, her toes finding and pressing between his until they were perfectly fitted and he could not be certain which parts were his alone, exclusive of hers. If he could not say the words, it would not matter, he thought, she was the same as him, surely she felt it, too. When the time came to fulfill his end of the bargain with his father, she'd trust him, she'd understand, he reassured himself, because that had to be how it was when people loved each other.

The horse lifted his tail and dropped manure, kicked at a fly, shifted his front feet as if to turn around, raised his head and snorted. "All right." J.B. lifted the reins and the horse took the first step down the hill, bracing its front legs while the rider leaned back and gave him his head. At the bottom, they made their way to the windmill whose noisy blades slowed to a stop as the wind died down. J.B. dismounted to give the horse a drink from the tank. While the animal plunged his nose and splashed the water, J.B. stared at the churned-up sand. A piece of stone stuck out, maybe something he could take to Hayward, who liked to collect Indian relics. He eased it out and brushed away the sand.

It looked like a hide scraper. Careless to lose such a good tool. He used the side of his boot to clear around the hole from the scraper. He usually found arrowheads in these blowouts, occasionally a broken spear or tomahawk head, sometimes used rifle shells. He hefted the scraper, admiring the balance that let it fit easily in his palm, his fingers in hollows where others had held, thumb, forefinger, until it became an extension of his hand, the sharp edge ready for scraping the fat layer from the hide. Most of the Indians used white men's knives now, axes, guns, the old ways gone. Then his foot nudged something else, almost like an animal. He stepped back and looked down, then cautiously shoved with his boot toe. It didn't move. The sweet scent of wood smoke and cured hide rose unexpectedly and drifted away before he could grasp where it came from.

He sighed and peered across the hay meadow and the distant hills sheathed in a faint green haze. He should get back on his horse and finish the ride to his father's ranch. He shouldn't spend another minute here. Cullen was waiting to come home.

A meadowlark whistled, a male calling for a mate, the black chevron on the puffed-up gold chest shiny and remarkably beautiful at that moment. The bird cocked its head and eyed him from the cattails at the edge of the marsh. Red-winged blackbirds shuttled back and forth across the meadow with the urgency of soldiers preparing for battle.

His horse snorted and shook the water from its face, worked the bit in its mouth, and gazed at the man.

A large flock of yellow butterflies bumped their way across the pasture, lighting on the blooms of flowers and tips of grass, then rising in a cloud like yellow ash sailing from a prairie fire, they continued past, on over the top of the ragged ridge of the sand hill. He had another hour in the saddle to reach Drum's place.

"To hell with it," he said and bent to work. His thighs and the backs of his legs ached against the unusual stretch, but he didn't dare kneel for fear his knees wouldn't straighten. "If I was a horse, I'd shoot myself," he muttered. As it was, he would have to start wrapping them in strips of muslin soaked in camphor of a morning. Dulcie would have a good laugh about that when she saw him. The thought stabbed him with regret and he dug harder against the sand that spilled back into the shallow hole.

He felt a piece of wood with his fingers and pulled out a pipe with a foot-long carved cedar stem hanging half broken off, the barred turkey feathers still fresh. The red pipestone bowl had never been used, and the stem, decorated with a line of crudely carved animals, appeared new. Tiny yellow, red, black, and white cut-glass beads hung below the mouthpiece along with the feathers. He squinted to make out the design scratched on its hard surface. Nothing that made sense, tall and short lines like a series of tipis or stars. Hayward would like it. J.B. figured he'd use it to encourage the boy to talk again.

He poked the toe of his boot into the hole, feeling for the thing he'd touched earlier. When he found the yielding mass, a chill crossed his forehead and prickled his scalp. Deer, maybe.

"Goddamn it," he muttered and knelt, this time on his hands and knees to carefully brush away the sand.

The open mouth was filled with it, as if

her last screams had solidified, the lips drawn back snarling like a wounded bobcat. She'd fought to the end. Her open eyes clotted with sand. An apron of darkness cradled her tangled black hair that had come unbound from the traditional hide strips. He wondered how long she'd been dead. As soon as the tips of his fingers touched the stained sand, he knew. Still wet. The tears in the corners of her eyes. Not long. He swiftly tried to clear her mouth, her face. Warmth lingered on her skin. Her hands were like claws stretching up. He put his finger to her throat below her ear, and could detect nothing. Then he leaned his head against her chest, listened. When he sat back on his heels, he slowly scanned the silent hills. How had he not seen the person who did this? He stilled his breath and concentrated for any sound at all. Nothing except the occasional whine from the windmill. How long had she lain here?

Then he heard it — the faint click of metal against metal and the grunting of a man in boots stumbling in the soft sand beyond the water tank. J.B. quickly looked toward his horse and the rifle in the scabbard before he stood to face the gun pointed at his chest.

"Oh, it's you —" He held up a hand against the finger squeezing the trigger.

Then a mere deep breath's time before he felt a hot burning fist plow through his chest, opening his body to the light, first a red flare across the hills, then a whole bonfire of black sparks, then a white blanket pressing so abruptly that he fell to the side of the grave, grasping the scraper he had grabbed the moment he heard the metallic click. Cullen, he thought, reaching for the boy and his mother as darkness swallowed them all. Then the wind gathered itself and the windmill began to spin, clanking loudly enough to be heard for miles.

CHAPTER TWO

Ry Graver bent almost double into the rising wind, holding a gray, dilapidated hat on his head as the old horse plodded along the dirt road. Scrawny and ewe-necked with a rough brown coat shedding clots of hair, the horse had lost almost all its teeth and could only mouth cornmeal and pulped grass to stay alive these days — something the man took care to give it, though it often meant going hungry himself. Without the horse, he might never put this place behind him. So he cared for the horse, as hopeless as it was. If he had any money, he could anticipate a night's lodging, food, and coffee laced with whiskey a man could get in the Cattleman's Hotel in Hyannis or that place in North Platte, a beefsteak that filled a platter, hot fried potatoes, imagine; he sighed and stared at the empty road stretched ahead, last week's snow already melted and dried and blown away.

Ranchers complained it was too civilized outside the Sand Hills. So much land to the south in crops these days, Nebraska was becoming a regular settled state. Too many people coming now that they'd gotten rid of the last of the Indians, moved them up to the reservations in South Dakota, then found that these hills, full of rich grass and plentiful water, would support cattle and horses. The first decade of the new century, and people poured in despite the drought the last ten years. You'd think this country couldn't hold any more. Winter wheat, they'd sold the immigrants on the idea of planting in the fall, let winter do the work of keeping the young seeds warm and wet, then sit back and watch the field green up with the spring rain. A person didn't have to lift a hand until harvest. Let dust be your mulch, the experts in Lincoln said. Unless it didn't rain. Unless they made the mistake of coming into the hills with their plows. Ry Graver, the man on the failing horse, had made that mistake even though he'd known in his gut it was wrong.

He'd set up two miles behind him and watched his young family slowly starve, growing exhausted, trying to eat the rats and snakes that lived in their soddy, the children setting snares for songbirds and rabbits weak with drought. Several times Bennett or one of his cowboys had driven a dry old cow to his doorstep, dropped it with a single shot, and ridden off in the night. Despite the tales of hostile ranchers Graver heard in town, he knew that J. B. Bennett wasn't trying to drive them out. He seemed to understand how hopeless it was. The hills didn't take to the plow. When Graver broke the ground, the wind took the thin layer of soil and left sand that crumbled around the seed. He saw that right away, but by then he didn't have a choice. Three little ones and a wife who looked at him with the heart torn out of her eyes. He had to keep going, if for no other reason than the hope that the work would kill him and it would all be over.

But he waited too long, waited until after the children began to die, picked off by disease, then his wife, leaving only the stubborn man, a bitter expression locked in his eyes as he hefted the small bindle of blankets and clothes tied to his battered rifle across his thin shoulders and walked away from his dream. Riding the old horse unfit to plow or work cattle, Graver planned to go as far out of the hills as the animal could travel. When it collapsed, he'd continue on foot until he reached railroad tracks where he could jump a train going east or west. It didn't matter.

His eyes were too dry to weep anymore. There was a point past which you couldn't, like a repeated blow to the head, you got dulled to other kinds of pain. His hand trembled as he took out the makings for a cigarette, the gray-pink tip of his tongue so dry the paper stuck for a moment. He had to pry it off carefully to keep the Indian tobacco from spilling. He rested the horse beside the road, watching the smoke from his cigarette curl into the air and vanish. At least it took the edge from the gnawing hunger in his belly. He couldn't remember when he last ate. It didn't matter.

When he felt the old horse's sides swell like a bellows, he feared it was about to die. Instead it gave out a high broken whinny, ending in a long, deep cough that jostled the saddle side to side. He grabbed the saddle horn. The reply came from over the low hill to his right and was followed by another whinny, this time more worried. His horse managed a couple of short, choppy sounds before it turned and started to pick its way toward the young chestnut that now stood at the top of the rise, reins trailing.

"That's not right." He nudged the old horse with his heels.

"Hello?" he called and immediately felt foolish.

As soon as he saw Bennett's body, he stepped down and tied the trailing reins of the rancher's horse to his old horse. Then he stood still and waited for any movement or sound. Nothing but the cursed scraping of the rough, homemade windmill. He narrowed his eyes to examine the shadows, looking for any deeper shade that would indicate a man crouched there. A bird taking flight from the hay field whipped his head around, but he could see nothing that had disturbed it. When he was satisfied he was alone, he moved close enough to see the body of a young Indian woman in the hole, and Bennett's figure curled like a boy asleep in his bed beside her with the bloody hole in his chest. He knelt, wet his fingertip, and held it in front of Bennett's nose, then his mouth, feeling no coolness at all. He tried to pick up the man's hand to feel for a pulse, but the body was rigid. Flies crawled in the thick black bloody spill on his shirt. A photograph with a dot of fresh blood on the corner peeked from his pocket. Graver pulled it out and wiped the blood on his pants. It was a picture of a handsome young woman who wore a smile as if she were about to burst out laughing. He'd seen her in Babylon a few months ago. Bennett's wife. She hadn't been so happy then, he remembered. He glanced at the man again, a man who had been lucky for so long it felt outrageous for him to die so effortlessly. Graver started to tuck the picture back in J.B.'s shirt pocket, then stopped and slipped it inside his own instead. He would have to find her, make sure she had nothing to do with this. He didn't want to get involved, but that was the hell of it, now he was.

The Indian girl looked much the same, only she appeared to be a more recent kill. Her eyes still moist in the corners, a silvery tear streak visible on her cheek, a fly drinking from it.

Graver waved away the fly, rocked back on his heels, and lit another cigarette, smoking it to the brown nub, the glowing tip pinched between his filthy broken nails. He remembered the day in March when Bennett had brought a mule to his soddy, and dropped the lead rope at his feet.

"What's this?" he said.

"Use him or eat him," Bennett replied.

"No." Graver had to swallow the spit rising in his throat at the thought of roast mule haunch. He could imagine his sick, starving children, sitting listlessly in the dirt, unable to muster enough energy to play.

Bennett put his spurs lightly to his horse and was trotting away before Graver could thank him. The mule brayed once, a long sucking roar that made Bennett's horse twitch its ears and bunch up like it might decide to buck and run. He reached down and patted its neck.

It was too late, of course. The mule made them all so sick it finished off the youngest the first night, and his wife lasted long enough to see to the other two as they passed, one by one, starving, stomachs bloated with indigestible meat. He was the only one who fought off the cramps and runs, eating his way through the nausea to a newfound strength. Enough to burn the few goods they had in a little bonfire that served to smoke and dry the rest of the mule meat in long strips for the trip out of the hills. With every bite he tasted the clothing, bedding, even the rag-stuffed dolls his girls made, tasted the peculiar bitterness of the bone button nose, the sharp, scalding paint of the blue eyes and red mouths.

Graver shook his head and looked at the midday sun in the cloudless sky. He wanted nothing to do with that Indian girl and whatever she was to Bennett. He walked back to the horses, stood staring at them for a minute, considering the value of the

34

saddle and bridle, the rifle still in its scabbard, and finally the sleek, high-bred horse that could carry a person quick as fire out of the hills. Then there was the picture of the wife, Dulcinea, he remembered now, and the sharp edges of the photograph scratching his chest.

He reached to untie the reins to Bennett's horse, only to stop and start to bend when he saw something that looked like the red pipestone Sioux used.

The shot passed through his old horse's nose and plowed into its chest with the sound of a fist punching a sofa, the noise echoing under the delayed boom of the gun as the animal simply dropped like a tree felled by an axe. Bennett's horse screamed and tried to break away, but the knotted reins held, and Graver used its frantic motion to grab the rifle off the saddle and slither over the crest of the ragged hill.

He lay there panting, gorge rising to his mouth, before he remembered to check the load in the rifle and chamber a round. He'd be damned if he was going to get left in these hills by some coward ambusher. He looked for the shooter. Judging from the bullet that took the old horse, the shot came from the north, which meant the shooter was somewhere beyond the windmill and

35

tank. Maybe he'd been lying in wait the whole time and Graver should have paid more attention to the shadows. He did a quick estimate of distance and figured it was twenty to twenty-five yards. He'd be ready if the man showed himself.

After a few minutes the gnats and flies found him, and he was brushing them out of his ears when the bullet took him, spun him half away. He almost blacked out, but gritted his teeth and used the wounded shoulder to brace the rifle on the hill, aimed, and fired at the spot where he figured the gunman was holed up, then ducked at the barrage of fire that followed. Bullets thudded into the ground around him, but nothing touched him. If he kept down he'd be fine, as long as he didn't give in to the dizziness. He looked at his shoulder leaking blood through the thin cloth of his shirt. Damn it, that was the last shirt his wife had made him. Now this son of a bitch had ruined it.

He raised the rifle above his head and quickly squeezed the trigger. The bullet pinged off the windmill. This time the gunman only returned a couple of shots before the silence grew around them.

"I can wait you out," Graver called.

"You ain't got the bullets," a young man's

voice replied.

"I'm saving the last one for you, my friend," Graver said. There was another angry spray in rapid succession, but nothing hit home. Bennett's big red horse had apparently grown used to the situation because he was busy eating grass now.

"Gimme the horse," the young man shouted.

"This about a horse then?" Graver said.

"This ain't none of your business."

Graver focused on the low mound behind the windmill. "What kind of gun you got there?"

"Remington." There was pride in the voice.

"Clean shot on him, but you were off on me."

Graver heard him curse. The voice sounded younger than he'd originally thought. Was he going to be taken down by some damn kid? After all he'd gone through? God had to be a real bastard.

"Is he dead?"

"You and him got into it over the girl, then?"

This time neither the young man nor the gun replied. Graver had to remind himself to keep his eyes open, to watch for an ambush, to not get distracted. His head felt cloudy, like it was full of milkweed seed, and he was beginning to find the buzz of flies collecting on the dead horse tolerable. There must be a lot of happy cows out there this afternoon, not a fly in a hundred miles. They were all here feasting. He watched the small pool of blood from his shoulder blacken with their bodies. Next the beetles would show, and if he didn't stay awake, he could end up eaten from the inside out. No, he knew that wasn't right. He shook his head to clear the downy logic. And that gave him an idea.

"Hey, kid," he called.

"Yeah."

Graver was right.

"Made a mess, didn't you?" There was another long silence, which a meadowlark took up with its calls.

"Maybe." The answer finally came.

"Look, I don't owe these folks nothing. Let's you and me saddle up and ride on outta here. Go our separate ways. I'm headin' south." Graver quieted his breath in case the kid made a move that could be heard above the whining windmill.

"What about the horse?" The kid sounded sullen.

"Well, son, seems to me you shot my horse. How am I gonna ride outta here without I take the red horse?"

"It'd be horse stealin'." The kid seemed to find humor in this idea.

"Take my chances on that one." Graver didn't point out that murder was a sight worse crime.

"Fine by me." A shot burned past Graver's right ear, reminding him to keep down. "That was just by way of farewell."

Graver checked his urge to charge. "Can't say I want to meet again." He kept his tone casual. "You go first, son, otherwise I won't feel right about it."

This time the kid laughed bitterly. He didn't sound as crazy as Graver expected. "You won't shoot me in the back?"

"You won't circle back and shoot me?"

"I get your point." A shot thudded into the ancient saddle on the dead horse. "And I ain't nobody's son!"

"I can see that." Graver grew drowsy in the escalating afternoon heat, could feel his eyes drift shut with the distant sound of hoofbeats.

When he opened them again, the sun had shifted so it poured right into him, and the damn blackbirds were all over the hay meadow, and the flies — there had to be thousands now, more than he could count — his eyelids started to drift down again, but he caught them with a shake of his head.

"Kid? You there? Hey, kid?"

Graver waited a long time; he might even have passed out again, he wasn't sure, he couldn't remember what he was doing there, what time he'd started out that morning. He knew his wife would be worried if he was late for supper. And he was so thirsty, that surprised him, how his tongue felt swollen twice the size so he couldn't quite close his mouth, but breathing that way made his throat all the drier. He thought about calling the kid to bring him some water, but decided against it when he remembered that the kid might be sneaking up on him. He heard a clink of metal nearby and turned so quickly his shoulder gave a vicious stab of pain, almost knocking him flat. He peered over the crest of the hill and saw a turkey vulture tear at the dead horse's face, pulling the eyeball from the socket so viciously the head lifted an inch and resettled. Graver looked at the sky to figure the time. It seemed so long ago, all the earlier events. He braced the rifle on the ground and staggered to his feet.

Although it had pulled off its bridle, the red horse hadn't gone far. Graver reached for the headstall, forgetting about his wound, and the pain took him to his knees.

He shook his head, it felt bloated and heavy, sloshing like a gourd of water, and the weight pulled him backward, his face to the unrelenting heat of the sky. The last thing he remembered was trying to straighten his legs because he didn't want them to have to break his knees when they put him in the box.

CHAPTER THREE

J.B. was found after midnight by the foreman Frank Higgs, Larabee, Irish Jim, and Willie Munday. After a hasty supper, Higgs had divided the men and searched to the east and south of the ranch for their boss, who had failed to return as he always did at the end of the day. The other men went north and west, and wouldn't return until early the next day. It was twilight as the men approached the windmill and water tank off the path to Drum Bennett's ranch and noticed the small herd of cows pawing and milling, refusing to approach the water. Then they saw the dead horse and the dark, irregular shadow of bodies.

Higgs quickly dismounted. "Willie, you and Jim go and pull some of those bulrushes from the edge of the hay meadow, make a torch, search these hills around us." He turned to Larabee, who dismounted, and paced the ground around the bodies, peering closely at the churned sand and grass glowing white in the dim light of the sliver of moon that inched past the shoulders of the hills.

J.B. was lying on his side, eyes fixed on a half-buried Indian girl who somehow looked like a fresher kill than the man. "What the hell, J.B.," Higgs swore as he knelt, touched the edge of the wound that had torn a large hole from chest to back. On the face of his employer and friend he saw both shock and sadness.

"Oh damn it," Higgs whispered and reached to rest his fingers on the cold forehead of the man he'd grown to love as a son over the years. This would kill Vera, who'd almost adopted the father and his young son as soon as she started working here. She bossed J.B. and the boy as if they were her own.

"Frank." Larabee held out an empty brass shell casing that glinted dully in the moonlight.

Irish Jim, bearing a torch of creosote-soaked cattails, moved his horse closer and peered down. "We all carry that one."

"Got another one over here," Willie Munday said from the outer edge of darkness. "J.B.'s horse just wandered in, too. Must've heard us."

Higgs brushed his fingers over Bennett's eyes to close the lids, but it'd been too long. They were stiff, unmoving. He looked at the men gathered around the small circle of light at the center of which lay a man. They'd all seen death aplenty, a couple of the old-timers had fought in the War Between the States, and Larabee back from that war with Spain, but this was different. Bennett was boss. Well-liked. The kind of man to ride the river with. His sons, Cullen and Hayward, now that was another matter. Higgs looked at the men, and then nodded toward the body. "Willie, get down and help Jim pick him up, lay him over my saddle."

It was difficult to lift a body the size of J.B. onto a horse. Higgs and Larabee stepped forward to help, but even with four men it was a struggle. They tied him to the saddle, and the horse danced and chomped nervously. It seemed for a moment that Bennett himself refused to leave the land. Higgs peered into the blackness beyond the wavering pool of light from the torch Willie had jammed into the ground. He sorted the sounds of curious, thirsty cattle gathered to watch the men — stamping hooves, grunting as one body pushed against another — and heard no telltale clink of metal spurs or jingle of bit, no flash of moonlight on rifle action or pistol barrel. Whoever did this was long gone.

"What about the girl?" Larabee asked.

"Hell." Higgs swung back to the grave. "Cover that up."

Larabee looked at the foreman, startled, then tipped his head and started kicking sand over the girl's body. Irish Jim took a folding shovel from his saddle and set to work, too, but the sand wouldn't stick. They no sooner had the body almost covered than it seemed to shift and slide off. Before long the two men stepped back, clearly spooked, their eyes on Higgs, who lifted his hat, ran his hand through his hair, and resettled the hat, tugging it more firmly in place.

"Maybe we should fetch her back to the ranch," Irish Jim said.

Higgs shook his head. There'd been trouble again with the Sioux lately. It was only ten years since Wounded Knee, and the Indians were still pissed about that mess. No good would come from having a dead Indian girl on Bennett land. Damn it, if J.B. were alive, he'd know what to do. But he wasn't, and Higgs could only face one thing at a time.

"Leave her," he said, ignoring the quick exchange of looks between Larabee and Irish Jim.

"Better come see this, boss," Willie Munday called from the darkness. They followed his voice to the small pool of light from another hastily constructed torch.

As he sank knee-deep in the sand, Higgs cursed.

Willie Munday knelt beside a body dressed in rags, peering into the face. "I know him. Name's Graver, Ryland Graver. Farmer with a bunch of kids and a missus. J.B. sent me over there with a beef last fall. Heard they busted out." Willie raised his head and looked at Higgs. "Think he did this?"

Higgs noted the dead horse beside Graver and shrugged.

"He has J.B.'s rifle," Larabee offered. "And that's Red's bridle tied to his nag's. I think he got caught trying to steal Red and J.B. and him fought and —"

Higgs held up his hand as the man on the ground groaned, his eyes fluttering open. His lips moved and Willie leaned down to hear, and then sat back on his heels.

"He wants some water."

The men watched Higgs deliberate and then slowly nod. If he was the killer, they'd want to hang him back at the ranch, where they could use the cottonwood trees J.B.'s wife favored when they'd built the house.

Once the man drank enough, he tried to sit, but Irish Jim held him down and bound his wounded shoulder. Graver passed out again and the men lifted and shoved him onto the horse before Irish Jim got up behind to hold him. There was something unnatural about leaving the Indian girl unburied behind them, and the four men stole glances over their shoulders as the procession moved into the darkness toward the ranch.

"Frank?" Willie Munday, their newest cowboy, rode up beside Higgs and leaned over in a whisper. "Looked around, noticed another set of tracks out there. Small-footed horse and a man in moccasins."

Higgs searched the man's face. "Keep this quiet. Soon as we take care of J.B. and this Graver fella, you, me, and Larabee'll come out here and God willing find something." Although he didn't know much about Munday, Higgs thought he could trust him. Man did his work. Wasn't hard on the horses. Good tracker. Kept his mouth shut, not like Irish Jim or a couple of others who wore a man down with their constant yapping.

It was eight miles back to the ranch but it seemed a thousand to the men flanking the foreman's horse, burdened with its double load. The sky had dropped into the darkness of extinguishing stars when they finally entered the ranch yard. Tired horses shuffled and sighed as they made their way to the barn. Jim and Willie stepped down with Higgs and Larabee outside the main house and unlashed the body, and while Willie held the gate, J.B. was borne up the brick path. They hesitated at the door. Higgs reached to rap his knuckles, and then realized the person who granted permission to enter was dead in their hands. He turned the knob and pushed it open. The room was dark. The boy asleep upstairs, Higgs's wife, Vera, likewise asleep in the foreman's house, some four hundred yards away.

"Wait." Higgs turned and felt his way through the dark to a kerosene lamp on the small table between the sofa and reading chair, found the sulfurs beside the lamp, and lit the wick. As soon as the gold glow pushed back the shadows, Higgs gestured, and the men brought the body to the brown-speckled cowhide sofa and carefully lowered it. Later the hide would bear the dark smudge of Bennett's blood, but it never occurred to anyone to get rid of it.

The men stood looking around the room, hats in hands, clearly uncomfortable to be in their boss's good parlor and in the presence of his body.

"Go on. Irish Jim, you take care of Graver's wound, but make sure you tie him to the bunk. Late call tomorrow; get some sleep." Higgs grimaced, laid his hat on the table beside the lamp, and promptly picked it up again. Larabee let the others pass, then looked over his shoulder at Higgs, who nodded.

At first, Higgs thought about going upstairs and waking Hayward with the news, but he thought better of it. You always knew bad news soon enough. Best to sleep while a body could. He glanced at the dead man, startled by the fact that the eyes had closed, as if he could finally be at peace now that he was home.

"Okay." Higgs breathed deep and sat in the big, overstuffed chair upholstered with a burgundy plush that had worn thin and dark on the arms and back where J.B.'s head had rested for years. The wife's doing. Something called "Turkish Victorian," all done up with tassels and fringe the dogs and boy had taken turns pulling off until the furniture sat like aging relatives, fat and old-fashioned, beside the dainty mahogany table with claw-and-ball feet and carved foliage up the legs. An heirloom from her family, J.B. had noted with a touch of humor one night. That, and the whatnot corner thingy that held Hayward's Indian relics and the silver belt buckle he'd won riding goats at the ranch rodeo when he was ten.

Higgs glanced back at the body, examined it more closely in the light now that he was alone. The chest wound was ugly. They were always ugly. He pulled up the lace antimacassar pinned to the chair arm, leaned over, and placed it across the wound. "Look like a damn preacher now," he said. "Sorry, J.B., Jesus," he hastily amended, his eyes filled.

"That's enough," Higgs whispered as the wet on his grizzled cheeks dripped down to darken the collar of his flannel shirt. "Sorry." He looked at his scarred hands, the permanently swollen knuckles, the index finger he couldn't straighten, beset with a trembling that wouldn't stop as it made its way up his arms, into his chest, his shoulders, and down his legs until he felt like he was about to shake into pieces, but still he held the great sobs within, releasing only the faint hissing sound of boiling water as he wept.

It was almost seven the next morning when the door opened and shut, waking Higgs to his wife's light tread. She looked straight toward the kitchen, and thus missed the figure of her husband next to the body

50

of their employer.

Higgs considered calling her, but she was already banging pots, starting the coffee, firing up the woodstove, humming softly, with the occasional chiding word for her own mistakes. Soon there was beef frying, biscuits rolled, and eggs whipped. She'd stop cooking once she heard. He knew she would. So he kept quiet. The men needed to eat. First and foremost, you fed stock and men.

The parlor was much the same as it had always been, Bennett being a simple man and his wife, while she'd lived there, not a fussy woman. There was lace on all the chairs and it hung in the windows — though it didn't do a damn thing to keep out the cold. Rather than newspaper and catalogue pages covering the walls for warmth as in the bunkhouse, the parlor walls were papered with garden flowers and framed pictures of sour-looking people from her family out East. Chicago, was it? Cleveland? Higgs couldn't remember. Why hadn't she taken her pictures with her, he wondered. And the kerosene lamp — he looked over, it had long since burned out — with the big pink cabbage roses on the two globes. He understood about the furniture — except maybe the little table between the two hulking pieces. The table's rich, dark finish glowed from the beeswax Vera rubbed into the wood.

But the rest of the stuff — even the piano covered with that tasseled scarf — why hadn't she shipped it home? Unless she planned on coming back or came from a place with things twice this good. He glanced at Bennett. That was probably it. It was sixteen years ago when that bad spell of luck came along and they damn near lost the place the first time. Cattle got screwworm, blackleg, scours, and every other damn thing they could think of, horses colicked or broke legs, and it stopped raining. Grass didn't green in spring. They were bleeding money and stock, J.B. told him. But in the middle of it Bennett and his wife went off for a month, then came home, a load of furniture and junk in a wagon behind theirs. Within a couple of months they were buying stock to replace what they'd lost and eating store-bought food when the garden died. The younger son was born six months later.

As other spreads went under, Bennett's thrived, with enough money to buy surrounding land at rock-bottom prices. It didn't take a schoolteacher to figure out the arithmetic. Even after the past years of drought proved almost fatal for the ranch, these days any number of men nursed a healthy dose of envy and dislike for Bennett. What would happen to Hayward now? At fifteen he still acted the boy, no hand at all with the stock and a joke to the men. Damn Bennett for getting himself kilt. Higgs sought the end of his mustache and brought it to the corner of his mouth to chew, a habit he'd developed of late since he gave up whiskey and tobacco for his wife.

He thought again of the boy asleep upstairs. He sighed and rose, straightened stiffly and held the small of his back until the grabbing pain reluctantly released. Best get this done before the men came up for breakfast.

Opening the bedroom door slowly didn't stop the hinges from squealing. Higgs froze in the hallway, waited to see if the boy would say something. Surely he was awake now, but when he pushed the door open the rest of the way and looked inside, the room and bed were empty in the dusty light. The lace window curtains were flung up over the rod, and the window gaped. A brown moth, stranded in the rising sun, fluttered weakly and tried to climb the inch from the frame to the sill. Upon closer inspection, Higgs realized the bed hadn't been slept in, although a body had at some recent time dented the blankets and pillow. The thought wormed into him that maybe he should be worried.

It was a boy's room to the extent that it contained the dusty trophies of hunting trips — antlers, brushes of rabbit, squirrel, fox, and deer, tail feathers of pheasant and turkey, and the two-foot span of an eagle's wing nailed to the wall. Higgs remembered that one — the boy shot the huge bird accidentally, he said. Bennett made him nail the wing to the wall over his bed so he had to endure the sweet rot as it slowly decayed to teach him a lesson, and Hayward never said a word. He kept the window open for the next year, even when it was thirty below zero last winter, so cold your snot froze your nose shut and stung your eyes, then froze the tears to your lashes. Maybe the boy was more like his father than either imagined.

His eye was drawn to the revolver on the top of the big oak wardrobe in the corner. What the hell — the boy wasn't supposed to use handguns. Higgs was in midstride when a door slammed shut downstairs followed by hurried boots on the stairs. He slid into the hallway, just in time to face Hayward.

"What —" The boy drew up short and

stepped back, his rawboned face, a younger version of his father's, darkened.

Higgs took in the jacket and pants stuck with burrs and bits of grass, the dirt caked on elbows and knees. Was that guilt on his face? Or merely surprise? The boy had inherited his mother's eyes, small, quick, capable of hiding things in their flat stare.

"Where you been, boy?" Higgs hadn't meant to question him, and it came out like the boy's father would have said it.

Hayward shrugged, glanced at his dirt-rimmed nails, and spread his right hand and rubbed the back as if it ached. The knuckles were raw. He'd been in a fight.

"Fighting?" Higgs raised his eyebrows. "Your pa know you've been —" Then he remembered.

"He don't care." The boy dropped his hands to his sides and straightened his shoulders as if his father watched. "What's it to you?" His voice had all the harshness of the young trying to sound brave in front of a man who knew what his tone really meant. Higgs remembered being that age. He stepped back and held up his hands in deference.

"Hayward, son." His voice shook and the boy noticed. His head jerked up and his eyes darted past Higgs, then swept into his room.

"Your pa's dead." Not once through the long hours of searching for, then finding, Bennett, then carrying him back and sitting with him in the parlor, had Frank Higgs felt the finality of those words. Now it was true. Now he'd told someone to whom it mattered. It was taken away, the fact, and made over, refashioned, then it would be remade, over again, until the J.B. he knew was in little pieces, vanished as surely as this afternoon when they would place him in the ground he had fought and loved and toiled for. This thought came and went in the seconds that it took the boy in front of him to blink, shrug, shake his hands at his sides, and then blink again.

"He's gone, son, J.B.'s gone." Higgs felt a cleaver sever the thought from the rest of his mind and patch it onto the side of his heart, where the weight made it hard to catch his breath.

"Where is he — where's my pa, Higgs, where is he?" The boy's voice rose into an anguished cry as he turned and rushed downstairs, stumbled, almost fell in the middle, caught himself with the railing he rode in a kind of free fall until the bottom, where he regained his feet, then bent in the middle, heaving bile and snot and tears while Higgs watched from the last step.

"He's on the sofa there." The man tried to steady his voice, and Vera charged in from the kitchen to see what the commotion was.

"Oh my Lord," Vera moaned. "Oh my sweet Jesus." She reached for the boy, forced his head into the soft padding of her shoulder and bosom. Together they sank to the floor, Vera's one arm cradling the boy, the other clasping J.B.'s jacket sleeve, stiff with the shawl of dried blood.

There was a knock on the door, the handle rattled, and Larabee poked his head inside. "Boss?"

Higgs glanced at his wife's stricken face and went to the door, opened it enough to slide outside and shut it. The men gathered on the porch and brick walk, hats in hands, faces somber.

Chapter Four

Following a dreary breakfast no one could stomach, Vera cleared the long table in the kitchen, and Willie, Larabee, Jim, and Higgs deposited Bennett's body on the bare boards. The three hands took one last look at their boss, bowed their heads, and left. Before Vera could do more than sniff away the tears and fill the dishpan with soapy water to bathe the naked body, Higgs took the washrag from her hand and sent her to find proper clothing to dress him for the burial. As he worked his way from the feet up the legs, Higgs imagined he was washing down a newborn calf or colt, rather than this other thing, but when he reached the genitals, shrunken, negligible, he paused, questioning the whole purpose. No wonder women did this job — what man could stand to see his kind so utterly useless, destroyed, and not despair?

"Jesus, J.B.," he murmured, "I mean, what

the hell happened to you?" The body Higgs had always known as powerful, as heavily muscled as that big red horse he rode, looked almost frail without clothing, drained, without purpose. It didn't look capable of any of the feats of strength and will for which J.B. was known. Was it will, then, that first fled for the dead? Then purpose and desire. The body was remarkably without yearning now.

Higgs scrubbed the dried flakes of blood from the torso of the man he had loved, then mopped at the pink water on the table, and watched as it ran over the edge. It puddled on the pine plank floor Vera kept so clean the wood was bleached light gray and so porous the blood-tinged water quickly soaked in a stain that would never disappear, although he would not know that.

While he scrubbed the left hand, separated the fingers, worked the dirt and blood out from under the nails, he wondered if he should try to find J.B.'s wife. He wiped the empty ring finger clean. She'd never make it back in time, he thought, even if he knew where she was. Last he'd heard, she was teaching Indian school up on Rosebud Reservation. Before that, she moved from town to town in the Sand Hills, circling Bennett land but never stepping foot on it.

The body wouldn't hold for her to be found. The rigidity was starting to leave the limbs and there was a distinct spicy, sickening sweet smell.

Maybe she'd finally gone home to her people out East. He remembered she was the daughter of a patent medicine manufacturer from Chicago, that was the place, with enough new money to have been wooed and won by a western rancher. He had to hand it to her, though, she stuck. No matter how the town women treated her because she was a Bennett and after her own father-in-law pronounced her too weak to be a good broodmare, she stuck. Made a good marriage and built the kind of family J.B. never had . . . until the day Cullen was taken.

Higgs grimaced and worked his way up the shoulders to the neck.

"Lift his head," Vera interrupted. She draped the suit over the back of a kitchen chair and held a comb and brush for his hair.

"I wouldn't —"

She elbowed him aside and lifted the back of the head with one hand, comb poised in the other. The flopping skull stretched the skin and groaned — Vera lurched backward. The head landed on the kitchen table with a resounding thump that sounded too much like a pumpkin being squashed. Higgs stood frozen, watched as a fly found the blackened flesh of the wound and tentatively probed the ragged hole with its front legs. Vera stared at the hole for a moment, and then backed farther away, shoveling the air with her empty hand.

"Turn your head," Frank ordered.

He quickly tied the flour sack he'd used to dry the body around the wound as if Bennett were readying himself for a duster. Higgs stepped back and surveyed his work. Most of the blood and dirt were gone. He took the comb and brush from his wife, wet the hair with the pink water, parted it down the middle, and flattened it as he'd seen his friend do for as long as they'd known each other. It felt more intimate than bathing him had — the last thing a man could manage to do for himself if he were still breathing and had at least one working arm.

With Vera's help, he dressed Bennett in the one suit he owned, the one he wore to meet bankers and to get married all those years ago. The black wool sleeves were moth eaten, the lapels faded, the collar dark with grease and dirt. Vera adjusted the high standing collar so it sat straight.

"A Bible, Frank? Where's his —"

There was a knock at the back door, followed by a muffled voice saying the wagon and men were ready. Hayward pounded down the stairs and strode into the kitchen as the men hauled in the hastily constructed coffin from the back porch. Irish Jim let his side slip and tilt, banging Willie's fingers against the doorframe as they struggled to keep it upright. Willie swallowed his curses and cast the other man a baleful expression.

They'd made the coffin with planks from the new barn door, and only guessed at the length. When J.B. didn't quite fit, they removed his tall black boots and bent his knees to one side so he lay twisted at the waist.

Hayward edged between them to stand beside the coffin, and that seemed right. It wasn't until he raised his hand that Frank saw the eagle wing, worm-eaten and brittle, so dusty it smeared the black wool coat when the boy placed it on his father's chest.

Vera let out a sobbing breath. Otherwise the room was silent, acknowledging what was imagined as the boy's benediction.

"Get his hat." Higgs crossed J.B.'s hands on the wing and placed the black cowboy hat on top.

"The lid will crush it," Vera said and lifted it out again. "Brand-new hat."

Higgs nodded to the other men to help

him with the lid. He didn't need to say any more good-byes. The sooner this was over, the better it would be for Hayward.

They fought the windblown sand to keep the hole deep and long. When they grew exhausted, they dropped the shovels and lifted the coffin over the hole. As they lowered it, the bulky box tilted and slipped, and then dropped so hard the planks split apart. They could see the black suit through the gaps. Higgs picked up the nearest shovel and heaved sand and dirt for all he was worth. They'd say a few words afterward. J.B. wasn't in a position to argue.

The graveyard, which until now held only a favored dog, Vera's cat, and the boy's first horse, stood to the left of the barn and corrals, far enough from the houses that a person could almost forget what was there. They'd strung barbed wire to keep the cattle out, and placed a couple of worn-out wagon wheel rims, bleeding rust into the yellow sand around the switchgrass and bluestem, and the cream separator that never worked right over the graves to keep them still. Now they'd have to find more trash to hold down the coffin. In a day or two, Vera would plant wild roses, see if they'd take with the water Higgs would carry there. They might do better to copy the people on Rosebud and leave a body out for the elements, he thought. With land like this, it was a lot of work to be so damn civilized.

"We done here?" Hayward asked. He clapped his hat on his head and drew the string under his chin to keep the wind from pulling it off. The cuffs of his jacket were so short they stopped halfway down his forearm, Higgs noticed with a jolt. The kid was shooting up. He'd top out at his father's height, six two or three. Old enough and big enough to get into some real trouble.

"Where you off to?" Higgs asked.

The boy glared at him, spun, and started toward the barn, picking up speed until he was running. By the time he made the corral, put a rope on one of the horses, fashioned an Indian war bridle, and sprang on its back, Higgs wasn't halfway there. At least the boy didn't turn all the horses loose when he leaned down, opened the corral gate, and went through. He swung it shut again and waited for the latch to fall.

As the men watched the boy leave the barnyard and lope down the road, Vera tucked her arm through Higgs's.

"Little bastard rides like his da," Irish Jim said.

"Let's get something to drink," a voice

behind them said.

Back in J.B.'s office, Higgs picked up the fresh brandy bottle, gave it a shake, heard the liquid slosh, and set it down, carefully positioning it next to the short glass. He sighed, picked up the small beaded turtle J.B. had bought at the trading post for Hayward. Below it were newspapers from Omaha, Denver, and Rapid City. Old stories about Wounded Knee. Higgs seemed to remember J.B. going up there for the ghost dancing before the massacre, or maybe it was afterward. He and Vera had taken the train to Denver that December so he wasn't around during that whole uproar. J.B. didn't talk about it much, but what he saw must have troubled him plenty. Higgs ran a light finger over the tiny beads crusted with dirt. A person could always give it back, Higgs had suggested when J.B. told him what the turtle held, but J.B. shook his head and frowned. He was ever a man to ponder a situation. That was for damn sure. Higgs pushed back from the desk and reached for his hat. On second thought he pulled a pistol from the holster J.B. kept hanging off the desk chair, tucked it in the back of his pants, and covered it with the black suit coat he'd worn for the funeral.

He glanced back at the bottle, wiped his

mouth and chin with his hand, and pulled open the door. He'd spent a good part of his life doing what J.B. wanted; now he'd have to spend the rest doing what he thought J.B. would want. It just never got easier, did it.

J.B.'s wife should've taken the second boy with her when she moved to town. He was a devil on animals and men alike these days. Running like hell's half acre was on fire. J.B. couldn't do much with him, and since he was the only son J.B. had after Cullen was taken by Drum, he didn't *want* to do much with him anyway. J.B. was raised hard, and he was caught between wanting to be kind to the boy and also thinking he needed the lessons that stuck with a person. It ended up being the worst possible way to raise a son. None of them Bennetts know how to raise a child, Vera swore at Higgs nightly. They ruin every one they get their hands on.

Now he had to deal with this Graver. A part of Higgs hoped he'd done the killing so they could hang him and clean up the mess before dark. It was never that easy, though, he told himself as he left the house, pulling down his hat so the wind wouldn't lift it.

The mulberry trees had grown rapidly.

They shaded the roof of the bunkhouse windows to the east and clumps of seedlings had sprung up, creating a grove. Only problem was the mess. Men ate the berries, but birds got to them faster, leaving splashes of purple all over the ground, the roof, and any clothes or saddle blankets the men hung out. Coyotes liked the berries, too, and late at night he'd seen a couple on their hind legs in the moonlight, pulling ripe ones from the limbs. Their scat turned loose and deep purple and made a terrific stink, but he never could bring himself to lift the rifle those nights he sat on his porch, unable to sleep for the deep ache in his back that shot pain so sharp along his ribs and into his shoulders it hurt to lie there next to Vera.

As he approached the bunkhouse, Higgs noticed a cracked pane in the window by the door that faced the big house. The building was long and low, made of the same brick they'd used for the house, with four small windows on each side. The roof was tin that rang like a cheap bell whenever it hailed. Rain produced a softer cadence, still so loud it was hard to think inside. The tin was streaked dark orange with ribbons of rust. Someone should check for holes.

The door, a thick pine slab dented and marred from years of angry men kicking it, stood open to let in sorely needed fresh air. The stink was worse than the barn. Added to the odor of animal sweat and manure was the meaty stench of unwashed bodies, long underwear that never got changed, half-rotted socks, and cigarette smoke. Rumpled, muddy clothes hung from nails on the walls, along with ropes, bridles, saddles, and halters in various stages of disrepair, and newspaper and magazine pictures with curling edges dotted with fly specks. Every bed stood in a puddle of the owner's belongings. J.B. would be in here with a — Higgs stopped. J.B. didn't have a say anymore. The thought made his mouth drier than sand.

He squinted in the dusty light to find the wounded man. There he was in the darkest corner, farthest from the stove, on the bed where the youngest or dumbest cowboy usually ended up. As Higgs eased down on the one opposite Graver, wincing at the warning stab of pain from his back, he studied the man. His long frame was thin and laced with hard muscles, his shirtless torso wrapped in Vera's ragged muslin. His face was a chiseled mask, lines etched at the eyes and mouth, the high cheekbones, and below the strong nose the generous mouth seemed to suggest a good-natured smile. But hard times had created a perpetual crease on his brow, which he wore even in sleep. From the little history Higgs knew about him, Ry Graver had endured all the hardship life had to offer a man willing to venture west. Too bad his youngsters had to suffer. Graver was thirty-eight, but his face looked ten years older or more and his dark brown hair bore silver streaks. Higgs's own hair had turned gray at twenty-five.

"If you're done looking, I'd like to tell you what happened." The voice was low and clear as his eyes slowly opened.

Higgs's face flushed. "I'm listening."

"Water?" Graver tilted his head toward his wrist, tied to the bed. The other arm was held against his body by the bandage.

Higgs stood and went to the crude bench by the door that held the bucket of water the men used for drinking, washing, and shaving. He filled the tin cup that hung on a leather thong from a nail in the wall, brought it to the bedside, and held it for Graver to drink.

When Graver was finished he sighed and laid his head back on the bed, eyes closed. A long minute passed before he said, "They're all gone, wife" — he swallowed hard — "youngsters." He paused for a long moment, then said, "I was walking out of the hills when I found the bodies."

"When was that?" Higgs leaned forward, elbows on knees.

Graver thought for a moment. "Late morning." He opened his eyes and looked at Higgs. "Spare another cup?"

Outside the crows were setting up a racket in the mulberry trees and made Higgs wonder if a coyote had been brave enough to come around in daylight.

After more water Graver closed his eyes and told his story. The image of the Indian girl's body came back to Higgs with startling clarity. He should have done something about that. Animals probably worked it over pretty good after the men left last night.

Graver shook his head slowly and looked at Higgs. "Don't see why he didn't finish me."

"So you didn't have a shootout with J.B.?" Higgs watched as Graver's face registered surprise, then anger.

"Hell no. Man fed my family."

The words and tone sounded true. Higgs sat back, hands flat on his thighs. "Any notion who shot you?"

Graver shrugged, and a grimace of pain followed, his face graying, his voice barely a whisper as he said, "Sounded young." Then his eyes drifted shut and his breathing quieted as he dropped off to sleep.

Higgs wanted to ask him about the blood-spotted picture of Mrs. Bennett Vera had found when she cleaned his wound. He studied the sleeping man. Why hadn't the shooter circled around to finish him? With the dead Indian girl, probably some brave hopped the reservation, maybe J.B. stumbled on the killer burying the girl. Or maybe J.B. . . . Higgs stopped and stood. He'd have to go out there again, examine the girl, look for clues.

At the door he glanced back at Graver. Best move him to the house so he could keep an eye on him. Drum would want to hear his story when he finally showed up. When Higgs sent word about the funeral, Drum had replied, "I'm working cattle today." Higgs would send a man to town for the lawyer tomorrow. Track down the widow. Tell the new sheriff, though he doubted the man would bother coming out for an Indian and a Bennett.

CHAPTER FIVE

Rose quickly undressed and cleaned her sister's body, biting back the memory of the times her hands had run the length of her sister's arms and legs when Star was a baby and it was Rose's job to care for her. The tips of her fingers lingered on the bruise around Star's neck, where the man had stopped her breath. When she eased Star's fingers loose, a gold locket on a chain lay nestled in her palm. Rose picked it up and found it was warm — as if she were still alive. Holding it out from her body, she stared at the object as she would a cluster of poison berries. What did it mean? Was it the killer's? She pried open the locket, the faces inside, a white man and woman, were faded strangers. She closed it and tucked it in her pocket. She'd think on it later when her work was complete and she could finally mourn.

As the eldest surviving woman in her family, Rose bore the burden of the funeral ritual. She cleaned the sand from her sister's ears and lips, then struggled to lift the shoulders and head so she could tug on the white deerskin dress, and cried out in frustration until Some Horses, her husband, rushed to her side. The dress was intended for Star's wedding day, as it had been for Rose's. The soft hide was fringed, beaded, and belled for the dancing that would take place. On the front, their mother, a fine artist, had painted a man and woman on horseback, wearing war paint and wielding spears to protect the new family. Now it would go to Wanagi Makoce, the spirit land, where Star would wear it proudly among the dead.

Rose smoothed the fringed arms and hem, and sang to force away the grief, but it didn't work. She wasn't ready to mourn. She wrapped the dark blue shawl her aunt had contributed around her sister's hips, and then picked up the star quilt she had made when she was twelve, the stitches surprisingly small and neat, the pieces of yellow and white cloth bursting from the center, and set it down again. Wrapping her sister in the quilt would be the final act before they moved her to the Buffalo Grounds. She ran her fingers down Star's arm, and then removed the silver bracelet Some Horses had won for her in a game at the last powwow and put it on her sister's wrist. She fastened the red-and-yellow quill earrings and kissed Star's lips one last time, jerking back when she felt their warmth. They had waited a day to see if she would revive after they found her in the Sand Hills and carried her to Rosebud, as was their custom, hopeful when they saw the fresh tears in her eyes, but new breath never came. Even now.

Rose glanced around the tipi. Some Horses was outside readying the travois to bear the body after dark. The old ones spoke of ghosts who would come back to bother the living, but Rose never believed them. She hated to see a good tipi or house burned after death to keep the spirit from returning. She welcomed Star's spirit, though she knew it was wrong. When another tear seeped from her sister's eye, Rose captured it on the tip of her finger and pressed it inside her blouse against her heart. As she wrapped Star in the quilt, rolling her so she could pull it tight, she thought she could hear her sister murmur, the voice so far away she could not distinguish the words. She made a choice then — one she would reconsider over the next few

74

months. She continued to wrap the body until the final edge could be neatly tucked and there was only silence. It was her sister's spirit calling, not a living Star. She'd heard stories of this, especially when the death was a violent one. Rose must work hard to keep the spirit in her sister's body so they could rise together and enter the red road as one.

She stepped back, pressed her hands together to keep them from removing the quilt and freeing Star. From childhood she had been trained to perform the death rituals, heard stories of ghosts wandering the earth because they were not properly sent to the spirit world. She knew what she was supposed to do whether she wanted to or not.

She tried to take a deep breath, but her ribs pressed in too hard, binding her body like a wet hide, and she could only form a gasp that ended in a cough. She could almost feel her sister slip inside her then, as if following the tear she had placed on her heart.

Without warning, the light outside began to fail, and the tipi sank into shadows. It was time. Rose folded her mother's ghost shirt that Star had saved and tucked it inside the quilt beside her sister. There was no bone comb or beaded mirror, nor fancy quilled hair fasteners or colorful beaded moccasins saved for courtship, only the bloody shirt to be carried into the next world as evidence of their people's unhealed grief.

Rose glanced at her own special things in their small parfleche box. She had nothing else of value for her sister's journey, her life to the next world. If she had only known, she might have, but it was no use. She found the sweetgrass bound with thread next to the tipi entrance, held it over the fire, then blew the small flame down to smoking embers, which she used to bless the four directions, the sky and the earth, and then swung the smoking grass around and across her body. When she was done, she called Some Horses and her daughter, Lily, to begin the final journey.

The night was dark with only a quarter moon to lead them through the woods to the ancient pine Some Horses had chosen, one he could climb with the body strapped on his back. The white priests had tried to stop their practice of placing the dead in the open air to encourage the journey to Wanagi Makoce, but there was no question as to where her sister belonged. Rose shuddered at the thought of ground burial or burning.

She listened to her husband's breath as he struggled up the tree, and tried not to think about what would happen if someone discovered the body. In a year they would end their mourning with a *wanagi yuha* to remember Star's spirit. What few relatives were left would tell stories about Star and distribute her possessions, except there was nothing left. Rose and Some Horses would have to buy and make clothing and tools to exchange.

"Now," Some Horses whispered from the tree, and Rose began a blessing song, torn even now between wanting to release her sister's spirit into the other world and holding it here until Rose could avenge her death.

The wind quietly grew around them and began to push the pine and cedar tops side to side, tossing Horses and her sister like a boat on a lake.

"Hurry," Rose called. Some Horses grunted with effort as he lashed the body to the limbs and trunk.

Rose tried to recall the other song in the burial ceremony, and couldn't. She was empty, numb; her own tears wouldn't fall though she could feel the salt warmth of her sister's drowning her heart. She knew she shouldn't, but while she waited for Some Horses to slowly descend, Rose looked up at the sky, the sliver of moon, and finally the dark mass of her sister's body, and whispered her promise.

The wind rose and quieted as if it had captured the moonlight that settled like a flock of silver birds around her. It was then that her sister's spirit began a tale that would send Rose on a journey for the man's heart. It must be taken so Star could rest:

I am Star of the Miniconjou. This is the story I never had the chance to tell, though I whispered it to the deer I spied fawning in the marsh grass one spring morning. The doe's pain fresh, like my mother's that winter morning ten years before, at Čhankpé Ópi Wakpála, what the whites call Wounded Knee. Later I wondered if I had ruined the world for that babe as it stood wobbly on long, spidery legs, gazing about at the dew-sparkling grass and the water alive with light while his mother licked him clean and dry. Did I curse him as my people have been cursed?

Would he fall prey too soon, as my sisters and brothers did that morning, the bullets finding their running backs and skulls as they stumbled in the hard dirt

78

and icy clumped grass? We gave thanks for the mild weather, believing Wovoka's promise that the world would open again as we sang, "The buffalo are coming, the buffalo are coming . . ." Someone looked up at the weary winter sky and said she could smell their hot, grassy breath, and then she saw their powerful legs galloping down a ray of light and clouds, and we threw up our arms to rejoice, and sang even louder, "The whole world is coming!"

Stosa Yanka throws dirt into the sky to make a road for the buffalo we can all see and smell and hear, dreaming already of the rich meat stews and the warm robes they will give us, and deer and elk and antelope and bear following, the eagles arrive, the air yellow with the whip of their wings, and then crows come, hundreds, they walk among the dancers, proud bobbing heads keeping time, and it is all happening as Wovoka has promised and the people sing louder in time with the animals, and the ghost shirts come alive, birds and butterflies and animals lifting off men's shoulders and chests and backs to join the dance, and the thrown dirt hangs in the air like a road to welcome back the world, and only the hummingbirds are shy and hold off, as they are wont . . . and then a sharp crack and the air is split, the dirt spilled, and the new world collapses down on us in pieces, the guns boom and the people fall, running, falling, screaming, falling, and I am away, my hand pulled by my mother as we follow the others up the ravine, running like deer now, light and bounding until we come to a place where badger dug a hole in the side of the hill and Mother shoves me inside, no matter what awaits me, stay, Star, she whispers with her finger to her lips, her eyes wild as a bird in a grass net, stay. I close my eyes so I will not see what is in the hole with me or watch her disappear, but soon they are opened by the men's voices.

"First you taste the meat, then you drink the blood," says the man with one eye that searches for me while the other eye looks at my mother, held by her hair, a knife at her throat. She won't look at me, but I can't stop seeing her. I feel at my waist for my small skinning knife, but I dropped it while we played chase the prairie hen, so already my story is not the story I meant to tell and I have confused that morning with the day before and the day before that.

Maybe the dancing had not yet begun . . . the sacred tree was in the middle where we danced but we were not allowed to include it in our game. Our older brothers in their mission school clothes played on the other side of the camp, their hair shorn, the backs of their bare necks embarrassed; they tried to act as if they were too old to play the fox and hen game. I saw Lame Dog, with the deep scar on his calf where he was attacked by a dog before he was taken away to the school. He was watching me the way he'd always watched me, knowing as I knew that one day we would share our tipi and have many fine children. I had seen it many times and not told anyone except my sister, Rose, who sees as I do. He was there playing a boy game, a contest of rock throwing, or stick fighting, or fighting. It made me happy, I know that, to feel him across the camp, my husband-to-be, and so we were not dancing, not seeing the buffalo, and in my haste to tell this story I have poured all the stories into one, so when the medicine man threw the handful of dirt in the air — and it must have been powerful, because we were seeing the road and also doing our morning chores, and also playing, and all of this in that moment when the buffalo hooves touched the earth again, and the birds cried out a warning of salvation and loss — the gun fired. At first we did not know what the sound meant, and then the big gun, the Hotchkiss, and the Springfields, the Colts, their horses branded front and back, numbers and letters, their hides scorched, shook their heads, the curb chains rattled, the flash of sabers and spurs and somewhere the tinkling of bells, of silver spur chains, of men loading guns, the guns.

The boys go down, all at once as if in a game, and I open my mouth to scream. The buffalo are running across the camp, over the hills, up the ravines, follow us, they cry, and we do, though people fall all around me, and the crying grows louder than the guns or the pounding hooves, and my mother is forced to lie with her legs spread and the other man, the tall, thin one with the blond hair and narrow face, holds a saber point at her heart and smiles while crooked eye pulls down his pants and shoves inside her, my mother keeps her eyes closed and bites her lip against the pain, blood drips on her cheek, and it makes crooked eye both hungry and angry, for he begins to beat her while he does his business, then he trades places with skinny man, and crooked eye mounts her from behind like a dog, holds her hair while she rears back but cannot throw him off, and crooked eye beats her about the head and that isn't enough so he curses her and pokes her with his knife and kicks and pulls her to pieces. By the time they are through, they have stabbed and cut chunks of flesh and each takes an ear, then crooked eye her scalp. Skinny man cuts off her breast and scrapes away the flesh to make a pouch, he says, for his coins. As he shoves it in his shirt, a small gold object falls out unnoticed and drops into the snow at his feet.

If this were your story, you might tell it differently, the pieces in order, the way I waited in that hole, crying without sound for hours, my shoulders shaking dirt loose until I hoped to be buried alive, anything but having to wait for dark when I crawl out, find my mother, and try to help her home. I start back to camp, must ease past bodies stiffening in the cold night air. I had not known so many were undone.

As I get closer, the field is alive with movement. Wovoka was right! We are reborn! The bullets didn't tear into our ghost shirts, didn't kill our flesh, we are unharmed! A man scrambles to his feet, holding up the eagle talon necklace that Black Coyote wore, and the beaded moccasins his mother made for him, ah, the scavengers, like crows they cover the dead, stealing what doesn't belong to them, sending my people into the next world naked and full of pain. They strip the bodies of everything, even the hair. This they do to women and children who have not made war upon them, while the cavalry eats and drinks at their fires like warriors who have done a good day's battle on innocents, sick and old, so few young men here anymore, and now I have no past, no future, the husband I am promised still running, though the back of his head is blown apart, his legs seem to churn beneath him in the dirty cold.

That night I go back to the badger hole, climb in, and dream half a dream, in which I tell the hummingbirds that they must fly in the four directions of the winds and tell all the people what has happened here at Čhankpé Ópi Wakpála, let the world know of the slaughter. It is growing light when I remember to look for the object the thin man dropped by my mother before he left. It is a yellow chain with a round disc that opens to reveal tiny pictures of a white woman and skinny man. I put it over my head and tuck it in my blouse. The murderers were too drunk on blood to search her, so I am able to find the beaded deerskin

84

turtle she wears around her waist that holds my mother's life cord. I find her large knife in its sheath on her thigh and wonder why she did not reach for it. I pull off her tattered, bloody ghost shirt, fold it carefully, and place it inside my dress.

There is nothing I can give her except to cut a hank of my braid and tuck it in her hand that she may use my life spirit to carry her home. I kiss her bloody cheek, cover her face with my blanket, and know that where I am going, there will be warmth and food. I begin to walk, carefully avoiding the men who search the dead for booty, half-starved for the last feather, the last bone necklace, the last deer-foot whistle, the last ragged pants, the last half-torn belt with the beads falling off like bread crumbs for the people to follow into the earth. We do not bury our dead. We do not! They need their funeral rituals! I want to shout at them, but I must stay quiet and scuttle along like a mouse, unseen, unheard, until I reach the church at the trading post, where I will find what people remain alive. I will tell them how our people were loaded on wagons like twisted limbs fallen off dead trees, and carried to pits and dumped while dirt was piled on top, their spirits crying out for help so loudly I had to cover my ears, and all the others cover theirs and weep silently. Finally we understand the malice of the angels their god sends.

You might think this is the end of my story, but it continues for the next ten years until one day I saw skinny man again. He came into the trading post, asked to speak with the Indian agent, and pulled out a coin purse, made a show of it as if daring anyone to ask. Our people recognized the shame and turned away. My heart thumped hard and seemed to stop. It didn't matter, I said my prayer to my mother's spirit, pulled out the locket, and let it sit on my blouse where he might notice it.

The night before I went to meet him for the third time, Rose, I told you that I was going to see a white man who had something of our mother's that he wanted to return. I never had the chance to tell you the rest. You see how you must send the story of wrong out into the world, but since the hummingbirds don't come when I die, I am telling you now.

I meant to taste the sweet white ends of ripe grass, to let the deep rock coldness of water rinse my mouth, and to marry the boy who was always meant to be my husband and have many babies suckling while I ground corn and dried berries and pounded the meat flat and laid it out in strips to dry rich and fragrant in the sun, I meant to have such a good long life, I meant to lie in the arms of my love and watch the stars I am named for wheel their great paths in the sky, telling of our years to come, I meant to listen to the wind and its messages, and to come to a fine old age, my body ready to be received back into the world, but I am only a girl, a wound in the earth that will not close, I unbury myself over and over until there is justice. Rose, it is up to you now.

CHAPTER SIX

Three days after the funeral, Drum Bennett strode through the kitchen door with his usual quick steps, his boots landing lightly on the plank floor. "Where is he?" His barrel chest pushed against his faded brown flannel shirt like a threat. There was nothing apologetic about the way his gaze swept over the foreman and his wife seated at the table finishing their breakfast after the men had been fed and sent to work. At five foot eight, it wasn't height that gave Drum menace. It was the thickness of his body, the arms as hard as axe handles, the thick-fingered hands with knuckles the size of walnuts that possessed the hard speed of a former boxer. Bennett had had to fight his way clear of his past, had taken to the road as a young man and staged boxing matches with locals in the small towns of Missouri, Illinois, and Iowa before coming west. Almost every man who'd ever worked for

Drum Bennett had felt the teeth-cracking blow from one of his fists. Drum was a man who hit first and didn't talk later.

Higgs merely lifted his chin toward the upstairs. Vera cleared her throat, drawing Bennett's quick eyes. She pushed back her chair and laid her hands flat on the table on either side of the plate of doughnuts she'd made for the men.

"Coffee?" she said without offering a doughnut. Bennett's gaze wavered, shifting to the plate. It took an almost visible will for him to shake his head and stiffen his shoulders. He hadn't removed his hat when he barged in, and he did now. Drum was preternaturally uncomfortable in the company of women. He blocked up like an old bull with a young cow. His hard eyes took on a surprised look that made him seem younger than his years. His nose, broken several times, seemed to collapse a little more, as if the sheer will of his cussedness was the only thing holding it up; his round, fleshy face shimmered briefly, showing a glimpse of a joyful, curious boy who had retreated too soon.

"Where is he?" Drum asked again.

"Hayward?" Higgs asked. Although his voice was neutral, a small muscle in his jaw tightened. He was already tired of Drum

Bennett's questions.

"You know who I'm talking about. Suppose the boy's up there with the killer, too." Drum was on the verge of beating the foreman to the floor.

"He didn't kill your son," Higgs spoke carefully. "He's just a farmer."

Drum wanted to fire this mealymouthed bastard right now, but he didn't have anyone to put in charge yet. Cullen wasn't ready, no matter what he thought. Nineteen and still unbroke as the day Drum took him. J.B.'s wife sure hadn't added any grit to the bloodline. Look how easy it was to convince her to leave and stay gone.

Higgs stood, forcing Drum to look up, another damned irritating thing about the man. "Look, Ry Graver found the bodies and got shot for his trouble. We need to be looking for the killer, not fighting each other. Graver said the shooter sounded young. Good shot, too."

"What do you mean, 'bodies'?" Drum tilted his head to study the man.

Higgs looked confused for a minute. "We found an Indian girl with J.B."

"What Indian girl? What the hell are you saying?"

Higgs ran a hand through his thick gray hair and shook his head. "Don't make a lick

90

of sense. Didn't recognize her. Fourteen, sixteen, you know how those women are, growed at twelve." He described the scene in a few brief sentences, his eyes fixed on Drum.

Drum nodded and searched the man's face, then let his gaze wander the kitchen. "What else?"

Higgs took his time, glanced at his wife, who lowered the coffeepot to the table. "I can't figure out why the shooter didn't finish Graver. Rode off and left him. Kills two, leaves one. Don't make sense."

"You're sure about this man?"

Higgs thought a moment, and then slowly nodded. A fly bumped the window glass over the sink, buzzed angrily.

Drum released a long breath and stretched his neck to the right until it cracked. "Reckon Hayward could come down here?"

"I'll give a call," Vera said.

Drum watched Vera's swaying hips as she left the room and again wondered if J.B. was blind.

"How's Cullen?" Higgs asked.

Looking around the kitchen, Drum let the question linger in the air. The fly buzzed louder, banging into the glass with tiny bumps hard enough to knock it down to the sill. J.B. hadn't done so bad for himself.

Curtains on the windows, swept floor, lamp chimneys shining clean, wild roses in a vase on the table. His own house was a lot rougher. He and Cullen too tired of a night to do more than eat the bland beans, beef, and stewed fruit on tin plates Stubs served up to the hired men. The smell of those doughnuts clung to the room, made his mouth water. Maybe he should hire Higgs and his wife to come work for him. He glanced at Higgs, standing with his hands braced on the back of the kitchen chair. When their eyes met, Higgs didn't shy away, as a lesser man would. He held his ground. Drum knew he tended to low-rate other men. The man would have to sharpen his spurs to ride for Drum Bennett, though.

The sound of hurried boots on the porch brought both men's attention to the kitchen door as Hayward burst through, already trying to assume an authority that sat poorly on his face and shoulders. There was something there, though, a worried expression that flitted across his eyes behind the defiance.

"What do you want?" He stood beside the door, arms folded, leaning stiffly against the wall.

Drum studied the boy he rarely saw. J.B. hadn't the heart to make a man out of him.

Though he and Cullen were brothers, four years apart, this one was a waste of good food. Drum thought briefly of taking him home, too, then stopped. He was already ruint. Fancy shirt, trousers, even his boots showed little wear. Kid had those dark circles under his eyes and pale skin from doing more night work than day jobs.

"What do you have to say for yourself?" Drum asked.

"What's it to you, old man?" The kid actually sneered and Drum was on him, slapped his face so hard his head banged against the wall. As soon as the boy started for him, Drum slapped him on the other side just as hard, and watched with pleasure as the pale skin flamed with his fingerprints and the kid shook his head to clear it.

When Hayward started for him again, Drum balled his fist and bent his knees, but Higgs caught his arm before he could throw the punch that would've broken the boy's nose.

"Let him be," Higgs warned.

"I'll get you!" With tears in his eyes, Hayward glared at his grandfather, turned and yanked open the door, and ran outside.

Drum snorted in laughter. "Kid's got some gristle after all."

"He just lost his father," Vera said in a

voice that let him know he'd stepped over the line. The image of the fleeing doughnuts made Drum a little sorry.

"Can't baby a half-grown boy, make a bottle calf out of him." He grabbed his hat and put it on, gave the brim a yank, and moved the slide up the stampede strap to his chin. Damn wind always blowing in the hills, trying to take a man's hat and his thoughts both.

"I'll be sending a man over in the morning to inventory the place before I decide who to keep on." He glanced around the kitchen once more. It might work out that he would move over here, run the combined ranches from the more comfortable place, let the boys have the run of the other house, which was so rough they couldn't do more damage if they tried.

"I don't think so," Higgs said.

"What?" Drum tilted his head like he hadn't heard right.

"You're not sending anyone over here." Higgs straightened his shoulders and raised his head so his four extra inches seemed to grow.

Drum chuckled and shook his head. He'd have to fire him now.

"J.B. left a will. Copy's with the lawyer in Babylon."

Drum's stomach churned unpleasantly and sent painful acid-laced food into his mouth. He swallowed and scowled at the other man. "What's it say?"

"Wife and boys." Higgs fought the faint expression of amusement in the corners of his mouth. "She's to look after the youngster, and Cullen takes over running the ranch."

Drum's skin prickled cold. "He did that. Left those no-count boys and a runaway wife . . ." He shook his head. "I don't believe it." He knew they hadn't seen eye to eye on things, but to leave it all outside the family this way. Was he drinking? Drum felt the flush of anger move up his legs, spread through his torso and along his arms, and threaten to choke off his breath. He fought to keep it from flooding his brain, making him do things he'd regret. He had to get out of here, go home, and consider his next steps carefully, away from Higgs's prying eyes.

He pulled open the door and hurried outside, passing Cullen, who lounged against the fence post bordering the yard. "Let's go," Drum ordered.

"Cullen." From the doorway Higgs said the boy's name loud enough that Drum glared at him. "You want to come inside a minute, son? I got something to tell you."

"Come on, damn it." Drum jerked his horse's reins loose from the hitching rail. Used to his master's impatience, the big spotted gelding stood, iron jawed and unblinking as the man tightened the cinch with short, hard pulls.

"I'm gonna see what he wants," Cullen said, already halfway up the steps to the house.

"Get back here!" Drum raised his quirt as if he could strike the boy from that distance, and the horse shied, aware that it might be the recipient of the blow. Cullen sneered at him and disappeared into the house, letting the door slam loud enough to spook the spotted horse.

"Hold still, you ignorant son of a bitch." Although his words were rage filled, Drum kept his voice and body quiet so the horse wouldn't shy and buck away. How was it that nobody was listening to him today? "I'll settle with that boy later," he muttered, all the while wondering whether it wasn't a little late for that now that Cullen was taller, faster, and meaner than his grandfather. Those days of beating sense into the boy were over. Now it was time to see what took and what didn't. The cussedness of J.B. giving the ranch over about knocked Drum off his horse. The wife would want to sell it, and Drum would have to come up with ready cash he didn't have unless he raided his gold stash again, and that was a dangerous proposition. Why couldn't his son have just died and let his father take over? They never had a need for lawyers and such. No high-falutin judge had ever put his thieving fingers in the family business and come out rich. Not until now. Next thing he knew, that damn wife of J.B.'s would sneak back and lay claim to everything. His threats wouldn't hold much water now with J.B. gone. A thought crossed his mind that made him so uncomfortable he shook his head and cursed. He hoped to God he didn't have to sink so low as to kill a woman.

"Damn you, son, what the hell were you thinking? How'd you go and get yourself shot anyways?" Drum put the horse into its running walk, the one that ate miles as if they were inches and stayed easy on his back.

It dawned on him slowly, spreading a smile across his face even as the horse sidestepped to avoid a prairie dog hole. He settled his seat again and gave the animal its head. Yes, Higgs would need his help convincing the men. No reason a man shouldn't go and help his grandsons and his son's widow. One thing continued to bother him during the ride home, though: Why was J.B. so unforgiving about his taking Cullen to be raised? Drum had gotten over it, as he guessed his own father had. It was what they did with first sons, took them to be raised right, like the old Greeks, the Spartans, so they'd grow to be men who could last, men who'd stand in a fight. Drum remembered his own cousins, how shiftless they turned out, running off to fight for the wrong side in the war, getting themselves kilt with a bunch of border raiders in Missouri. Drum's great-grandfather drank himself into steady decline until he swole up like a pillow, turned yellow, and died in the front porch rocker *his* father had made when their people first came to the Missouri Ozarks. It was Drum who pushed west to the Sand Hills of Nebraska and used his gold to buy as much land as he could before anyone else found out about the place.

Drum stopped at the windmill that marked the end of J.B.'s land and the beginning of his, where his son had been murdered. The cattle had trampled the grass into sand, and only the water tank kept the place from blowing out. The wind was a low, steady hum in his ears, but he could still make out the bellering of a cow to her calf beyond the nearest hill. His horse pricked up its ears and snorted, shifting its weight back and forth between its front legs. Drum lifted the reins and the horse broke into a lope, heading for the noise.

While the rest of the herd grazed their way up the next hill, a brown-and-white cow paced frantically in front of a small blowout, where her calf churned its legs in a futile attempt to stand on the dissolving surface. The calf's sides were heaving wet and its tongue hung outside its mouth, but it wouldn't give up. Drum hoped the cow wouldn't charge him as a threat to her baby. He untied his rope, built a loop, and edged the horse closer. But as soon as the rope settled around the calf's neck, the cow charged his horse, butting him with her head so hard the horse lost its balance and went down, rolling on Drum's leg before he could free himself from the stirrups. The cow ducked away and stared at the spectacle from some distance while the calf on the end of the taut line, still fastened to the saddle, fought the rope cutting off its breath.

Drum's leg was numb as the horse lay on top of him, and for a moment he was content to stay there, not wanting to know what lay beneath the numbness. Then he swore and slapped the horse's neck. "Get off me!" It rolled onto its belly, propped its front legs straight, and raised its hind end with a big lurch. When it was on its feet again, it gave a whole-body shake like a dog and looked down at its rider, who had managed to slip his boot out of the stirrup just in time.

"Hold on. I'm coming." Drum sat and looked at his boot toe turned unnaturally inward. Then the pain swept up his leg and nearly flattened him.

"Damn it all to hell!" He began a long string of curses at the broken ankle. The cow started bellering again, drawing his attention to the calf choking to death on the end of the rope the horse pulled taut as it had been trained to do but wouldn't half the time. Now, of course, the damn jughead decided to do as it was told.

Drum searched for something to use as a crutch, but without trees in the hills, there weren't any fallen limbs or sticks. He considered the tall dried stems of the soapweed around him, but they wouldn't hold his weight, and he couldn't afford another fall.

The cow pawed the ground like she meant to charge the horse and man again. Drum struggled to drag his pistol from the holster he wore on rides into the hills. He'd shoot her if she tried to pull another stunt like that.

"Get away!" he shouted at her and waved his arms. The horse rolled its eye and tossed its head. "Not you, you damn fool," he crooned to the horse. He wanted to put a bullet in him, too. "Ease up, now, easy," he coaxed. The horse miraculously obeyed, and stepped forward to slacken the rope.

Drum's next maneuver was the real test. He tucked the shooting pain from his foot in a corner of his jaw, like a plug of stale tobacco, and dragged himself to the horse with a steady stream of words so the animal kept its mind on business. As soon as he was under the stirrup, he pulled himself upright, almost falling down again when his foot accidentally swept the resistance of the grass and new pain roared up his leg and burst in his head. But he fought it, as his grandfather had trained him to do with repeated beatings. "Don't you show a thing," he muttered.

"Whoa now, son, steady." He talked his way around the horse, used the animal's body, tail, and saddle to stand upright until he was on the far side and could mount using his good foot. He swung the bad foot over the horse's rump, miscalculated, and grazed it, nearly knocking himself off the saddle. He had little control of the broken foot, and could only rest it near the stirrup, knowing the heavy wood would bang the broken bones with every stride.

Even though it was a mild day, his shirt was wet and sweat ran into his eyes. He removed his hat, which had miraculously stayed put, and wiped his face on his sleeve.

Lifting the reins, he backed the horse, tightening the rope and slowly dragging the calf out of the sand bog, but he couldn't jump down to remove the line. He felt on his belt for his knife. Fortunately, it hadn't slipped from its sheath. He nudged the horse as close to the calf as he could, and kept an eye on the cow, who again pawed the ground. He was half-inclined to shoot her and be done with it, but then he'd lose two animals instead of one — he was in no shape to carry a motherless calf back to the barn to put it on the bottle. The horse tilted its head and rolled its eyes at the cow and danced lightly in place, ready to launch if she moved.

"Hold still, damn it." Drum gathered as much rope as he could into loops until the calf was just below his stirrup, then he slashed the line, leaving the calf with a collar of about three feet. With any luck, it would fall off or he could send someone out to fix it. Now, the question was, could he make the three-hour ride to his place? The foot was starting to throb like a son of a bitch. He wished he'd cut his boot before he mounted but a man hated to ruin something still of use. He looked over his shoulder at the thin path he'd just trod between the two ranches. Maybe there was something he could salvage here, he thought, and turned his horse back toward J.B.'s place. He should be there when that damn woman showed up throwing all kinds of fit.

CHAPTER SEVEN

Dulcinea Bennett closed *Grimm's Fairy Tales* and smiled at the boys and girls sitting stiffly at attention at the wooden desks before her. A few wore fearful expressions as the result of one story after another in which mothers and fathers betrayed their children, or acted foolishly and lost them. The animals weren't much better. She hated these stories. As she looked across the room, her eye caught on Lily, Rose's daughter, whose small round face was filled with enthusiasm as she raised her hand, something that almost never happened among the Indian children at the Rosebud Reservation school.

Lily burst out, unable to contain herself. "Our spider is smarter than the one living with the flea in your story, Mrs. Bennett. Iktomi is powerful. He does things backwards to fool you. He can trick you, too."

The other children glanced nervously at each other. The use of Lakota language was forbidden, and they must never speak of their old ways. Willow, a tall, reedy girl with bowed legs, leaned over and whispered to Lily, who blushed and dropped her eyes.

"What a wonderful creature! Can you tell me about any others?" Dulcinea glanced at Crooked Tail, seated next to last in the row by the door. He opened and closed his mouth indecisively, and his hand fluttered at his shoulder. When she nodded at him, he spoke so softly she had to move closer to hear.

"Rabbit Boy. Hero," he said, his hand collapsing on the desk with a soft thump.

"*Wagnuka*, red-headed woodpecker," Sarah Sweetwater said. Dulcinea looked at the girl seated across from Crooked Tail. She had spent the entire year in silence, but now spoke clearly and confidently. Her large eyes made her thin face seem narrow and she kept her lips closed to hide the fact that her baby teeth had never fallen out and now crowded her larger ones. Her cousin, Lost Bird, had been adopted or bought by General Colby after Wounded Knee, depending on which story one believed. She was taken to Colby's home in Beatrice, Nebraska, and raised by a white family. Sarah's aunt never recovered from the shock of the killings at Wounded Knee or losing the child. This past summer, Mrs. Colby tried to enroll her adopted daughter with the Cheyenne River Agency for full tribal rights, including an allotment of land.

"Don't forget *kangi* the crow and the turtle *keya,*" Billy Blue Horse said in his distinct high, clipped voice.

"*Ptan* and *capa,*" a voice called out. It was the tiny, sickly Otter girl who sat in the front, as far from the windows as possible to stay warm. Dulcinea turned and smiled at her, and the girl said, "Wakan Tanka," in an awed whisper, her face alight as she glanced shyly at the other children, who grew quiet, caution in their eyes. A couple of the oldest watched for Dulcinea's reaction. She had heard the words before and knew they were sacred, a reference to the great mystery, the creating power of the Lakota people. She closed her eyes and nodded.

An angry male voice said, "Hestovatohkeo'o." It was Stone Road, a fourteen-year-old who was held back for not learning his numbers and letters. He spent most days locked in the cloakroom or working in the kitchen, punishment for using Lakota or practicing his religion. The Indian agent had tried punishing the families of children like him by withholding food allocations and other supplies, but in his case it did no good. This was his last year in school. He was one of the children Dulcinea had tried to reach, to tutor privately, but it didn't work. In a way, she was relieved he wouldn't return in the fall.

"And who is that?" she asked in a tired voice.

"Double Face. The second one grows on the back of his head. Make eye contact, you die!" The boy smiled and opened his hands while the other children shifted uncomfortably and whispered to each other.

"Your fairy tales have anyone that powerful?" he demanded.

She was about to answer, then closed her mouth and looked at her students — dressed in plain cotton clothing, hair shorn, lacking ornament as if they had taken the vows of a strict Christian order — and shook her head. It was self-evident who had the power here. She recalled the supervisor's warning last fall. She was hired to introduce them to white culture and teach them to be of service in white families.

"By six and seven, Indian children have stopped playing with toys and are considered adults, working as hard as any grown person. They don't need coddling. Teach them how to be good citizens, how to follow rules, and about the consequences of poor decisions. And let's hope they go home and teach their families so we stop having all this trouble." The supervisor had looked out the window of the classroom at the bleak sweep of rolling hills nearly devoid of trees, with only the tall grasses and the empty mindless blue sky to relieve the eye. He wasn't a bad man. Dulcinea had heard him called saintly for his Christian convictions. He had fought to keep the school open when whites wanted to empty the reservations after Wounded Knee. He'd ordered the doors locked during those dangerous times, and the children were unable to join their families at the Ghost Dance. Although he was praised, Dulcinea wondered at his strategy. She'd worked at the school for a year now, and suspected that much of what she was asked to teach the children was useless or worse.

She glanced at the gray walls neatly lined with pictures of happy white children playing with farm animals, baking cookies with their mother, decorating a Christmas tree, ironically drawing turkeys and Indians for Thanksgiving — calendar pictures from previous years. She had been instructed not to allow the students to express their tribal culture with Lakota language or customs, and under no circumstances to celebrate their primitive rituals or display their drawings or handicrafts unless they reflected white culture. It was a ridiculous order, and she spent the year afraid to violate it. Now, in ten minutes' time she had undone the year, and felt relieved. It was the last day of school and she could feel the rising impatience in her charges, who sat twitching like horses under the burden of required stillness. When they returned in the fall, they would struggle to refrain from smiling, to maintain blank faces, and she would once again feel the weight of their obedience. Her friend Rose often hinted at the richness of Lakota life but was hesitant to reveal much. Dulcinea suspected that Rose met with the students secretly to share news of home and their culture. She had no real proof, though, except for Stone Road.

Dulcinea hadn't seen Rose in more than a week. The woman had disappeared without a word, leaving the kitchen shorthanded. She was startled at how easily the other woman slipped away and by the hurt she felt. Rose was her only real friend since she had been forced to abandon her husband and sons.

Half-strangled by guilt and grief, she tried to live close enough that she could ride into the Sand Hills to watch over her family, Drum Bennett be damned. He always caught her, threatened her again, and she resolved to stay away, move to another town. Before long, it would begin again. A few times J.B. found her in the town and brought Hayward to spend time with his mother, which drove her wild with regret. When J.B. came alone, they fought for hours about Cullen and about her leaving, and then fell exhausted into bed to punish each other's bodies, ending in silence side by side in her rented room like a long-married couple waiting for a train.

Only Drum would tell her about her son, and his stories were as dark and bitter as any the Brothers Grimm could conjure — injuries, accidents, misfortunes. These were the hallmarks of Cullen's life, as far as she could tell. The last time Drum found her, she was waiting for a glimpse of Cullen out by the old line shack on Drum's land. She knew her son went there to escape his grandfather's tyranny. It was only a matter of time. She camped there for two weeks last August, fighting biting flies, heat, and loneliness. She spent the time training the little ranch horse she'd bought from the livery stable in Gordon. She wouldn't give up this time, she vowed; she'd be there when Cullen arrived and they'd talk until they understood each other. Drum be damned.

Drum arrived at dusk one evening, standing in the stirrups so the horse's jarring trot wouldn't pound his back and hips. He courteously stopped and dismounted far enough from her tent and fire that she was not disturbed. But when he stood in front of her and let his eyes sweep her figure, she felt shame, as if she didn't measure up.

"Here we are again," he finally said with a slap of his reins across his palm. He sounded tired, and his wolf white-blue eyes glinted like mica as they took in her tent and her hobbled horse grazing nearby. "Having a time, aren't ya? Picnic? Campout?"

She remained silent.

"Got nothing to say, do you. We're going round the same ole mulberry bush." He put his hand on the butt of his revolver. "You're like a dog keeps coming back where it's not wanted." He slipped out the gun and let it hang in his hand between them.

She should have been afraid, but she wasn't. "Where's Cullen?"

"By God, I'll burn this place down if you don't keep away!" He raised the pistol and pointed it straight at her.

She shrugged and moved so close she

could lift the gun he held and press the barrel against her heart. When she smiled, he shrank back, and the gun trembled in his hand. "You're crazy."

She raised her eyebrows and smiled again. "I'm going to have him back."

"You'll get nothing. I'll finish off the lot before I let you touch any one of them." He spit to the side, as if he could rid himself of the bitter taste. "You don't care nothing about yourself, but your men are another matter. Keep that in mind. They might not get themselves kilt, but there's a world of hurt they can be in unless you stay off Bennett land."

That was the problem. She couldn't be sure that Drum Bennett wouldn't cripple his own to prove a point. He couldn't kill her, it wasn't in him to hurt a female for some reason, but males were another matter. As she watched him mount his horse and ride away, she thought it might be a relief to be done rather than continue living like a ghost, haunting the lives of loved ones, unable to reach out and touch them. Maybe she was going crazy. She packed up and left after that, hadn't seen Cullen since.

The last time she saw J.B. was during the warm spell in March when she rode down to Babylon to arrange the surprise shipment she'd bought for her husband and sons. They met in the room that was always reserved for the Bennetts at the hotel. For once their argument was halfhearted and they ended seated side by side on the bed. She traced the lines on his forehead with a finger and teased him about his sore tooth. For the first time in years, there was playfulness between them instead of grief and sadness at the separation. He asked, "Can you forgive me?"

"When you bring Cullen home," she said. Unlike the other times she'd made this request, he nodded. Then a spring blizzard came through and nobody could get out. April was cold and rainy, travel was hard. Finally May arrived, bright and fresh, and there was no more waiting. J.B. would bring her son home, she knew it.

He was especially busy this time of year with calving and culling, branding and fencing. Ten years ago, when they first separated, they sent coded telegrams, full of anger and threats and cajoling. That stopped after a while. God, she missed him. She couldn't believe it was years now since she left. Years that old man had held her family hostage. This year, she vowed, this year she would put a stop to it. Soon as the Kentucky Thoroughbred horses she'd bought for her husband and boys arrived, she'd tell J.B. the whole story and let him deal with his father in his own way. She planned the horses as a gesture of hope to bring their family together again, to signify her return and . . . and she didn't know what . . . She'd made the purchase on impulse and now it seemed foolish. She folded her arms and glanced out the window.

The American flag on the tall pole outside swayed in the wind as thin clouds skimmed the flat blue sky, causing waves of shadows to roll across the grass like the edge of a hand sweeping crumbs from a table. She walked over, unlatched the window, and turned back to the class. She wanted to invite them to climb outside and run through the new grass with her, as she would soon do on the ranch. She had felt a kind of wildness all morning, an anticipation. Something was coming toward her and she felt the urge to run.

"Mrs. Bennett?" A senior teacher poked her head in the doorway. Dulcinea turned and noticed the critical expression the woman wore that pulled her face into a narrow line like a ruler. "It's time."

Dulcinea nodded to the disappearing head, dropped her gaze to the patient faces of Lily and Willow and Billy Blue Horse and all the others. She beckoned to them. Each row rose and filed silently to the front of the room, where she shook their hands and gave each a little brown sack of penny candy she'd paid for out of her own pocket. Lily pulled out a cinnamon gumdrop and shyly licked it with the tip of her tongue before shoving the whole piece in her mouth, where it sat bulging in her cheek as she turned and skipped toward the door, then stopped and walked slowly, head down. Stone Road paused, hands at his sides, and refused to accept the small reward, until Billy Blue Horse tried to take the sack from her hand.

"Hestovatohkeo'o," he said, nodding toward the older woman outside the window, who was yelling for the children to be quiet for the photographer's picture.

"Maybe," Dulcinea said. It wasn't a bad description of the woman, at any rate.

Stone Road smiled and lifted the sack of candy in salute before he sauntered down the aisle, flipping some books open and slapping others shut. Dulcinea felt a sense of calm in her chest. The boy would be fine. He could survive without her or the school. She smiled as the children broke for the doors, shouting and laughing and shoving as they ran to meet the families gathered to take them home.

She turned away from the happy reunion, unable to stop the tears that filled her eyes. This was the cost of her bargain, and she wondered if it was only the scene outside that caused her unease. She surveyed the empty room one last time. Would she return next fall? She stuffed her pencil case and protractor, blackboard chalk and eraser, books and ruled paper, sketchbook and watercolors, scissors and colored paper in her flowered brocade satchel and pushed the chair against her desk. As she started down the row of student desks, she paused at one that bore the freshly carved outline of an elk with huge antlers and body and tiny legs. She knew whose it was, and she was glad to see him finally take the challenge she'd given them to draw what matters most. Little Elk had steadfastly refused to use the charcoal or pencils she gave him for anything except scribbling across the paper until all the white was extinguished. She might as well have given him the cheap lined graph paper he could buy at the trading post, instead of the quality drawing pads she'd ordered from Omaha. Next year, if she was still teaching, she'd offer him woodcarving tools, yet even as she thought it, she knew it probably wouldn't happen.

"Mrs. Bennett? Dulcinea?" Rose stood in the doorway, arms hugging her chest as if it were February, not May.

"Rose." Dulcinea peered into the hallway for Lily. The child was nowhere to be seen. Must be with her father, Some Horses. As she drew closer, Rose wouldn't meet her eye. Her face seemed swollen and chalky.

"What is it?" Dulcinea reached out, but her friend dipped away. Dulcinea took a half step back, swung her satchel in front of her body, and held it with both hands while she waited.

"No one's talked to you yet?" Rose lifted her head and searched Dulcinea's face. Without waiting for an answer, she said, "They're dead. Both of them." Her tone was harsh. Dulcinea didn't understand.

"What are you saying? Who's dead? Where?" She was seized by the image of Rose's daughter and husband lying in a pool of blood, but no, it was only a minute ago —

Rose tried to take a deep breath, but it seemed she couldn't. She brushed the tear from her cheek with the back of her hand and straightened her shoulders. Without looking at the other woman, she said, "My sister, Star, and your husband."

Dulcinea felt the silence settle into her, as if everything in her body had stopped mov-

117

ing, and every sound in the room and outside ground to emptiness. If she did not take another breath, the stillness would make this bearable.

"They've been looking for you."

"What?" Dulcinea couldn't understand what Rose was saying and didn't want her there anymore.

"Your people, the men at the ranch, they don't know where you are. My cousin heard about it in town yesterday and remembered you were up here. They buried him ten days ago. My sister was left out there —"

Dulcinea stared at Rose, and the other woman seemed older, dark circles under her eyes, her hair matted with grass and pine needles. She recognized that she should feel sympathy for her but couldn't move to express it or even open her mouth. Her chest was full, tight, and the noise rose up her throat, which tried to close against it, until a sound burst from her that was half howl, half sob, and still the tears would not come.

CHAPTER EIGHT

For ten days Drum ran them ragged, countering the orders Higgs gave the men at meals, directing Vera, too, though that didn't go well. Higgs smiled at the thought of Vera's stiff back and quick hands as she chopped potatoes for frying while Drum harangued, wheedled, flirted, and finally gave up trying to convince her to make him more doughnuts while he was laid up on the sofa with a broken ankle.

The boys were pushing at each other again, playing slap tag among the horses shifting nervously from leg to leg, tied to the corral, while the hands got ready to ride out for the day's work. Drum tried to send Cullen back to his ranch, but he refused. As Higgs watched, the boys swung up on their horses and spun them at the same time. Hayward took after J.B., tall, rangy, developing powerful shoulders and a broad back. He'd be grown in another couple of years, but what kind of man would he become without his father? What kind of man would either of J.B.'s sons become?

The boys glanced at each other, sat deep in their saddles, and put their spurs to their horses' sides, holding the reins tight so the animals had nowhere to go but into the explosive bucking and rearing that followed.

"Damn it," Higgs yelled. "I told you boys to leave those youngsters alone. You're wrecking perfectly good cow ponies with that nonsense!" He sent his horse loping toward theirs. The young horses stood, legs planted stiffly, heads thrown up, eyes rolling, bits foaming. "You think this is a gol-darn game?"

The boys glanced at each other and grinned, then shook their heads and shrugged, more alike than anyone would have guessed despite being raised apart. The sun was coming up over the hills, a red-orange ball in clear blue light, promising a day of searing heat.

"You two are riding fence." Higgs made an instant decision. "Go pack your gear, load Molly Mule."

"Not her," Hayward said. "It'll take for-ever."

Higgs nodded. "Just what I was thinking. And those horses you're on better come back rode right and broke to death. Now get going."

Head bowed, shoulders slumped, Cullen stepped off his horse and tied it to the rail. Maybe there was such a thing as breaking an animal too hard, Higgs thought. Hayward slid off the back end of his young horse, spooking it to kick, but the boy merely laughed, swatted it with his hat, and held on to the reins as the horse plunged and reared away from its tormentor. There was definitely such a thing as not being hard enough on a boy.

"Make quite a pair a hands, don't they?" Larabee stopped his horse beside Higgs and began to build a smoke.

"Week riding fence with that mule should take some stuffing outta them." Higgs glanced at Larabee. "I been thinking we should take Graver with us today."

"I'll get ole Sandy saddled up for him." Larabee put the cigarette in his mouth, struck a wood match on his saddle horn, lit it, pulled a smooth lungful of smoke, and let it trail out slowly as they watched the boys try to lead, then push Molly Mule out of the corral.

"Them boys got a task ahead of 'em." Larabee chuckled as the mule bit Hayward's shoulder and tore his shirt after he punched her nose. The boys stood off then, more respectful as the mule eyed them, teeth bared, ears flat. Then she dropped her head to snatch hungrily at the sparse weeds and grass.

"That Cullen thinks he's man enough to run this place, he has some to learn. I'm barely holding him back as it is. Less said about Hayward, the better." Higgs heard the kitchen door shut and turned as Graver came walking out the yard gate, stopped, and stared across the ranch, taking in the big barn, stable, corral and dry lots, winter pastures, bunkhouse, toolshed, chicken coop, foreman's house, all nestled in the small valley between the grass-covered hills, sheltered from the worst of the winter wind and snow. Graver finally turned his gaze to the boys struggling to settle the pack frame on the mule. Without a word, he walked across the dusty barnyard and took the halter rope from Hayward, who was using the end to battle Molly's slashing head and teeth while Cullen tried in vain to snatch the cinch strap and draw it under her belly. Graver put out his hand to stop the boy. Cullen hesitated, and then stepped back with a shrug.

The mule went motionless, watched warily out of the corner of her eye as Graver reached out and rubbed her withers, working his fingers up her neck, pausing at the poll behind the ears to lift the leather halter so it wasn't cutting into her head, then sliding his fingers down her jaw, scratching his way under her chin and up her nose. She blew hard and sighed, and her left hip relaxed. Graver fashioned a quick rope halter that passed behind her ears and looped over her nose, rubbing and talking to her the whole time. Then standing by her head, facing her hind end, holding the halter under her chin, he flicked the rope end toward her haunch. She lurched, kicked out, and finally took a step forward, which he rewarded by rubbing her neck and head before asking for another step. This time she swung her hind end, fought to free her head, and bucked before she came forward. The command-praise ritual was then repeated for a good half hour, until the mule complied and trudged forward whenever asked. The two boys watched until they grew bored and went to the bunkhouse for their bedrolls. By the time they returned, Graver had the pack frame secured and was attempting to lift the spool of barbed wire onto the mule's back with his one good arm.

Even from their distance, Higgs and Larabee could see the oily sheen on his pale face.

"You two take that wire and get that mule loaded," Higgs yelled. Hayward opened his mouth to talk back, but Cullen elbowed him and together they lifted the wire spool and tied it on while Graver held the lead rope.

"Ungrateful little bastards didn't even thank him," Larabee said.

"Saddle J.B.'s horse. Graver'll do fine," Higgs said.

Larabee raised a brow. With a slight shrug, he lifted the reins and loped across the ranch yard to the dry lot where the red horse had stood since they brought back J.B.'s body two weeks ago.

As soon as the boys mounted and rode out, Molly Mule trotting behind them, her rolled eye showing white and head held out stiffly in front of her, Higgs walked to where Graver leaned against the side of the barn, head back, eyes closed.

"Ready for a ride?" Higgs asked.

"I reckon," Graver answered without opening his eyes. "Got a hat I can borrow? Heat's already eating into my skull pretty good."

"Did all right with that mule."

Graver shrugged.

"Thought we'd go out there again, where you and J.B. ran into that trouble."

Graver folded his arms and opened his

eyes enough to see the foreman. "Why's that?"

"Something might come to you."

"I didn't kill anybody." Graver's voice was soft but firm.

"Black hat on the hook right inside the kitchen door. We'll meet you at the house with a horse."

As soon as Graver started walking, Higgs noticed that he wore flat-heeled farmer's brogans. "Ask Vera, Mrs. Higgs, to fetch you a pair of boots, too." No use in having a man dragged to death or worse if a horse shied and his foot went through the stirrup when he fell off.

CHAPTER NINE

Before he rapped on the door, Graver could hear the old man yelling and the sweet-voiced woman laughing. They'd been going at it since the day Drum Bennett was deposited on the overstuffed parlor sofa. Sometimes Vera's sweet tone took on a knife's edge and she'd cut the old man off at the knees; this was usually followed by a few hours of blessed quiet, during which Graver would be able to sleep.

"What does *he* want?" Drum yelled.

"Hush," Vera hissed. Pushing the strand of damp hair off her forehead, she gave Graver a quick smile and tilted her head. Her eyes had a touch of green like the water in the hay meadows. Sometimes, when she was angry, a dark cast appeared like the morning sky before rain. She was a handsome woman with light tortoiseshell skin that shone in the new summer light. When he told her about the hat and boots, she hesitated, and then reached for a hat, quickly brushing the brim and crown and holding it up to glance inside. Before he put it on, Graver saw J.B.'s initials stamped in the leather sweatband, and paused. The hat fit perfectly.

As soon as she left to find him boots, Drum Bennett started in.

"You may have the rest of these farmers fooled, but I know you. I know what you did. Don't think I'm not gonna do something about you soon as I'm on my feet again. Now take off my son's hat!" The old man's face had lost color, as well as some of its tautness, beginning to sag into wrinkles that made his threats seem more bluster than warning. Graver removed the hat and held it in both hands.

"Sir, I'm sorry you lost your son. It's a hard row to hoe. But I did not kill him, and I intend to find out who did. Same man shot me, a thing I cannot tolerate."

The old man stared at him, as surprised at the length of the speech as anything he'd said.

"I just knew you'd grow to liking one another." Vera bustled in clutching a pair of high black boots with long mule tabs. Almost new, they had a waxy shine and barely scuffed soles.

"Ma'am, I can't take those." Graver started to back out the door.

"I don't have time to go looking again, Mr. Graver. I'm in the middle of making doughnuts, so you'll oblige me to take these boots and let me get back to my cooking." She held the boots out with one hand and rested the other on her hip.

"Take the damn boots," the old man growled. "Man's dead."

Graver shook his head and took the boots. They fit just about as perfect as they could without being made for his feet. When he stood and stamped, driving his heel home, he straightened his back and shoulders, despite the twinge from the healing wound, and felt something new settle in his mind.

The chestnut kicked out behind as soon as it was asked to lope, and tried to put its head down to buck, but Graver was ready for it and sat light in the saddle, not giving the horse its head until it settled down to work. He felt the deep satisfaction that came from riding a good horse again, one with powerful hindquarters that reached under the body and a good sloping shoulder that grabbed at the distance. J.B. hadn't spoilt the horse's mouth either. The animal responded to the lightest touch on the reins, and Graver was careful to sit back when he asked for a walk or a halt, the response was so immediate. He smiled in appreciation. For all he'd sacrificed to become a husband and father and farmer, this was probably the only thing he truly missed, but he rarely allowed himself to dwell on the series of choices and mistakes that had brought him to this desolate land.

The recent loss of his family overpowered any kind of regret and seemed petty compared to the lives he had seen finished. In the end, his wife hadn't asked anything of him, no terrible return to her hometown for burial, no message to her unforgiving family. How quickly we are taken, he remembered musing, and was then brought back by the wails of his small children as they passed. His wife had simply slipped under the dark waters of her death without a sound. They never had a chance. Their lives fluttered away like milkweed seed on the wind. He couldn't catch and hold a single one. Now, as then and the whole time afterward when he was digging their graves and burying them in the sand, and laying the rusty iron bed frame over them so the animals couldn't dig them up, he hadn't allowed the luxury of tears, of self-pity as it were, because he was alive, and he couldn't do a damn thing about it.

Graver couldn't help feeling that no matter what he did, he kept traveling the same circular road as they topped the hill and looked down at the windmill and water tank. The red horse snorted, tossed its head and reached its nose around to stare at his boot. Wrong man, it seemed to say. Graver felt an unnatural apprehension in his gut, as if he was about to hear gunshots echo in the still morning air and feel the bullet rip into his body again.

The grass was especially green here because of the water, and cropped by the cattle that came to drink and stood swatting flies. The herd was elsewhere this morning, though, and the men had the area to themselves. Other than that, it was the same as the day he was shot. What did Higgs want? Graver didn't have any answers, at least any he wanted to share, and he noticed that Higgs and Larabee had drawn up on either side of him as if to block an escape.

A meadowlark on one of the windmill struts puffed its chest and sang its courting song, then glared defiantly in case any other suitors showed. Graver thought of his wife's passion for drawing the creatures in the world around her, how heartbroken and brave she had been when the two oldest children had taken her box of pastels and scrubbed them on the table until there was nothing left. There was no money to replace them. After that she had drawn with pencils until they wore out, too. He watched her hands toward the end, anxiously sketching with her fingernail in the packed dirt by the fireplace, staring into the fire. While the fever was on her, she drew on the mattress ticking and the dirt floor, until her nails wore down, and her fingertips bled from the scraping. Even after he bound her hands, the motion continued, sometimes scrawling the air between them, sometimes the front of her nightgown, or the bed again. He was glad to burn the bedding when it was all over, afraid he might recognize the portraits.

He shook himself. Why had he never asked her if it was worth it, what she gave up for him? He knew he didn't want the answer, and was glad she never offered. The truth couldn't be known until the end of a person's life, and then what's the use. He should never have taken her love, like a gift that was out of proportion for the occasion. But it was a young man's mistake, one he'd never repeat. He wiped his face with his hand and wasn't surprised to find it sweaty. Ever since he was shot, he felt chills and twisting cramps in his gut like his body fought to rid itself of the poison. His mind wandered, too, right when he needed to pay attention to things at hand, like it was trying to trick him.

"Can you think of anything else about that day?" Higgs asked Graver while Larabee smoked and watched. Graver shook his head. A breeze drove the windmill blades, producing a high, persistent squeal, and then quit and they slowed to a stop. "Larabee, you got any grease on you?" Higgs asked. "Might as well fix that son of a bitch while we're here."

The man sighed, finished his cigarette, and rubbed it out on the toe of his boot before climbing down and searching his saddlebag for an old tobacco tin.

"What's that?" Higgs asked with a frown.

"Hair grease, hand healer, leather protector, waterproofer, bag balm, wound dressing. Want some?" Larabee grinned.

Higgs waved his hand. "Get going." He shifted his eyes to Graver. "You get down and show us how it happened. Every inch of it."

"Thing is, my knee's been giving me fits lately, and climbing's . . ." Larabee stood next to his horse and glanced at the windmill as if it were a Wyoming mountain peak.

132

Higgs snorted and shook his head.

"I'll do it," Graver said.

"You up to a climb?" Higgs asked.

Graver maneuvered his horse to Larabee's side, took the can of grease, and headed for the windmill on the far side of the tank. Anything was better than acting out the shooting again. Maybe they were going to finish him here, the thought had occurred to him several times throughout the ride.

"Can't fault a man for wanting to work," Larabee said as he stepped into the stirrup and settled back into the saddle.

"Hope that arm's healed enough. Hate to have you haul him back on your horse, you walking the whole way," Higgs said.

"Looks like he's doing fine." Larabee lifted his chin to the windmill, where Graver was straddling the crossarm and digging into the grease tin.

"You need to get back down there and start looking for clues," Higgs said.

Graver slowly worked his way around the scaffolding of the windmill, pretending to examine the machine while he memorized the way the small hills folded into the larger ones that were actually sand dunes underneath a thin layer of soil and grass. To the east a series of shallow hills like steps cut into the front of a tall hill. The killer must have waited there, Graver thought, where the grass was cropped short by his horse. He tried to remember the voice from that morning. At the time, he'd thought it was a young man, but maybe it was a woman? Or perhaps the shooter had been lying in an uncomfortable position, say on his back, where the soapweed took over the hillside. Person'd have to be cautious of rattlers sleeping in the shade of those wide stiff leaves. And the prickly pear cactus, the yellow blooms peeking out of the spiny ears, he'd have been careful not to roll or kneel in those.

Graver's fingers felt the gears, the drive shaft of the windmill, dry as a bone. He didn't remember that noise, but it must've been there. He peered closely at the housing for the drive shaft and saw that a stray shot had pierced the metal, allowing the grease to clog and dry. He stuck his finger in the hole and felt the bullet. Have to come back and dig it out, see which gun it came from. Had they saved the bullets from J.B.'s shoulder or checked his guns to see if he'd fired back? He quickly glanced over his shoulder. Higgs was focused on Larabee. Graver circled the windmill struts one more time, examining the murder site from every angle. The puzzle wasn't only J.B.'s shooting, it was the Indian girl's death as well. Why was she there? Where was her body now? And why had the shooter left him alive? For days, he was haunted, thought the killer might change his mind and come back for him. Another reason to figure this out, to be ready when the shooter realized his mistake. Then Graver had another thought — what if he tried to draw the killer toward him instead? First rule he'd learned in his past life: trust no one. Second rule: have a fast horse nearby. Always. He glanced at the chestnut gelding as it restively stamped and tossed its head against the no-see-ums chewing bloody clots in its ears. Third rule: stay out of family problems. Well, he'd blown that one to hell, hadn't he.

He tested the blades and was rewarded with a nearly noiseless spin. He threw the grease tin to the ground and began his one-armed descent, pausing halfway to rest. His shoulder throbbed wildly. Dizziness came through his head in a wave and ate up the day around him. He closed his eyes and leaned his cheek against one of the main wooden supports. Be lucky not to end up with a face full of splinters like his hand. He should have asked for gloves, but he was so used to doing without that the thought hadn't occurred to him. He wished to hell he were someplace else. Wished he'd kept going that morning, hadn't been drawn into another man's fight. But now it was his fight, and no matter how he felt about the Bennetts, he had to help set things right. A vivid image of his wife and children suddenly swept over him, and he closed his eyes against the sudden moisture. When he reopened them a cloud of dust was rising to the top of the hill. He quickly jumped down and ran to his horse.

"Damn those boys!" Higgs stood in the stirrups. Graver sent his horse up the small rise behind him to see more clearly as cows and calves spilled down the hill and crowded the water tank.

Higgs removed his hat, bounced it against his thigh to clear the dust from the brim, put it back on, and gave the front a final tug to guarantee it was tight. "Nothing to see here now those cattle come through. Let's get back."

"I need a job," Graver said.

Higgs squinted at him and gave a short nod. " 'Less you got a better offer, you can bunk here. Thirty a month and found to start."

Graver glanced at Larabee's patched saddle and bridle, and the worn pants and shirt he wore. "I'm grateful for the offer, but . . ."

"Just stay until we get this killing sorted out, then."

Graver nodded. He stared at the place he'd found the girl and the man that morning.

Larabee spoke up, "Wonder what J.B. was doing up here with that girl." He glanced at Graver.

"Probably saw something, same as me." Graver returned the look. "Where's the girl buried now?"

Larabee ducked his head and glanced at Higgs.

"We don't rightly know. Came back to get her and she was gone." Higgs lifted his hat. "Can't put the rain back."

Graver surveyed the little meadow one more time and wondered how it was the girl was gone. Did animals drag her off? Or did the shooter come back for her?

CHAPTER TEN

Dulcinea and Rose stopped their horses on the last hill overlooking the ranch and stepped down to stretch their legs after the long ride. Yesterday they left Rosebud, crossed into Nebraska, and stopped in Babylon for the night before coming into the hills. It was the end of the day, and Dulcinea could see lone cowboys on horseback driving cattle slowly out to summer pastures. They must be late this year because of J.B.'s . . . she could not say the word yet. Glancing at Rose, she felt the kinship of sorrow and could not begin to imagine the loss of a sister. There was no hierarchy to grief, she realized, and her knees nearly buckled as her feet sank into the sand underfoot, where the horse-and-wagon traffic had killed the grass. She was almost home and something made her pause.

To the right was a vast blue lake, the surrounding marsh alive with birds feeding and mating. The air bore the moist scent of water, so blue it put the distant white-blue sky to shame. She shaded her eyes to stare at the lake where pelicans floated peacefully. Nearby a pair of swans stretched their long necks searching the waters for food, and farther on, ducks dove and flapped, green necks glistening in the sun. Myriad red-winged blackbirds perched on dried cattail stalks with brown heads shredding into the new green shoots below. Nearby, one bird straddled two cattails, feet clenched fiercely to hold its territory against the loud, hissing wind.

After she rode down this hill, nothing would ever be the same. Right now, Dulcinea was between two worlds, but soon she would be in the one without her husband. She stuck her hand in the pocket of her traveling coat, fingered the crumpled yellow paper that carried J.B.'s last coded message from March. *Soon the birds take wing with my heart.* She hadn't known about his poetic nature when they first married, or even after the boys were born. It took their separation for his silence to become eloquent in the anonymity of the telegram's compressed language. She fingered the paper's edge. She was wearing it soft as flannel.

Beyond the lake, the hills rose green and humped like ancient fallen beasts, their grass remorseless and brutal hair. There were few trees that thrived naturally here, the occasional cedar the men hacked down because it drew too much water, the sand willows, mulberries, wild cherry, and cottonwood by the small creeks and rivers. She used to miss trees terribly, their casual interruption of the sky, until she returned to Chicago for a visit, then she missed these ragged hills instead. She stooped to pick a wild pink rose, avoiding the tiny spines that slivered like unseen glass hairs into one's fingers. There was little scent, but the creamy softness of the petals like the inside of a dog's ear more than made up for it. She placed one on her tongue, and imagined she could taste the hills, the bittersweet tang of life.

"Those three men don't have any cattle." Rose pointed east where the cowboys trotted their horses. Two of the men slumped in the saddle while the third rode with shoulders high and firm.

"Where did it happen?" Dulcinea asked. Rose would know. She'd already been out there.

Rose tipped her head at the three men.

"That way. Water tank between Bennett lands."

"Why was my husband there with your sister? How old was she?" Dulcinea regretted her question the moment it left her mouth and Rose grimaced like she'd been slapped. "I'm sorry —" Dulcinea reached out, placed her hand on Rose's arm. "I don't understand."

"I don't either," Rose admitted. "She was going to meet a man who could help her —" She paused and picked up the reins she'd dropped to ground tie her horse. "She was a good girl. Told me he had information about our mother." She appeared lost in thought as she watched the three men near the ranch yard. "Maybe it wasn't your husband she was meeting."

Dulcinea stared at the other woman, who bit her lower lip to stop from saying more. She stepped back and picked up her own reins, then pretended to check the cinch on the saddle before she mounted again. What could J.B. know about Rose's family? She'd told him about befriending Rose when they met in March, and he seemed ignorant of her family. She looked westward, where heavy clouds lay above a gray veil that meant someone was getting the luck, and the rain. The sun hung near the lip of the horizon like a red ball at rest, and a low bush beside her suddenly exploded with lavender butterflies that clouded around her long skirt, washed up her bodice, and splashed against her face, their wings like an exhaled breath of powder as she closed her eyes. Something about the moment, its unexpected tenderness, made her long to hear him say her name again, just once more, "Dulcinea, Dulcie May," as he'd whispered in her ear when last they'd met, in March.

A red-tailed hawk glided up and over the hill, the white winter belly almost obscured by summer brown, and then dipped toward the valley they traveled, swift as an arrow. It hit a rabbit running a ragged pattern through the switchgrass along the road ahead. The rabbit uttered a single choked scream, then went limp and hopeless, back broken, eyes fixed as the bird swept upward. A single drop of blood splashed Rose's faded-gray-cloth-covered arm, the edges feathering out and sinking, already permanent. Rose followed the hawk's flight until it was out of sight. "Star," she whispered. "Star is making sure we're safe."

Dulcinea knew they should go down the hill to the ranch. It would be dark soon, and late for supper. She used to be the one

142

cooking, along with whatever cowboy's wife they could hire. She knew what it meant to have extra mouths at the table. Rose didn't eat much, though, and she hadn't been hungry since they'd left the reservation, but she'd have to eat to keep track of things. She was going to find the person who killed J.B. They were alrcady sentenced to death in her heart. She glanced at Rose. What kind of vengeance did she plan? In the years she'd known her, Rose had been a fair person, but anything to do with family was outside fairness. Dulcinea felt the same.

"Your husband left you a lot of land," Rose said, her eyes squinting into the distance.

"I wish he hadn't." Dulcinea was surprised by her bitter tone, as if she blamed the land itself. She had thought of nothing except getting home and making certain that Rose was right. Stranger things happened. Maybe J.B. was still alive and it was — she couldn't think what.

She half expected her husband to see her from atop another hill, to gallop toward her, waving hat and arm, as he had every other time she arrived.

"What are we going to do?" Dulcinea turned to the other woman. Rose stared at the ranch below, and then shifted her eyes back to Dulcinea.

"We're going to find out who did this. Look and listen. Someone knows something. My sister will help us." Rose looked down at her mount's wind-tangled mane, combed it thoughtfully with her fingers as the horse gazed longingly at the others going home for the night.

Dulcinea pulled up in front of the house and Rose stopped beside her. Her gaze followed the picket fence around their first home, where the foreman now lived, and then on to the second, larger house J.B. built for her when she was pregnant with their second son. It needed paint, but the windows were intact. The lilacs in the side yard had grown tall and straggly, the blooms spare, purple and white glimpses amid the dark green leaves. She hadn't been this close in years. She was too afraid of Drum catching her or her husband forcing her to explain why she couldn't stay. She dismounted and started for the house, then shifted her gaze to the fenced-in pasture beyond the barns. He wasn't in the house. He'd be out there. They couldn't wait. She lifted the skirt she still wore from school and started toward the cemetery where her husband rested.

The sound of the house door closing made her glance over her shoulder as Vera Higgs strode to the gate, lifted the latch, and stopped with her hand shading her eyes, taking in the new arrivals. She was a tall, slender African, dressed for work in men's canvas pants and a faded blue shirt cinched with a wide leather belt. She stared at Dulcinea without expression, as if the wind in the hills had picked up a feather and blown it to her doorstep. A few years ago, J.B. introduced them in town, and it was a painful, awkward moment with him tongue-tied between them. Dulcinea nodded without speaking to the woman, whose gaze shifted to Rose, who still sat atop her horse.

"I take it you're with Mrs. Bennett," Vera said. "If you ride over there, one of the men will take your horses. You're welcome to have supper with us." Her low contralto voice held a music Dulcinea envied, and she was jealous that another woman invited her friend into her own house. She immediately shook the notion from her head.

She started toward the cemetery again, took only three steps before she heard, "Vera! Who is that? Vera?" Only one man had a voice like that: loud and harsh enough to wake the dead. Her eyes flitted from the

145

cemetery to the house to Vera at the yard gate, and her mind filled with a roar.

"Do not tell me that Drum Bennett is in my house!" She glared at Vera standing in her way as she half ran to the gate and then yanked it out of the other woman's hand, marched up the walk, climbed the rotting steps, crossed the porch, pulled open the door, and strode inside.

"Get out!" she shouted at the figure on the parlor sofa, leg propped on a pillow while he yelled himself red in the face, white spittle collecting in the corners of his mouth like a rabid dog.

He blinked, mouth gaping. "You!" he growled. He had a full head of greasy white hair, and a mustache hung with a curd of egg over lips so thin they looked to be drawn on his fleshy, boneless face. The brows were thick white, too, as if he had fallen in a boiling laundry tub of lye soap. His skin was shiny hard, brown as a beetle's, and his eyes were the same ugly white-blue. To ask for any kindness would be as fruitful as inquiring of a bolt of fabric how the day was progressing. It pleased her to see the sweat bead his forehead and dampen his chin. If she could pry open those razor lips and jam her traveling pistol down his throat, she would do it.

She pulled off her hat and tossed it on the rocker across from him. "You need to leave." It was then she noticed someone sat in the corner of the room, legs clad in dirty, torn denim stretched out in front of him as he slouched in the chair, hat pulled halfway down his face as if napping. Slowly the legs pulled under his body and the figure thumbed his hat back and sat up, still managing to slouch. Cullen. The same wolf white-blue eyes as his grandfather, the same insolent sneer on his lips. She couldn't catch her breath, felt like she'd run a footrace and was on all fours panting.

"Hello, son," she said, keeping her voice soft as she would for a young child. He stared at her as if she were a stranger.

"We had a bargain, woman." Drum pulled himself more erect and wiped his mustache, the egg curd dropped to his sleeve.

"That bargain's lying out there in the ground. Call your men. Get on your horse or wagon for all I care, but get out of my house."

"You're the one needs to stay gone, missy. Soon as I'm up again, you —"

"You'll what? J.B. is gone." She folded her arms and rocked back on her heels.

"I didn't kill him," Drum said in a low voice.

"However it happened, you killed him," she said. Cullen's laughter from the corner made both adults glance over. Drum's face paled and his mouth hung for a moment, then his expression darkened.

"You're out of your mind —" He licked his lips.

"You didn't protect him, did you? Look at you, you're a used-up old man. You can't even take care of yourself now." She gestured toward the broken ankle, and he stretched his hand down his leg as if to protect it from her.

"Cullen, get the hell out of here," Drum said. The boy laughed again, shook his head this time, as if realizing he was out of everyone's reach.

Drum glared at her. "Think it's safe here now?" His whispery voice made her shiver.

"Oh no." She braced herself on the back of the rocker. "I talked to the sheriff in Babylon this morning. He's coming out here to investigate. I said it was more than likely your doing."

His eyes settled on the glass of water on the table beside him, then glanced quickly at her. He let his hands drop in his lap and stared at the wall. "You have to sleep sometime," he said.

"I'm not worried about an old cripple."

She pulled her traveling pistol from her skirt and held it loosely in her hand. He saw it and shook his head. There was a sharp intake of breath from Cullen's corner as he straightened with hands on the chair arms and feet under him, ready to spring.

They waited in silence. It reminded her of the special musk of the reptile house at the zoo in Chicago when she was in grammar school, a dry, fetid stillness fueled by the unwashed and unrepentant man and the long stewing rage of the woman beside him. She wondered what Cullen thought. She cursed the fact he was here to see this. She'd meant their reunion to be much different.

"Too late to take the boy, lady." Drum's smile was more smirk. "Maybe he's the one you have to watch out for now."

She had to pretend he lied because his words came too close to her fears. She saw the mirth leave Cullen's face, replaced by the alert expression a hunted animal might wear. Had he —

She turned abruptly and went to the kitchen for coffee. The coffeepot was in its usual place on the warming shelf on the back of the woodstove, which turned the contents to bitter black soup by end of day. J.B.'s favorite, a bitterness that made a person's tongue swell and teeth brittle as if they'd been grinding sand.

"Cup would be fine by me," Drum called.

"Same for me," Cullen's singsong mocked the two adults.

She took a sip, savored the harsh bite with the tip of her tongue, and glanced around the well-kept kitchen, noting the orderly arrangements and feminine blandishments of flowers and her old lace curtains.

"Cup a coffee, sister," Drum said. Cullen slouched again, hands folded on his lap, his expression amused. Where was her boy, her sweet boy of old? She shivered, and then stopped herself. Couldn't afford to show weakness in front of the old man.

She went to the chair across from Drum and moved it closer to the low table on which rested his sundry goods: a battered metal comb one would use on a horse's mane and tail, a pair of tiny wire spectacles, a smooth pebble veined with gold and silver, and a book whose spine and cover were so worn, the printing was a series of gold hieroglyphs, unreadable to her eye. Drum Bennett with a book. Truly he must be at wit's end. No sympathy rose in her heart. She recalled the weeks and months after giving birth when that old man arrived to browbeat her out of bed, weak and ill, into cooking for him, despite the boys crying hungrily. "We'll make a ranch woman out of you yet," he'd declared.

She sat, lifted her skirt, and placed her left foot on the table, kicking the pebble and comb onto the floor. When he saw her right foot about to join the other, he rescued his glasses from being crushed, although the book slid off and landed with a spine-breaking thump, loose pages flittering. She settled her skirts and leaned back, allowed the muscles sore from riding to find the contours of the chair. Her knees protested when straightened and her calves took a minute to relax their contraction.

"He took up with an Indian girl, you know, that's what got him killed. Found her out there right beside him."

She responded with silence, and he nodded. Cullen shifted restlessly in his chair, then rose and went quietly through the doorway to J.B.'s office. They listened as the cork hissed from a bottle and liquid sloshed into a glass. He reappeared with a half-full glass of brown liquor in his hand and began prowling the room with catlike grace, silently weaving among the chairs and tables while taking small sips. He stopped at the whatnot shelves and picked up the belt buckle Hayward had won riding goats as a boy and let it drop with a thud on the walnut shelf. He took a longer drink.

"You didn't know he was seeing that girl?"

She gulped the burning-hot coffee to scald the lump caught in her throat. Cullen stopped behind her chair, rested his hand on the back of it. She was unsettled, she wanted to lean forward but remained still, even when he began to play with the chignon at the back of her neck. When his ragged fingernail scraped her skin, she couldn't stop her shiver and he placed his hand on her shoulder. She waited a moment before reaching up to touch his fingers, afraid he'd jerk them away. He sucked in his breath but held still, and she stroked his fingers three times before he lifted his other hand to drink again. She could smell the heavy spice of their wedding brandy. That's what they'd always called it.

"She was fourteen. Tiny slip of a thing . . ." Drum grinned, as ugly as he knew how, like he'd just made her stick her hand in a gunnysack full of rattlesnakes. "What do you think of that, sister?" He rubbed the thigh of his good leg and chuckled. She closed her eyes and turned her face from his. That kind of meanness needed a witness to really be enjoyed. Cullen squeezed the back of her neck with his hand and remained silent.

A part of her knew J.B. deserved more

152

happiness than their miserable meetings of‐
fered, but a child? J.B.? Rose said her sister
was a good girl. Why would Drum lie, un‐
less he was responsible.

Drum glanced at Cullen. "He's not com‐
ing to live with you, you know that, don't
you?" Drum's mood and tone changed
abruptly and Cullen began to prowl the
room again. "Don't bother pretending,
sister. I know why you're here. That boy is
mine, that's all I have to say on the subject.
You'd have him ruint in a month. Turn him
weak and mewly like J.B. was until you left.
Took him a while, but he grew a pair and
managed to keep this place going. More
than I predicted." He paused and looked
out the window at the ranch yard, where
the hands were gathering for supper.

"What have you done to find his killer?
Anything? Or have you been sitting here
planning on how you're going to take over
everything J.B. and I built?"

Drum almost flinched, his face reddened.
Cullen stopped at the end of the sofa and
watched her, the drink halfway to his mouth.

"I sent men out to look." Drum stared at
his hands, his mouth a grim line.

She stood and paced between the kitchen
and living room, hands clutched in front of
her as if she were going to be sick. Her mind

flooded with protest and argument, but it did no good. Not now. Not then when Drum arrived that morning for his "legacy," as he called it. Family curse was how she'd always referred to it, as if the vampire of Bram Stoker's novel had come to life in the Sand Hills of Nebraska, a place so remote the rest of the state rode out of its way to avoid it. There was no justice here. They were all merely blooded creatures waiting for the fatal bite. Even J.B., the man who loved her more than she loved herself, could not change his father's mind. And so she was forced to leave without him ever knowing she paid for his safekeeping, and the price became her burden, the forfeiture of their future together.

She stopped behind the chair she had sat in and clutched the back. Cullen had returned to his father's office for another brandy and stood in the doorway drinking and watching them.

"I will find out who murdered my husband. You don't need to concern yourself. He would want it that way. He never trusted you, Drum. Not for a minute. I wouldn't be surprised if you were the one pulled the trigger. If you did, I'll hang you out there myself." She pointed to the cottonwoods behind the barn.

"Just because you're the cow standing in the pigsty don't mean you're not dirty, missy." Drum used both hands to lift the splinted leg, pivot, and ease it to the floor, grimacing at the effort that brought sweat to his pale cheeks and the backs of his hands.

"Here, Cullen. Put that glass down and help me. I got to visit the outhouse," he yelled, then glanced toward the homemade crutches at the end of the sofa. He wouldn't ask. He studied the table blocking his access. His only choice was to hobble around it. Somehow he pushed himself upright, swaying with the bad leg propped out in front of him, balancing with his arms outstretched, on one foot, like a man on a wire in the circus. The first hop on the good foot brought his toe under the braided rug and he crashed to the floor, crying out as he tried to twist away from the broken ankle, resulting in a loud snap as his arm broke beneath the weight. Cullen drained his glass, set it down, and hurried over to help.

Dulcinea was on her feet before she could stop herself. Shifting him to lie on his back, she accidentally grabbed the hand of the injured arm, and moved the bone with a grating sound. He moaned through gritted teeth.

"Lie still!"

"Help me, boy," Drum groaned.

Cullen rocked back on his heels and looked at his mother, the amusement again in his eyes as he raised his brows. She nodded and together they tried to raise the old man to a seated position. When that failed, she rose and went to the door to call for men to help. Rose was still at the gate, holding the horses. Both looked played out from the long, fast ride, their heads down, coats rough with dried sweat. She watched as the hands started for the house and then paused at the door to peek at the scene inside, uncertain what was expected of them.

"What happened?" Vera asked as soon as she pushed her way through the crowded doorway, followed by her husband, who stepped forward and knelt beside the old man.

"Frank Higgs, ma'am. We met in town couple years ago?" The foreman tipped his hat to Dulcinea.

"Still have to go out back," the old man muttered as Higgs directed the men to lift him. "That damn woman did this to me! Keep her away from me!"

"I told you to use the night jar," Vera scolded.

"He needs to go home," Dulcinea said. "I

156

don't want him in my house."

Her words were greeted with expressions ranging from surprise on Frank and Vera's faces, to bemusement on Cullen's, and finally to fleeting triumph on Drum's, before he fainted in their arms.

CHAPTER ELEVEN

She blew in like a hard west wind, the kind that dropped a man's bones to zero, froze his hair to his skull, and clogged his eyes with ice. Graver shook his head at the scene. The old man on the floor, pee darkening his trousers and the braided rug beneath him, Vera and Frank Higgs standing helpless while the widow paced, her small black kid button boots thudding firmly on the parlor rug, her arms folded, as if Drum Bennett's every ragged breath caused her affront. In a plain gray bodice and full skirt, Dulcinea Bennett was a handsome woman with only a few small lines at the edges of her light brown eyes. There was a rich glow to the strands of auburn hair falling out of her chignon. She possessed a slender build that spoke of inner force, more than equal to her father-in-law, Graver suspected. She appeared cool despite the heat that put a moist sheen on everyone's face. He wondered what made her leave her family.

Higgs called Larabee and Willie Munday to move Drum upstairs. Cullen followed.

"I don't see why he can't stay on the sofa," Mrs. Bennett muttered to their retreating backs.

"Hard to keep that arm right," Graver said, intending to elaborate from his own experience until she caught him in a gaze that would freeze a man on a hot stove. She was definitely Drum Bennett's equal, and certainly more than Graver could handle.

"And who are you?" She stopped behind the rocker, her hands gripping the black lacquer. He noticed they were the kind of hands that had seen work, the nails short and irregular despite the small thin fingers. On her left hand, she still wore her wedding band. Well, Graver thought, that was something.

"Sir?" She tapped her fingers against the back of the chair. She was like an overbred mare, likely to bolt at any moment, not reliable enough to work except maybe as a fancy horse some lazy owner could step out for show. She opened her mouth to address him again, but he interrupted with a wave of his hat.

"Ryland Graver, ma'am, Ry." She closed her eyes and nodded.

"I'm sorry, ma'am. Shall I fetch you a glass of water?" He moved toward her with the intention to catch her if she fainted, but she waved him away.

"Please. Get yourself some water." She opened her eyes and tried to smile. It came out a tired grimace. "I just need to know who my employees are and what jobs they perform." She inspected him, dressed in J.B.'s clothes, from the tall boots to the black shirt to the new black hat that Graver worked hard to keep the dust from settling into. "Judging from your attire, I'd say you have some elevation above the other men. So I repeat my request, what do you do here, on J.B.'s, our, ranch?"

He picked a piece of cottonwood lint from the brim of the hat, wondered what to tell her. He didn't want to shock or offend her with the fact that he was wearing her dead husband's clothes, but he didn't have any others to wear. He was in a quagmire. From upstairs groans and then a shouted string of curses commenced when Drum apparently awoke as they set his arm.

Frank Higgs hollered from the top of the stairs, "Graver, bring that bottle of brandy from the office."

Graver lifted his hat. "This is what I do here, Mrs. Bennett, whatever they tell me."

As he edged past her to the office tucked off the parlor, he smelled the musk of a woman's body unwashed from travel beneath the sweeter scent of her perfume and felt, for the first time in more months than he cared to think, a surge in his own body that made him pause for the briefest moment behind her, her back inches from his chest. His breath caught in his throat, and he swallowed hard. He wasn't sure, but he thought he saw a tremor pass through her.

"I'll keep your accommodating nature in mind, Mr. Graver." Her voice had a rich deepness that ran itself up and down his spine before settling in his legs, made it just a bit more difficult to walk with the assurance of a man who carried his own water in the world. Hell, it made a person want to carry his and hers and anybody else's she had a mind to invite along. He smiled and shook his head as he moved inside the office and spied the brandy on the desk.

"That's our wedding brandy," she said when she saw the bottle in his hand. "That man never even bothered to come over when we got married." She reached for the bottle, but Graver lifted it away.

"They need this upstairs, ma'am."

She stamped her foot, but her arms collapsed to her sides. "This really is the last straw. I am going to march up there and make them take him home. He's never going to leave at this rate!" When she started to push past, he stood in her way and reached to take her arm. A surprisingly strong and muscled arm it was, he had time to consider before she shook herself free.

She pulled herself to her full height, all five and a half feet, and seemed able to look down her nose at him despite his advantage in size. A schoolteacher look, definitely, he thought. "Give me that bottle."

He was about to give it to her when Higgs thundered down the stairs, startled when he saw the two of them, grabbed the bottle, and rushed back up. Graver suppressed a smile, focused on his own battered hands while she took a few deep, restorative breaths. When he peeked up, her cheeks were aflame and she rubbed tears from her eyes with her knuckles like a child, a look his own daughters had worn on occasion. The thought stung his nose and throat like vinegar.

He wouldn't offer her the pieties she would hear from others. He knew how grief poured out your life like so much night soil and left you empty as a piss pot, the stink and rancor bubbling your skin to open sores that only you saw and felt. No one who truly

grieved wanted to be touched, held, rubbed
on . . . it was like being boiled alive. He
didn't know how anyone survived. Getting
shot was hardly a scratch compared to what
happened after his wife and children passed.
Maybe a part of him deserved it. Maybe
she felt like that now.

He glanced at her tilted head, listening to
the cursing and voices upstairs, the creaking
of the bed as they struggled with Drum.
There was a faint dew of sweat under her
eyes now, across the pink sunburn and
freckles on her cheeks, on the bridge of a
nose that had a bump in the middle, which
some might consider a mar on its beauty,
but he did not, and the lips, though she'd
seemed angry or pensive since he'd met her,
had corners that curved upward despite her
mood. He could see how a young J.B. would
want to court and win her, as Graver had
his own wife. Always there was that one
feature, that one small detail that seemed to
bring a person to another person, something
private and endearing. With his wife, it had
been the peculiar points of her ears, which
made her seem fawn-like, like some benign
creature he should protect, but despite his
fierceness, he had failed, as J.B. had failed.
There was nothing a man could do, apparently. He sighed. She shook herself and

163

glanced at him, then back toward the stairs. It had grown quiet.

"I'm sorry. I, it's just —" She opened her palms and looked at him as if he could do something to fill her empty hands. "Have you met my other son, Hayward?" She held him briefly with those light brown eyes rimmed with violet, then shook her head and peered out the window.

Graver nodded cautiously.

"What's your judgment of him?" She looked at him again, her face solemn, the suggestion of a smile on her lips, hoping for a good report. It broke his heart.

He hesitated, glanced up the stairs, then back out the door at the men drifting down to the bunkhouse until supper call. Vera's stew was ready, cornbread sitting under flour sacking, butter softening on the plate. "The boys, well, they pretty much have the run of things here." He took a deep breath. "They sit a horse pretty good, rope decent, sometimes they even put in a day's work you stay on them, but they're youngsters yet."

She waved her hands at the description. "Never mind all that. Soon as they go away to school, they'll learn other skills." She hesitated, and then in a rush, "I need your help with something."

164

"Ma'am?"

Her voice trailed at the sound of a horse arriving, accompanied by yelling and loud laughter from the barnyard. Her face brightened and she strode out the door with Graver behind. "Hayward," she whispered.

The boy rocked unsteadily in his saddle, unmindful of the lathered horse's sides heaving for breath beneath him. Finally Hayward slumped sideways and slid off his horse, landed with a soft thump in the dirt. Struggling upright, he unbuttoned his trousers and pissed, ignoring the wet splashing. Finished, he worked at buttoning his pants until finally giving up with a shrug and turning back to tug on the exhausted horse's reins.

Cullen pushed past them in the doorway and sprinted down the walk to where his brother tried to stand without weaving. "You were supposed to wait for me!" Cullen pushed Hayward's chest and he fell back, landing in his own piss-soaked dirt. They fought for a few minutes until, being the bigger of the two, Hayward pinned his older brother and held him while they argued. In the end, they lay side by side, gazing at the sky, giggling, no doubt about some mischief they planned. Graver kept that to himself.

"High spirited," Graver said. His hands

clenched his hat to keep from walking out there and throwing the two of them in the stock tank until they sobered up. They could take care of the horse afterward, too. Probably ruined it, spent its heart and mind on foolishness. He was pretty sure he wouldn't be able to help the widow with these two.

"They need some refinements, I can see that, but they come from good stock." She wasn't going to give up on her boys. Her lips formed a smile that wanted to become broad, and though she held it back, her eyes were alight with joy and her shoulders fairly trembled with the urge to reach out to them. She was their mother, despite having abandoned them, peculiar as that seemed to Graver. "Hayward? Cullen." Mrs. Bennett started down the stairs toward the gate, calling their names, her deep voice higher than before, the question in her tone letting the boys know they could ignore her.

Cullen half pulled, half shoved his brother upright, then stood and brushed at the pissy mud on their clothing, which only resulted in smearing it. He picked a glob off his cheek, threw it at Hayward, and followed with a shove that nearly sent the boy sprawling again. The wrestling match threatened to restart until Hayward glanced at his mother, ran a muddy hand through his long hair to push it off his face, and dipped his head at her. Cullen glanced at her, too, and let his body slacken, not bothering to push his brown hair back or wipe his face on his sleeve. His face wore a pout, the mouth a replica of hers except the corners turned downward in a perpetual state of dissatisfaction. His white-blue eyes were small and quick, like a wild animal's. The Bennett nose, strong, slightly hooked and crooked from being broken, sat squarely on his face, making him not so much handsome as possessing the possibility of character. Without taking his eyes from his mother and Graver, Cullen snapped his fist out and punched his brother in the arm. Hayward's yowl brought a smile to Cullen's mouth, leveling its corners.

"Boys." The widow ran out of words as she searched their faces. Neither boy moved. She started to open her arms to them, then thought better of it and let them settle at her sides. "I'm sorry about your father."

Hayward dropped his gaze to the ground and shoved the toe of his boot through the sandy dirt. Cullen stared at her with his small flat eyes, tilting his head and lifting his chin the way his mother did. Suddenly Cullen lurched forward and wrapped his arms around her, rubbed his muddy cheek

167

against hers and nuzzled her hair, then stepped back and held his arms out and performed a deep bow. His mother's expression was startled, then grateful, but quickly turned to anger when she saw that filth stained her dress from his mocking embrace.

"Mother —" he began. "May I call you that? It's so kind of you to come calling." His mouth curled in a sneer and he gave Hayward a quick cuff on the back of his head. "Say hello to your mother, stupid! You remember her, don't you?"

Hayward stretched out a hand, realized how dirty it was, rubbed it on his pants, and then held it out again. She ignored his hand, stepped closer, and embraced him, casting Cullen a defiant glance, while Hayward kept his arms at his sides as if suffering from her touch.

The older boy nodded once, looked away, and the meanness fell from his expression, replaced by something that made his lips tremble. When his mother dropped her arms and stepped back, there were tears in her eyes, and neither boy would look at her.

"Need to take care of that horse," Graver said.

Hayward sighed and started to turn. Cullen caught his arm.

"Who the hell you think you're talking

to?" Cullen took a step toward Graver, who shifted his left leg back a few inches, preparing to fight.

Hayward grabbed Cullen's arm and muttered something that made the older boy glare at Graver and then turn away. Graver almost followed him when he yanked the reins and pulled the horse off balance so it about went down before managing to steady its spent legs.

"That wasn't necessary." Mrs. Bennett turned toward him, her chin high, face pale. When she swept past him in her dirt-streaked dress and muddy hair and face, there was an overbright glitter of tears in her eyes and it struck him to the quick. He wanted to whip those boys within an inch of their lives, make them apologize to their mother, make them comfort and care for that poor broken horse, make them sober and clean and respectable. He wanted her world to be just what she needed it to be. He would do that for her.

But she paused at the gate and called back, "Graver, help them with the horse."

It was enough to make him feel like he'd taken a mouthful of flour, dry, tasteless, impossible to swallow. He should walk away, and he would, he thought, except he didn't own so much as a horse, let alone the clothes on his back. And there was still the question of who shot him and killed J. B. Bennett and the girl. He meant to find out before he left.

■ ■ ■ ■

PART TWO:
AND STARS
CONFOUNDED

■ ■ ■ ■

CHAPTER TWELVE

Fall of 1889 Rose got a job in Rushville, Nebraska, which sat below the Pine Ridge Reservation in South Dakota. The school gave her a letter saying she was able to perform the duties of a servant. In other words, she swept and cleaned, washed clothes, and sometimes cooked for Crockett, the white man who ran the telegraph office. He slept in the back rooms of the little house in a nest of his own sweat and alcohol and sometimes waste. No matter. Day and night, the chattering key like a trapped ground squirrel could only be escaped through drink, in his case, or by sleeping in a tipi behind the livery stable, in Rose's. The two did not speak. He believed her mute, and he signaled her work with broad hand gestures or shouted single words. For some reason he thought she might be deaf as well.

It was the telegraph that drew her to the

job. She studied his stained fingers as he tap-tapped, and then the book beside the key, the one that formed the words. It was a secret he did not want her to have, but she watched and memorized. Practiced at night while he was passed out drunk, the moon spilling a slender column of light on either side of the window cover and knifing across the counter where she sat, learning to tap the code.

Rose had always been drawn to secrets. She was a member of the Turtle Clan and knew their stories, which she would later tell only to the next in line, her daughter. She didn't tell her the "Morse code," though. After the taps brought the troops against her people, she wouldn't spread its poison. She only wanted to know its power. The next year, 1890, was the summer of the "Ghost Dance," as the whites called it. Indians on their way to Pine Ridge Reservation passed along the edges of town, and she often met with them, shared food or goods they needed after their long journeys. Word spread across the West, and the Cheyenne and Paiutes, along with her own Lakota, hurried to Pine Ridge. She longed to join them, but her mother sent word by her nephew that Rose was to stay away until she sent for her. Even then, her mother was uncertain about the white men who peered restlessly at the dancers through their glass eyes, some intent on dragging the older girls behind the tipis. Her mother feared for Rose's safety.

The keys never stopped chattering in those months, and as Rose learned the code, she discovered what foolishness the army believed, fed to them by frightened white ranchers and townspeople who feared Indians whenever they saw more than two at a time. In their eyes a family with children became a raid, a potential massacre.

Rose could not enter most of the stores in Rushville if she wished it. She gave drunk Crockett a monthly list of goods and he purchased them for her, giving her the few coins left over as her remaining pay. She knew he cheated her.

By late summer, the number of dancers had doubled, and Big Foot, Short Bull, Kicking Bear, and Sitting Bull's names appeared often in the telegraphs. A man named McLaughlin, Standing Rock agent, called the Ghost Dance "demoralizing, indecent and disgusting" before he'd even witnessed it. The white men wanted her people to become Christians. They called Wovoka the devil, because he predicted the whites and their soldiers would drop dead if the people danced.

Sometimes her nighttime studies left her sluggish for work. Soon Crockett started to empty her pockets and remove her shoes at the end of each day, sometimes force her to lift her skirt and let him pat her blouse in case she was stealing — only his codes, only secrets too small for her pockets, too large for the heavy, stiff shoes with laces he made her wear instead of moccasins, so he could hear her clumping heels on the bare wood floors.

At night, she wore the moccasins her mother had made, beaded with wild roses, and she wove sly as a snake. She opened the wood file drawers and found copies of telegrams starting that summer, from the agent to Fort Niobrara and Fort Robinson to General Miles and from there to the president, congressmen, anyone who would listen, so great was the fear of a half-starved people, broken, in ruin, who only wanted to dance in hope again. The son of God is come, they said, and they danced to hold off the belly hunger, the desire of the spirit so much greater. By fall of 1890, the tone had grown harsher still, demanding the immediate deployment of troops to finish the business on Pine Ridge. She shivered in the night coolness as she read the messages.

She thought of her days in the Indian boarding school, staring out the tall windows at the corner of the cemetery where the small white crosses and short beds of humped soil sat row after row, too close together, and told the story of other Lakota children. She vowed not to be one of those who withered and died there. She pretended to be patient, obedient, and dumb so they would trust her and leave her alone.

Soon more and more troops arrived, their camp crowding her tipi until she had to sign to Crockett for permission to sleep on the office floor. He dared to pinch his nose and point at her bundle to suggest it smelled, and she smiled her not-smart smile and nodded. He shook his head, shrugged, and returned to his room to drink and sleep, despite the chattering key he couldn't keep up with.

It was early October, and she was sweeping the worn wood planks, listening to the code, writing it in her head and deciphering the words, more news about Sitting Bull, who was an old man with little influence except over his Hunkpapas. Kicking Bear visited him and now the Hunkpapas had joined the Ghost Dance. It seemed possible the army would kill Sitting Bull, and her heart was sick as she tried to think of a way to warn her mother, who still didn't understand about the telegraph, or the newest invention, the telephone, which captured a person's voice and sent it across the land. Rose wondered if the voice would sound the same when it returned from its journey. The whites created tendrils like bindweed that trapped their lives together. She had to do something.

At dusk she watched for her people on their way to the dance and sent a message to her mother, who never replied, which meant Rose was to remain in town. When her cousin finally brought word, Rose asked about Star. "She is young enough to be safe," her cousin explained. "Your mother says, 'Too many white men here now. You must not come back yet. I will tell you when it's safe. When the buffalo return, when we are free.' " Rose never heard from her again.

By late fall, the town had doubled and tripled with soldiers, men and women making money from the troops. Photographers from Chadron and Omaha and news reporters from Chicago and New York rode the train to Rushville and came to the telegraph office daily to send their stories home. Much of what they wrote was wrong or made up or both, but there was often a seed of truth Rose could find if she looked carefully enough. Big Foot grew lung-sick and Buffalo Bill Cody visited Sitting Bull in late November to convince his old friend to co-operate with the white men and come to the Indian agency to be arrested, but the visit ended with Cody giving up in disgust. The old leader was finally killed during his arrest in the middle of December. More troops poured out of the trains. The stories grew wilder. Rose didn't dare walk outside during the day for fear of being pushed, cursed, spit on. At night the danger was drunken white men seeking a fight, even if it meant an Indian woman.

She realized from the telegrams and the increasing troops that her people's world had changed too fast, too hard, to make a return. Crockett would send a telegram to Washington, D.C., one day, and mere days later, more trains arrived, hissing and clang-ing, to disgorge soldiers and guns and horses and provisions. Her people had a few rifles and old muskets, though the army tried to take them, but they had nothing like the big Hotchkiss guns that could kill so many so easily. Her people had little am-munition, too; they couldn't afford to shoot randomly on the chance that a bullet would strike home, no matter how much they prayed. She could see the end before it began. Again and again, she tried to send messages to her mother, begged her to flee.

Rose couldn't bear to think of those last days in December. The troops chased the dancers to Wounded Knee, surrounded them, and when the signal to dance was given, opened fire with rifles and cannons. Afterward the troops patrolled the reservation, preventing a flood of people in search of loved ones, so she waited and heard Star was safe with relatives, but her mother was dead. Later, when she met her sister again, she learned their mother's fate and began to plan her revenge.

The troops left as quickly and smoothly as they'd arrived. By February, Rushville was quiet and the telegraph man drank harder and fumbled through her clothing for stolen items more often. She took to wearing her skinning knife under her blouse and stole a gun from a cowboy passed out in the alley behind the saloon. The gun she wore snug against her chest on a string around her body, spinning away from Crockett before he could find it. As game flees before the hunter who has not prayed and spoken to the animal spirits, men began to avoid her. She could walk day and night across town and no one dared meet her eye. Since she'd found the pistol on the cowboy in the alley, Rose had taken to waiting in the dark outside the saloon. Sometimes she searched and stripped the unconscious men, sometimes she helped them asleep. She chose only what she needed or fancied, and would make a tiny cut on their hand or neck to count coup. Without a coup stick, she amended the ceremony to the use of her skinning knife and drawing a single drop of blood. Upon waking, the man would guess he had scratched himself when he fell. Rose thought of the old warriors feasting on the liver and heart of a downed enemy to gain his power, but she could not bring herself to even taste the blood. She learned enough from the telegraph to know the enemy was everywhere, the people vanquished.

There was a white woman who came every week to send a telegram that fall and into the winter. By spring she sent a telegram only every two weeks, then once a month. Her name was Dulcinea Bennett, and while Crockett was full of courtesy when he took the message, afterward he would laugh at the garbled words he was too stupid to translate. Rose knew they were code, such a simple one it took her only a few nights to break it. The messages, so full of longing, made her miss her own mother and sister. Soon Rose made a practice of

181

remaining in the room when Dulcinea visited. Pretending to sweep or dust or wash windows, she watched the white woman, and, as if she could feel the eyes on her, Dulcinea began to nod and smile at her when she came and went. Once the white woman dropped a coin and it rolled behind the potbellied stove they used for heat, and Rose used her broom to edge it out and picked it up. Dulcinea gave her a surprised, grateful smile and thanked her when Rose held it out to her. Forgetting Crockett, Rose smiled, too, her eyes catching the other woman's in a quick exchange of understanding despite their differences.

"Back to work!" Crockett yelled with a wave of his hand. "She's mute," he explained. Dulcinea lowered her head to hide her smile as she placed the coin on the counter as payment for her message.

As she left, the white woman placed her hand on Rose's shoulder and thanked her again. "It's nothing," Rose murmured with an eye on Crockett, who headed to the back room and his whiskey.

Then one evening in late winter, Dulcinea invited her to tea. Rose followed the woman to the back stairs over the notions store, where there were several rooms to let. Inside the tiny room was a single bed, a battered wardrobe, a small pine washstand with a chipped white pitcher of water, and a table with two chairs. The white woman turned up the lamp on the table and went about pouring tea. It must have been some time since she had spoken to another because she began to talk about her life and continued until dawn, even weeping once over her sons. They continued to meet, and their unlikely friendship bloomed as they walked quietly through the hills, catching the scent of new grass and wildflowers. They didn't speak a great deal after that initial conversation, merely spent time together.

One evening in late April, the telegrapher finished his meal of eggs, fried potatoes, and bacon and sat at the table with a whiskey bottle and glass, drinking more than usual. After a while he grew talkative. He didn't expect Rose to respond since in his mind she was mute and stupid. Finally, he spoke of last winter and Wounded Knee.

"Needed to clean them out," he said. "Look at you —" He took a drink. "Inbreeding. No morals to speak of. Can't be taught." He finished his glass. "Best Indian I ever knew. Can't talk and not too lazy. I'll keep it!" He whooped with laughter and slapped the table with both hands. He gazed at her, and there was a shift in his eyes.

Despite her efforts to stay ugly, dirty, to keep temptation from his mind, he took out a small tortoiseshell comb and cleaned the food from his mustache as he did nightly, winked at her, and demanded to know what she was stealing.

Then he swiftly wrapped his arms around her so tightly she could barely breathe and pushed her backward onto the bed, landing on top of her. She couldn't reach her knife or gun while his hands groped and his body pushed the air from her lungs. He had to roll off to unfasten his pants and she was able to slip on top, grab the pillow, and press it over his face, leaning with her entire weight. Much of his fight had been spent getting her on the bed, and his limbs were heavy with drink. She fought off his clawing hands and bucking torso by hooking her feet and hands to the sides of the bed. When the scratching sound of his breath beneath the pillow quit, and his body shuddered, and then softened again, she lifted it. She had meant to put him to sleep, but was angry and now his hands lay carelessly at his sides, a shred of meat nested in his mustache.

She left him there and went to the front office, determined to find anything that would offer clues or names of the men who'd killed her mother and massacred her people. She found Bennett files listed by individuals and ranches. Drum Bennett wrote short, blunt orders for land and cattle deals, which made him richer over the years, but J. B. Bennett's were coded like Dulcinea's. Some she sent to him from Rushville, but others came from Gordon, Chadron, Cody, Valentine, Ainsworth, towns that sat above the Sand Hills. Hers was a restless spirit, Rose had already concluded, and she did not bother to decipher the code. She did wonder why they thought it necessary to hide their messages. And why Crockett kept them. She never found a message to or from a Lakota.

In the bottom drawer, tucked behind the other files, and without a name, she found the pictures. Photographs and newspaper drawings from before and after the massacre, some dated back ten years. A picture of Rose with the other children at the school. She stared at the photo from the Ghost Dance village for a long time until she began to hear their voices chanting, her mother's, see the dogs circling, whining, tails down, looking for food when there was little to eat, the picture said, yet the people built fires and cooked big kettles of stew from commodity meat, wild rabbits and birds, roots and vegetables to keep the dancers going. She rubbed her thumb across the image of the bodies frozen in a ravine, arms reaching out, legs still running in the mass grave. Photos of soldiers lying with guns at the ready and onlookers behind them. She pounded that picture with her fist. Didn't they realize, didn't they know what would happen? The priests told the dancers to go home. Jesus is coming! The Savior is coming, the dancers insisted while the soldiers cleaned and loaded their guns, and the cannons were rolled to the top of the ridge for a better field of fire on children playing games, dancers, old and crippled ones watching. So few escaped. She searched the images for her mother and sister but didn't find them. Finally she tucked the photographs and drawings into the large envelope with the newspaper clippings, stood, took one last look around, and poured lamp oil on the floor. She touched a burning candle to the oil and it smoldered so long she wondered if there was some white witchcraft at work, but when she opened the door, the fire swooshed alive.

When they found Crockett's body, the sheriff said it was a mishap caused by too much drink, and no one remembered the stupid mute Indian girl who used to work for him.

Rose went to Dulcinea that night and the two of them rode up to Pine Ridge Reservation for the first time since the massacre the winter before.

CHAPTER THIRTEEN

J.B. was always on his way to Dulcinea. First, that fine April afternoon in 1880, as he walked along the Lake Michigan shore in Chicago, marveling at the water that extended past the horizon, flat instead of hilly like home. Although he would never see the ocean, he decided it must be like this, no way for the eye to comprehend the vastness before it. He half expected to see steamships bound for Europe and the Far East, and was momentarily confused by the freighter that appeared to crawl sluggishly along the line where water met sky. Then he saw a young woman, half dragged by a pair of small white curly-haired dogs who leapt and ran, straining to swim at the water's edge, jumping on passersby and snapping at the toy balls she threw ahead of them.

He admired her grace and beauty, but most of all her patience handling the dogs. She was unafraid of appearing relaxed and awkward when they tangled her in their leashes or muddied her long skirt with their paws. When the fatter of the two managed to slip off his collar and wade in fearlessly, the waves up to his ears, she threw back her head and laughed, then followed to retrieve him and give the other dog a good soaking, too. J.B. looked up and down the beach. She was the only woman in the water. It was too cool for swimming. He'd been warned the lake stayed cold until mid-summer, but she didn't seem to mind. The dark line of the water wet her gray dress past the long bodice to her small waist. It must have weighed on her, yet she still moved with grace. Once she'd secured the collar around the dog, he bounded out of the water, bouncing up and down with his paws waving in the air as J.B. approached.

Fortunately, the little rascal slipped out of his collar again and headed straight into J.B.'s arms, licking his face as if they were old friends. J.B. never forgot that dog, and felt as brokenhearted as Dulcinea when he finally passed.

"My dogs won't bite," she called with a smile.

"Might get licked to death." He laughed and stood with the dog in his arms.

"You're getting wet," she said, her own

long gray sleeves dripping.

"J. B. Bennett," he said. "Nebraska Sand Hills. Cattle. That's what I grow, I mean raise, cattle." Stop, he warned himself, hush now. He grinned foolishly.

"Dulcinea Woodstone," she said with a tilt of her head as if to get a better view of him. "Three blocks away. Play with dogs, read books, attend boring parties, theatrical and musical performances. What are the Sand Hills?" It was her humor that capped it for him.

They saw each other every day after that, as long as possible until her parents began to worry, then he'd gone home for a month, only to return and ask for her hand in marriage. She'd been waiting, packed, her trousseau consisting not of dresses and furs, but of specially ordered ranch clothing as she called it. The only outfitting he had to do in Omaha when they stopped on the train out to North Platte was to buy her a pair of cowboy boots and a real cowboy hat. He didn't care if she wore a coronation crown and a ball gown, but she insisted that she be ready for her part in their western adventure. Years later he wondered how their life had changed so easily, from this to that, and from that to this: He'd spent the last ten years tracking her to some rooming house or hotel in a town above or below the hills, or a few times to a tent she pitched far from their house. He never knew when she'd summon him for another argument, never knew if he could leave work to meet her. Last time, she told him he must bring both their sons if he expected them to be together again. He'd held off as long as he could, intending to wait until after branding and culling, then woke and decided today was the day he'd ride to his father's ranch and retrieve their eldest son. It was Drum who'd taught him to always do the hardest work first thing in the morning.

On the last morning of his life, J.B. rode out to retrieve his son from his father, deep in memory. He remembered that Dulcinea had waited until after breakfast that final May morning ten years ago, when the hands had ridden out to collect the cattle for spring branding. It was a day like today. As soon as the last hand mumbled thanks for the breakfast and with hat clutched against chest backed his way through the door and carefully closed it, she stood and walked with a determined step, shoulders back, chin high, and stopped in front of the big Union Pacific calendar he kept on the wall above the baker's table and pie safe, despite her objections. He liked the western themes. This month a lone cowboy rode hell-bent for leather across the sagebrush after a wild-eyed longhorn. J.B. never tired of that picture, even though it was already mid-May and he'd faced it every morning and evening. Later he would wonder that he never thought to ask why she'd written a small *x* in each day for the past two weeks. On May 15, she drew a slash across the whole box rather than the small, discreet *x*. He'd always been a little slow on the uptake, Drum assured him later that day when he rode in for the cow sorting since both their herds ran together each winter. After Dulcinea left, he spent money he didn't have to build a fence between his land and Drum's, but the cattle still broke through on occasion. Too little too late.

"Looks like she was wishing it was your throat she slashed rather than that little ole paper. What did you do to that girl, J.B.?" Drum's mouth had widened into a grin when he'd heard. J.B. remembered her preoccupied air, how she ignored Hayward as he tried to lift another ladle of syrup onto his pancakes, succeeding in dribbling it across the table and dropping the large wooden spoon on the floor without any of it landing on his plate. The child had looked fearfully at his mother, his lower lip quivering, and J.B. had picked up the spoon and wiped down the table without a word. Dulcinea stood watching them, a thoughtful expression on her face, arms folded, then she turned and walked swiftly to the stairs, lifting her skirt as she hurried up almost soundlessly. J.B. thought he'd seen tears in her eyes.

She came down wearing a long ivory linen duster over one of the two traveling dresses she had brought with her all those years earlier.

He slammed down his coffee cup, pushed the chair away so hard it fell backward to the floor, and strode across the room to grab her arm.

"What is this?" He knew it was the wrong tone, the wrong words, because her eyes flared then flattened and her mouth settled into a grim line. He dropped his hand.

Hayward began his peculiar sobbing-hiccupping that was much too babyish for a five-year-old boy, his father would later assure him.

"Go outside, son," J.B. told him, but he sat quietly, stubbornly at the table, kicking the legs of his chair and scowling at his mother.

Dulcinea took a deep breath, squared her

shoulders, swiped at the corner of her eye with the edge of her gloved hand, and peered around J.B. "Come here, Hayward, come to Mama."

The boy picked up his fork then purposely dropped it on the plate to produce the clanging sound the adults hated, but which he seemed to understand he would not be reprimanded for in this moment of crisis. Satisfied, he ran his forefinger once more through the syrup and melted butter smeared on his plate. She had made his favorite breakfast — donkey pancakes, including the bacon packsaddle that he'd gobbled first.

"Son," J.B. said.

"Leave him alone." She adjusted the black-plumed hat on her head, draping the veil across her forehead so it could be pulled down and tied in back.

"Hayward, go outside. Tell Jorge I said you could have your new horse." J.B. hoped she would hear what he suggested, that he meant to give their five-year-old his own horse, despite her objections, that she daren't leave, but she only looked over her shoulder at the stairs behind her.

"I'm ready to go," she called and immediately the sound of a large, heavy object thumped down the uncarpeted steps. J.B.

194

counted each one, four to the landing, ten to the bottom.

"Who is that?" he asked.

Hayward bounced off his chair and ran to the door, pulled it open, and clambered down the three steps to the stone walk, his miniature cowboy boots clopping loudly. Her steamer trunk landed with a thud at the bottom of the stairs, and one of the men, Stubs, who later went to work for Drum, followed.

J.B. looked at Dulcinea, her expression grim, while her hands busied themselves with a large floral brocade satchel stuffed with necessities for a long journey. After rummaging for a moment, she extricated an ivory envelope he recognized as her stationery from before they were married. She handed him the envelope but stopped his hand when he moved to open the unsealed flap.

"You're leaving then," he finally managed to say. He could hear the jingling harness and creaking wood as the wagon pulled up outside the gate.

He knew better than to ask how long she'd be gone, just as he had known better than to ask if she was staying when she arrived ten years ago. He felt something small inside him, a shard of resentment that wanted revenge, and fought to keep it silent until she was halfway to the gate.

"Nobody's going to water the lilacs," he called to her.

She brushed it off with a wave of her hand over her shoulder. She wasn't even going to look at him?

"Or those mulberries, nobody's going to . . ."

She spun and marched right up to him, the expression on her face so fierce he took half a step back before he caught himself. Staring at him, eyes filled with tears, she clasped the back of his head and pulled his mouth to hers, kissed him so deep and long he began to hope, until she released him. Did she think that would keep him until she returned? He wiped his mouth with the back of his hand, worked to keep the anger out of his voice when he told her that she shouldn't leave; though it hurt him to beg, he came as close as he could, pulling her into his arms, smelling her sweet iris perfume, willing himself to remember their first night together under the coarse wool blanket with another folded for a pillow on the ground beneath the stars.

"I'll bring Hayward to visit," J.B. said. Hope jumped in her eyes before she caught herself, smoothed the front of her duster and tugged on the black kid gloves that snugged her fingers too tightly now, her hands nearly ruined by the harsh weather, rough land, and hard chores. She'd have to cut her wedding ring off someday, he thought with a pang.

She shook her head.

"Do you have enough money for the trip?" He half turned toward the house. "I can —"

"You go get Cullen from your father and I'll come back," she said.

She shifted her gaze to the man beside her on the wagon bench. "Mr. Stubs?"

When he didn't move, she lifted the whip from its holder and cracked it over the horses' backs. Lunging forward, they swept against J.B. and pushed him backward.

"You'll never see Hayward again," he yelled as the wagon left the barnyard. He couldn't fetch Cullen and his defeat slumped his shoulders as he watched the ball of dust churn down the road, until finally they were a mere speck disappearing over the last hill on the horizon.

Hayward rode happily around the corral on his new spotted horse, which trotted three steps for every ten it walked to keep the swaying rider on its back. J.B. watched his boy and felt both pride and sadness swell in his chest, and soon another feeling, one that made him spin on his heel and hurry inside the house, run up the stairs two at a time, and yank open the door to their bedroom, where he discovered that she'd left her perfume bottles, the silver-backed brush, comb, and mirror set he'd given her, and the glass jars of creams and powders he was helpless to understand, sitting on top of the clumsy dressing table he'd made for her. Cottonwood. He brushed the dented surface with the edge of his hand. Wood so soft it bore the impression of everything she'd ever set down too hard. Had she been so angry? He'd waxed the wood to bring out the soft yellow hue, but over the years it had darkened along certain grains, and small dark spots dotted the surface like tears. Had she wept here? Suddenly, he knew with a force that punched the breath out of his chest that if she wept, it had not been for him, anyone but her husband, who had given his eldest son to his father. Cullen, this was all about Cullen.

He grabbed one of the jars, spun, and threw it with all his might at the wall over their bed. It didn't smash and splinter into greasy shards like he'd hoped, merely thumped harmlessly and bounced across the bed she'd so carefully made, folding his mother's wedding ring quilt at the bottom, to be drawn up in the night chill, as if she would return on the morrow, as if she would return at all —

He ripped the quilt from the bed, yanking at the end to tear it to pieces, but heard only the barely audible pop of a stitch or two before he threw it down in disgust. She had taken nothing of their life together, he noticed, as soon as the red mist cleared his eyes. There was the lithograph of the carriage on a misty Paris boulevard, trees swept up and away over the streetlights. The coatrack in the corner where he hung his hat and jacket and she the thick wool robe he'd given her that first Christmas, when it had been so cold she fussed about getting out of bed of a morning. It still hung there, dusty, unused. They had laughed that he so misjudged her size, and the rough blue-and-black weave made her skin prickle. His face reddened as he remembered her smile, the one he mistook for pleasure, and now saw as derision. She'd been laughing at him every day of their life together.

There had to be something he could hold as hostage against her return. She was determined, and when she put her mind to a thing it would take a train to stand in her way. That's why he'd been surprised when she'd let Cullen leave, let Drum convince her. What had that old bastard said? Had he told her about their bargain?

He took a deep breath, smelled the musk of the face powder encircled with its own dust, and the perfume bottle she hadn't bothered with, as if she would change herself so completely that he couldn't even recognize her scent should they ever meet again. He sat on her bench covered with needlepoint roses. He didn't even know where she was going. Maybe running off with some cowboy. The thought made him gasp, and he stopped. He would never believe that about her.

Facing her vanity table, he picked up the silver-backed mirror and laid it back down, then the brush, with silver handle wrought into twining flowers, he didn't even know what kind, his big callused palm could barely register the texture, and he wondered if she had put her fingertips in the curves of the stems and leaves, what she had thought as she lifted the brush, as he did now, and drew it through her hair, as he did now, with long and even strokes, over and over, as he had watched her do on countless nights. Had he ever once asked if he could do it for her? Surely she would have enjoyed letting her exhausted arms fall loose in her lap, hands cupped, while he brushed and separated and finally plaited her heavy auburn hair into a braid that would last almost the entire night if they didn't make love. He stopped, set down the brush, and looked at its fine bristles, embedded with a few of her long auburn hairs, and three of his own shorter, thicker black ones.

Five years after she left, her old one-eyed horse began its decline and J.B. spent a week of cold nights in the corral with it. "I'm always on my way to her," J.B. spoke aloud. "I boarded the train that first summer and got as far as Council Bluffs before I got off. It was as if I was drunk, the blow of not seeing her staggered me. She let me know she was in Chicago with her people, in case I cared to send the boys. She knew I couldn't do that. It got so bad I couldn't stand the ranch and found myself in town more than was right. Heard about the business up on Pine Ridge and decided to take a look. I don't think I much cared what happened to me and the boy, but she kept writing and messaging and reminding me to take care of Hayward, so when I went up to watch the dancing I took him, too. Thank God he was home safe the next time, in December."

He bowed his head to the horse's neck and breathed in the coarse, dusty hair, tried to dislodge the pictures of bodies falling before cannon and rifle fire, red roses blooming in the snow, soldiers riding down stragglers with their guns and sabers. "She came back to North Platte the next March and sent word to come, but Hayward got the measles, and a freak late snow stopped the wagon on the way to town. Remember that? I unhitched you and rode you back in a blizzard. We were both half-froze."

He stroked the old horse's neck, burying his fingers in the thick, brittle coat that hadn't shed out the past spring, a sign the end was near. J.B. had kept the horse close the past summer, fed her special mashes when she couldn't chew hay or grass because her teeth had fallen out. Now the horse lay wrapped in the wedding ring quilt from his own bed, its breathing labored as he spoke.

"Then cattle prices went south, and I had not a dollar to spare. I couldn't see her without I could pay for her dinner. The next summer she set up camp just west of the line between Drum's and our land and sent word to meet her at the windmill by the gumbo flats. She's different every time, but the same, too. We fight so hard I think we'll kill each other one day. Hayward's a hand-ful, don't dare leave him much. I keep try-ing to tell her that. He won't come with me anymore. Doesn't see why his ma isn't here raising him. He doesn't understand what losing Cullen means to her. How she's try-ing to force me to make it right. But I can't, I just can't."

J.B. rubbed the old horse between her ears and worked his fingers down the short neck, massaging until she relaxed and dropped her head with a sigh. He pulled the blanket off his shoulders to cover both their bodies and laid his head on the horse's side, letting the deep lift and release of the animal's harsh breathing lull him into a rare dream-less sleep. In his mind, he repeated the words as if they could be released into the world and travel on their own to her: "I'm always on my way to you."

CHAPTER FOURTEEN

The day Dulcinea returned, she dropped her hat and coat on the bench at the end of the bed and wandered around the room, opening curtains and running her fingers through the dust on the vanity surface, wondering who had positioned the tarnished silver-backed set she had forgotten when she fled. She picked up the brush and paused before running it through her hair, shorter now, then registered what she had seen, the black strands tangled with her auburn ones. Neither of them had thought themselves to this moment.

"My God, how we are destroyed," she whispered, a line from some forgotten drama, or maybe she had written it in her head as she entered the room where she had slept with J.B. all those years ago. She had carried on an internal dialogue with her husband for so long that his death did not alter the conversation. It merely expanded across time and space. The dusty swaths of yellow lace and silk at the windows stirred slightly despite the glass being closed.

When she first left the hills and went home to Chicago, she was maddened by grief for her sons and husband. She tried prayer and found it lacking in formality. She attended churches of every denomination — except for the synagogues of Jews, which would not have her — and found religion empty as a spring potato bin. She sought advice from every manner of psychic, spiritualist, palm and card reader, and finally discovered an entire church of spiritualists whose service consisted of any number of individuals standing in front of the congregation on wooden chairs and receiving notices, like telegrams, from the departed, with messages for random members. She received hers the last night she attended. In the form of a flowered horseshoe, the sort draped over a winner at the racetrack, or sometimes over a coffin at a funeral, it read GOOD LUCK. The message, from an uncle she'd never heard of, mentioned a journey west. The congregation clapped and imagined the best while she broke into a cold sick sweat that chattered her teeth as she hurried to her parents' house three blocks away that hot August evening, praying her sons were safe, and never imagining that it would be J.B., despite Drum's vow.

She always wanted to come home, always meant to explain her bargain with his father and listen to him explain his, waiting all the while for Drum Bennett to die. The old man drove them apart. It was his fault. They had both made a pact with a devil who knew them better than they knew themselves.

"Dear God," she whispered. "I hate him."

When her fingers pushed into the familiar grooves of the brush handle, she felt a light pressure back, and wondered if the long journey remained in the nerves of her body, and made her arms tingle as if someone stroked the fine hairs beneath her sleeves.

"You're giving yourself the frights," she scolded and rubbed at the tarnished silver back of the brush. She couldn't remember why she'd left the set. She'd been so surprised when J.B. gave it to her in the middle of summer, the package arriving with canned foods and tools and barbed wire and barrels of kerosene from Babylon. He was not a man given to surprises, so she was moved beyond words when she opened the pale blue velvet half-moon box that contained the brush, comb, and mirror fitted in their watered-silk-lined berths.

The pressure on her fingers grew. She

used her other hand to pry away the handle, and dropped the brush. Then the oversweet scent of iris rose from the table. She glanced in the mirror, then at the cut-glass perfume vials. Some were empty, others reduced or dried, as if the tops had been left off for days on end. Did he spoil them on purpose?

The scent of iris grew stronger, like the flowers were in the room. She leapt to her feet and rushed to the window to scan the ground outside: nothing but weeds in her old gardens. Then she remembered, she'd left when the dark purple iris heads had started to break open, the air heavy with their syrupy-sweet scent. The memory was like a blow to her back. She bent double and wept as she had when Rose first told her of J.B.'s death.

For two weeks, Dulcinea waited for word of her surprise to arrive. When Hayward burst into the house that morning with a message from the train station about the horses from Kentucky, gifts she'd bought for her husband and sons, she pushed aside her chores and ordered the runabout readied. She was sick to death of the constant thumping of Drum's cane on the floor above with one damned demand or another, an hourly reminder that she had done nothing to remove his presence from her home and worse, to find her husband's killer. The sheriff hadn't made an appearance at the ranch either, and she intended to see him. She had interviewed the men and made Graver take her to the site of the killings, yet still had no clues, no place to start, while Drum's lewd assertion about J.B. and the Indian girl sat like a jagged rock in her chest. Rose said ignore him and that he was a crazy old one, not worth the piss in his pants. But Rose wasn't getting anywhere with her spying either. Apparently, no one on the ranch knew a thing. With spring roundup under way, the men had little time to devote to a mystery. Cow work always came first. That was going to change, the two women vowed. Rose had sent for her husband and daughter to meet them in Babylon, and Dulcinea had plans of her own.

The boys jumped at the chance to go to town, and with Graver along to bring back the wagon, she would arrive with her sons at her side to answer all the questions in the eyes of those who knew her story. She was home now. She was a mother again. She ignored the nagging reminder that the boys still showed no interest in her. Today at least, she could pretend. She glanced at the boys riding on either side of the runabout, their heads up, necks and shoulders stiff as they imitated the solidity of grown men — and her heart pumped wildly for a moment. They would be lovely, strong men like their father, she thought with a smile. He would have been proud.

As the horses trotted smartly under his hands on the reins, Graver pointed out items of interest as if Dulcinea and Rose hadn't spent years riding these hills. Eventually the land flattened and houses staked out the road as they turned north down the main street, where the mercantile center was framed by a raised plank sidewalk on either side. Driven cattle herds had left the road splashed with sloppy green manure. Dulcinea glanced at Graver's grim face. Did he expect her to raise a lavender-scented silk handkerchief to her nose, as her sisters or mother would? Instead she took a deep breath, shook her shoulders and head, and declared, "It's a lovely day, is it not?"

He raised his brow and, in that moment, reminded her of J.B. — it was like a punch to her stomach. It happened that way. In the midst of a pleasant scene, she would be tossed back into a pool of grief. She breathed deeply and kept her eyes on Cullen, who was a small, wiry version of his father, but quicker, more agile. She had to get to know him better. Anything to keep her mind off the way Graver's long fingers contained a certain beauty as they handled the reins with confidence. He was considerate of every creature, she observed, as she let her gaze drift to the profile of his sun-browned face framed by thick gray-streaked hair that hung unevenly below his black hat. His quick brown eyes caught every detail, and she saw the muscles in his neck and shoulders shift in response. A wheel of the runabout sank into a hole and briefly tilted her against him. She felt his arm tense to hold her upright as he whistled for the horses to pull harder. She leaned the other way and he let out a breath, and she knew right then that despite everything a time was coming for the two of them.

The livery stable and rail yard were a block west, then north again, but she had to visit the Cherry County Emporium first and pointed toward the massive storefront. Two ladies stopped and stared as they pulled up to tie the horses. Dulcinea glanced around; they were the only runabout or conveyance of any stature other than the ranch or farm wagons along the street. Single horses were in plenitude, ridden by men who appeared in striking similarity regardless of whether they were ranch hands or bosses, attired in worn pants and high-heeled boots, ranging from those with soles held to the foot with twine or wire or strips of rawhide to those whose scuffed appearance indicated they'd never made the acquaintance of polish. Graver's tall, shiny boots were an exception.

Graver climbed down, unhooked the check reins, and tied the team to the railing. With a pat to each wide neck, he turned, and seemed uncertain whether to help her down. She solved the crisis by opening the knee-high door, unfolding the three steps with a shove of her boot toe, and descending with her skirts held above her feet the required six inches. Her mother would be proud that all the money spent on private tutoring had produced a lady able to exit a carriage on her own, even though she then stepped squarely into a cow patty with both feet, breaking through the dried crust to the green slop beneath. Only by the grace of God was she able to maintain her balance. When she laughed, Graver visibly relaxed and held out his hand, which she gratefully accepted.

She turned to her sons, who still sat on their horses watching the activity. They were half-grown children, she thought, what harm could find them here? "Boys, be back here in two hours. I'll need your help then."

Hayward nodded nervously and glanced at his brother. Cullen shrugged and dismounted.

"Take care of the horses," she said to Graver, who rolled his lips and nodded. "I have a few errands."

Graver stared at his boots an infuriatingly long time, then nodded again and turned toward the store.

"Where are you going?" As soon as the words were out of her mouth, she knew the tone was all wrong.

"Vera gave me a list." He smiled unexpectedly and her mouth responded before she could control it. He wasn't afraid of her. He wasn't even interested in keeping a job with her. Maybe Drum was right. Maybe he was the killer. Dulcinea noticed that Rose watched him closely from the back of the runabout, where she still sat, posed like a visiting dignitary.

When she entered, the store assaulted her senses in a multitude of ways — first it was the riot of stink, the high crafty stench of a half circle of pale cheese the size of a wagon wheel, the myriad smells of harsh black bars of store soap and braids of garlic so old the dust hung in long strands as if the gray-white bulbs wept, barrels of apples and squash and potatoes with the rich scent of ripeness turning to rot, the dry stale odors from bins of flour and rice and beans and sugar, the acrid aroma of coffee beans, the half-rancid layer of lard and butter and milk left too long in the warm room, the damp ashes in the stove, the deep-smoked grease of bacon and ham strung on rope that had begun to carry the green hue of the molding skin rind, the thinner, sharper tang of sausage loops that spanned the corner of the meat counter like Christmas tree strands, the rich shine of the brown-red casings decorative against the drab browned plaster walls.

In the women's goods, a thin layer of cheap perfume hung in the air, a too-sweet idea of flowers that clung to the nose and mouth, competing with the odor of bran mash, straw, and hot downy bodies from the feed area, where the baby chicks, goslings, and ducks were corralled in separate pens, crowding and cheeping in the corner under the heat of kerosene light. She leaned over and inhaled the manure-and-mash smell, reached down and cupped a downy black chick and brought it squirming to her face. It flapped and protested, its tiny eye blinking furiously as it paddled the air, and stabbed its beak at her fingers. She cooed and stroked its head until its eyes drooped sleepily, then held its body against her cheek, closed her eyes, and she was there, that first spring when J.B. brought the chicks home from town in a wooden box he had wrapped in burlap against the cold — fifteen chicks, and she insisted they keep them in the corner of the kitchen where it was warm. She never minded their stink, because she never tired of watching them chase each other until they collapsed in a heap in the corner of the pen, eyes squeezed tight against the light, tiny chests pumping slowly in and out. She wanted to make them her pets, to press that plump downy ball into the hollow of her neck and feel the soft search of its tongue against the underside of her chin — but the coyotes and snakes took every one as soon as they put them outside. For the next batch they built a coop and a large pen to contain them until they were grown and smart enough to be turned loose. They only lost five of those. Were the chickens now at the ranch descendants of those survivors?

Near the implements she noted the source of the oily smell that put a sheen over the whole store — the leather, guns, shovels and rakes and hoes, the spools of chain and rope and wire all wore it: saddles, harness, strap goods, boots and shoes, even the long waxed coats shared it — the odor of preservation, of what it took to keep their lives out here, if not smoothly, then at least withstanding. It had been so long since any of this mattered to her that she wanted to pause, run her fingers over the goods, and let the rich scent soak into her skin.

Suddenly, the indefinable spice of her husband after a day of hard work, the heavy sweet sweat that smelled so intimate it could be coming from her own body. She turned abruptly, and Graver was watching her, his arms spread across the aisle, hands resting on the plank shelves. She blushed and dropped her eyes, opened her mouth to speak and found the words had disappeared. In the dimness, he looked ever so slightly like J.B. Nonsense, she chided herself and blinked away the tears.

CHAPTER FIFTEEN

At the post office window tucked in the back corner of the store, Dulcinea loaded Graver's arms with packages and directed him to the runabout, but as he stepped off the plank walk, the stack began to slide. He felt like an inept clown juggling parcels while a couple on the walk watched the spectacle.

A tall, narrow dog sauntered over, sniffed a box lying in the muck, licked his chops, daintily picked up an edge in his teeth, and turned to run.

"That's my chocolates! Here, give that back!" Dulcinea shouted at the dog, a black-and-white long-haired creature with a whip-like tail and jutting hips. It turned to stare at the commanding figure on the walk, and with eyes down, ambled over, hesitated in front of Dulcinea, and then carefully placed the box at her feet. Only then did the dog look up, its red-rimmed, watery eyes hopeful. Dulcinea stared back for a full minute before bending to retrieve the package with one hand while she stretched out the other to let the dog sniff her fingers.

It leapt onto the boardwalk with an awkward, shambling grace, more akin to grasshopper than deer, and immediately sat with its head at her waist, tongue lolling as it opened its jaws in a happy, panting grin, eyes bright, tail thumping a steady rhythm like a person knocking on the door to a house.

"Why, he's somebody's dog! He's such a good boy, aren't you, aren't you a good boy?" Dulcinea cooed and rubbed his head, cupping each ear in her hand and massaging with slow, circular motions that brought groans of appreciation from deep within the animal.

"I'm afraid he *was* someone's dog," a tall stranger paused to remark. "A family of homesteaders who returned to Missouri last month. Dog couldn't keep up with the wagon. Sore leg. They weren't of a mind to pack him in with the kids and furniture, so they tied him up outside of town and left him. He's been living high on the hog, as you can see." The stranger gestured toward the ribs that sprang out when the animal sat.

Graver deposited the packages in the empty back of the runabout, stepped up to the walk, and brushed at the dirt on his trousers.

A Mormon ranch family edged by the group, turning their heads to stare even when they were well past. The woman and her daughter wore old-fashioned sunbonnets and the group dressed entirely in black and white. Behind them came a Negro couple, the man in a carefully fitted dark blue suit, the woman a sky-blue gown. Dulcinea stared openly at the passersby.

"Every color and faith out here. Live and let live, I say." The stranger lifted his hat and resettled it.

She studied him for a moment, then returned her attention to the dog. She was going to keep him, Graver realized, and the stranger seemed reluctant to move along.

"Percival Chance, ma'am, attorney-at-law." He bowed slightly and touched the brim of his gray cowboy hat. The pants and coat sleeves of his black western-cut suit were shiny, threadbare at the edges, and the once-white shirt a dingy gray. The leather of his black-polished boots was so worn, there was a brown undercast to the shine, and the soles were thin as cardboard. Must not be much money in lawyering, Graver decided.

Dulcinea nodded. "Mrs. J. B. Bennett."

The lawyer glanced at the riding costume she wore instead of a black mourning dress. "My apologies, Mrs. Bennett. May I extend my condolences?"

She tipped her head. "You may do anything you'd like, Mr. Chance, but I thought Mr. Rivers was the only lawyer in town."

Chance's fair, handsome features tightened, his skin stretched over the sharp cheekbones and fine straight nose. "It's a mistake I am correcting."

Graver studied his face, the sardonic mouth, almost smug with secret amusement at the world's expense. Maybe he was being too hard on the man, but he could not shake the sense they'd met before, and that it hadn't been an altogether pleasant encounter.

Dulcinea patted the dog a little too hard on the head. To his credit, the animal merely squinted and flattened his ears. "If you'll fashion a collar and leash for him, Mr. Graver, and tie him in the runabout. Wait, here, use this." She unclasped the buckle and slid the belt from her waist in a single motion, while the men stared, and wrapped it twice around the dog's neck and fastened it. "And now a leash. Maybe a piece of harness? I'm taking him home. Can you go ask the storekeeper for some meat scraps and a bone?"

Dulcinea turned to the lawyer. "Since my husband used Rivers, perhaps it would be best for me to hire you instead. Do you have an office?"

He tipped his head to the right and they walked past the Emporium to the next building, where his rented office was a small, stuffy room on the first floor, divided from a patent medicine retailer and dentist by a flimsy wall that forced both men to conduct their business in melodramatic whispers.

Dulcinea paused in front of the open door Chance held and glanced back at Graver. "Will you complete the order at the Emporium and meet me at the livery stable?" She gazed at the dog, who watched her with growing love in its eyes. Then, as if realizing the two boys had been missing and quiet for some time, she looked down the street, stared at the door to the beer parlor. "And find the boys. We'll need them at the stable." She picked up her skirt and swept through the doorway.

Inside the Emporium Graver found the bolts of fabric Vera had requested; noting the array of colors and textures, he fingered the plush velvets. His wife, Camellia, came to mind, how pretty she'd been when they'd first met at a soiree. She'd worn lilac silk and velvet, a complicated dress that favored her wide hips and narrow waist and small bosom — and she smelled like a heady, sweet flower, her namesake, she'd told him with a laugh. She'd always preferred pale shades that complemented her white-blond hair and skin that burned in the harsh prairie sun as soon as she'd left her parasols and broad-brimmed hats behind in Kentucky. After they came west, it burned over and over until only the raw red skin remained, even in winter, and her fine hair turned brittle, lifeless. When she died she was like a locust shell, the remains left behind after her real self crawled away. He vowed that day he'd never remarry, and never again bring children into a world that would kill them as easily as flies.

He searched his pockets for the lists from Vera and Dulcinea, whose paper irritated him with its sweet perfume, and he held it between two fingers, away from his body as he walked. Everything about that woman irritated. Scented paper. French soap. Boxes of chocolates. Marshall Field's, when they had a perfectly good wish book from Sears, Roebuck. She wouldn't last, he concluded, though a nagging buzz in the back of his head said she might. So far she'd proven herself tougher than most women who lost a husband and had a man like Drum Bennett to deal with. He smiled at the way the old man raised her hackles.

"I cannot sell goods to you if you insist on coming through the front door. I told you to come round back, hand me your list, and wait by the steps." Haven Smith, the store owner, had to look up to stare into the bland face of the man beside Rose. A Southern Methodist preacher with a tendency to thump the Bible he kept by his register when all else failed to impress, Haven stood only five feet four inches and had the poor luck of never convincing a woman to leave Kansas City for the fortune of life in the Sand Hills. Now he took his loneliness out on everyone, especially Indians and homesteaders, whose poverty was a sure sign of disgrace in the eyes of the Lord, at least that was how he preached it to his congregation on Wednesday nights and Sundays.

The Indian pushed the scrap of packing paper, covered with thick letters scrawled with what appeared to be the burnt end of a stick, toward the white man and muttered a word Graver couldn't hear.

The storekeeper clenched and unclenched

his fists and made no move to pick up the paper. The Indian had exceptionally large hands with powerful fingers. His face was puffy as if from drink, but the small determined mouth, stern eyes, and square jaw suggested he was not a man prone to weakness.

"I'm not touching that filthy thing," Haven Smith growled and shook his head, the gray hair curled in tight, possessive knots, glittering in the poor light of the store.

Graver stepped forward, leaning around Rose, who stood with head high, her shoulders wrapped in a black-and-red shawl trimmed with ribbon work, elk teeth, and tiny bells, and then reached over the head of the small girl who accompanied them, whose eyes were fastened on a jar of candy sticks. Picking up the list, he held it under the lamp and read aloud the small necessities. Smith blinked through his smudged square glasses and did not move.

The storekeeper ignored Graver and fixed his gaze on the Indians. "I told you to get out and come through the back there. Now git." He started to turn, but Graver grabbed his arm.

"You want the Bennett Ranch business, you fill this order right quick. These are

Mrs. Bennett's guests," Graver spoke in a low voice, his lips near Smith's ear. Then he picked up the man's hand, shoved the paper into it, closed his fingers around it, and squeezed with his own until the man's eyes watered, then released him. "Understand?"

Smith shrugged, glared at Rose's family, and stomped away to fill the order. It took a few minutes, during which Graver lifted three candy sticks from the big jar and handed them to the little girl, receiving a shy smile as reward. When Smith returned he opened his mouth to protest, then glanced at Graver and thought better of it.

When the order was assembled and wrapped, the Indian reached for it, but Smith raised his finger and shook it like a schoolmaster at a child. "No no no." He smiled. "You pay this time." He swung his eyes to Graver and lifted his brow. "Unless your benefactor wishes to contribute something more. Sir?"

Graver had nothing, which he suspected Smith knew, and wanted to back away, but couldn't now. He'd overstepped. He could try to put it on the ranch account and repay it working without wages. Before he could suggest it, Smith said, "Ah, I thought not," and pulled the order back across the counter.

"I paid. I have credit here. That picture —" He tipped his head in the direction of the dusty penny postal picture cards that stood on the counter for travelers and hill folks.

Smith smiled, the lamplight reflection on his glasses hiding his eyes, and leaving two burning holes. "Only one left. No more credit unless you take another. And this time, I want your wife and little girl, too. Indians are real popular now. Especially in fancy regalia, so bring that with you next time."

Graver pulled the postcard from the rack. The man was dressed as a chief with full eagle feather headdress. Over the front of his beaded shirt a bone bib hung from his neck past his waist, and around his hips a wide beaded belt with long streamers. He wore beaded leggings and moccasins, and a fine quill-trimmed blanket over one arm. At his neck he had tied a cowboy-style kerchief. The same determined face looked beyond the camera without a trace of embarrassment.

"This does not include my family," the man said. "And I think I will not be posing for more of your pictures." He leaned toward Rose slightly and said something in the quick, husky syllables of their language.

She lifted the beautiful shawl from her shoulders, revealing the shabby, stained blue man's shirt she wore tucked into her patched skirt, which was held by a belt decorated with red, black, and yellow beaded stars on a white background. She laid the shawl on the counter without looking up to see the storekeeper's greedy expression as he eyed her belt.

"The belt, too, and we'll call it even."

Rose murmured to her husband, who shook his head. Reluctantly, she untied the piece and set it on the counter next to the shawl, but kept her eyes on it. The little girl solemnly placed her candy sticks on the counter, too.

"Get those dirty things off my counter." Smith shoved them toward the child, who wouldn't raise her eyes, and let them fall and shatter on the floor. The child's chin quivered, but she remained quiet even as tears rolled down her cheeks.

Graver took a deep breath. "That's enough."

Smith was enjoying himself. "Oh, and what is it you need?"

Graver took the package and placed it in the Indian's arms. Then he reached into the jar of candy and pulled out a handful of sticks and gave them to the child.

"I hope you can pay for —"

"That will do," Graver said. "Put it on the Bennett account." He placed Vera's crumpled shopping list and the scented one on the counter. "And while you're at it, fill these lists for Mrs. Bennett and load it into her buggy out front."

Under his watchful eye, Smith left to gather the items, weaving in and out of the many customers with questions. Graver went to inspect the ready-made spectacles in the second aisle, figuring he could use a pair for reading in the dim light of the bunkhouse, before wandering over to examine the slightly used clothing along the back wall.

He caught sight of Rose's family as they moved toward the back door. Graver shook his head, nodded toward the front, and led them out. For the first time, her husband gave a tiny smile. Outside on the boardwalk, a ranch couple split to walk around the little family, and the man spit into the street. Graver took a step after them, but the Indian touched his arm to stop him.

"Thank you," he said, and turning to Rose, he said something in Lakota that brightened her face.

"Ry Graver." He held out a hand and the man took it.

"Jerome Some Horses." He held up a hand and nodded wryly. "I know, I know, but I like walking." Both men laughed, and for the first time Rose smiled. The child detached one of her candy sticks and began licking it.

"I think you know my wife, Rose at Dawn, and this is my daughter, Lily."

"Your English is good," Graver said to Some Horses and removed his hat and bowed slightly, which made Rose snort.

"Boarding school in Mission. Jesuits. If it doesn't kill you, you learn to read and write and do sums. Still doesn't get you a job, though." Jerome looked down the street where half the windows held signs that read NO INDIANS ALLOWED.

"I can ride pretty good," he continued. "Used to break horses for my uncle on the reservation. Don't much care for cattle. And I can keep books with my eyes closed. But nobody would hire an Indian for work like that around here. Rose said Mrs. Bennett needs help on her ranch, though."

Graver nodded and let his gaze wander to the spotted pony tied to the railing, the family's belongings hung cleverly from a pack fashioned of rawhide and bone. The horse seemed in good flesh, but Graver's eye caught on a series of gashes on its front and hind legs. He frowned and stepped closer for a better look. The deeper cuts were sewn shut, the smaller ones coated with grease, and the horse didn't appear to be in any pain as it dozed in the afternoon sun. He turned to Some Horses, his eyebrows raised.

"Tangled in barbed wire."

"Did a good job doctoring it. What's the greasy stuff on the cuts?"

"Ask Rose. She's the horse doctor and everything else with those darn animals." He laughed and shook his head. "She should be Some Horses, and I should be Not So Good With Horses."

Graver looked at Rose with new respect, but when she smiled, he couldn't be certain she wasn't laughing at him. He'd been aware of her eyes on him at the ranch, and now realized she was someone he should keep an eye on, too.

"Mrs. Bennett needs help," she said.

CHAPTER SIXTEEN

Inside the lawyer's tiny office two wooden chairs sat against the dingy plaster wall cut off by the temporary partition. Despite the attempt at privacy, Graver could hear the conversation between Mrs. J.B. and Percival Chance as he sat down. There was nothing to entertain, only the grimy window of the outside door that gave onto a blurry street. He looked down at the floor, its rough planks, hastily nailed in place, separating and warped. Soon be a hazard to see your lawyer, he noted with a wry smile.

"You see we were in correspondence over the years," Dulcinea was saying, "as these letters prove. And J.B. deeded the ranch to me, as this document supports. It's dated last year, drawn up by an Omaha attorney who came out here to deer hunt. It's all clear in this letter. J.B. had second thoughts about his boys and their ability to handle such a large enterprise, and their grandfather's nature. I had a lawyer in Chadron look them over already, but I'd feel more comfortable having someone local." Graver could hear the worry threading her voice.

"What do you want me to do, Mrs. Bennett?" Chance's voice was as smooth as river-polished stone, except for the hint of amusement underneath.

There was a brief pause, followed by the click of her purse snapping shut and the chair scraping back. "I want you to file this deed today and notify Mr. Rivers that the court should set aside the will he has on file. Then, write a letter to Drum Bennett and my sons explaining the terms. They need to hear this from a lawyer, not me. Do you understand?"

Chance cleared his throat, and the chair groaned as he apparently leaned back, stretched, and then pushed himself upright. "Perfectly clear. Would you prefer to pay me now or . . ."

From the looks of his office, it was obvious the man needed money. Too many in the hills settled their differences by means other than lawyers. It would be years before the signs that hung in Omaha and North Platte advising men to leave their firearms at home appeared here. The excuse was always rattlesnakes and coyotes, but folks

231

were generally more respectful toward a man with a pistol belted around his hips or a rifle on his saddle.

"Of course, but I would not appreciate a delay or a disclosure of our conversation until you file the will and transfer the deed. Do you understand?" This time her voice was low and even. Woe to the man who didn't do her bidding. Graver smiled.

"You needn't worry about my desire to converse with my fellow townsmen. I have been here five years and have yet to be invited to share a single meal or drink. There is little society for me here."

This news surprised Graver. Chance was a tall, handsome man, a bachelor.

"You're lucky then," Dulcinea said. "This town is a sore on the rump of Balaam's ass, as far as I'm concerned. You should move to Denver or Omaha, Ainsworth even. After you file for me, of course." She laughed, and Graver could imagine the tilt of her head as she did so.

"Would *you* care to take a bite with me at the Cattleman's Café?"

"I must decline today, Mr. Chance, but I'll return in a week to discuss the reaction to my filing if you can send a rider out with the letters. I imagine there will be some noise from Drum Bennett, who is recuperating in my home at the moment."

"I'll bring the letters personally in a day or so, Mrs. Bennett. I'd be interested in seeing the ranch, and there's nothing as soothing to the weary mind as a sojourn to the country."

There was a moment of silence as the door opened, allowing him a glimpse of the office, the walls covered with an assortment of handmade Indian goods.

"What is it?" she said when she saw him waiting.

Graver didn't need reminding that she was the boss, and her tone embarrassed him. "Wahl, boss, we got all them chores done."

Her head jerked at his exaggerated servility.

Over her shoulder, Graver saw Chance grin. It put him on guard. The man found too much humor in things, as if he always had a hidden card to play and was never in danger of losing the game.

Outside the office Mrs. J.B. stopped, then looked up and down the street. "Have you seen the boys?"

"Not lately," Graver admitted.

"Please find them." She consulted the little watch that hung from a pin on her dress.

He opened his mouth to protest, then shut

it and jammed on his hat as she turned and started for the livery stable.

"But first bring the runabout with my dog," she called over her shoulder.

"Hello." Dulcinea dug in her pocket, pulled out a lump of sugar, and offered it to the gray stallion. The horse looked at her, ears twitching back and forth. He blew high through his nostrils, arched his neck, and bared his teeth as if to bite. Then he grabbed the sugar from her palm and backed away to chew. Dulcinea pulled another lump from her pocket and offered it. This time the horse lowered his head, snorted, and edged over to take it carefully, chewing without backing away. Dulcinea reached up and rubbed his jaw and the side of his neck, working her way up to the ears, which she stroked between her fingers. The stud relaxed and nuzzled her shoulder.

"I'll be riding him. Graver, you take the runabout. The boys will be on their horses," she said. "And we'll pony the two mares."

"Ma'am." Dun Riggins, the livery stable owner, cleared his throat, spit, bit down on the chew, and then shifted it to the other side of his mouth. "Where you want them boxes?"

She looked startled and glanced at the

stack in the aisle. "We'll need to rent a wagon from you."

A crafty look stole into his eyes, and his lips set in a grim smile. "Yes, ma'am, we got us a wagon." He paused, spit, shifted the chew again, and glanced at the stallion. Graver could tell he was toting up the cost of his general irritation at being ordered about by a woman.

"Yes?"

"Only one left in town, I'm afeared, and it's seen better days."

Graver almost groaned aloud.

"Will it make it to the ranch or not, Mr. Riggins?"

"T'aint no other," he said in a mournful voice.

"I'm sure. Fetch it with a team and I'll have my men load." She opened her purse.

The wagon was a shambling wreck, the wood warped, cracked, and paintless, the wheels wobbly, the seat brace broken on one side and shored up with a log that meant the driver sat on a downhill slant. The team was a mismatched pair that would fight each other the whole way, Graver could tell, since the paint was a barely broke youngster with a small pig eye and Roman nose, already humping its back and trotting in place. The washed-out strawberry roan was an old broodmare whose ponderous belly swung so low to the ground, it looked as if she'd knock into it when she trotted. Judging from the bog spavins in her hocks and the hooves that hadn't been trimmed in so long the toes were starting to curl, Graver knew she couldn't do much more than a plodding walk. It was going to be a long journey home.

"This the best you can do?" Graver asked.

Riggins nodded, eyes sly, infuriating little smile in place as he harnessed the animals. He had a short club tucked in his belt that the paint eyed with disdain. Graver thought the horse probably deserved it as his teeth snapped the air beside the man's head, and its hind leg snaked up and out in a swift cow kick that would have nailed Riggins had he not been agile enough to jump out of range. Graver saw Rose's family standing beside their horse, which the child now rode, watching the spectacle. Jerome and Rose whispered and nodded to each other, until Rose came forward and stopped at Graver's side without speaking.

"I can drive them," she finally said in a flat voice.

Graver handed her the patched rein.

Mrs. Bennett saddled the gray stud, which looked to have Thoroughbred racing blood from its long body and fine head but was too heavy-boned for speed, and Graver brought out the two mares. He would ride the prancing black one with the too-alert eye, and tie the bay mare to the wagon, as she appeared calmer and less ambitious. Both were clean-legged and well set up. Where had she found Kentucky racing stock?

Graver took the boys' horses back to the Emporium while Jerome tied his to the runabout and followed, driving as his daughter sat beside him and the dog rode in back, chewing a bone among the packages.

Graver found the boys at the Emporium in front of the glass-encased gun display quietly discussing the merits of the Smith & Wesson .44 Russians. Hefting the guns, Hayward pointed toward the target on the far wall, an Indian chief in war paint and full eagle feather bonnet. An old Spencer .56 and a Berdan sharpshooting rifle sat on the counter. Haven Smith peered at them over his round glasses between customers, and when he saw Graver join the boys, he seemed to sigh in relief.

"You boys starting a Wild West show or planning on joining Buffalo Bill's?"

"This ain't none of your business," Cullen said. Lifting the big Spencer to his shoulder, he sighted on the target and squeezed the trigger, and then mimicked the sound of the Indian's head exploding. The boys gave a short, mirthless chuckle, and Graver smelled the alcohol.

"You want you a nice Winchester you're going after deer or antelope. No point in blowing the thing to pieces and ruining the meat." Graver picked one with an engraved barrel off the wall. "Here's a good used one." He held up the rifle, rubbing his hand along the satiny finish of the stock, and quickly sighted down the barrel. "Looks true." He turned it over in his hands, suddenly squinting at the memory of the shooting at the windmill. He looked at the boys, who watched him but now glanced away as if they didn't. Was that guilt on their faces?

"But you boys already own one of these, don't you? Your pa give it to you?"

Ignoring him, Hayward laid the Russians carefully on the glass and pulled a wad of dollars from his jeans. "Think he'll take eighty for the pair?" He began smoothing the bills with the side of his hand, larger than his brother's, Graver noticed.

"You don't need those," Cullen muttered to his brother. "That Berdan's probably

238

seen better days, but it'd get it done. I'm taking the Spencer." Cullen slipped a thick pack of folded bills from his back pocket. "Come on. Cash money talks, baby brother, cash always talks." He hefted the long rifle over his shoulder and pushed past Graver, who had to lean back to avoid being hit in the head with the gun barrel.

"Your mother's waiting for you," Graver said when they'd completed the transaction.

"Tell her we're staying in town tonight." Cullen glanced at his brother and the younger boy nodded.

"Tell her yourself." Graver walked toward the door.

"Do as you're told or get packing," Cullen called after him.

"You didn't hire me, boy, and you don't fire me." Graver half expected Cullen to shoot him in the back as he walked out the door, carefully closing it behind him so as to not rattle the etched glass. He stood on the boardwalk, took a deep breath, and lifted his hat to wipe his eyes on his shirtsleeve.

Astride the stallion, Dulcinea was speaking with Rose, who drove the dilapidated wagon. He studied the way Dulcinea sat, waiting, her big horse restive, chewing the bit and nodding his head up and down, each upward swing slightly higher so that eventually he would hit his rider in the face. Graver was about to intervene when she tweaked the rein and told him to stop. The horse tucked his nose to his chest and rattled the bit with his teeth. Sweat broke out on his neck and around his ears.

"Did you tell them we're ready to go?" she asked.

He nodded. She sat a horse well, astride, in full command with a deep seat and straight back. "How long do you think they'll be?"

He wanted to respond that they were spoiled, disrespectful brats, and they needed a good hiding, but shut his mouth and shrugged. Her hands held the reins firm and light at the same time. In English riding, they kept the reins short with constant contact on the bit, which wouldn't do for cow work where a person had to handle a rope and sometimes a whip, too. A horse had to be trusted to carry itself, to work off the leg and shift with the cowboy's weight.

"That horse isn't real cowy," Graver said by way of making conversation. Jerome smiled.

"I should hope not," Dulcinea said. "We're going to breed a new kind of horse out here, one that will, well, one that will be a pleasure to ride and possess greater beauty and intelligence. And it can be taught about cows." She dropped her chin and frowned. "Where are those boys?"

"You could give them a holler," Graver said and leaned against the post that held up the porch overhang. He studied the stallion, a tall gray with four white socks, and wondered about its bloodlines.

"We'll go and set up some bottles and try them out." Cullen exited first, cradling his new rifle across his chest like an orphan calf, followed by Hayward, adjusting how the new holster rode his hips.

"These sit a little heavy. Maybe I should just wear one. Leave the other one on my saddle. It's hard to walk. Maybe I should —"

"You bought guns," Dulcinea said, her expression flat.

"Aren't they something?" Cullen held up his rifle so it pointed at the stallion's chest. Graver straightened. Even Hayward looked startled and reached a hand toward his brother, then let it drop.

"Hayward's too young for those pistols," she said.

"I am not! Watch —" He drew the guns so quickly she gasped. "I got a cross draw, too." He flipped the guns into their holsters and just as quickly pulled them out cross armed, wearing a big proud grin.

"But how accurate are you?" Graver said. "Doesn't matter how fast you are if you can't shoot straight."

"I hit everything I'm aiming at." The boy pouted.

"And I get anything he misses," Cullen said.

"We'll have this discussion at the ranch," Dulcinea said.

Cullen stared at the horse, fascinated, as he slowly shook his head.

She fixed the boys with a hard stare. "I need you to help get the wagons home. You can come back tomorrow or the next day if Higgs doesn't have work for you."

"Can I ride him?" Cullen asked.

"In a few days. The mares are a gift for you boys. The stud was for your father, so —" Dulcinea hesitated.

Cullen's eyes darkened and he looked away.

"I need your help in exchange, though." She glanced at Graver.

"Can I ride him now, on the way home?" Cullen asked.

"Nooo, you have to earn his trust first. Now what I do need help with . . ."

"Get off the horse," Cullen said, and his

carelessly held rifle swung upward and pointed at his mother. Without thinking, Graver shoved past Hayward and slammed into Cullen hard enough to knock him backward. He grabbed the rifle and flung it away as the boy fell against the Emporium wall, rattling the plate-glass window. Then he pulled him up by the back of his shirt collar, shook him like a puppy, and slapped him hard across the face.

"A man doesn't point a gun at a lady," he said with another hard slap, leaving a bright red imprint on the boy's cheek. "And don't point a gun at anything you aren't going to kill."

With tears in his eyes Cullen yanked free and whispered, "Then you're dead!"

Graver raised his hand to slap him again, and Dulcinea cried, "Stop! Cullen, Hayward, get on your horses now."

Hayward looked at his brother, who shook his head as if to clear it and was about to retrieve the rifle when Graver stepped in his way. "At the ranch."

Cullen slowly released his breath and straightened to stand eye to eye with the older man. "I been beat so hard I couldn't walk, you think a couple little slaps mean anything? These hills are big, lonesome country — you better ride loose from now on. And you interfere with me and my mother again, I'll kill you on the spot." Graver could see tears in the boy's eyes.

"Anything I can do for you folks?" The sheriff leaned against the wall of the Emporium, watching them.

Mrs. Bennett hesitated, then stepped down from the gray and handed the reins to Graver. "I need to speak with you," she said, and the sheriff nodded toward his office a few doors away.

"Go on ahead, I'll catch up," she called back to Rose and Jerome Some Horses. "Boys, you go on, too."

CHAPTER SEVENTEEN

Although she didn't ask Graver to wait, he did, as he attempted to puzzle out where he'd seen that lawyer before. Then he remembered the December day ten years ago when he'd gone up to Wounded Knee, hitching a ride with a wagonload of whiskey for the extra troops, who arrived so quickly they outran their supplies, especially nonessentials like liquor. The merchants in Rushville had telegraphed an urgent order to Babylon and John Parker had decided to take matters into his own hands. His plan was to drive all the way to Wounded Knee and sell directly to the troops. It was a spur-of-the-moment decision on Graver's part. One moment he was listening to the talk in the livery stable, where he'd come to have a broken wagon wheel repaired by the blacksmith, the next he was helping Parker heft the barrels and bottles of whiskey on the wagon and climbing up beside him.

The ride there was bitter cold, and the wind bit into his face and through his coat. He and his bride had just moved into the hills, and it felt like a fine adventure to finally see an Indian encampment and the soldiers he'd heard so much about. His wife was safe; he'd kissed her good-bye and left her in a room at the hotel with a book and plenty of blankets against the cold. He'd also left her with the last of their cash in case she needed anything. Even then, he shook his head at his ignorance. She was seventeen. Of course her eye would be taken by the bright playthings the stores displayed.

They arrived just after dark, pulling behind the last row of tents so as not to attract the attention of the officers. The sentries let them through as soon as Parker revealed the wagon's contents, and word quickly spread through the enlisted ranks. For a few hours, they did a land-office business, and by nine o'clock they were rolling out blankets in the bed of the empty wagon. Parker had saved one bottle for himself, and Graver took a couple of quick swallows to warm his empty stomach. By the time he drifted off to sleep, the drunken noise of the camp had grown so loud it formed a disturbing barricade that brought bad dreams and little rest.

He awoke at dawn to find his blankets and hair coated with heavy frost. Parker shook himself off and climbed down to piss. Graver followed, shaking in the damp cold that had settled in his clothes. Parker tilted his head toward the cooking fires and the two men were able to find coffee and plates of bacon and beans without much trouble, even though the soldiers, holding their swollen, battered faces in their hands as they fought hangovers, were less than eager to see them again. Graver could feel the ill will and short tempers ooze around the camp like a yellow pestilent cloud. Then the Indian drums began to pound and the heads of the men near them jerked up, eyes wild.

"Are they comin'?" one soldier whispered as he reached for the rifle on the ground beside him.

Another soldier stood and brought his telescope to his eyes. "Just dancing." He sat down hard, as if his legs gave out.

"They're comin'," said the first soldier, who stood and cocked his rifle, his face covered in greasy sweat, a sour stink rolling off him in waves.

Parker stabbed his fork into another piece of bacon and jammed it in his mouth, then stood, placing his metal plate in a pile with

the others. "Let's take a look before we go."
He nodded toward the small valley where
the tipis had been hastily rigged. The camp
was alive with playing children, romping
dogs, and figures collecting at the dance
site, the drummers gathering on the circle.

Behind them a bugle sounded and the
hungover men clumsily prepared arms. The
Indians seemed to ignore the soldiers,
although Graver noticed some officers in
conversation with a couple of their elders,
while their few young men acted guard, pacing nervously behind them.

This went on for a while until the young
men went back to their tipis, retrieved their
old guns and pistols, and dropped them at
the feet of the colonel in charge. The steady
drumbeat and pulsing rhythm found its way
into Graver's body — thud, thud, thud, the
sound pumped in his blood, up his legs, into
his chest, down his arms, and inside his
head, knocked against his skull and the
backs of his eyes until he felt both restless
and lulled. The din of the soldiers behind
them grew louder, and the young braves
standing guard paced, keeping one eye on
the soldiers. Graver saw the big Hotchkiss
cannons wheeled into place on the rise
above the camp. Surely they didn't mean
to . . .

A dancer threw back his head, chanting in Lakota, and tossed a handful of dirt to the sky. Then a rifle fired. There was a moment of stunned silence, and then all at once every gun roared in reply. Parker pulled him flat and they watched as the cavalry fought the Indians. The big guns mowed down dancers, tipis, children, dogs, old people, and women alike. At some point Graver clamped his hands over his ears and squeezed his eyes shut. Behind him, he could hear soldiers hit by gunfire cry out.

When the Hotchkiss guns finally went silent, Graver rose to his hands and knees, looked out across what was left of the camp, now strewn with bodies and burning tipis, and threw up. Parker stood, his expression dazed. He shook his head, made a sound of disgust in his throat, spit, and turned away. "I've had enough. You coming?"

Graver paused, uncertain, and then followed. They didn't speak all the way to Rushville, where they were forced to spend the night because Parker had driven the horses too hard the night before.

They bedded in the livery, since it was already snowing. The New Year coming, and his wife alone. At the time, Graver had no idea that night was only the start of the disappointment that awaited her in married life. Warm at last, nestled in the straw of the loft, he couldn't stop replaying the morning's bloody images, and finally he rose and walked down the street to the hotel. Although it was coming on midnight, the town was awake with dangerous energy like they rode an electrical current that would never release them. He could hear men swearing and fighting up and down the street. Whatever they had done up there, he was sure they would never be free of it.

At the hotel saloon he stood at the bar and ordered a beer. The stranger next to him turned and raised his glass in a toast. Graver stared at the man, tall, blond, and handsome with unearned amusement in his eyes, like he had won some game without having to play too hard. His lips were pursed as if he held in outright laughter and Graver's first instinct was to punch him in the face. The man dropped something on the bar and Graver stared at a pair of child's moccasins, beaded, the bottoms barely worn. He raised his eyes to the stranger, who shrugged and drank from his glass of whiskey.

"You there today? Thought I saw you there. Yes, you were the one brought the whiskey to the troops." The man nodded and a conspirator's smile, small and confident, appeared on his face.

Graver thought to deny that it was his liquor, then said nothing and looked at his beer. He didn't want to be here. Didn't want the man to say another word.

"We were lucky to be there. Spectacular show. Never saw anything like it. Especially afterwards . . . some wonderful pieces to be had . . . I found these on a young girl." He spread his palm over the moccasins.

Graver lifted his fist, then dropped it, turned, and walked out. The man's smug laughter followed him all the way into sleep when it finally arrived around dawn. The memory still chilled him, made him feel as if he had somehow used a gun on those people, too.

The lawyer, Percival Chance, was the man in the bar, Graver was certain. He would never forget the amused expression on the man's face as he gestured toward his trophy.

Chapter Eighteen

As soon as she reached the end of the block, Rose turned the uncooperative horses and circled behind the Emporium. Tying them to the rail, she eased around to the back door, the one Indians were forced to use. White people paid little attention to the comings and goings back here. She pulled the door open slowly so it didn't squeak and let it settle behind her without latching.

The storeroom was in twilight compared to the next room, and she took her time, gazing around at the bags of flour, sugar, and coffee alongside barrels that held whiskey and pickles. She had never understood pickles, and she hated whiskey. She was of half a mind to stick her skinning knife in the barrels to release their contents, but had more important things to do. She edged to the door and peered into the main room, where Smith hustled up and down aisles waiting on white customers, too cheap to hire help. She could do it, she knew every item in the store, where it was, and what it cost. She'd spent that much time studying what she couldn't afford. If he caught her now, he might ban them forever. As it was, they were only allowed in on Mondays and Thursdays, never the weekends when most ranch families came to town. And they had to be gone from town by five P.M.

She thought of pulling her shirt over her head and half covering her face, knowing that it wouldn't make her invisible to others, that it would only make her feel better. In fact, it might make her more distinct. She took a deep breath and edged into the main room, eyeing Smith as she ducked behind the counter.

A yellow-haired white woman in a plain white cotton dress filled the aisle ahead, speaking over her shoulder to the store-keeper as she shook out a remnant of gingham cloth. "I want something original, handmade. I'm surprised you have nothing made by Indians here. Surely you can put them to work beading and sewing. Why in Denver, I visited the most wonderful store full of Indian crafts."

The yellow-haired woman wanted to buy a headdress, a pair of moccasins, a quilled or beaded medicine bag. She only wanted handmade. Rose imagined more women like her collecting tribal goods for their houses, putting her people on display as curiosities. These people stuffed the animals they killed, and would stuff Indians too if they could. Although whites thought her slow-witted, Rose was known as a wise woman on the reservation, one who could read English on her own. She'd read all the contracts her people had made with the U.S. government. She spoke with the tribal elders about the laws that changed constantly, and the ways the government cheated them out of their allotted land and food. But none of that mattered after Star was found murdered. Now she had one job: to find the man who had killed two women in her family. From what Star had said that last day at the trading post in Mission, Rose believed she had found him. Then she was killed on Bennett land. Rose knew the answers were out there, and hoped, for Dulcinea's sake, that it wasn't J. B. Bennett or her boys. She planned to take her revenge. No counting coups this time.

Rose searched the shelves under the counter. She had to hurry before Smith came back for the shawl and belt to show the white woman. She hoped he hadn't the time to put it away in his storeroom. She'd made the belt for Star, but her sister was killed before she had the chance to give it to her, and Rose had vowed she'd wear it forever when she learned of her death. There it was, the white stars glowing under her shawl. He could keep that, it meant nothing. She pulled out the belt and wrapped it around her waist, pulling her shirttail over it before standing and quickly leaving the way she'd come, shoulders stiff against the fear of his voice demanding that she stop.

Some Horses waited at the edge of town, and the boys were nowhere in sight. Rose's heart thumped at the sight of her family. Lily was the leader in the games and tricks the children played on their elders, and Some Horses was popular for his funny stories and quick schemes. He made money off any whites who happened to cross his path. Their history was a tale of survival, whether it was recorded as the winter count on the tipis or in the stories and songs they passed along their generations. Even now, the Lakota held hidden gatherings to practice the peyote religion that had made its way from the Southwest, while the Christian converts decorated their churches in traditional Lakota colors. Some of the priests understood, learned their language and studied their beliefs so the two could merge without harm. She'd even heard of one priest who secretly entered traditional life, living in his residence only when his own elders visited. Otherwise, he was a married man who supported a family, attended sweats in the lodge behind the church, and observed the traditional calendar alongside the Christian one. It wasn't especially confusing to her people. She wasn't so sure about the whites, who seemed able to grasp only a single thought or belief at a time. She pitied them in that.

As she drew up beside the runabout, the paint tried to buck in its traces, and she checked him with the rein, so instead he reached over and bit the fat mare's neck. She squealed but slumped her head in defeat. Rose picked up the whip and gave him a stinging cut across his wide buttocks and cursed him in Lakota. He stood trembling, and then hesitantly twisted his head around to peer back at her. She commanded him to move in Lakota. He put his shoulders into the harness and trudged forward. She wondered where the pony came from on the reservation.

With time to think on the ride back to the ranch, Rose said a quick prayer to Star, and waited, but received no reply. It was discouraging. Either the ghost was with her or not. She had entered into a fearful bargain with her dead sister, violated all of their teachings about death. If her people knew that she'd invited the ghost back to live with her, they would shun her, or worse, insist she spend time alone, without family, and undergo a cleanse in the hope that her sister could be persuaded to the red road and home.

"I know what I'm doing," she whispered and lifted the reins to urge the horses faster than their plodding walk so the runabout wouldn't get too far ahead. Ten years ago, she'd learned that no one cared about her people's dead. Seventeen soldiers received the Medal of Honor for their killings at Wounded Knee and at White Clay Creek the following day. She spit to the side of the wagon. She alone was responsible for finding her sister's killer. Dulcinea would ask the sheriff for help, and involve the white courts, but Rose knew it was worthless.

She thought about the Pine Ridge Indian School, where she'd been forced to board, where the doors were locked night and day, the grounds surrounded by barbed wire, and the children imprisoned for their own good, or so they were told. They were punished for speaking Lakota and could not practice their religion, but their families found ways to continue their traditions. Once her mother sent a doeskin bag filled with healing plants, their uses outlined with beads and signs that a white would interpret as mere decoration. Rose still had the bag, the last gift she'd received from her mother. It was for her also that she must undertake this vengeance. A flood of warm anger spread across her chest and she lifted her head to scan the hills.

This was not her first act of vengeance. Rose was known as a fierce warrior among those who attended the school. While the whites mistook her as untrainable, she worked against them and held secret classes where the children spoke their language, performed the pipe ritual, observed the moons, and practiced dancing. They were almost never discovered, and when they were she always took the blame, which would usually be light since she was considered too dumb to learn. She found her weapon, though. In February of 1894, she set fire to the school and burned it to the ground. The snow around it melted and the earth welcomed the new freedom from the weight of the building that had held so much wrong for so long. She sang prayers for her mother's spirit that night as the sky burst yellow and red, strong colors, from the burning building. It wasn't enough.

Her need for vengeance was a rank seed she watered daily, until even her husband grew afraid. After Star's funeral, she spent two days sweating and praying, her husband and child left alone. Then she consulted the oldest woman on the reservation, the one person who held enough wisdom to help. The visit did not go well, and she left feeling more alone than ever before. It was her task only, she decided, although the woman told her that the world would die in a flood many lifetimes beyond, and that all creation would be called to justice, so there was no point to vengeance. She said too much wrong had tilted the people into chaos that would not be righted in her lifetime or her child's or her child's child's. Her task was to survive, merely to survive. Rose jumped up from her chair and rushed out the door.

She had thought hard as she and Dulcinea rode back to the Bennetts' ranch, and sent a message to Some Horses to meet her in town. She assured him she would not take any action that would endanger their family, their child, and that she merely wanted to bring the killer to the attention of white authorities. They both knew she lied, but in a marriage, one agrees to certain stories in order to survive. She would be careful, she promised herself. Her husband and child were part of her spirit and she theirs. She would die before seeing them harmed.

The runabout slowed and pulled to the side as Dulcinea and Graver galloped up and hauled their horses to a prancing stop. The two boys came whooping out of the little draw ahead and Rose saw Dulcinea watching her sons, a fearful expression on her face. Had they done the killings? Rose had asked around the reservation about Star and heard strange tales from her aunt's husband, of some Lakota boys and white boys at the last rodeo. She wondered if these were the boys. She would find out.

As she drew up to the runabout, Some Horses glanced down at Lily squirming on the seat, then out into the flat expanse. The girl needed to pee. "Traveler's stop. You go on ahead," Rose said as she pulled up beside them.

Rose climbed down, handed the lines to Graver, and took her daughter out a ways, finally stopping in a patch of soapweed tall enough to screen the squatting child. Lily was about to stand when they heard the warning rattle behind her and both froze. Rose waited, tried not to hold her breath, and was on the verge of greeting the snake in Lakota when it uncoiled so she could see its huge head and thick body as it stretched to its full six feet. It gazed at her, tongue fingering the air, then oozed away, leaving a signature trail etched in the sandy dirt.

"Thank you, sister," Rose whispered. Lily stared at her before she dropped her eyes and whimpered.

■ ■ ■ ■

PART THREE:
FALLING TOWARD
THE WOUND

■ ■ ■ ■

CHAPTER NINETEEN

Dulcinea slept long and hard after the trip to town. She woke to find breakfast over and the ranch yard alive with men, horses, and bawling cattle. She paused on the front porch and looked for her boys. Were they already working? Somehow she doubted it, and the thought troubled. Then she recalled Cullen's reaction to the stallion and trotted down the walk to the gate. Two men on horseback were coming down the road toward the ranch. Where was Graver? Or Rose and Some Horses?

Inside the cool shadows of the barn she stopped to let her eyes adjust, and then headed to the back, where they'd stalled the new horses. Relief washed over her as the gray stallion poked his head over the stall door and nickered. The black mare paced uneasily, her coat damp, while the bay munched hay with a contented eye. They needed to stretch their legs. She searched for the halters and found them in the dust on the ground.

Sloppy. J.B. wouldn't put up with hands treating equipment this way, and neither would she. Time to stand up to these men. She raised her head and straightened her shoulders. They'd hate taking orders from her, but they'd learn.

She led the mares out one at a time, starting with the bay, who helped settle the nervous black. The horses needed names. Maybe she should let the boys decide. She recalled Cullen laughing at her and knew it was likely a waste of time. She turned them loose in the big square pen beside the barn, and each let itself down with a groan, rolled over and over, then stood, shook off the dust like a dog, spun and galloped and bucked around the pen until it tired. It had been a long train ride from Kentucky for the two pregnant mares, but they seemed in good shape.

She went back in the barn for the stallion. As she caressed his long neck, she wondered what J.B. would have thought of her gift, bought with her own money. She had planned it so carefully. He would bring both boys to her, the three of them reunited, a family. Of course, they'd have to work out the problems, but it would be a fresh start.

She'd used an old acquaintance of her father's, who owned racehorses, to procure these three from a reputable breeder. The gray was just below the rank of top sires. He'd broken down his first race with a badly bowed tendon, so he was cheap. The two mares were of the same quality: good, not excellent. Perfect for her plan. She imagined J.B. walking through the stable door, whistling, hands thrust in the pockets of his jeans, smiling to see her. She started to think of good things to tell him, but the illusion faded and foamy salt filled her mouth like blowback from a running horse. He had written her about the spotted mare, a brief note she'd pondered, wondering if he had killed her himself or had one of the men do it, or maybe done as he'd suggested so many years before and turned her loose to die of cold, starvation, or mountain lions. It was another stone she stacked on the wall between them. Go get your son, she'd ordered him in March. Now he was dead. Drum had to be the killer. She felt a chill on her face, stopped and heard the men yelling and whistling at the cattle in the branding pen outside. Cullen was home now, yet the thought gave her little comfort. Something was wrong with the boy.

"Damn you, J.B.," she cursed under her

breath as the stallion swung around and headed toward the water bucket, shoving it with his nose so it splashed. It shouldn't be so full, Dulcinea thought, why wasn't he drinking?

He pushed the bucket again, and more water slopped over the sides. "Stop it," Dulcinea said and pressed her hand to his chest, backing him away.

The mouse was a small brown field variety, with a long tail that lay on top of the water like a thick piece of string unfurled, weaving back and forth as if steering the exhausted body between scrabbling attempts to climb the slick sides of the bucket. It didn't seem to notice the woman watching. It was far beyond that scale of worry and menace.

Dulcinea cupped her hand underneath to lift it, and it managed to swim over her fingers. She tried again, this time with both hands, raising it up, water streaming, the soft mewling exhausted and angry. She thought to close her hands, but didn't want it to bite or scratch. The mouse had suffered enough. She released it by a small hole in the corner of the stall. Outside she heard a commotion of voices rise then quickly fall. Maybe it was the boys. She should let them grieve, although a part of her wished they were more like their father and didn't put themselves on display so much. Without her family's social courtesies, and lacking the code of western men, they were more like dogs let off the chain. Although she would not admit it to a soul, they frightened her. If only she and Rose could find the killer. Then she would leave these hills and take the boys with her; they would improve with education, she was sure of it.

When she led the stallion out to his pen, she saw Larabee, Irish Jim, and Willie Munday resting in the shade beside the barn, their clothes and faces streaked with dirt-soaked sweat, three shovels propped next to them. They'd been working on the road between the ranches since Drum demanded they improve it. She wanted to tell them not to spend much muscle because she intended to put a stop to his plans this week. As she turned the horse loose, someone called her name from the hayloft window. Rose stood in the opening, pointing toward the house, where Percival Chance stepped down from a tall, narrow bay mare with a crooked white stripe down her nose that veered to the right at her nostrils. Beside him, Alvin Eckhart, the sheriff, struggled to dismount from a nondescript shaggy brown horse that could only be another refugee from Dun Riggins's livery stable. Overweight and unused to riding, the sheriff looked pale and sweaty as he stumbled to maintain his feet and stand beside the horse to loosen the girth.

She ignored the newcomers and turned to the resting cowboys. "Why aren't you men working? There's a lot of daylight left." She found herself imitating J.B.'s manner of address with the men.

They stopped talking and averted their eyes as they brushed the dirt from their trousers and shirts.

"We're waiting on Higgs." Larabee indicated the foreman's house with a tilt of his head.

"Go knock on the door and find out what he wants you to do, for heaven's sake." She was tired of these men and their mincing rules.

The other two looked at the ground while Larabee shrugged and shook his head. "Rule one: don't bother Higgs in his house."

She snorted. "Rule two: don't expect to get paid for standing around half a day. So here's work: Willie, you clean the henhouse, pull out the old bedding, line the laying boxes with fresh grass, and wash the waters and feeders. Irish Jim: You clean the horse stalls and lay down fresh bedding.

Then scrub out the water buckets and refill them. Larabee: you shovel the manure out of the corrals and clean the water tanks. When you're done, you can start taking down the cobwebs in the stable, and I want the tack hung up properly in the tack room. No more throwing equipment on the ground. If you still have time on your hands, check with me. I don't mind being bothered if it means you earn your keep."

She blushed at their surprised expressions, yet knew from teaching school and every other job she'd held over the last ten years that she had to stay firm or they'd spot her softness, and that never did anybody any good.

Chance wore a small grin, and his eyes appraised her anew. She took in the pink glow on his cheeks from the ride in the full hot sun that produced a sprinkle of freckles over his nose and on the backs of his hands. She was surprised he didn't wear gloves like most of the town men, but when she put out her hand the way a man would, she recognized the reassurance the callused palm gave his grip. He was a handsome man, yet her body felt uneasy around him and she couldn't say why.

"That'll teach them to sit idle when the boss is around," he said with a laugh.

"Ma'am." The sheriff managed to tip his hat and wipe his face with a big blue square handkerchief at the same time.

"We'll go inside," she said and looked back at the barn where Rose stood in the shadows. It would help if she'd come and hear what was said. She tipped her head, gave a small wave of her hand, and hoped Rose understood.

Seated in J.B.'s office, Dulcinea, Chance, and the sheriff examined each other for a moment. Chance was the first to break the silence, reaching inside his coat and withdrawing a thick sheaf of folded papers. "I think we're well within our legal rights on this, Mrs. Bennett. I went to the length of consulting by telegraph with a colleague in Omaha. We all agree that the letter and subsequent will should take precedent. Since Mr. Rivers could see nothing flawed in my argument, he's allowing the documents to be filed." He opened the folded papers and smoothed them with the edge of his hand. "Provided you attend a hearing when the county court is next in session, it should turn out fine." He leaned back and looked at the plaster ceiling. "That should be in late fall, I believe. Too much ranch work until after first snow." He glanced at her. "Is that agreeable?"

She gazed at him, noting the too-straight nose, as if it had been drawn on his face by a skilled artist re-creating the ideal proportions of an ancient Greek statue. His longish face had a more Byzantine aspect, or Spanish Inquisition. El Greco's long-fingered, hollow-cheeked noblemen with pointed beards that seemed too carefully groomed. Still, there was something about the lawyer that pleased the eye if one ignored the almost constant amusement in his.

She shook her head and picked up a large, crudely made knife J.B. had used as a letter opener. It surprised her by fitting neatly in her hand, and the rawhide-wrapped grip immediately warmed her fingers. She tapped the flat of the nicked blade against the stack of unopened envelopes and assorted sheets of paper before her, watched the balance shift, the pieces separate and slide off, revealing a small beaded figure that resembled a turtle. She picked it up and turned it over. It was unlike J.B. to own such artifacts. Hayward's perhaps?

"Your husband seemed to have an interest in Sioux culture. I happen to have a number of artifacts in my possession. If you like, I can show —" He reached into his coat pocket, and she held up a hand to stop him.

Again, she heard the sound of men's loud voices and ignored them. She pushed the papers back over the beaded piece.

"Mr. Chance, my case?"

"Yes, well, I suppose we could petition the court for an early judgment. Contact the judge, send him the papers, explain the exigency, and so on. No guarantee he'll want to take it on, but it's worth a try. I'll explain that you have traveled a great distance and that deferring the ruling means detaining you and creating great discomfort in your current, ah, situation, when you are accustomed to a life more accommodating to your, ah, feminine nature." He cleared his throat as she glanced at the dust and horsehair on the front of her blouse and began to brush it off.

She smiled and looked directly in his eyes, the color of her old dark blue velvet opera cloak. "I suppose it wouldn't do to appear before him in my current state?"

The lawyer dipped his head in a slight bow. "Although it has its charms, perhaps you are right. Helpless is a better tone to set with Judge Foote." He paused and appraised her for a moment, which made her uncomfortable. "I myself prefer a woman who is unafraid to take command of her surroundings." He leaned back and clasped his hands behind his head. The sheriff cleared his throat.

"Have some things to tell you," he began. Her heart leapt at the possibility that he'd solved the murder. She was quickly disappointed, then angered by what he said.

"Well, I asked around town, nobody knew nothing. Then I thought about the Indians since one of theirs, you know —" The man dropped his chin and looked at his hands. "At first, none of them knew a thing. Then I got this boy in jail for fightin' and he spins a tale about —" He glanced over his shoulder, then back at her.

"What?" she asked.

"About those boys of yours coming up on the rez and causing trouble. Might be that girl was part of it, too." He took a shallow breath and let it out with a shake of his head. His face was damp again, and he pulled the big blue handkerchief from his jacket, patted his cheeks and forehead.

"You're not serious," she said with a quick glance at the lawyer, who seemed amused.

The sheriff studied her a moment while outside they heard the boys whooping as they clattered into the ranch yard at a gallop.

"They're children," she said. "Do I have to hire Pinkertons to come out here and find my husband's murderer?" She laid her hands on the desk and leaned forward.

The sheriff looked at his hands, plucked his hat off his knee, and stood. "Don't know what to tell you, Mrs. Bennett. My money's on the boys. You hire anyone else, they'll come to the same conclusion. My advice: hire you a good lawyer. Good day." He nodded to her and Chance, put on his hat, and left. She spun her chair and watched him struggle to mount his sorry horse and put it into the slow trot that would eat the miles to town.

"Mrs. Bennett?" She turned at the sound of the lawyer's voice.

"Could I help out?" For once all the features on his face matched in seriousness.

She shook her head. "I can't believe this."

"He's a dentist, not a trained investigator. Undertaker too. Not much experience aside from pulling teeth and putting people in holes. I wouldn't trust him to find a stray cat." The lawyer eyed her, started to say something else, and then stopped.

She picked up a brittle yellowed newspaper from a stack on the desk and saw J.B.'s notes on the Wounded Knee massacre. Rose had told her about losing her mother there, and that her sister, Star, was close to unmasking her killer. She had repeatedly warned Dulcinea not to mention the story to anyone, but she thought she should tell the lawyer the one fact that might help his investigation. As she opened her mouth to speak, her nerves sang to stop.

"I recently hired a Sioux woman whose sister was the girl killed with my husband. Star was her name, I believe. Perhaps you could discover how —" She paused, her throat closed. She coughed to clear it and found she had to hold her fingers against her neck to continue. "What their relationship was." She felt her face flush, and couldn't look at him.

Chance stood. "Of course." He put on his hat and paused at the door. "You can count on me to be discreet." He studied the doorframe for a moment. "What's the Indian's name?"

After he left, she resolved to tell Rose what she'd done. In some way, it was essential that Dulcinea know if her husband was having an affair with the young girl. She was haunted by the terrible notion that he'd deserved to be killed by the girl's family if he had corrupted her. She shook her head. No, she couldn't believe it, no matter what Drum said. And the idea that her boys could kill — that was ridiculous. But even as she thought the words, she felt uneasy.

Could Cullen? Hayward was too young, but his brother? What would she do if it was true? She'd have to protect him from Rose as well as the authorities. She'd have to leave the hills with both boys and sell the ranch, hide as far away as possible. Europe or South America.

Her shaking hands rattled the newspaper she held and her gaze fell on J.B.'s underlined sentences that described how the bodies were stripped and thrown into a mass grave. On the second page, J.B. had underlined the names of whites who'd been there — and written Harney Rivers and Percival Chance in the margin. It sent a shiver across her shoulders, and she swiveled her chair around to look out the window. Chance was talking to the hands on the porch of the bunkhouse. She gathered the papers, tucked them in the bottom of the lowest desk drawer, and locked it.

The boys were sullen at supper, eating quickly and sloppily with their faces a few inches from their plates, refusing to answer the lawyer's polite inquiries. Although she hadn't wanted to, she'd invited him to stay the night since his interviews with the men had taken the rest of the day. Rose was silent when Dulcinea told her about the lawyer's offer without mentioning the sheriff's initial conclusion. Maybe Rose already knew, maybe all the Indians believed it was her boys. The thought made her frantic.

Chance raised his voice to be heard above Drum's constant thumping overhead. "Do you find many Indian artifacts in your blowouts?" The boys glanced at each other.

"Hayward, I saw a collection of arrowheads in your room. Why don't you tell Mr. Chance about them?"

Her son's face reddened with the effort to remain silent as he pushed at the half-eaten slab of chicken with his fork. A sly smile widened Cullen's mouth. Was it possible to dislike her own flesh and blood so much she wished them ill? She wanted to tell Cullen that she didn't even recognize him. She wanted to announce that he had to leave her table and never return. She hated herself for it and turned her attention to him with a smile.

"Cullen, perhaps with your greater experience, you wish to speak to Mr. Chance's question." She touched her lips with her napkin and lifted her chin. He glared at her with such pure hatred it made her skin clammy. How did her lovely towheaded boy become this Cullen? She looked deeper into his eyes, searching for that boy, but they remained bottomless, empty, as if she could see through the dark tunnel to his skull.

Then he pushed back his chair, stood, lifted his hand and dropped the linen napkin on the gravy laden plate, shoved the chair against the table, rattling the glasses, and strode toward the stairs, mounting them with the litheness of a cat leaping from limb to limb. The pounding on the ceiling stopped, and those left at the table absorbed the silence in its wake.

Higgs and Vera studied their plates. Hayward looked confused as to whether he should follow his brother or finish the food he eyed hungrily. With a sigh he cut a large chunk of chicken breast and stuffed it in his mouth, chewing rapidly. When he tried to swallow and commenced to choke, it was Chance who thumped him on the back and handed him a glass of water. Hayward almost thanked him when he could breathe again, caught himself, and settled for a quick nod. Chance looked at Dulcinea with a twinkle in his eyes. She glanced at Vera in time to catch her watching them with an odd, distracted expression.

Cullen still hadn't reappeared when they'd finished the meal, so Dulcinea invited Hayward and Percival upstairs to the small porch J.B. had built off their bedroom when they found they couldn't sleep inside in the summertime.

She opened the French doors, stepped out, and pulled the cover from the telescope stationed at the railing. Since the porch was at the back of the house, the light from the men's bunkhouse and Frank and Vera's did not interfere with its view of the night sky. Chance gave an appreciative chuckle. Hayward stepped closer and stroked the long brass barrel with the wonder of a child. Apparently he had not known about his father's obsession.

"What is it?" he asked.

"A telescope." She explained its use. "Want to see?"

Chance stepped back as she positioned the eyepiece, moving the barrel to focus first on the moon. When its cratered surface appeared, she waved Hayward to her side and showed him how to place his eye. He gasped when he realized what he saw, quickly looking up at the distant moon, almost full, and then placed his eye back at the scope. "The shadows are canyons!"

"And it's not made of cheese or little green men or fanciful creatures," Chance said. "Or lovers' sighs or wishes either." He smiled at Dulcinea.

"Here, there's something else you can see." Hayward stepped back and she peered into the scope, moving it slightly to focus on the Archer with Orion's Belt. In his eagerness, Hayward stepped on her foot, and looked aghast, quickly uttering an apology. She placed a reassuring hand on his back and he didn't shrug it off. When he bent to scan the stars she pointed out to him, she rested her hand on the back of his neck, thrilled at the soft down of his hair. He was busy observing the Milky Way, so she dipped her head and caught his scent as she had when he was a babe in her lap. It was different now, a young man's sweat, complex with tobacco, horse, and whiskey. She was caught in a terrible tide of regret. How could she have left him? Drum's threat loomed again, and she remembered the sickening bargain she was forced to make. She wasn't prepared for what followed, when no amount of arguing with J.B. mattered. He wouldn't allow her to take Hayward and he wouldn't rescue Cullen from his father. Her breath came short and shallow as she felt the lost years with her sons, and she looked up in an effort to keep from crying.

The sky over the hills was so close tonight,

as if a person could reach up and pluck the stars one by one and tuck them in her pocket for safekeeping. Somewhere close by, a coyote called, running up and down the scale like a musician opening an instrument, then another joined and another, and before long, the sky filled with a joyous, triumphant ululating that ran from horizon to horizon as the coyotes gave chase. It ended abruptly with the almost human scream of a rabbit, then silence as the animal was quickly torn to pieces. The ritual was nothing new, but it seemed to shake the group as they released their collectively held breaths and glanced at each other uncertainly. Hayward stepped back from the telescope. The spell was broken, and he mumbled, "Good night, Mother," as he slid around her and left.

Chance stepped to her side. "May I see?"

He moved the telescope from place to place, then straightened. "Very good instrument. But I notice it's positioned for the northern sky."

As she shrugged, she became aware of something she had not thought of before. J.B. had positioned the telescope for the northern sky, the sky over her head on Rosebud. The peddler had recently delivered a new eyepiece, too, stronger, more

283

carefully ground, from Germany. Perhaps it was merely coincidence that he last scanned the sky over her. Next, he might have turned to the west or east, or taken the telescope out of the house for a clear view of the southern sky from the roof of the barn. She stopped the sentiment. J.B. didn't just give his oldest son to his father, he abandoned her, too, even if she was the one who had left.

"My husband had a curious nature." She lifted the canvas cover from the floor and spread it over the telescope. "Let me show you to your room."

It was a relief to be rid of him. She wondered if she was a cold woman. When she first returned home to Chicago, she spent sleepless nights on the widow's walk of her parents' house, peering west, as if her husband were a sailor adrift in an ocean of grass, and making his way to her, he could arrive at any time, and she had to be the one to catch first sight of him. She was still young then. She hadn't realized how long it would take. She thought again of the piece of paper Drum had shown her. It took three days for her to fully understand what it meant, what J.B. had done, and what could never be undone. She thought again of Rose's sister. Had J.B. taken solace there despite the girl's young age? Had he been unfaithful? She pushed the thought aside and dragged their wedding quilt out to the balcony, content to spend the night as he must have, lying alone with the stars overhead, and the rush of the wind rustling the grass, and the steady throb of the peepers beating along with her heart.

CHAPTER TWENTY

At first light Drum Bennett slowly gathered himself for the task ahead, easing one leg, then the other out of bed and planting his feet on the floor. Cullen had helped him with his trousers the night before, and the arm was healed enough that he could discard the sling and slide into a shirt. Buttoning it took time until his shoulder, stiff from inactivity, gave with a few noticeable crunches and he worked the hand that had stayed immobile for so long. In the old days, when he was younger, he'd worked cattle with a broken arm. Now he was weak as an orphan calf. He wanted to bellow his rage at the injustice, but knew better than to wake the household. Dulcinea with her fancy-man lawyer spending the night. Oh, he'd heard them talking. He knew what they were up to. Rivers sent him a message. He'd fix her. That was number one. Number two was joining the ranches. Number three, and he knew this was a distant possibility, was finding his son's killer. With all the time laid up, he'd had some unwelcome thoughts on the subject. Now he needed to prove himself wrong, or he'd never feel safe again.

Drum waited for the lightness in his body to recede before he could muster the strength to pull on his boots. Last night, Cullen brought him rawhide strings to tie around the upper portion that they'd had to slit open to release his swollen foot four weeks ago, and he'd be damned if he was going to throw away perfectly good boots. He would fix them himself if he didn't have this work ahead of him. As it was, he'd give them to Stubs to mend. Man was too old and worthless on a horse anymore, had to earn his keep mending equipment. Drum bent over to wrap the boot with rawhide, and grimaced at the way his belly had grown fat and wobbly, making it difficult to breathe at this angle. Hell, come to that he was next in line after Stubs for a bullet to the brain. Look at the shape he was in. Fat as a tick and snake-poison mean.

He straightened and pushed his feet firmly into the boots, despite the protest they made. What did a man come to, a bag of bones and a waddle of fat, all disarranged and helpless. He glanced at the picture of

287

J.B. on the dresser and the thick envelope that lay beside it.

"Damn it, son, you never did amount to a pile of crap, did you?" He took a deep breath, released it slowly, and straightened his spine as he did so, then using the cane Cullen had fashioned, pushed upward, forcing the wobbly ankle to hold his weight despite the pain that shot up his leg into his back. Although the arm was still weak, he made it do its job, and pressed down on the cane to support the bad leg. It felt like the healing arm threatened to snap again, but he ordered it to get to work. With just a few more steps to the door, the words to an old-timey song started in his head. *Old Joe Clark was a mean old man . . .* He couldn't remember more than the refrain, which he repeated with every step. *Old Joe Clark was a mean old man . . .*

By the time he made it down the stairs, he was panting and his shirt soaked with sweat. "J.B.," he mumbled. He had to stop talking to his son, to remember he was dead. He blamed too much time sitting around without work to wear a body out. He knew his son was gone. Some son of a bitch shot him. Just like Drum's grandfather, in Missouri, a lifetime ago. Shot him dead, right in front of Drum, when he was only a boy of thirteen. His father was killed by Indians out West, he was told, and his mother died in childbirth, left him to be raised by her father. After the old man's death, Drum struggled to keep the homestead going. He was too young, and no one would help a boy his age alone. They wanted him to stay with the neighbors down the road, a large family of girls who could use another strong back to do for them. Store wouldn't extend him credit till he could bring in the crop. He had all he could do keeping meat on the table and milking the cows. In all the years they lived together, his grandfather, another mean old man, had two things to tell his grandson: "This land is everything. Don't ever sell, lose, or walk away from our land. And, boy, never trust nobody, not even me." Then he'd slapped him so hard the boy wore the finger welts on his face for a week. From then on, Drum flinched every time his grandfather or anyone raised a hand. After a while, it wore on the old man until he made him stand like a stone and take his punishment. Drum hadn't meant to lose the land. He had struggled long and hard to keep it, but there was no chance. He was fourteen when he walked away, carrying the shame on his back like a rock-filled pack.

Drum stood, hands on the back of the

chair at the kitchen table, bracing until the tremble left his legs and his breath returned to normal. He was the first in three generations to reach sixty and he had no idea what to expect. Usually he didn't think about his age, and just pushed himself harder when the joints ached and the lungs felt small. The breakfast dishes were laid out, the coffeepot ready for the fire in the stove to be lit. No reason he couldn't do that himself. Vera would be over soon. Damn, he hoped Higgs would take his offer to get rid of Dulcinea in exchange for the foreman's house. Get things back to normal here. He lit the fire and found himself staring into the flames, something he avoided as a rule. No point in going back there. What's done is done.

But this morning the past wouldn't go lie down in the corner like an old dog. The scene appeared again and again, in waves of ever greater detail. The faces at the window with the flames in the background like a painting of the last judgment, then the terrible collapse of the roof before he had time to — He always told himself he was going back inside, he was, he would fight his way through the fire and save them. He hadn't known they were there when he went back with the kerosene and rags. Drum groaned, and then glanced around to see if anyone had heard him. The coffeepot burped and murmured as the water heated. The fire crackled and the stovepipe ticked as the rising smoke heated the tin.

By the time he was fourteen he was skin and bones, too tired to cook, let alone eat. He could barely shoulder the pack onto his mule, and the walk to town took twice as long. He hobbled then, too, he thought ruefully. He'd lost a toe to the plow. And that was another thing he counted against the man. In town, he sat to rest behind the livery stable under a big sugar maple, and fell asleep in the dense summer heat. By the time he woke, it was coming dark and he had to hurry. Bennett Shear was just going to supper at Shadow's Tavern to celebrate his new acquisition, which solidified him as owner of the entire valley. He'd already moved a tenant farmer onto Drum's farm. When Shear heard his name called, he glanced at the boy without understanding that he should be afraid, then turned back to speak with a man leaving the tavern.

The bullet caught him midsentence right through the heart, spun him slowly down the boardwalk steps into the muddy street where he lay on his side like a man gone to sleep. There was such harmlessness in the final picture that people stopped and stared for a moment, unable to determine if Shear was dead or alive. Drum had been too exhausted to move at first, then some instinct told him to walk slowly away, holding the pistol at his side, finger on the other trigger he intended to cock and pull if anyone moved to stop him. But by some magic, people were too curious about the dead man to notice a boy. When he gathered the mule's rope, his first thought was to head west through the woods where trackers would have a harder time. Instead he went north, back the way he'd come, picturing the kerosene barrel in the corner of the shed and the rags that were his grandfather's clothes in the other. He didn't know about the tenant family. The five little ones on the pallet bed he'd left in the sleeping loft. He didn't have time to warn them that it was too hot in the summer and too cold in the winter, that they would spend their nights hugging each other to keep warm.

Since that time, Drum couldn't stand the smell of kerosene. He kept coal oil lamps, candles, and cow chips for fuel at his ranch. He'd avoided civilization after that, choosing game trails and outposts. As he walked, he planned. First he changed his name to Drum Bennett, after the man who had ruined their lives. No one would expect him to take the dead man's identity, so that's what he did. Even J.B. didn't know his true origins. That was fine.

The day he came for his grandson, the past was wound around his insides like a tapeworm, eating itself full while the man starved, belly distended. Drum had rebuilt the family fortune, seized the land from Indians and other settlers, fought fiercer than any animal could to hold on to it. When his place was secured and his son's also, he started thinking toward the future. He couldn't be sure J.B. was strong enough to make the boy into a man who could hold the land against the Bennett Shears of the world. Sending J.B. to his wife's folks in Missouri to be raised hadn't worked out so well. His son was too soft, too generous when he should hold the line against others. That woman he married was evidence of what happened when the right stamp wasn't put on a boy. No, Drum knew how it had to be. That day he got up, told Stubs to fix a pallet bed for the boy in his own room, saddled two horses, and set off for J.B.'s. He hadn't reckoned on the disturbance she'd make. Drum's own wife had been a sullen, quiet woman who obeyed him without speaking, had done so until the day she disappeared, just like that, off the face of the earth. He found no tracks, no evidence that she had walked, ridden a horse, or driven a wagon. Within days, it was as if she'd never been there, and he felt enormous relief. Since she was a poor cook anyway, he was happy to eat the victuals prepared by Swensen the Swede, who had lost a foot in a blizzard and needed other work after a winter of lying around eating. Over the years, Swensen had perfected the plain food Drum preferred, neglecting salt and pepper even. It was food meant to toughen the boy, he'd explained to Swensen. The ancient Greeks and Romans knew better than to baby a male child. Make them sleep on the ground, without clothing, teach them to take the blows without speaking.

The coffee began to boil and Drum hobbled to the bread safe to cut a couple of slices. The saucer of butter had been left on the table without a cover and bore the impression of a tiny mouse paw and the twin gnawed furrows of teeth. Waste. It made him so mad, he smeared over the soft surface, obscuring the disturbances, and positioned the plate so no one would suspect. He'd eat his bread with mulberry jam. Another of J.B.'s fancies. If he'd paid more attention to the future, and less to every little comfort, he might be alive today. Drum cursed under his breath and knocked his fist against the table. Goddamn it.

He poured a cup of coffee and hobbled outside to the porch to sit and wait for Vera, Higgs, and the men. Something about this morning reminded him of the day he'd come for Cullen. Except then, he rode with his back to the sunrise, and the gray-blue around him gradually turned rose, then yellow, and finally full color at almost the same moment the full bright heat began to warm the back of his shirt. Today, the sun took its time, stabbing the bunkhouse windows with light that seemed to sink, then bounce back, sharp and brittle, like a signal sent one place to another to another. He'd read Homer's *Iliad* and *Odyssey* the first winter he'd spent in the hills living in a tipi on the Niobrara River. He'd found a spit of land with an artesian well that never froze and the river itself only took a skim of ice in places, and he'd found an old tipi he patched and used. It was cold as the dickens, but the wild plum, willow, and burr oak kept off the worst of the wind. Sheltered in the lee below the hills to the south, he learned to drive the tipi poles deep into the ground, to keep a fire going, and to not touch the sides of his tipi with his body. He would have starved except for the river, which drew deer, antelope, and turkeys during the long cold months, even when the snow was deep. He came close to eating coyote, too, but didn't. Once he found a stray cow and, nearly starving, was torn between killing it and trapping it to begin his own herd in the spring. His stomach hurt so bad he chewed willow bark and boiled grass to drink the broth that played havoc on his bowels, but he kept the cow alive, and come spring he would turn it loose and track it to other cattle it would find. On one particularly cold, still night when the tree limbs crackled as the sap froze and he could make out the pad of coyote paws circling the camp, he coaxed the cow into the tipi with him. When he woke in the morning, the animal was lying by his side, providing the warmth he had dreamed about.

It was right at the end of that bad cold spell when he and the cow almost died that he found the Indian woman mired and exhausted in a chest-deep drift she'd plunged into coming off the hill on a little buckskin mare. Try as they might, it was clear they couldn't free themselves and were doomed when darkness fell. Drum watched their feeble struggles for a few minutes, and then waded through the deep snow toward them. His own horse had taken off the night of the first snowfall, and he wore snowshoes he'd fashioned from strips of willow branches and bark. The churned-up snow made it hard to keep from sinking, but he managed to get close enough to grab the war bridle and pull the horse's head. Although she stretched her neck, the game little mare didn't have the strength to raise her forelegs high enough to strike out into the snow in front of her, so Drum went around to the side and lifted the nearest leg by hand, placing it ahead of the horse, then repeated the action on the other side, then went to the haunches and pushed and swatted until the horse was driven to a desperate lunge. In this way, he half dragged, half pushed the horse out of the drift. The woman, sunk into the snow beside the mare, he dragged to safety.

He nursed her until the thaw finally arrived in the middle of a late March night and they woke to a warm wind and snowmelt creeping into the tipi. She stood, shook out her waist-length hair, tied it with a strip of buckskin, and began to roll their bed before it got soaked. He realized then that she had been waiting for this moment to leave, and he hastily signed for her to stay as his wife. He assumed that no white woman could survive the hills with him. She was plain, with broad flat features and expressionless eyes so dark he always seemed to be looking at his own reflection when she stared at him. There was a small thick scar on her chin that she often covered with one hand when she knew he watched. She had not said a word in the weeks she'd been with him although he had tried English, then a smattering of Ute, Sioux, Omaha, and Ponca. He didn't know any other languages. Still she soundlessly joined with him in the deep cold nights of that winter. It kept them alive, and she showed him other ways of boiling bark and grass, of spearing fish that waited sleepily at the bottom of the small pool under the young cottonwoods, of smoking the deer meat in strips, sucking the marrow from the bones and grinding them for soup. The cow somehow found enough forage to stay alive, fatten even, he realized that morning of the March thaw. Her sides bulged and her coat had a glossy sheen. The Indian looked at the cow and burst out laughing, the first he'd heard from her. When he raised his brows and shook his head, she tugged the ragged sleeve of his coat and gestured to the cow's stomach, then her own, using her hands to draw a round pregnant shape. He looked at the woman's stomach pushing hard against the deer hide dress, then the cow's heavy stomach hanging just above the newly revealed earth.

"I am Mary Morning," she said in carefully enunciated English, and her black eyes softened for the first time as she glanced shyly at the cow's stomach again. When her face relaxed, it became almost pretty, and Drum felt a brief quickening in his heart. But he wasn't a boy anymore. He had already lived a hard life on his way to the Nebraska Sand Hills, and she wasn't the first woman to claim something from him.

He thought now of how different it might have been had he not been raised by that mean old man, had he not shot Bennett Shear and fired the homestead, killing those youngsters, there, he'd said it, had he not done any number of wrong things before they were done to him afterward. For two years before he came to Nebraska he made his way around Colorado and what became New Mexico, prospecting, fighting, barely scraping by, and he'd done some things out there that still haunted him. One in particular, the mine he stumbled upon in the Spanish Peaks, on the way to Fort Morgan. It showed some color, and he couldn't figure out why it was abandoned until the afternoon the owner showed up with two pack mules and a scattergun aimed at his belly while he slept in the man's bed in the lean-to at the front of the mine opening. He was sure he'd die that time, and given how hungry and tired he was from trying to scratch a living out of rock, he wasn't sure he cared.

Drum drained the coffee from his cup and struggled up to pour another. Not a soul stirring. Lazy so-and-so's. He stood on the porch, surveying his son's ranch. He had to hand it to J.B., the buildings were placed right where he would've done it — so no matter the weather a man could tend cattle and livestock in the home pastures and corrals. The hay yard wouldn't be snowed in, and water was always close by. Drum had to admit that when he built his own spread, he wasn't so circumspect, and extra work was needed in the winter to keep the stock watered. If he had it to do over — He bit off the idea with a quick grimace and a shake of his head.

The gold weighed more than he expected coming down that Colorado mountain and crossing Wyoming and up into the Sand Hills, but he was still a young man then, strong as an ox, and the mules were from Missouri and wouldn't quit. He had stayed

300

almost a year with Wilke, and they'd dug out enough gold to keep them from despair. Wilke said he'd split it down the middle when the time came, but Drum saw how that left them each with merely a small mound. "I know there's a big vein in there," Wilke always claimed when the boy grew despondent. Tomorrow, he promised. When the vein finally showed itself, it was too late, really. Drum had planned on leaving for weeks. It was his pick that pulled down the soft stone shelf, revealing a wide vein that Wilke attacked, heedless of the rock trembling above him. It didn't all come down that morning, and they were able to pull out a sizable amount of gold before they quit for the day. The vein widened, which seemed impossible to the two men who labored carefully now, scooping up the gold gravel and crumbles along with the nuggets.

Wilke was beside himself, slapping Drum on the back, swearing they would be millionaires now, as soon as they could haul their find down to the assayer's office. That night as they lay on beds set on either side of the fireplace, Wilke insisted they plan for their fortunes. As far as Drum could tell, there still wasn't enough for the ranch he intended to build, to show his dead grandfather who suspected he was too weak to hold the land. Drum could never admit to himself that night was the beginning of it. Even now he couldn't be sure that he was the one who caused the cave-in, with Wilke trapped on the other side. They worked for three more weeks. The vein was wide and some of the purest ore either man ever saw. Their fortunes were substantial with no end in sight. Then the entire roof gave way. Drum escaped with a couple of broken fingers and cuts and bruises, but he was in the front and plunged outside as soon as he heard the first crack. Wilke went deeper that morning to follow the seam along the roof into the mountain, picking here and there to reveal the gold. At first there was silence as the dust rose into the still morning air and then the birds in the jack pines around them started yammering again.

He called Wilke's name and pulled rocks out of the way, but heard nothing so he gave up, resting on his heels as he surveyed their little camp and imagined the trip down the mountain for help. Except there was nowhere to go. By the time he made it to La Veta or Fort Garland, Wilke would be dead if he wasn't already. Drum thought of Wilke's last words, "Good Lord, the whole roof is gold, Drum, it's a gold dome!"

He heard the first sounds as he was rolling up his bed and figured it for imagination, the wind or the birds whose voices could sound human in the peculiar angles and depths of the mountains. As he packed the camp utensils onto the mules, he heard the voice more clearly. Wilke calling his name. He stopped, and stared at the wall of rock plugging the mine. Wilke was hurt, he could tell from the weakness of his voice. There was too much rock. The pieces too big, even if they were riddled with gold. He had enough now. He began to load the gold equally on the mules, and when it appeared to be too much, he unloaded them again, put a few cooking utensils into his pack, and discarded the picks, shovels, and tools. Then Wilke's voice grew louder, more demanding.

"My legs are busted, Drum, you got to get me outta here." When that didn't raise a response, the voice whined, "I'll give you my share, boy, I swear, you can have it all. I can dig more. Just help me . . . You have to see this gold, Drum, it's more than we ever imagined. We'll be kings. Just help me . . . Drum? You there, boy?"

Drum started back up the slope to the opening, then stopped. A man with two busted legs would have to be nursed for months, right into winter. They'd be stuck

303

here, low on food, regardless of the piles of gold. They might not make it. Probably wouldn't. So there'd be two dead instead of one. Maybe Wilke could dig himself out, though Drum doubted it, maybe he could get himself down the mountain, though Drum knew that was impossible. There was nothing for it. He surveyed the lean-to and in a last impulse grabbed Wilke's pack and shouldered it, feeling the wooden Hopi kachina doll the other man had set such store in digging into his back. He picked up the mules' lead ropes and started down the mountain.

At La Veta, just over the mountain pass, he tied the mules in an arroyo outside town and took a small cache of money Wilke had hidden among his clothes. He bought a decent horse, a rifle, a pistol, and the supplies he would need for the trail. His story was that his horse ran off in a thunderstorm coming through the pass and he was on foot. The man at the livery nodded. He'd seen it happen. He sold Drum a bay horse with three white socks that had wandered into his corral wearing a saddle and bridle late one night. No brand to speak of after Drum blotted it with a hot cinch ring. He cropped the mane and tail and fed the animal corn and water to bloat it. As soon as the brand scab fell off, he used a root dye to darken the white sock on the front leg. He'd wait awhile to sell the saddle and bridle.

Making his way across Colorado, along the high plains and down into the Sand Hills, Drum had time to consider the problem of the gold, especially those nights coming into winter when the wind blew Wilke's voice. Even now, sitting on the front porch of his son's house, he could hear his name when the morning breeze caught the edge of the roof. Sometimes it made him so mad he had to hit something. Most of the time he pushed it aside, willed the sound to stay buried with the rest of it.

He sipped his coffee. It was cold. He got used to cold coffee and cold jerky that first winter in the hills. By the time he decided to settle in the Sand Hills, it was too late to build. He deposited a small amount of gold in the Cattleman's Bank in Babylon under the pretense that he had made his stake in the California strike. He buried the rest, planned to use it only when desperate, to avoid drawing attention. Plenty out there would take advantage of a lone man holding a fortune in gold. The mules were stolen almost immediately, leaving him with the horse that ran off the first big snowstorm, true to its nature. Drum hunkered down then, figuring to winter on the Niobrara, where he was told the season was usually mild with thaws following storms. It was not that kind of winter.

He looked at his hands, the two fingers he couldn't quite close, and the dark nails that never regained normal color after frostbite. Come spring, with the cow pregnant and Mary Morning gone, he found his land and began to build a small house, spare and plain. He figured he would build a bigger one later, using some of the gold. He tried not to touch it, kept it in reserve to back up any play he made to acquire more land, cattle, and horses, but as it was he went twice a year to the hidey-hole, always toward dawn. He was lucky the rattlers that frequented the mounds of stone chose not to bother him. He figured it was part of a grim blessing on the gold, on his fortune and life. Except for women and the boy. No blessing there. Mary Morning had stayed until spring, helped him with the chores and cooked his meals. They shared a bed in the silence that grew from winter on, no whispered endearments, no declarations. She must have known how he felt, he reasoned. He wasn't a man to give things away to just any passerby. Later he would realize that he loved this strange Indian woman more than anyone in his life. He would have shared his fortune with her, he told himself, although he wondered if that was true. He certainly would have cared for her and the child. He would have done that at least. No reason for her to slip away on the buckskin mare. How she even mounted with the belly in front of her, he never knew. Maybe she walked away leading the horse. That image always made him sad, and he shook it off. He could have bought her material to make a dress, combs for her hair, shoes or beads or whatever she desired. A mirror, a better mirror than the small cracked one he used to shave his face. He thought less about the child she carried. He couldn't say why that was, either.

CHAPTER TWENTY-ONE

As he watched now, the rooster came out, inspected the sunrise, and commenced crowing. When nothing happened, he clucked to himself and minced back into the henhouse. That new dog of Dulcinea's came down the stair, pressed its face against the screen door, and whined to get out. Drum hooked his cane on the door handle and pulled it wide enough for the dog to slip through. An ungodly mutt, it gave him a courtesy nod, then ambled down the stairs and out into the yard to relieve itself on the lilac bushes.

The white woman he married was a whole different story. Drum shook his head and grinned ruefully. What the hell was he thinking? On a horse-buying trip to Missouri, he stayed with a family that raised fox trotters and before he knew it he had foundation stock and the man's only daughter to herd home. Turned out she wasn't much interested in Sand Hills ranching and as soon as she dropped the baby boy she took off to Omaha and beyond. He told J.B. she died so he wouldn't have to answer for it later. She did die, he learned from her father, on a ship that sank in the Atlantic, on its way to Europe. She married a duke of some sort and was going to live the life she'd always wanted. As far as Drum knew, they were never divorced, but it hadn't mattered. Silly woman. If she'd waited long enough, he would have used the gold to buy her pleasure. At least he told himself that when he was in a generous mood.

Which brought him to his current problem. He reached inside his shirt and pulled out the envelope that had been sitting on the dresser upstairs. J.B.'s new will and a copy of Drum's. Who was he going to tell about the gold? Who was he going to leave it to? He never trusted his lawyer enough to put the fact of its existence in his will. He certainly didn't want Dulcinea to have it. Cullen wasn't ready, it would spoil him. Hayward wasn't old enough. He'd be damned if he was going to ruin those boys with too much money. He had spent the last month in bed ruminating on the problem and still hadn't come up with an answer. It was time to ride out and check on it.

And it was time to put his plans into action, before the county judge held his hearing. Right now he could do just about anything to bring the two ranches together and J.B.'s widow couldn't do a thing to stop him. He smiled grimly, slapped the envelope softly in his palm. Maybe the gold could buy the judge or even pay off the woman so she'd leave the Bennett men in peace once and for all. Today he'd get word to Stubs to come over to help him ride out for the gold. Have to blindfold the old fool, or get him so drunk he couldn't find his way there or back. Doubted he could ride yet with this damn foot, though, need to take a wagon, pretend to go to town or some —

"You're up." Dulcinea's voice startled him. Damn woman to sneak around like a thief in the night.

"Coffee's on the stove," he said gruffly, flinging the cold remains from his cup off the porch. The dog came up the steps and wagged its long tail at him briefly, saw the disapproval in the man's eyes, sighed, and flopped down beside him, bones hitting the wood floor with a cracking thump.

"I'm not your friend," Drum said and felt like those were some of the truest words he'd ever uttered.

When she returned with the cup in her hands he wished he could've asked for another. He leaned back and raised his bad leg to rest on the porch railing covered in curls and scales of old white paint. His son hadn't done much work these past few years. Drum had to admit the cattle and horses were in good shape, but the rest of the place had taken on that run-down shabbiness of a man about to give up. Who would've guessed J.B. would take on after a woman like that? Fortunately, Drum had been there to do the right thing.

"Do you have any idea who killed him?"

Drum looked at her for a long moment. "Don't you think I'd be the first to put a rope on his neck if I knew?" He thought about the Indians lurking around town, the sense he was always being followed on his way to the gold, the rough lot he employed — any one of them would slice his throat for a dollar — the lawyer fella he encountered twice riding their land with a shovel and a pair of binoculars, this Graver who showed up at just the right time, and finally, Cullen. Would he shoot his own father? Drum couldn't be certain — maybe he'd bred too much meanness into that boy.

"I thought you were supposed to protect

him . . . that was our bargain."

"I did the best I could." He felt a quick stab of guilt in the middle of his back. He couldn't very well tell her that he'd made up a bunch of lies to get her to leave.

"You lied." She grimaced and sipped her coffee. The silence between them grew more uneasy as the corralled horses began to mill and argue like their morning hay was late. A flock of sparrows wheeled up and out of the cottonwoods, then splattered down again and began furiously pecking at the ground beneath.

"Is the sheriff from Valentine doing anything?" she asked.

Drum snorted. "Man's about as useful as a three-legged horse. Told me it wasn't his concern if we hills ranchers want to kill each other off."

She shook her head. "Babylon sheriff believes it was the boys. I'm thinking of hiring Pinkertons."

He glanced at her. "That's a goddamned bad idea."

She stared straight ahead now, her shoulders rigid, voice flat. "You have something to worry about?"

Drum ignored her. Damn wastefulness. Sometimes it seemed that was all life had to offer. A man worked hard, too hard even, only to see what he'd built sheer away and dissolve like salt in water. Did he want to find his son's killer? Had it made a bit of difference when he avenged his grand-father's death? Maybe Wilke had survived after all, waited all these years to track him down and finish off his family. The thought, crazy as it was, made him uneasy. He thought of his gold and some Pinkerton fol-lowing him around. He shook his head.

"Won't nobody talk to a stranger out here. You know that." He hadn't meant to antag-onize her, but could tell from the flush that rose up her neck to her cheeks that she took it personal again, like she always did.

But when she spoke her voice stayed even. "You might be right. I just don't want to let it go, act like it was an accident. We're living with a murderer. Who knows what his plans are?"

"You don't think it was someone passing through?"

She turned toward the corral again and shook her head. "That Indian girl and Graver. Maybe J.B. was the innocent by-stander. Something's odd. Who was the killer's intended victim? Or was he a mad-man of some sort, but wouldn't there be others then? It can't be the boys."

She'd thought about it more than he had,

Drum had to admit. Maybe he was too old, too used to the way things happened out here in the hills. Maybe he was more concerned about the ranches and his money than about why his only son was killed, or who did it. Think harder, he scolded. What had J.B. done to deserve killing? What did he have that another person would want so badly they'd kill for it? Drum couldn't think of a single thing so he sat silent, conscious there was a force out there moving against him and his that he might not be able to stop.

"You remember that last time I came to take Cullen home? You told me there could be accidents in the hills. It was a dangerous place to live and you were the only one who could keep my family safe, but I'd have to leave? You even said you'd take Hayward if I didn't stop. And J.B. wouldn't stop you. Is that what happened? He decided to stop you?"

He stared at her.

"I think maybe you shot J.B." She stroked the coffee mug with her fingertips. "I just have to be sure, and then I'm going to kill you."

CHAPTER TWENTY-TWO

Graver was assigned to check fence, windmills, water tanks, and cattle in the pastures between the two ranches. Some Horses and the other cowboys were finishing the branding while Drum's men were spot branding almost a day's ride away. Cullen had made it clear that he wasn't taking orders anymore now that Drum couldn't raise a stick or hand to him. Hayward was simply gone. Dulcinea hated to leave, but she and Rose had to seize the opportunity.

They moved swiftly on the gray stallion and the Indian pony, eating up the miles past the round and contented cattle that dotted the hills with calves gamboling nearby, butting each other and splaying their legs in imitation of their mothers to snatch at grass they didn't want. The hills were green and rain came often enough to keep them from turning golden brown.

Drum's ranch was quiet in the early

afternoon, chickens nesting in the shade through the heat, horses sleeping in the corral, hind legs cocked, heads down. There were no dogs to greet them. Instead they saw a big orange tomcat lolling on the porch of the plain square house as if he were enough to scare intruders. The house had never been painted; now the boards were warped and pulled away from the nails. Dulcinea tied her horse to the hitching rail and walked up the dirt path to the step made from an old buggy seat with Rose beside her. When they stepped on the porch, the unpainted boards sighed, threatened to drop them through until they moved to either side. Twists of grass and oilcloth and newspaper were stuffed in between the boards where the wood pulled away, and nails had been driven randomly to stop the siding from springing off the house, leaving only the black tarpaper beneath. Dulcinea pushed open the door, half expecting to meet with a gun as the squealing hinges announced them. The cat darted inside, and she reminded herself to make sure the damn thing was out when she left. Apparently Drum left his door unlocked because he figured his reputation would deter thieves.

The smell hit them like an axe handle to the nose, and Dulcinea could feel it soak into her skin and clothes. Glancing around, her first thought was a dead body, but she saw the culprit immediately. The sink was stacked with dirty dishes and pans, crusted with rotting food, and blackened with the bodies of flies. On the table, the plates and bowls were filled with squirming maggots. They left the kitchen area and glanced into the parlor, where a desiccated gray striped cat curled into a painful howl of death on the sofa, mouth stretched open in rictus snarl, teeth bared. The orange tom prowled the furniture, sniffed the air around the gray body, and avoided it by rope walking over the top of the sofa, meowing loudly.

Rose ducked her head and went through the doorway to the three rooms in back. The first, clearly the old man's bedroom, was as spartan as the house, wall cracks stuffed with newspaper and rags. The floor was covered in mouse droppings, and the over-sweet smell of dead mice added another note to the fetid air from the front room. On pegs along the wall hung the old man's few clothes, including an ancient black suit, thick with dust. A barely worn Stetson hung on the peg next to it, and a pair of black boots sat on the floor beneath. Dulcinea picked one up and turned it upside down. A flattened brown field mouse, with big, paper-thin ears and long tail hardened by time, dropped to the floor. Big flies thunked lazily against the filthy windows on either side of the bed, and when she went to open the nearest window, the frame came out in her hands. It'd never been properly sealed. Rose shook her head and nodded at the candle wax stuck to the edges. She set the window down on the floor, waiting for the big flies to find their way out. On top of the small bureau beside the bed sat a candle in a pool of melted wax, a pair of store-bought spectacles, and a battered journal of some sort, all wearing the light powder of abandonment. Was Drum Bennett a keeper of memories?

Dulcinea reached for the journal, then pulled back her hand. If she took it, the old man would know. When she leaned in, she saw a *W* embossed in the scratched brown leather cover. She opened it, careful not to tear the brittle pages. The only contents were crude drawings of mountains and what looked like maps. She closed the book. Then she opened the top drawer of the bureau, which held extra socks and a pair of long johns. Nothing hidden underneath. The second drawer contained a woman's ivory-colored camisole and silk stockings with lace tops. She drew the silk length between her fingers and the two women looked at each other.

When she picked up the camisole and held it to admire the pale pink and ivory roses lining the top, she saw a small silver bangle. A closer inspection revealed tiny marks — it was a baby's teething ring. In dim letters on the inside, she made out *J.B.* and a date obscured by the teeth marks. Hard to fathom Drum being sentimental. She thrust it back inside, covered it, and closed the drawer. They went across the hall to a smaller space, which turned out to be a storeroom, the walls lined with shelves of canned goods and supplies. Either the smell had lessened or they were getting used to it. Rose pointed to the poison set out on scraps of newspaper beside the bags of dried beans, sugar, flour, and cornmeal. No mice in here.

They almost missed it in the dark corner of a lower shelf behind a box of candles. The pack was old, the canvas stiff and cracked with dirt as Dulcinea untied and opened the flap. First she lifted out a six-inch-tall wooden figure that looked Indian, but not like something from the local tribes. Rose took it before she could set it on the floor, turned it over in her hands. A green snake twisted in the fist of a man, if he could be called that — a creature with a large square head, black stripe down its face, turquoise earrings and necklace, fur ruff around the neck, small carved bird feathers tacked to the head, a leather tail, and a red-and-black canvas skirt with a black snake oozing across the front. The legs of the figure were clad in red felt boots. There was bulk and overpowering energy in the form, coming partially, Dulcinea realized, from fierce black eyes that seemed to rage against all they saw. The mouth was open, too, a black maw that promised only ill will. "Kachina," Rose said and pulled out a tattered shirt to wrap around the figure cradled in her arms, an uneasy expression on her face.

Letters addressed to someone named Arthur Wilke fell on the floor, along with a string-tied packet of photographs of a young woman, several people in a group on a white porch of a farmhouse, and a group of cocky men gripping rifles and wearing Union uniforms. Dulcinea picked them up and quickly tied them together. There was a razor and strop, a small round metal mirror cloudy with corrosion, and a silver pen knife of the sort gentlemen carried, engraved with the same *W* as the journal in Drum's bedroom. She pulled out a book, *Plutarch's*

Lives, and felt along the bottom of the pack. Out of frustration, she turned it upside down and shook it hard, releasing a brief shower that sparkled in the dim light. Dulcinea knelt, wet her fingertip, and picked up some of the grainy dust.

"Gold. Someone named Wilke had gold in here." She shook the pack again and flung it to the floor, kneeling to look at the meager goods. "Drum's hiding something." She looked at Rose, who glanced at the wooden figure in her arms.

"Are you taking that?" Dulcinea asked.

Rose looked horrified. "Nooo —" She pulled the faded blue cotton shirt tighter and lifted her chin for Dulcinea to hold open the pack. "These spirits — I don't mess with them." She carefully lowered the figure inside, untied the bag of cornmeal, reached in, and sprinkled a small handful over it. "Put those other things away and close it up," she ordered. "We need to leave." She stood and walked quickly from the storeroom while Dulcinea restored the pack and thrust it back into the dark corner. Returning to the bedroom, she replaced the dirty window, plunging the room into dusk again. When she left, she caught a quick glimpse of the bare room that her son must have used at the end of the hall. The sight made her stomach knot.

Outside Rose had untied their horses and was already mounted. "We need to get away from here," she said, putting heels to the spotted pony. Dulcinea swung up on the gray and followed her at a gallop. She was disappointed in what they'd seen. There was nothing but evidence of a spartan life that bore down on the men until they broke or ran. She understood her son better now. Maybe even to the point where she could imagine him killing his father for betraying him.

They slowed the horses and were circling a small hill when Rose put out her hand to stop, then pointed to the far side of the meadow, where a man was digging with a shovel. As they watched he straightened and peered closely at something in his hand, then opened it and let dirt and sand fall. The women looked at each other.

"Chance," Rose whispered. "That's his horse."

"What's he doing?" Dulcinea asked with a frown.

Rose shrugged. "Something he doesn't want you to know about."

They watched as he mounted and left the valley in the other direction.

CHAPTER TWENTY-THREE

The hands rode in just before dark, quiet and tired from the day's work. Irish Jim had a bum knee from a roped steer that had twisted back on him as he dismounted to doctor its eye, and the new hire, Black Bill, wore a bloody scarf tied around his neck from a gouge when the barbed wire he was tightening had snapped. The flies followed the blood scent and buzzed lazily around his face and his constant slapping, waving hand startled the horse he was trying to unsaddle. Finally Graver took over and Bill nodded his thanks.

"Get Vera to look at that," Irish Jim advised. "She's more doctor than that yahoo in town."

Jorge, the oldest hand, walked his horse in so quietly he startled Graver. A good man with a horse, he'd already tamed the little dun mustang so he could slide off its back end without getting kicked. He wore the traditional large rowel spurs but never gave a horse more than a flicker. Most of the Mexican cowboys Graver had known were good horsemen and fearless around cattle. He'd rather have Jorge than almost anyone else back him in a culling pen. The two men nodded to each other, covertly noted that their horses weren't as wrung-out tired as the others. Jorge was always the last cowboy in because he walked his horse at the end so it'd be dry enough to get a quick curry before he grained it.

It was Saturday and the men would be cleaning up, grabbing a bite, if they could stand the wait, and riding hell-bent for leather to town. J.B. had usually kept the men closer to the ranch on Saturdays so they could quit while it was still light and make it to town before dark, but Dulcinea wanted them to put in a full day's work and Higgs hadn't figured out how to explain the situation to her. Graver had overheard the men mutter about it the past two weeks. They were beginning to see Higgs as weak in the face of a woman, but they were all united about steering clear of Drum and his ragtag outfit of hard cases.

"You coming?" Larabee asked Graver as they stood side by side at the washbasin. "You should come. New girl at Reddy's

Place. She sings some, but it's hard on the ears." He glanced at Graver, who slicked back his wet hair with a broken-tooth comb. "Man gets too meditative . . . well anyway, we need another hand. Townfolk aren't taking to us much these days. Elected their first peace officer in ten years, and he promises to throw us in jail we do more than talk polite to the ladies and drink tea."

Graver watched the excitement in the other man's eyes and nodded with a grim smile. This was what he was now: thirty dollars and found. Not even riding his own horse or wearing his own boots. Hell, he might as well go bust up town on a Saturday night. Might could talk to the sheriff about the killings. Maybe someone with authority would take an interest before they all died of old age. He'd seen the sheriff out here, but nothing came of it. Leastways, nothing was said to him. Was he in the clear, then?

As they trooped in to supper, the men drew up short, milling uneasily as cattle at a sullied water tank. The table was set like always, but it was clear the men were eating alone, while Dulcinea, the lawyer, Drum, and Higgs waited in the parlor to partake of a more leisurely repast without the hired help. He noticed that while Rose placed the food on the table, she kept an eye on him.

The bread Graver usually enjoyed stuck in a muddy wad in his throat, and he quickly made a sandwich with the steak and left the table. The other men followed until they were all out on the porch chewing the last of their hasty meal and not speaking. By the time they saddled up fresh horses and loped out of the ranch yard, their mood had turned sour and Graver was sure they'd find their fight in town. He hoped the new girl was something to look at, and he hoped he wouldn't bust up his healing shoulder. Clouds that had moved in before supper now lay in a thick, ropy mass overhead, and the wind gusted enough that the men had to tie on their hats as they rode toward town. The blowing dust was heavy with the smell of rain falling somewhere in the hills.

Although he hadn't been invited, Some Horses appeared at Graver's elbow as they ordered their first round of drinks. The bartender hesitated, then asked for the Indian's order and passed on to the next man.

"At least Fleming serves Indians," Some Horses said. "Reddy usually doesn't even let me in the door. Mex or Negroes neither." Then he added with a small grin, "Prices so high it's probably lucky."

Graver had wondered why they stopped at Fleming's first. He'd never had the liquor habit and knew little of the saloons in town. The men were well on their way to liquored up when they decided to move on to Reddy's. The bartender looked relieved as they quickly drank and shoved each other stumbling through the door into the dark wind that blinked the kerosene lamps and made it hard to push the door shut behind them. Outside the men tightened hats on heads and leaned into the sand and dust the wind blew into their faces, making it hard to talk without getting a mouthful of grit. Despite the string of new streetlights, the night seemed especially dark as the wind tossed flowerpots and wooden shipping crates and burn barrels in their way. Larabee was already staggering and too drunk to notice as he trudged across the street toward the small cave of the saloon on the corner a block down. Black Bill tucked his head and turned sideways to protect his face with an arm while he held on to his Stetson. Jorge imitated him while Irish Jim strode forward, face up, inviting the elements, hat nailed on head. Graver glanced at the black clouds boiling above and the wall of darkness that steadily advanced from the west, backlit by lightning that raced across the sky. When it struck the ground he felt a queer tingle up his legs followed by a nearly deafening roll of thunder. The men picked up their pace, walking faster until they broke into a run as the glow of the windows drew near.

Here it comes, Graver thought as he felt the rush of cold wind on the back of his neck, followed by icy drenching rain. By the time they reached the overhang of the porch roof, his boots had filled with water, and his feet squished with every step. The men around him shook their arms and hats and took turns shoving each other out of the shelter of the porch into the hail that pounded the metal roofs up and down the street, stinging the tied horses so they milled and bumped each other and tried to break loose. Finally, Larabee, as self-appointed leader, pushed open the door, and they crowded into the dimly lit room so filled with smoke it sat in layers that the three girls floated through as they brought drinks to the men seated at the small round tables.

The woman behind the bar seemed composed of various parts, a left arm, a right shoulder, one breast, half a face that arranged and rearranged in the fog. Graver glanced around to see that Some Horses, Jorge, and Black Bill had silently separated from the group and disappeared. As he came to the smooth oak bar, he saw the sign barring anyone of dubious origin, including those with skin darker than the bartender's palomino horse. Graver guessed it was probably sun bleached, too.

He got a beer and leaned against the bar with Larabee at his side. "So where's this girl?"

Larabee grinned, somewhat sobered from the dousing. "Downstairs." He put his hand on Graver's arm. "Wait a few drinks. It's better that way." There was a peculiar light in his eyes. Graver thought about leaving, but the prospect of the long ride back to the ranch in a downpour rooted him to his spot. Every cowboy stood in a small pool of water dripping from his clothes. They were a sorry lot, soaked, battered, half sporting some sort of bandage. The hands holding drinks told the tale of hard work: swollen, misshapen knuckles, fingers that wouldn't close or had pieces missing, marred with seesawing scars and rope burns. The faces around him were burned into deep brown or permanent red, making it almost impossible to determine any man's age, let alone race. How could Reddy be so sure about skin? He wondered where the three men had gone.

Graver felt a stab of regret that he hadn't

gone with them as the smoke lifted briefly to reveal tobacco-colored walls. Yellowed newspaper photos, articles, and posters of rodeos and particularly two white horses with a young girl standing on their backs, Roman style, filled the wall to his left.

"That Reddy?" He nodded at the poster and nudged Larabee, who was staring at one of the worn-looking women, a skinny brunette wearing a thin, shapeless dress whose red shine had been washed to a faded pink. Droopy gray lace along the bodice revealed the slight cleavage of her small, tired breasts. She waited for the reluctant drinkers to drop a few coins on her round tray, straightened her back, brushed a hank of limp brown hair from her eye, tilted her head, and closed her eyes as if her own touch were the only comfort she knew. A pair of silk stockings with a run laddered up the side revealed narrow, trim ankles.

Larabee shook his head and nodded at the tired woman. "That's Nance. Her old man went rodeoing, left her with three youngsters and a cardboard shack at the edge of town when the bulls finished with him." Larabee took a swallow of beer, sounding more sober by the minute, as if the beer countered the effects of the whiskey. "She's working dark to dark putting food on the table for the little ones. Shame to see her like this." He glared at the cowhand who tried to pull her onto his lap and fondle her breasts at the same time as she pushed him away with a tired smile.

"Damn fool Lister, married her and worked for Drum a time, couldn't cut it. Never did grow up. Guess he figured it out about the time his brains were stewed with arena dirt." Larabee turned to lean his elbow on the bar and direct Graver's attention to the wall of photos and newsprint.

"That's Reddy's daughter Imogene on the poster. Genie, they call her. Followed Lister right down the road, she never came back neither. Guess she met some young fool and stayed gone, the way I heard it. Made a bundle trick riding. Enough for Reddy to sell this place to his other daughter, Lucille, and retire to drinking full time. Lucille lives outside town with a pack of half-wolf dogs and a herd of Indian ponies, while he holes up here in town, street behind this one, over by the firehouse." He took a sip of beer as his gaze followed the skinny brunette making her way between tables to the bar, where Lucille waited.

The woman barkeep wore a plain black skirt and a black shirt, ironed crisp but faded, that came to a V at the neck over skin already developing the matted texture of a country woman. Her face wore a neutral, manly aspect with its oval shape and slightly shadowed upper lip and jaw. Her eyes revealed nothing as the thin brunette dropped the round tray on the bar and shoved the change toward her. Lucille swept it into her waiting palm with the edge of her hand and dropped it in a cigar box on the back of the bar. She drew four beers in a row, topped each with a perfect crown of foam, and placed them precisely on the tray. When she was done, she considered the woman propped on an elbow with her eyes closed. Lucille reached out and looped the lock of spent hair under a long finger and lifted it back across the woman's head. When Nance raised her face, she wore a tired smile, and Lucille gave her arm a quick squeeze and nodded to the men at the table in the corner, who had begun to wave and stomp their feet.

Lucille wiped the bar, lifting glasses and mugs and working her way to Graver. When she stood directly in front of him, she stopped and measured him with her eyes.

"You need something?"

Graver wasn't sure what impulse made him raise his chin at the sign barring Indians, Mexicans, Negroes, Chinese, and anyone of mixed blood. "What's that mean?"

She looked at him carefully. "You can't read?" She turned and moved to the other end of the bar to serve a couple of cowboys so drunk they held on to the edge of the rail to stay standing.

Annoyance rolled over him and he was opening his mouth to respond when Larabee elbowed him in the side and tilted his head toward the door that had just closed behind Black Bill, Jorge, and Some Horses.

"Ah shite," Irish Jim swore.

Larabee beckoned the three men over and shoved the pitcher of beer toward them. Without glasses, they had to pass the pitcher from man to man for a quick gulp while Lucille wasn't looking. Some nights she was inclined to let the nonwhite cowboys drink if they didn't ask for much.

Over the back door hung an enormous buffalo head, moth eaten, battered, shaggy to the point that it must have been going through summer molt when it was killed. One ear was twisted nearly off and dangled from the side of the head. The black marble eyes gazed almost drunkenly at the drinkers, and some wag had stuck a hand-rolled cigarette in its mouth.

Larabee leaned across Some Horses and

said, "One of them English lords came out here and shot him a while back. Not much sport. He was the last old bull, not bothering nobody. Pretty tame. But he shot him, had him stuffed and crated to ship home. Then a funny thing happened." Larabee's eyes lit up as the whiskey and beer were set in front of him. He lifted the shot glass, toasted Graver and Some Horses, and drank it down in one swallow.

"So this lord decides to go on one final hunt. And having shot the hell out of every living thing in twenty miles, he heads on up to Pine Ridge Reservation. Right after the Wounded Knee massacre, it was. Heard there's a big den of mountain lions up there and he wants one. Now nobody bothers telling him that these are cougars, and they don't live in big family houses, they're more loners. We figure to take his money and follow him around scraping up the bodies. Easier than cow work."

Larabee took a longer draught of the beer. Beyond him the men began to talk loudly and laugh for the first time since supper. Irish Jim and Jorge wore evil smiles as they played stick pig with a knife and their hands on the bar.

"So first thing happens, this lord runs into a man claims to be chief who says he needs payment for permission to hunt on Indian land. Dumb cocksucker pays. Not even an argument. Well, you can see how that was gonna play out. We ride a little further. Another chief. More money. By about the fifth time we're stopped, the lord asked the chief how many there were, figuring he should be about done paying. Indian smiles and says, 'Why, we're all chiefs in this tribe, sir.' "

Larabee laughed and slid a glass of whiskey to Some Horses, who smiled and shook his head, his eyes on the steady lift of his hand with the drink.

"But that's not all. The lord got so mad, he started shooting dogs. And you and I know, one thing you don't do is shoot reservation dogs. Hell, you don't shoot any man's dogs." Larabee shook his head. "And this after them troops shot hell out the women and young'uns.

"So we hightailed out of there, figuring things were gonna go Wild West show soon as those chiefs mounted up. The Englishman saw our dust and followed suit. He wasn't feeling too comfortable pulling this bull crap by himself, I guess. That lawyer fella, Percival Chance, was with him, tried to follow. Turns out, it was too late."

Some Horses nodded, eyes half-closed,

and held the glass under his nose as if the bouquet were Cognac instead of the cheapest watered whiskey. Larabee drained his beer and nodded at the bartender for another round. Graver finished his and shrugged.

"So you're wondering what happened." Larabee glanced at Graver while he took a drink from his fresh glass. "See, here's the strange part." He drank again, swished it in his mouth as if rinsing his teeth before swallowing. "We don't know." He grinned. "Never saw the man again." He drank. "We rode out of there like Old Nick was on our tails, and didn't stop till the Nebraska border. Ruint three good horses that day. When we looked back, there was nothing. No dust, not a thing." He drained the beer and nodded at the bartender.

"So we rode on into town, had a good night of drinking, in the morning saddled up figuring to go find the dumb bastard. We guessed that lord'd learnt his lesson by then, so back we go. We're still carrying rifles, you understand, and we've got pistols strapped on, just in case. And it's a miserable morning, rainy and cold as hell. It's fall and you can feel an early snowstorm tapping its boots over Wyoming way waiting for a good push from the wind to set loose over our heads. But we'd talked a little and worked ourselves up to going back to that last village for him. We knew nobody'd dare harm a hair on his head."

Larabee drank a shot and ordered another without touching the beer. His face grew thoughtful.

"It was miserable, getting colder by the minute, wind picking up. I remember turning to my brother, Grayton, and saying, 'We're in it now,' and his face had already started to freeze. Last I saw of him. Early blizzard took us down so fast we might have been twigs in the wind. Three days I hunkered in the little cave I dug with my bare hands in a ravine where some puny wild plums hung. Made my horse lie down to block the wind, and prayed. Ate snow, couldn't get no fire, and only had dried biscuits and a bottle I finished the first night."

Larabee drained his whiskey and raised two fingers again.

"I don't know how I lost Grayton, he just up and disappeared. Never saw that English lord again neither." He stepped back from the bar, pulled up his pants, and took a deep breath he let out slowly before he stepped up again.

"Reddy got the buffalo for next to nothing. Nobody felt good about it. The English-man's family sent a message that if we found a body, stick it in the ground. Guess they didn't care too much for him neither."

Larabee raised his whiskey in silent toast to the cracked mirror on the wall facing the drinkers. "Couple months later Lawyer Chance showed up, fit as a fiddle. Spent the winter in the Chadron hotel, living off what he packed out — hides, antlers, handmade Indian junk."

Some Horses gazed at the mirror behind the bar and met Graver's eyes, worry riding hard between them. It was the kind of night frayed the nerves of animals and men alike.

"Raise a glass to J.B., best boss we ever had!" Irish Jim shouted into the silence the men had fallen into. They automatically saluted the dead man and drained their glasses. Irish Jim glanced anxiously at Graver and ordered another round.

"You ever run into my brother up there on the reservation, Chief?" Larabee's face had suddenly gained that unfocused, doughy quality of the nearly drunk: his mouth fighting to hold itself while the skin around it loosened and collapsed. "I mean, after that ruckus at Wounded Knee, guess a man can't expect much from you people." Some Horses's face grew still as he stared into his drink. "Still, if you heard of a white man —"

Jorge leaned out from the bar and Graver caught his gaze. Black Bill was minding his own business at the end by the door, hat perched back on his head, latigo leather skin taut around the cheekbones and eyes, which he kept on the plank that served as a bar, and where his stack of coins stood in sober attention.

"Easy to get lost up there," Some Horses murmured.

"How come we never found no body?" Larabee slurred his words slightly. "A bad thing never dies, Chief."

Graver caught the bartender's eye and held his hand over the glasses to cut off the liquor. She shrugged and moved down to the other men. Four cowhands playing cards at a round table along the back wall looked up, uneasy.

Some Horses stared into the mirror, unblinking, as if he peered into a great distance. Graver saw his left hand relax and ease toward the knife sheath on his belt. He dropped his hand and let it settle on Some Horses's wrist as the wind howled louder and the building seemed to sigh and release dust from the rafters, which drifted down on the hats and shoulders of the men.

"Something you don't know," Some Horses said in a near whisper. Graver leaned in and stared at the side of the man's face, which held an unusual tension. "Girl found with J.B.? My wife's sister, Star."

Graver thought about what he'd seen. Was Some Horses the one who shot him? He watched the man carefully. Maybe that's why they'd seemed so eager to work at the ranch. "I'm sorry for what happened to her," he said.

Some Horses waited a beat too long, then said, "Rose is real upset. Says she's looking for the person done it. She's a hard woman for vengeance."

"What about this new girl at Reddy's you've been bragging about?" Irish Jim lifted his hat, brushed it off, and resettled it, smiling at Larabee. The man's head came up like a horse done drinking water and a slow grin spread across his slack face.

"You reckon my brother's taken up light housekeeping with some squaw?" Larabee said in a voice loud enough to be heard by everyone in the room.

Some Horses stared at the bar as if examining the quality of the wood, then backed up a step, hand on his knife. Larabee started to step back, too. Graver grabbed his arm and shook his head.

"Storm's getting bad," Black Bill said and glanced at Jorge, who nodded. "We better tuck the horses in behind here out of the wind."

The men hastened out the door into wind that roared like a train coming a couple of streets away, just as a roof sailed over their heads trailed by ladies' underwear and dresses. Graver and Some Horses glanced at each other, spun, and rushed back inside, shouldering the door shut after the last man.

Graver could feel the building pushed back and forth like a plaything between some giant's hands. The thin brunette stopped and looked around, a stricken expression on her face. The barkeep eyed Black Bill and Jorge and reached under the bar for a scattergun.

"Cyclone's coming!" Larabee pounded the bar, took off his hat, and whipped his hip like he was riding a bronc, whooping and spinning in a circle until Graver caught his arm.

"Downstairs everybody, quick!" Graver leaned across the bar to shout over the sudden roar of the wind battering the front of the building.

"Not him." Lucille pointed her jaw at Black Bill as the door crashed open. It took both Some Horses and Jorge against it with

341

their shoulders to push it shut again. The two men shook themselves like dogs flinging water on nearby drinkers who protested with dark expressions and muttered threats.

"Not them neither." Lucille shook her head as the storm grew louder, then suddenly there was a silence more terrible than the noise of a minute before.

Jorge shook his head, glanced at the ominous creaking of the ceiling, as if the building were being pried loose of the ground it sat on as the wind returned, and this time the engine of the freight train bore down on them, loosening another shower of dust over their heads. The thin brunette dropped her tray of empty glasses and wrapped her arms around herself, her mouth open in a silent scream.

"Run!" Larabee's eyes grew wide and he grabbed the pitcher of beer and the thin woman's arm and scrambled to the narrow stairs leading down, followed by the other drinkers shoving and pushing each other.

"You men care if our cowboys come along?" Graver called after the men plunging into the dark shadows of the basement.

"Long as you buy the next round," someone called. "I wouldn't care if you were Drum Bennett himself."

Graver nodded toward the stairs and the

three cowboys were soon swallowed by the darkness. He glanced at Lucille with her hands flat on the bar, head down, shaking it back and forth like she was trying to stop herself from doing something.

"Best grab a couple of bottles and get downstairs unless you want to spend the rest of the night in North Platte when the cyclone finally drops you."

Her head came up as the wind bellowed again, twice as strong, and rocked the bar. She grabbed an armful of bottles, handed four to Graver, grabbed more, and the two of them made it down the stairs as the door ripped off its hinges and chairs and tables were sucked away.

In the middle of the basement room was a low wooden platform holding a pallet bed on the floor, a chair, and a large wardrobe with a full-length mirror. The wind gusted down the stairs, pushing sawdust and trash onto the people and flattening a stray cowboy hat against the mirror.

The three bar women huddled together in the farthest corner, behind an overturned table. The tired brunette wept silently, rocking to the sound of the storm battering the walls apart overhead. J.B.'s men sat on the floor with their backs against the stone wall to the right of the women, and the other men were dispersed to the left, as if they all were willing to fight to keep the females from violence.

The one exception was a girl of sixteen or seventeen who sat by herself at a table almost directly below the stairs. She was a plain girl with regular features that would coarsen in years to come, but for now, she still had smooth skin that seemed to bloom despite the shadows cast by the few kerosene lamps hanging from the low ceiling. She was wearing red high-heeled shoes, silk stockings held by black garters festooned with tattered red velvet roses, and a short red silk robe that fell open revealing an elaborate bustier and panties in black-and-red brocade that lifted and barely contained her full breasts and seemed too big for her narrow hips and tiny waist. Every man worked hard not to stare too long at the shapely figure on display. She twirled her forefinger in the glass of whiskey on the table, then lifted it and sucked the end like a child, and never bothered to look at anyone. It was mesmerizing, and the men forgot to worry about the sounds of breaking glass and splintering wood overhead. The wind fought down the stairs, swirled her silk robe into the air, and let it settle like a bedsheet around her.

The girl continued to dabble in the drink. She seemed to enjoy sucking it off the ends of her fingers, ignoring the storm around her, and Graver realized she was probably on some sort of drug, opium or laudanum. She dipped three fingers in the glass and slowly wiped them across the tops of her breasts. If she kept this up, the men would be killing each other despite the fact nobody was drinking anymore.

Finally a new silence settled, except for the tinkling of falling glass and the creaking of shattered wood. Outside a dog set to howling and a horse whinnied and the people stood, shook themselves, brushed their clothes, and laughed uneasily. Lucille started for the stairs, Graver touched her arm and took the lead.

Halfway up the stairs he could barely make out the buildings across the street in the darkness, streetlights were gone, and he knew what waited for them. Only the back wall stood, bearing the newspaper articles and photographs of the girl on the white horses. The bottles, beer kegs, glasses, tables, chairs, the bar itself were all gone, along with the three walls. The cedar floor was scoured raw, the orange red of the wood revealed for the first time in decades. The air smelled dense with mildew and sweat, vomit and smoke, as if all the corruption of the bar had been set loose upon the town. Across the street, people gathered to stare at the devastation of the cyclone, which had torn down one side and left the other untouched. Then a breeze began to blow in the fresh sweet scent of wet grass from the hills, and overhead the stars appeared. The cyclone had skipped a few buildings the next block down, then squatted on the church, grabbed it up and shattered it into pieces that were sprinkled all the way to the edge of town. The spire ended up whole, unscathed, cross leaning slightly to the right, on the train tracks in front of the station.

As the shock wore off, the noise began, families shouting and crying, and animals screaming in fright and pain. Graver and Larabee quickly dispersed the men to help wherever they could and to find the horses, although they all knew the animals would head back to the ranch and their own herd as soon as they got beyond the storm.

Graver watched Lucille wander the edges of the floor, pausing in front of the wall bearing her sister's story, then continuing until she had traced the entire perimeter, before she turned and retraced her steps. This time when she stopped at the remaining wall, she seemed to stare for a long time at one picture, and then she reached up, snatched it off the wall, balled it in her fist, and dropped it. A frenzy seemed to break loose inside the woman because she began ripping down the posters, newspaper clippings, and photographs, shredding some, dropping others to be picked up by the breeze and sent across the floor into the street.

When the wall was bare, she stepped back, nodded, and said, "There." Then she turned and walked across what was left of the room, stopping on the boardwalk to shake off the few bits of paper that clung to her long, faded black skirt. She squinted into the dark and tossed her head, then stepped down into the debris-littered street and headed east toward home. She didn't bother to glance at Dulcinea, Rose, and Chance, who led a string of horses past her. The women looked around anxiously, while Chance seemed unmoved by the chaos.

Graver turned away before they spotted him. The girl from the basement still hadn't appeared. He thought about leaving well enough alone, but it wasn't in his nature, he supposed, so he sighed and went back down the stairs.

There was a half-full bottle of whiskey on the table in front of the girl now, and she was drinking from it with a determined rhythm, setting it down between each long swallow. Graver stood at the bottom of the stairs, watching. He wasn't sure she even knew he was there. Finally, he simply lifted her off the chair and cradled her in his arms. When he turned toward the stairs she lifted the bottle off the table and pressed it into his chest with her head. She weighed next to nothing, only a little more than his eldest daughter had, and he was still thinking of his girl's hazel eyes, like her mother's, when he rose up out of the basement and stopped at the top with the girl in his arms. The whole street could see him, and when he lifted his eyes, Dulcinea, Rose, and Chance were five feet from where he stood, glaring at him.

Chapter Twenty-Four

The lawyer tipped his hat with a smile. "See you found Pearl Stryker. Family's probably looking for her."

Dulcinea appeared puzzled and the gray stallion chomped the bit. The girl in Graver's arms stiffened and banged the bottle against his chest so hard he almost dropped her.

"Seems she's done being rescued," Chance said as he stepped from his saddle and handed the string of horses he led to Larabee.

"Put me down," Pearl slurred and pushed against Graver's chest. When he let her legs drop, she gave him a shove and almost fell. Her head came up and she squinted her eyes. "Where am I?" She turned to Graver, raised the bottle as if to crown him over the head with it. "What did you do?" she screamed. Larabee stepped up, took the bottle from her hand, and awkwardly patted her back. She snatched the bottle again, cradled it against her stomach, stepped off the boardwalk, and fell flat on her face in the muddy street in front of the horses.

"You men certainly have a way with women," Dulcinea said. "You just going to leave her there?" Rose smiled and covered it with her hand.

The lawyer looped his reins over the hitching rail and stepped carefully through the mud to the girl. "I'll take her home. I know Stuart and Mary must be worried sick about her." He eased the girl onto her side and tried to sit her up, but she was floppy as a set of old clothes, so he bent down and lifted her over his shoulder and stood, ignoring the mud smearing his shirt and pants. Dulcinea beamed with approval and patted her horse on the neck.

Rose's gaze followed the man. "Not many houses that direction . . ."

Graver pulled his hat lower and started down the block, where a crowd had gathered.

"Graver!" Dulcinea called after him.

He stiffened his shoulders and thought of that Tennyson poem he'd memorized when he was eighteen and living in a line camp one winter in Wyoming, nursing cows and trying not to go crazy. *Into the valley of Death*

He heard the stallion huff up next to him as he strode along the boardwalk, skirting debris. "Mr. Graver." Dulcinea's voice was high and nervous. "Please —"

Graver knew he should keep walking. "Lady," he began. "You don't own me. I'm going to see if those people up there need any help. If they do, I'm going to stay until the job is done. Now you take that fancy horse and your fancy manners and your orders and . . ." He looked at his hand, realized he had grabbed the rein and Dulcinea was trying to ease it away. When he suddenly let go, she tipped back and the horse rocked on its hind legs and reared.

Her face blanched as she urged the horse forward and down.

"I'm sorry —" He put one hand on the rein, the other on her foot. He could feel the tremor through her boot.

"I just wanted to know if you've seen my sons? They left right after you —" She turned to search the faces along the street.

"I'll start looking now." He knew in his heart those two would be fine. They were the kind always came away clean while everybody around them got taken down.

"I am sorry," she said so softly he wasn't certain he'd heard it. Rose, on the other side of her, stared intently at the scene. He remembered what Some Horses had said earlier. He'd have to convince Rose he didn't murder her sister or J.B. before she made a mistake.

Irish Jim trotted up the boardwalk that had miraculously survived the powerful winds, waving at them. "Ma'am? Mrs. J.B.?"

Dulcinea turned her horse to face the cowhand, her eyebrows raised, a smile on her lips.

"It's the blacksmith, Tom Farr, forge fell on him. Got himself a broken leg." Irish Jim was sobered by the storm, and blood streaked his shirt and pants. "Doc's busy with Omar's wife gone into labor and Omar got himself a good knock on the head when the porch roof was took by the storm and the five little ones all tossed and tumbled around like to have barely survived they got so many cuts and bruises but no broken bones and their dog —"

Dulcinea held up her hand. "Where is Mr. Farr?"

Irish Jim looked confused for a moment, and then pointed toward the livery stable at the end of the street with the blacksmith shop beside it.

"I'm not a doctor, but I'll do what I can." She touched the stud into a light trot.

Graver glanced around at the torches and bonfires people had lit since the new electric streetlights were taken out by the storm. The two men cast huge jittery shadows that paced them across the buildings on the opposite side of the street as they followed the cyclone's path.

"Where's this new peace officer I keep hearing about?" Graver asked.

"Went to North Platte with the family. Says he thinks he's solved J.B.'s murder." Irish Jim shrugged. "Not sure about that. He's the undertaker, you know. And dentist." He opened his mouth and pointed to a black gap where one of his upper teeth used to be. "Slick as a whistle, that one."

The men caught up with Dulcinea at a pile of debris that blocked the street, and their shadows paused briefly over her with a deeper darkness. It was the kind of moment Graver would later recall and ponder when Larabee's drunken words came back: a bad thing never dies.

Tom Farr's leg was crushed from the knee down, almost cut in half by the weight of the forge that had struck with quick annihilation and continued to pulverize the bones as he awaited rescue. When the men lifted the forge off his leg, he clamped his mouth shut. He was a massive man with bull-thick shoulders and neck, his broad face as red as the torchlight overhead. He'd had the foresight to wrap a harness rein above his knee and pull it tight to stop the blood flow, which probably saved his life. His foot flopped unnaturally free on the crushed leg. It was obvious the tendons were severed.

Graver tried to thread his way back to where Dulcinea was tying her horse, but the group around the injured man was too tightly packed. She doesn't need to see this, he repeated in his head, this isn't necessary. But the crowd briefly opened its ranks for her with Rose following and then closed as if a trap had been sprung.

She staggered for a moment, her hand at her throat, at the sight of the thicket of bone shards bristling out of the torn flesh and dark thickening blood. Rose took her arm to steady her. Silent courtesy descended on the group, and Farr unclenched his jaw and spoke for the first time. "Ma'am? I won't be any trouble, I'll be taking a little nap now so you don't have to worry yourself none." His eyelids fluttered briefly and he fainted, mouth going slack, head rolling to the side.

"Nothing for it," Haven Smith declared and began pushing out. "Thought I could bring him to heavenly ground, but sinners

354

go the path they come through this life. Rare's the day they give up their soiled ways."

"He's not fecking dead, Preacher," Irish Jim said loud enough to raise a laugh from the other men.

Haven Smith stopped and shoved his way back to where Irish Jim and Graver stood. "I'm speaking of his spirit, you fool!"

Irish Jim's face took on a serious expression, though his blue eyes were too bright. "You're dead on, Father, and what say we have a toast to the dearly departed?" He pulled a battered tin flask from inside his shirt and, unscrewing the cap, started to drink, thought better of it, and offered it to the preacher for first honors.

Smith shoved the flask out of his face and glared at the crowd until the men separated and let him through.

"Never knew a man of the cloth to turn down a drop," Irish Jim said and toasted the body again before taking a long drink, only to be interrupted by Dulcinea, who reached over and plucked the flask from his hand.

"We need this." She gathered her riding skirt out of the way, knelt on the ground beside the injured man, and carefully doused the wounded leg with the whiskey.

"Get me a knife," she said and the man next to Graver pulled a bowie knife from a sheaf on his belt and handed it to her.

Graver stopped himself from stepping forward to take over when she lifted the remains of the pant leg to cut it away clear to the upper thigh. When the cloth was gone, she rocked back on her heels and looked up at their faces.

"Are you certain the doctor isn't free now?"

A voice from the back of the group called out, "Just checked, ma'am, Omar's wife's in bad shape and Omar still hasn't come round."

"He's the lucky one," a voice commented.

Dulcinea sighed and looked at Tom Farr's sweaty face gone pale now that he wasn't fighting the pain. She used the sleeve of her blouse to blot his forehead and cheeks, took a deep breath, and released it slowly. "Here's what I need, then."

With Graver kneeling and holding the saw and a man sitting on his other leg and one on each side of the massive arms and Rose at his head holding it steady in case he awoke, Dulcinea directed the removal of the ruined lower leg. At the first bite of the blade below the knee, Graver felt a wave of weakness and wondered if he'd be able to

356

do this. Despite her calm voice, Dulcinea's hand trembled when she placed it on his arm for encouragement.

"I'm not strong enough to get through the bone quickly," she said and lifted her hand. Graver pushed the saw forward and back, blocking the sound as it tore through skin, ligament, and bone. The men around him released a collective sigh of horror and fascination. He felt her breath on his ear, on his hair, on his neck and wanted to gather her away from the grisly scene.

"My mother's father was a surgeon," she said in a low voice. "I've seen this many times. Thought I would follow in his footsteps, you see, until I met J.B. Now take the knife and finish cutting the tendons cleanly."

Graver tried to imagine haunches of beef and venison, anything but a human leg. Beside him he could hear her breathing in time with his effort and almost felt her hand on the knife as he worked the blade through the ropy tendon.

"Yes, that's right, thank God that knife is sharp. Ah, there, now we're done with that part. Now press this cloth over the stump while Rose and I prepare to suture. I only hope this heavy cotton thread is strong enough. Haven Smith isn't very forthcoming to save a sinner, it seems." She held up

357

a spool of thick waxed black thread that looked like it could hold a saddle together. Graver kept his mouth shut. It was a damn sight better than he could come up with. She knelt beside him and lifted the rag over the stump, noting how the bleeding was now a slow leak. He wondered if she'd cauterize the wound, but she decided against it when Rose leaned forward and whispered to her. He rocked back on his heels, and then stood to give his aching knees a stretch.

Graver watched the two women, working opposite each other, take neat stitches, tucking the skin in around the stump and closing off the tendons and ligaments. He noticed how strong and efficient their fingers were despite the blood that slickened the needles and thread. Dulcinea swiped at a fly buzzing lazily around her face and left a smear on her cheek. There was no nonsense about her now, no hauteur, and Rose had lost her shyness. They were in charge, the men around them silent as they watched. How was the blacksmith to work now? What would become of him and his business? Graver looked into the shadows, thought he saw the two round frightened eyes of a dog cowering inside the first straight stall.

When it was done, Dulcinea stood and stretched her cramped legs, then rested a hand on Rose's shoulder, and they stared at the still unconscious man. A tortoiseshell cat rubbed against Dulcinea's ankle, edging closer still until its head shot out and it began lapping the puddle of congealed blood as if it were milk.

Rose picked up the cat and handed it over her shoulder to one of the men, ignoring the animal's loud protests. She gathered the ruined limb in one of the rags that had been produced for the operation, wrapped it, and looked up at the men, who had given way somewhat, finally repulsed, made fearful by the spectacle.

"Sometimes a person wants to see the severed limb, make certain of its injury. Can someone pack this in ice for when Mr. Farr awakens?" Dulcinea said.

Haven Smith reappeared, pushing his way forward again. "I'll take it."

Dulcinea hesitated. As Rose handed it over, Irish Jim said, "Now you can start converting, you wee bastard," but there wasn't much humor in his tone.

The storekeeper blinked furiously behind his dirt-speckled glasses and cradled the leg in his arms like a newborn babe. "And you are a damned sinner, and a nincompoop."

He bowed his head as if he prayed over the baby Jesus, and then walked slowly toward his store. The men around Irish Jim slapped him on the back and nodded.

When Graver offered Dulcinea his arm, she refused, instead linked arms with Rose though she faltered as she turned to face the group. Irish Jim watched her with wonder on his face, as if she had performed a miracle and he was now her servant for all time. He glowed with pride while she looked at the blood caking her hands, filling the tiny cracks and pores and flaking off when she rubbed her palms together. Her fingernails were rimed in black-red, and the gold of her wedding band had disappeared.

"He needs to be helped to his bed and watched the next few days," she said.

The men looked at the heft of the man, then the stairs leading to the set of rooms over the blacksmith shop, and finally at the ground.

Someone in the crowd said, "Might be best to leave him here till morning. We can take turns setting with him. Don't think we can get him up them stairs in the dark, ma'am, that's a mighty big man."

She inspected them, not skipping a single one with her singeing gaze. "Make sure you tend to him. He dies, it's on you, and you, and you —" She nodded at several of the men. "He wakes up, you get the doctor to give him some morphine for the pain. You have to go find him, you do it, and you don't let this man suffer, you hear? Part of his survival depends on the pain not over-whelming his body. Understand?"

At the sternness in her voice the men straightened their shoulders, lifted their chins, and resettled their hats.

Graver cupped her elbow as the men parted for her. "You and Rose did good, Mrs. J.B. Real good."

She stopped next to the stallion, who dozed hipshot at the rail, and said over her shoulder, "And you make sure Haven Smith lets him see his leg if he asks."

In the days to come, she was never told the town wags passed the withering, rotting leg between them like an artifact from a carnival freak show, leaving it on one man's doorstep in the middle of the night, drop-ping it on another's lunch table at the café, and strapping it to a saddle as if the rest of the body were invisible as the horse was led through town. Tom Farr never knew that his leg continued its journey into the larger world, made it all the way to Leadville and the Black Hills gold camp of Deadwood, then back again. Tom never asked for the limb, and it was finally lost on a deer hunting trip when the men got so drunk they thought it was driving away the animals. They took it out to the Badlands and threw it as far as they could, watching the hard blackened flesh topple end over end as it descended into a mudflat that later would yield the skeletons of animals so ancient they no longer walked the earth. Eventually, it ended up on the shelf of an amateur Sand Hills archaeologist/rancher who spent the rest of his life searching for the animal large and odd enough to possess such a severed limb, despite being told by the experts at the Museum of Natural History in Lincoln that it was from the remains of a human, possibly killed by a wild animal or Indian raid judging by the violence done to it.

Rose, Dulcinea, and Graver made their way down the street, looking for the other men. The bonfires were dying with only a few torches set here and there in the dirt. It would take daylight to determine the rest of the storm damage. When they reached the ranch horses, they found Larabee, Irish Jim, Black Bill, Jorge, and Some Horses sober, tired, and eager to be shut of the place.

"Best Saturday night I ever had," Larabee declared. He spread his hands wide to show he was untouched by fight or liquor or loose women.

"Now ya got no excuse for lying about the bed come Sunday morn," Irish Jim said.

Dulcinea stood beside the stallion holding the high stirrup of the English saddle, and leaned her head against the leather flap.

Irish Jim started to step forward, but Graver shook his head, bent over, and placed the cup of his clasped hands at her knee. "I'll give you a leg up."

She glanced at him, surprised and relieved, placed her foot in his hands, and allowed him to hoist her into the saddle as he used to do for the exercise riders at the Kentucky racehorse farm. She nodded her thanks, exhaustion so deeply etched on her face her eyes seemed sunken into darkness and her mouth was a thin line. He noticed when she was tired a frown deepened on her brow, making her look stern when she was merely in need of sleep. He felt a wild urge to climb up behind her on the horse and hold her in his arms so she could lean back and rest after the night's ordeal. There was much more to this woman than he had imagined. She had real bottom and in no way deserved the poor treatment of Drum Bennett and her boys. He untied J.B.'s chestnut, grateful she had brought the best horse in the string for him, and led it out of the way of the others to mount. When he turned the horse back he realized Rose seemed to follow him. He was about to ask her why, then thought they'd had enough drama for one night. He couldn't forget what Some Horses had said. On the long ride home, he glanced at her when her attention was elsewhere, and saw that a deep sadness showed when she thought no one was looking, and he understood how the two women were so close, and he wondered what would happen if the Bennett boys were guilty.

CHAPTER TWENTY-FIVE

Rose woke at dawn, looked at Jerome and Lily asleep in the tipi, dressed, and walked outside, since it was the only time she would have all day to be alone. She passed the graveyard on the side of the hill, where the big spotted dog joined her, and kept walking. Across the new green pasture lay hundreds of webs that tented the Sand Hills grass with tiny silver beads, so many spiders, invisible, at work all night long to capture the equally tiny insects, a speck or two the meal until the hard hooves of cows and horses trampled the morning, breaking trails in long, dark lines. The dog padded through the grass, meandering as if a straight line could not be found in his mind. The webs so fragile they tore without a whisper, the slightest contact shredding the light.

"Iktomi," she whispered to the spiderlike man, the trickster who might be watching. Perhaps this was his doing, this field of webs. Her mother appeared to her as Rose had last seen her ten years ago, a serious person who cared for her elders and raised two daughters despite a husband who was lost in the past among white people. Rose remembered her mother shading her eyes and watching as the priests took her children away the first time. She thought her mother would fight, slash the throats of the men and free them, but she didn't. It was years before Rose understood. Years to forgive her, and just as she had, her mother was swept away forever. Star was the lucky one, she thought bitterly as she ran her hand across the webs until her palm was wet and sticky. No, Star wasn't lucky. That was a terrible thought. Star was brave, braver than her. She was going to find the man and punish him. Rose thought of her daughter, Lily, and hoped she was never given such a task. She would have to tell Some Horses that no matter what happened to her, he was to keep Lily from following her path. She wouldn't allow the daughters in her family to be sentenced to vengeance forever, barring their restless spirits from the red road. This crime must be settled in her lifetime.

She made a list of every man who might have killed her sister, and her mother. First, the man had to be part of the massacre at

Wounded Knee. Then he had to recognize the locket on the chain Star had worn that Rose now kept in the hidden pocket of her skirt, where she could feel it burning even now. Sometimes at night she wondered it did not scald her husband when he lifted her skirt. Last, he had to meet Star at the windmill on Bennett land, which meant he had to know the place. She didn't include the fact that he had to be capable of killing. She assumed every person was, given the necessity. She watched as the sun dried the webs and they gradually disappeared as if they had never been. And he had to be clever, a trickster.

"Help me, Iktomi," she prayed, even though it was dangerous to enlist his aid. He could easily help her enemy first.

CHAPTER TWENTY-SIX

Dulcinea awoke early, too, restless after the excitement of the storm and its aftermath. She rose, grabbed the wedding ring quilt, and went to the balcony, where the telescope waited like a falcon under its hood. She wrapped the quilt around her shoulders, sat in the wooden chair, and thought of that morning years ago when she saw the figure ride up the long road to their ranch. It was a memory she replayed constantly, wondering what she could have done to make their lives turn out differently. Now that she was back at the ranch, the memory had become especially painful. At first the figure was merely a speck floating in a ball of dust, but as it grew near, the old man was revealed, sitting rock hard in the saddle, unbending with the horse's motion, as if the saddle and the man were welded in a permanent iron fixture. She saw that he led another horse, saddled.

"What is it?" she asked Drum from the porch rocker where she sat with her two boys, one in her lap, the other beside her. Drum, realizing J.B. had said nothing, began a stream of invective.

"J.B. is in the barn. I'll call him."

As soon as she spoke, she saw in his eyes that he knew something she didn't, and his narrow lips twitched below the carefully waxed mustache.

She was rarely alone with Drum and was foolish enough to assume he abided by the rules of civilized society, though why she imagined that she could not say. She was still a young woman then, with a child at her knee, another at her breast on the porch of her own home.

"I'm takin' that youngster," he said and used his chin to indicate Cullen, who quickly hid his face in her skirt. She should have rushed inside for the rifle by the door, she should have called out. Instead, she tried to bargain, though her heartbeat was too slow and loud, as if it would strike the wall of her chest and burst.

"Taking him for a ride? He's too young to be on a horse by himself."

The triumph in his eyes made her look down at Hayward and jiggle him in her arms, hoping his cry would give her an excuse to flee inside, though she doubted she could stand at that moment. Her legs were shaking and weak.

"No, ma'am. Taking him to live with me. Be raised the way a boy should be, grow up and run the ranches as they ought to be run."

He gazed at the boy a moment, his lips pursed with thought. "You think a boy clinging to his mama's skirts grows up to be worth a damn? You think I was raised soft? Or J.B.? Well, never mind about him." Drum looked at the house with its curtains at the windows and bushes and flowers and herringbone brick walk. "Made a mistake sending him to the wife's kin, shiftless as they come. Took me five years to put some sense in that boy once I got him back."

Drum's expression, the frown and tight lips, said it was her ruining the hard work he'd put into raising his son. She didn't say a word. Truth be told, she couldn't. Her heart beat too fast now, drying her breath so she couldn't raise enough moisture to unlock her lips or her tongue that stuck to the roof of her mouth.

Cullen whimpered and clung harder, digging his tiny fingers into her leg, leaving bruises that took weeks to disappear, though she never wanted to lose them and found comfort in pressing her nails into the purple marks he left. Hayward ignored her efforts to wake him, merely smiled in his sleep while his brother broke into hiccupping sobs and stamped his feet as if he knew the days that lay ahead would forbid his tears. Still she did nothing, didn't believe her ears, simply sat in the rocking chair J.B. had given her when she was pregnant with Cullen. She had rocked both her babies in that chair, and by the time his brother was born, Cullen had learned to stand on it and ride up and down, laughing, his head thrown back, eyes closed. Drum dismounted and walked toward the porch.

"I would have you leave now," she said, finally standing and half turning, but he was too quick and snatched her son before she could stop him. The boy kicked and punched and scratched. Dulcinea grabbed the metal dipper on the water pail on the bench by the door and slashed it across Drum's face, smashing his lips against his teeth.

With the momentary distraction, Cullen escaped and ran not to his mother, but around her into the house, with her on his heels. She barred the door, placed the baby in his cradle, took down the rifle, checked the load, and aimed it at the window so

Drum could see. Blood dripped down his chin onto his faded gray shirt and she felt a wave of satisfaction when he spoke because the split in his lip garbled his words.

"This ain't the end of it, missy. Not even halfway. I'll be back — tell J.B. to have the boy ready."

He didn't bother touching his hat brim, a courtesy afforded even the most vile female in the hills. And he left the little paint gelding tied to the front fence. When J.B. came in for the noon meal, he took the paint to the corral, unsaddled and fed it. She stared out the kitchen window while it whinnied and paced to be taken home.

"What's this all about, J.B.?" She demanded an answer and was met with silence and a shrug. It took her a while to find the reason, and by then it was already too late.

"You're up early," Vera said, her hands coated with flour from rolling and cutting biscuits as Dulcinea entered the kitchen. Rose glanced at her without smiling, like she had something on her mind. Rose usually said nothing while Vera and she talked, but Dulcinea heard her conversing with Lily whenever she thought they were alone. This morning, however, Rose spoke.

"You were up early, too," Rose said. Vera's

shoulders stiffened, and her hands paused as she lifted the flour-dusted glass to cut the next biscuit shape. Vera's mouth opened to respond, and then she stopped and merely shrugged.

"Nearly summer solstice," Dulcinea said, "nobody can sleep."

Vera glanced at her with her eyebrows raised. She finished cutting out the biscuits and placed the tin sheet in the oven while Rose sliced the bacon and Dulcinea greased the big pan and began to fry the meat.

"Here." Rose handed her a bib apron and helped her with the tie so she wouldn't splatter her clothes with grease. Fifteen minutes later, she forked the strips onto the platter beside Vera's scrambled eggs and set it on the back of the stove to stay warm.

"We taking the horses out today?" Rose asked.

"We'll clean stalls first."

"I can do that," Rose said, "I'm fast." She meant quicker. "I promised Jerome I'd help him with the young horses this afternoon. Maybe Lily can stay with you, Vera, if you aren't too busy."

Something passed between the two women, but Dulcinea didn't know what it was.

When the coffee was boiled, Rose set the

giant pot to the side while Vera removed the biscuits and rolled them onto a plate for the table. They'd learned to work as a well-oiled machine in the kitchen, made the meal chores quicker. Sometimes she marveled that Vera had done all this by herself for years. She should be sick of it by now, and Dulcinea was half-convinced her suspicions were true as Vera watched the men file in for their meal. When Black Bill entered, she studiously averted her eyes and fiddled with food already cooked and washed dishes already clean. It was only after everyone was seated, women included, with heads down shoveling food and chewing as quickly as possible, that Vera fixed her attention on Black Bill. Her skin grew dewy and her eyes shone bright. There was a tremor in her fingers, and she merely picked at her food, spreading it around on her plate. Higgs didn't seem to notice. Dulcinea wanted to say something to her, but didn't dare.

"I won't say nothing," Rose muttered when she and Vera were shoulder to shoulder at the wash sink. Vera ignored her. Nor would Vera permit Dulcinea to help with the cleanup, so she got ready to ride.

"Someone's here." Rose glanced out the window and opened the door as the lawyer dismounted his horse.

"Now what's he doing here again?" Dulcinea murmured as the two women started down the walk to the gate.

"I thought we might go for a ride this fine morning." He swept an arm toward the sun-dappled hills and smiled at Dulcinea.

"You come, too," she said to Rose and they exchanged a knowing look.

Surprisingly, Rose looked at Chance and said, "Did you find that girl's home last night?" Her eyes glittered.

Chance shrugged. "Close enough," he said and went inside as Rose and Dulcinea hurried to the barn to tack up their horses.

"He's carrying a pickax and shovel on his saddle again," Rose said as she tightened the cinch on her horse.

Dulcinea frowned and slipped the bit in the stallion's mouth. "Seems a long way to come for a pleasure ride."

They took the cow path to the southern pastures to run the horses, then paused to let them catch their breath at the top of a hill that offered a view of the vast hay marsh and grassland stretching into the distant horizon.

"You sit a horse well, Mrs. Bennett." Percival Chance touched the brim of his hat as he pulled up alongside them. She ignored the comment.

"Our land stretches from the Dismal River almost to the Niobrara, Mr. Chance. What is it you're looking for?" She squeezed the reins to maintain the stud's attention. She realized with a growing unease that the lawyer's keen eye missed nothing as he searched the hills. Rose followed some distance behind.

The lawyer peered across the land. From his good but worn clothing, his air of educated romance, it was clear that this was a man seeking a way home, but first he must procure his fortune — an old story in the West. The roads to the Black Hills gold were strewn with skeletons of horses and mules and oxen driven to death in the mad hurry to reach men's destiny. Furniture discarded, empty barrels, crates of clothing and me-mentos, even toys left behind once the babe itself was gone. It was a hard land for those without patience. Time ruled this land, and in time everyone was wounded, and every-thing of value disappeared.

But in time, everything was born again, J.B. replied in her head, a man so in love with the Sand Hills and their vast silence that he allowed his father to take his oldest son to avoid an argument that would bring words into being that could not vanish, that hung in the air forever. In the hills grudges never died, they remained as they took place, as the words were uttered, since there was nowhere for them to go, nothing to break them apart, the soft edges of the hills offered nothing hard enough to smash the anger, nothing sharp enough to cut through the Gordian knot, so it lived fresh, undeniable as the first day. In the hills there were only first days, no history. Nothing was allowed to die. They marked time by the growing list of wrongs until its weight pulled them under and they vanished, smothered with the breath of sand in their mouths. "Don't leave me here," she had told J.B. before the birth of Hayward. "If I die, don't put me in this ground. Build me a mausoleum, limestone or granite, something that will stand aboveground. Don't consign me, J.B., don't."

He had smiled. "You don't understand this place, dear."

The contractions began in earnest then and soon enough the baby was born, in its own bloody sac, relentless and loved and given utterly to the destroying world. How could she leave him? That day she saw that nothing she did could stave off the future, the grinding of time that would yield him up to a fate already determined and inexorable; although she kept both boys as close as possible, they were already not hers. Drum made sure of that.

"You're thoughtful today, Dulcinea," Chance said, crowding her with his horse's body. The stallion lifted his back, arched his neck, and blew softly out his nostrils, his shoulders breaking into a sweat, foam on the bit flecking her dark brown riding skirt.

"I'm wondering when you're going to share the nature of your visit," she said. "And if you don't move that mare, you're going to find yourself under my horse's hooves." She glanced behind to catch sight of Rose, who kept her distance. She could feel there was something wrong about the lawyer, but couldn't quite put her finger on it yet. When she asked about his investigation into J.B.'s death, Chance made vague references to Indians who held a grudge against him and white people in general. When she asked, "Not my boys?" he smiled and shrugged, leaving her angry and uncomfortable.

They wove around patches of prickly pear cactus. She had it in mind to send the men out to dig it up and burn it, even though the fruit was palatable to man and beast alike. Eventually the grass would give way to the cactus.

"I hope my presence affords you some

comfort, Mrs. Bennett. I know you to be a capable, intelligent woman, but out here —" He stretched his arm to include the undulating sea of green before them. The grass was alive with the buzzing and sawing of insects and birds, and the wind only a faint brush across the bridge of her nose, the lobes of her ears, not enough to even ruffle the horses' manes. Above them, the sky was a soft, pleasant blue, despite the line of thick, dark clouds to the west. They got their weather from Wyoming and their trouble from Omaha, hills people said.

"You are alone, and there are forces arrayed against you." He clasped his hands around the saddle horn and let his horse drop her head to graze, a freedom Dulcinea never allowed the stallion. He chomped the bit impatiently and shifted his weight from foot to foot. Dulcinea squeezed her calves, picked up the reins, and resettled him.

"And isn't this a pleasant day," she said with a toss of her head.

"If you will allow me to —"

"I wonder what Vera has planned for supper?" She turned and smiled brightly at him. He looked at his hands, sighed, and shook his head. Rose drew up a few yards behind them and watched.

"Okay." He lifted his rein hand and

dropped it back on the saddle horn with a dramatic sigh. "I've been retained to look at the oil and gas resources out here. On your land there's a possibility." He gazed at her, his eyes reluctant.

Holding up her hand, she said, "Surface rights only? Mineral rights too?" She looked at the crest of the stud's neck and repositioned a handful of white mane that had flopped to the other side. "Or do they want the entire ranch?"

He shook his head again, and she touched her heels to the stud, eased down the slope of the small hill and up another. The lawyer was on her heels, choosing to be quiet for a change, a blessing, since she needed time to understand this new problem. She had no doubt he had found evidence that supported the purchase of her land. For a fleeting moment, she considered inviting her father for a visit to help, but truth be told, she wasn't certain she could trust him not to cheat her when it came to making a fortune, especially now that he needed money after the stock market's ups and downs. It would be worth it to see Drum and her father go head to head like bull elks. Very western. Very Shakespearean. Chance was an opportunist with a minor role, she decided. She'd have to meet the people behind him on top of her other problems.

CHAPTER TWENTY-SEVEN

When they came around the turtlebacked hill, the horses cantered eagerly to slake their thirst. Her two boys romped naked in the water tank, their horses grazing nearby, clothes in a heap beside saddles flung carelessly to the ground. Only their pistols and rifles were placed carefully within reach.

Their well-muscled bodies gleamed in the sunlight, Cullen the slighter of the two, wiry, while Hayward was taller, rangier, despite being younger. While they watched, Cullen jumped on Hayward's back and pushed his head under water with all his weight on his brother's shoulders. Hayward flailed while Cullen laughed but did not ease. Any moment he'll let him up, she thought, and her chest squeezed so tight she could barely raise her arm to shout and wave while she spurred her horse toward the tank.

When he saw them, Cullen frowned and flung himself into the water, letting his legs float up as he laid back so only his head and toes were visible. Hayward jumped up, sputtering and thrashing, staggered to the rim of the tank and threw up over the side, then laid his cheek against the top of the tank with his eyes closed, breathing raggedly while Dulcinea drew her horse to a stop facing the two boys.

"What was that, Cullen?" she yelled.

He glared at her and picked up a handful of the thick spongy black-green algae they'd set loose from the sides of the tank and threw it at his brother's head.

Hayward shook it off and opened his eyes, blushed when he remembered he was naked. "We was just horsing around, Ma," he said.

The stallion pawed the ground and snorted at the boys in the water he badly wanted. "We have to water the horses, son. Can you step out?"

She ignored Cullen, who lay back and exhaled all the air in his lungs so he could sink to the bottom of the tank. The tips of his pink toes were the last she saw of him. Was he holding his breath? Three bubbles burst on the dark surface amid the islands of algae gathered there.

"I hope you boys checked that tank before you climbed in." She sounded prim, motherly, and hoped Cullen could hear her underwater. "I wouldn't want you getting sick from swimming with dead animals."

Cullen burst to the surface, spit a stream of water that hit his brother in the face, and flung a handful of bottom muck writhing with pale pink worms. Hayward howled and lunged for him and the two thrashed until they tired of the game and leaned back in the water again.

"Boys, we need to water our horses." Chance had moved his mare closer and she fidgeted with thirst.

Cullen stood and water streamed from his bare bronzed shoulders and head, as if he were Poseidon, angered enough to send their ship onto the rocks. The illusion was brief but lasting. In his streaming locks and enraged eyes she glimpsed an ancient, unforgiving god: the betrayed child.

"Would you mind closing your eyes?" Hayward asked. From the noise that ensued, she gathered they climbed out and drew on their clothing, so it was a shock when she opened her eyes and found Cullen sitting naked on a blanket, rolling a cigarette while Hayward finished buttoning his blue shirt.

She couldn't tell if it was disappointment in Cullen's eyes when she ignored him and urged the stud forward to drink. He focused his attention on striking the match off his saddle horn and touched the flame to his cigarette. Drawing deeply, he held the smoke in his lungs and eyed the glowing tip, then let it out gradually with a long exhaling breath. He could hold his breath longer than anyone she'd ever known. When did he learn to do that?

A dark shadow came over them as the clouds along the western horizon that earlier only threatened flooded the sky overhead, moving swift as water overflowing a dam. Dulcinea searched for Rose, but she must've already headed back.

"Storm coming!" she shouted. A gust of wind bearing the moist breath of rain pushed the grazing horses away from the boys, and they grabbed for the trailing reins. While Cullen quickly dressed, Hayward held the horses with one hand and tried to saddle his animal with the other, but they edged in a circle. Then lightning flashed down on the hill behind them, leaving the air tinged with sulfur, and the distant rumblings of thunder walking the hills suddenly cracked like cannon fire.

Cullen grabbed his horse, quickly saddled it, and then helped Hayward with the skittish gelding. The boys were careful to wrap their guns in the waterproof sheets of their bedrolls. Dulcinea wondered why they needed all those guns. Were they frightened of whoever killed their father? Then a horrible thought struck her: What if they were involved somehow? She could almost imagine Cullen . . .

Her thoughts were interrupted by the sudden cloudburst, a downpour so heavy they had to ride side by side to not lose sight of each other. None of the horses were savvy enough to find their way back to the ranch house, and they had to rely on their own senses. By the time they reached the stable, horses and humans alike were shaking with cold.

Some Horses appeared at Dulcinea's side, quietly took her reins, and motioned toward the door with his chin. "Did Rose come back with you?" he asked.

"I, I don't know —" She turned to go back out as Rose rode into the barn, ducking low through the doorway, water streaming off horse and rider. "I thought you were ahead of us," Dulcinea said.

Rose shrugged and wouldn't look at her as she unsaddled and rubbed down the horse, steaming in the close air of the barn. Some Horses threw hay into the stalls as the boys looked after their own horses. In the semidarkness of the stable Dulcinea became aware of Chance standing beside his shivering animal, waiting.

He caught her eye. "If your man is finished there . . ." He held out the reins as Graver led in his own soaked horse, followed by a stranger.

"A man takes care of his own animal in this part of the country," Graver said with a hint of amusement in his voice. He unfastened the cinch of his saddle, lifted it off the horse's back, and hung it over the rail with the others. Every motion was fluid and precise, nothing extra, and Dulcinea had to admit, it defined him in a not-unpleasant fashion. The wet shirt outlined his lean muscular torso and made her turn away. For ten years she'd been alone, a voice in her head intoned, wasn't that long enough?

The lawyer unsaddled the mare while the stranger took his horse to an empty stall.

"When in Rome, Mr. Chance, when in Rome." The stranger had a loud, clear voice just this side of booming.

"Judge Foote?" Chance turned and stared.

"In the flesh," he said and flung the saddle over the rail as if it were a handkerchief rather than fifty pounds of soaked leather. He was a tall, broad man who had to duck his head slightly in the stall area with its low ceiling. Everything about the judge was large, even his full face and the thick gray-streaked blond hair he always forgot to cut so it hung well below his chin and he had to constantly tuck it behind his ears. His wide hazel eyes made a person feel scrutinized, catalogued, and shelved. She'd heard he was a man with an extraordinary education and an even better sense of recall for both spoken and written language. He was reputed to be careful and thorough with no tolerance for ignorance. His big solid jaw looked like it could break a fist, and his large mouth and formidable nose made for an arresting face. It was said that he still broke his own horses, and little wonder. She watched his big, capable hands wipe down his animal, straightening the mane and pulling burrs from the tail, all while patting and rubbing and talking in a low, reassuring voice until the animal sighed and commenced eating. Then he checked the water bucket, saw it was full, and left the stall.

"You run a tight ship, ma'am," he said. His eyes were bright as a bird's and when he smiled he had big horse teeth, stained like a horse's, too. "Judge Clayton Foote. And you would be the redoubtable Mrs. J. B. Bennett." He bowed slightly and when she offered her hand, he pressed it to his lips in a courtly fashion. "If I could trouble you for a place to dry off? I was riding out to see you when the storm broke. Fortunately, I ran into Mr. Graver here and he brought me in. Couldn't see a damn . . . sorry . . . darn thing."

"I'd be most happy if you'd stay the night, sir." She turned to the lawyer. "You're welcome to stay, too."

She looked at Graver, who was searching for a burlap bag to dry his horse. "Perhaps Mr. Graver will join us for supper?" She didn't know what possessed her, but it was worth it to note the irritation on Chance's face.

"I'm not dressed for company, ma'am," Graver said.

As they walked to the house under the clearing sky, Graver touched her shoulder and she paused to let the men pass.

"I mean I don't have any business with those men," he said with a pained expression on his face. Western men and their peculiarities.

"I would appreciate you being there tonight, Mr. Graver. These men want something I'm not prepared to give."

His face darkened. "Well, I . . ."

"No, I mean they have plans for the ranch apparently. I need you to stand with me. You're the only one I trust." She hadn't realized she felt this way until she uttered the words, and now she felt them deep in her chest, gathering with an odd force under her ribs. "Something might slip out about my husband's killing, too. I need another set of eyes and ears."

"Ma'am, I think they've come courting." Graver pushed his hat back on his head with a forefinger and smiled.

She waved the idea aside. "That kind of nonsense won't get them what they want. No, they're after much more than a middle-aged widow with two unruly half-grown boys." She hadn't heard those two since they returned. Had they already snuck off to the bunkhouse? She must work harder to tame them. In the meantime, she had to convince Graver.

"I'll go change into dry clothes."

Turning to leave, she heard him mutter, "Sooner haul a wagonload of skunks."

Dinner progressed about as expected: The hands had already eaten, and her sons acted brutish and sullen the entire meal because they'd had to wait. Frank Higgs didn't help when he insisted on questioning their whereabouts this afternoon when someone took a shot at him and put a hole in his favorite hat. The boys looked guilty, heads down as they sawed at their meat, pretending to have manners for a change. Dulcinea said they were at the stock tank and that turned the discussion for the time being.

When the meal was over, and seven bottles of wine later, the men were in fine spirits. Vera and Dulcinea had a glass apiece, the boys half a glass and they made much of how terrible it tasted, like children given a privilege they hadn't earned. The men retired to J.B.'s study to smoke and drink his brandy, and Rose and Dulcinea cleared the dishes, since Vera disappeared as soon as the men stood.

"Having suitors is a lot of work," Rose said in a deadpan voice.

"Suitors?" She stopped, accidently tilting the platter of congealed steak grease, blood, and bones that she was about to throw out to the dogs whining outside the door.

Rose looked over her shoulder and smiled.

"I think they're here on business."

"Yeah, the business of a handsome woman with enough land to make a man feel good about himself." Rose took the platter from her hands and carried it to the door. She opened it and kneed the dogs away.

"That lawyer is the one to watch," Rose whispered and slid back inside. They stood there for a moment, listening to the Sand

Hills night, the call of a barn owl into the darkness, looking for a mate perhaps, or simply announcing itself to the world, the breeze rattling the cottonwood leaves, the occasional whoop from the perennial card game at the bunkhouse, and the low laughter of the men in J.B.'s study as they imagined how to divide what was not theirs. It would not surprise Dulcinea to hear buying and selling in a minute, as if she were a blooded mare. It occurred to her that only Graver seemed to want nothing from her.

"Have you seen Chance doing something suspicious? What about Graver?" Dulcinea kept her voice low.

Rose shrugged.

"I think Graver's all right, don't you? The lawyer though, what was that business in town about the girl Chance took home?" Dulcinea asked.

Rose paused, her hands deep in the soapy dish water, and she seemed to think over her answer before saying, "She ended up another place."

Dulcinea stared at her. "What do you mean?"

Rose turned to face her. "He took the girl to his room."

Dulcinea's mind flooded with unwanted

images, and she shook her head to rid it of them.

When the dishes were done, the two women sat at the table with cups of tea.

"Have to butcher another cow, these men stay much longer. We've run through the spare chickens. They sure eat." Rose raised the cup to her lips, blew at the surface, and sipped.

Dulcinea shook her head. "They'll drink the cellar dry at this rate. I don't know what's gotten into them. Drum's not objecting either. That makes me nervous."

"We'll need more help they stay on. You decided where they're all sleeping?"

"They'll have to double up, and that might convince them to go home. Drum too." They laughed and were so relaxed in the moment that the sudden bang on the door caused them to jump and spill their tea.

Dulcinea stood and yanked open the door, thinking it was one of the hands with some injury from horseplay. Instead, it was Larson Dye, owner of the Box LR, hat in hand, hair oiled back, and freshly shaved since there was a white line halfway up his face like a high-water mark on a post. The rest of his skin was burned dark red, his fox-brown eyes permanently bloodshot; he looked like he had weathered a sandstorm. He was dressed in a brown suit and a yellowed white shirt. He rubbed the toe of each boot against the back of his legs, as if they wouldn't notice. His hands were the same beaten red-brown as his face, and he was missing the little finger on his left hand, and the tip of the ring finger on his right.

"Larson Dye, ma'am," he introduced himself, although Dulcinea used to know him and his wife, who died in the diphtheria epidemic years before.

"Yes, I remember, Mr. Dye. Please come in."

He nodded at Rose, and she ducked her head shyly.

"We were just discussing whether we could purchase some chickens from you tomorrow. If you have any to spare?" Dulcinea said.

Larson Dye appeared surprised, his head startling to the side as if she had slapped him. He struggled to form the words, and she remembered he had a slight stutter when nervous. He must have practiced his greeting on the way over.

"See, that's just it!" he managed to say. "I brought you a whole crate! I, I didn't figure, since J.B, and you come back, and all."

"Why thank you." Dulcinea offered her

hand, which he stared at as if he had no idea what to do with it. Then he daintily held the tips of her fingers, moved them up and down two inches, and let go.

The men in J.B.'s study burst out laughing, and Larson Dye's head swiveled in their direction, confusion on his face.

"I'm sure you know the other men. Care to join them?" She gestured for him to give her his hat and he handed it over reluctantly, nodded once to Rose and once to her, and ambled through the parlor to the men.

"At least that one brought something. Crate of chickens won't last long, though." Rose was interrupted by the sudden wild squawking of the chickens and the cracking of wood.

"The dogs!" The crate, chickens, and dogs were rammed against the door, and by the time they opened it, the crate was reduced to splinters, chickens running blindly into the dark, and the black-and-white dog stood with a dead bird hanging half out of his mouth. Since they were better trained, the other dogs simply whined and barked at him.

They closed the door and leaned against it, shoulders shaking with laughter they didn't want the dog to hear.

"Guess there'll be a hunting party tomorrow. Fresh deer or antelope. Turkey if they can get close, or grouse." Rose stretched and yawned. "I should leave you to your suitors." The merry expression returned to her eyes and a smile tugged at her lips.

"If anyone else shows up on this doorstep, shoot them," Dulcinea said.

■ ■ ■ ■

PART FOUR:
THE NOISE OF
THEIR WINGS

■ ■ ■ ■

CHAPTER TWENTY-EIGHT

When the Sioux family stopped at the ranch in late November of 1890 to trade for food, their story of the coming messiah and the dancing that would welcome him stayed with J.B. until he finally left Higgs in charge, took Hayward, and rode up to Rushville, arriving midmorning. He wasn't a religious man, but he'd heard rumors of the Indians gathering since summer and decided to see for himself. If he could find Dulcinea, he'd leave the boy with her. He tried the telegraph office, but couldn't give them her address so he gave up on that notion and thought maybe he'd see her in town. The place was teeming with cavalry troops, newspaper writers, politicians, and curious citizens.

Unable to secure a bed for the night, J.B. had to choose between returning to the ranch and pushing on. Despite the boy's cries of hunger and sobs of Mama, Mama,

J.B. held him in the front of his saddle. By the time they rode up to the military encampment, Sibley tents stretched wide across the flat landscape, while the thin winter light outlined every object as if it were drawn by a sharp pencil. The tents glowed white against the brown grass and dirt, and the horses in the rope corrals were silent, hipshot, heads down. The smoke from cooking fires and mess tents rose lazily into the white-gray sky.

On a small rise to his right, J.B. saw a man with a box camera on a tripod sighting on the camp in the late-afternoon light. Across the country newspapers printed drawings based on photographs of the Lakota encampment, the dancing, and the cavalry. He figured their reports were largely exaggerated. The *Omaha Bee* one of the worst for rumors and outright lies. The *Omaha Herald* tried harder for the truth, but it eluded them when there were powerful money and business interests at stake. He wondered what the government wanted here. He'd heard the Indian agent, Royer, was a fool and a coward, and called in the troops as soon as he could to stop the dancing. Some of J.B.'s men bragged about coming here to fight the "murdering redskins" and to save the white women and children who had earned their rightful place on Indian land. Another reason to come see for himself. If he had to hold his men at gunpoint, he would.

After a night on the hard ground, J.B. woke covered in blankets soaked with cold dew and frost. He saddled their horses and woke Hayward at sunrise. He didn't want any further discussion, and refused to gratify Hayward's desire to spend time with the rough soldiers. Once the boy was mounted, J.B. handed him two cold biscuits stuffed with bacon and a canteen of fresh water. He could eat like a cowboy on the trail. Last night he heard that Drum was prowling, and he wanted to avoid him if possible.

The dancing was well under way when they reached the Indian encampment, and J.B. was stunned by the number of tipis and people. Pulling up beside two white men in a buggy along the ragged edge of spectators, he used his binoculars to scan the dancers and supporters. The only guns seemed to be in the hands of young men acting as guards, who blocked anyone who tried to break into the circle and disrupt the dance. Women wore white cotton dresses with blue around the V-neck, painted with flowers and birds and animals. Men wore pale blue shirts painted with butterflies, buffalo, deer, and flowers . . . the life they would bring back when the road to the spirit world opened again. Later, he was told the people believed their garments bulletproof, but that story only appeared among whites after the cavalry drew close and trained their guns on the dancers, who fled to the Stronghold and Wounded Knee Creek.

The dancers moved slowly around the circle, lifting legs with the beat of the big five- and six-man drums. Soon J.B. felt the drumbeat move into his own body; his blood pulsed in his veins, throbbed in his head, demanded he keep count. Beside him, Hayward lifted his feet and knees in rhythm, too. Powdered by months of dancing, the dirt gave beneath his feet, springing back as the earth answered his step. Thoughts began to recede in the distance, and he was on a long road away from the land he knew. The ground itself carried the thudding rhythm into his feet and up his legs. It climbed his spine and encircled his chest, shoulders, neck, and finally smothered his skull until he almost danced himself, his heart beating as one with the others.

"Stay with your pa, boy." A stranger pulled Hayward back. J.B. nodded his thanks and looked down at the boy, who was as dazed as he was. Maybe they were both tired of being alone. He felt the hope here. Hope in the people dressed in rags, without shoes even in the cold, beloved children running and playing, dogs bouncing at their sides, patched and torn tipis with smoke trickling from the tops, big kettles of watery stew for the dancers outside the loose circle, old men and boys returning from the hunt with barely enough rabbits to feed themselves, the elderly and sick lying on the ground or propped on blankets around the circle so their spirits could encourage the dancers. None of it mattered as much as continuing the dance that would redeem their land and heal the rents the whites had torn in its fabric. J.B. was overwhelmed by the profound sadness: a vision of so much hope in a doomed world. What had he done? It was the first time he questioned his right to the land his father claimed, the land for which he had paid a terrible price.

"That's a scalp dance," the bearded white man next to him announced.

"No, that's an Omaha dance. It's harmless. Women aren't part of a scalp dance," another man said. J.B. glanced at him, noticed the priest's collar and black robe under the heavy black wool coat. Mission priest. He might know something. J.B.

introduced himself and discovered one was a storekeeper from Gordon named Swan, and the other a Jesuit from the Rosebud mission school named Hansen, a tall, thin man with thick blond hair and pale blue eyes.

"There's that photographer fellow again, Morledge, he's been here since summer." Swan pointed to a young man in dark clothing who drifted between groups, apparently welcome by all. "Goes out among them like he's on a Sunday picnic. Lucky if he doesn't leave that fine head of hair behind." Swan was not to be persuaded about the dancers, despite the women and even children who danced through the next several hours without respite. If anything, the rhythmic chanting and steady nodding shuffle took them to the edge of transport, such as J.B. had seen in Missouri tent revivals as a young man. He had never felt it his place to decide another person's religion, and if the messiah appeared to other folks, so be it. He just hoped to make it through a day.

"Can I look?" Hayward stretched up a hand for the binoculars.

The priest nodded at J.B. as if to say he was doing a good job bringing the boy here to witness.

"Sure hope those troops get off their duffs

and put a stop to this nonsense." Swan pointed to the steady stream of Indian families making their way into the encampment. "Folks around here, whites that is, are scared to death they'll lose everything they've worked for now. Religion, my ass." He snorted loudly.

"Those whites are squatters wanting to carve up more reservation, Mr. Swan," the priest said, his tone dry.

"Indians don't use a tenth of what we gave them. They got no money and they won't work, what good are they? We beat 'em fair and square. Now the government gives them food so they don't have to farm. Beef so they don't have to ranch. Wish I could join up!" He gave a war whoop and did an exaggerated dance step, knees rising like the great pistons of a draft horse.

The priest shook his head and glanced at J.B. with a smile. "Maybe you should."

J.B. thought about the beef issue on annuity days that he'd witnessed last summer when it was so dry and the ranch struggling. He'd culled the best steers he could find and driven them to the reservation. The families standing on the perimeter looked half-starved and tried not to appear anxious for their cut of beef once their relative rode it down on horseback and shot it, a poor replica of their buffalo-hunting days that made the white spectators cheer and clap as if at Buffalo Bill's Wild West show. A quarter of skinny beef was to last each family a month, regardless of the number of children or relatives. Last month Royer, the Indian agent, suspended the allotment until the people stopped dancing, and now the families must be hungrier than ever. J.B.'s stomach clenched. If he could, he'd find a way to push some cattle to the reservation, maybe in a place that wasn't so heavily guarded. He'd think on that. Maybe the priest would help, unless he was starving them to accept his Christian god.

"Will you look at that young fellow!" Swan pointed toward the photographer, who had loaded his equipment on his horse and made his way toward the dance. The guards immediately stopped him, but after some negotiation, allowed him to join the crowd as long as he didn't unload his camera. J.B. nodded to the two men and led his horse toward the dance, his son behind him.

They stayed a day, talking and watching, sharing the food cooking in big pots over campfires in front of tipis. J.B. liked how his son seemed interested and open to anyone who came near, soon joking and sitting with younger boys and girls resting from the dance or joining in their games. Close to dark, J.B. accepted the priest's offer to spend the night in his tipi. At least they wouldn't wake to wet blankets. After a supper of cornmeal in a thin meat broth of some sort, a Ghost Dancer named Jack Red Cloud, son of the famous chief and one of the first dancers, came to the tipi to discuss the increasing presence of the cavalry. A handsome young man with strong features, he posed the question that had bothered J.B. for months. Jack Red Cloud refused to look at the stranger as he addressed Father Hansen, and asked, "You have your religion, why won't you allow us to have ours?" The Jesuit shook his head once and stared at the fire in the center of the tipi, until finally he said, "It's not up to me. Ask the president. Ask Congress."

"American Horse agrees with them, says don't fight the white government. We'll all be killed. How can that be right?" When the priest didn't reply, instead staring moodily into the fire, Jack Red Cloud stood and left, muttering to himself. J.B. was torn by the argument. He thought every person had the right to believe as they wanted, but the Indians were in a tricky position. Was it really so important to continue a doomed cause? The government was wrong to starve the families, but maybe the Indian leaders should consider their survival, instead of insisting on make-believe. But if it was make-believe, why were white people so upset about it? Surely they didn't believe the Indians regained their power by dancing. J.B. threw a stick on the fire, watched the flames lick then gather it in until it turned orange and powdered into red coals. He glanced at Hayward asleep in his blankets, dark blue circles under his eyes like bruises.

"They have to be careful," the priest said with a sigh. "Big Foot is very sick, in the hands of the military. Who knows what they intend to do with him. Tribal factions and the military want Sitting Bull dead. Royer wants Little arrested, but the dancers protect him." He hunched, holding himself. "This isn't going to end well. More people arriving daily. Indian agent calling for troops to stop the dance and the so-called threat. Man's a fool!" He suddenly stood and flung something into the fire that looked like a rosary. J.B. couldn't be sure as it sank into the ashes and disappeared.

J.B. left Pine Ridge after three days and felt he'd witnessed a historic moment: the conversion of thousands of people to a new religion. Everywhere he sat and talked to Indians who spoke only of living in peace with creation again, without war and hunger, a world where their children could return to their families and be raised in the traditional ways in harmony with the animals and all people. It was a Christian vision without hell and damnation. On his way back through the cavalry encampment, J.B. stopped at the tent of General Brooke. He explained his assessment, saying, "The Indians are only practicing their religious beliefs. It's peaceful. No threat at all."

Brooke laughed openly at him. "All respect, sir, but you have no experience with these people."

"There are a lot of elderly, women, and children out there. Hardly anyone has a gun. Most of the young men have died or run off," J.B. protested.

The general nodded and stared at him. "You're lucky the hostiles didn't slit your throat or steal your guns, my friend. You don't know the force we're dealing with. They have weapons hidden all over that camp, and I intend to find them, or they will be made to pay."

A glint in his eyes assured J.B. that the general believed his words, and would happily massacre the entire camp without a thought. The military seemed bent on retribution for Custer and the Seventh Cavalry's defeat at Little Bighorn. And when the Indians were finally blotted out, the Black Hills and all the reservation lands would be open for white settlement. The argument still raged in Congress. There was money to be made here.

J.B. went through Rushville again, and noted the train that arrived loaded with more troops, horses, and supplies, as if a major battle would soon be fought. It worried him, but he reassured himself that it was a religious celebration, nothing more. Surely the military would eventually recognize that. He stopped at the telegraph office again, noticed the Indian girl tidying the place. The operator, Crockett, was notorious for his slovenly ways, and it was a treat to enter the room without the stench of sweat and garbage. When he asked after Dulcinea, Crockett shook his head, and from the waves of alcohol coming off him, J.B. felt he probably didn't understand the question. The Indian girl paused after Crockett stumbled to the back, and motioned him closer.

"Chadron," she whispered. He thanked her and quickly composed a message saying he'd be in Rushville late December if she sent word. The girl looked at him, read the message, and glanced toward the other room where Crockett's drunken snores rattled the dishes. J.B. laid the coin on the counter and left reassured.

Over the next month, he followed the mounting alarm over the Ghost Dance on Pine Ridge. He read papers from Chadron, Gordon, and Omaha, and rode into town as often as he could get away. Elaine Goodale Eastman, an Indian agent, said the ghost shirts only became bulletproof after the army arrived, and that should be evidence this was a peaceful gathering. He couldn't rid his mind of the images: gaunt children in threadbare clothes playing happily while their families danced and prayed to change their futures. At night he held Hayward for longer than usual and let him sleep with him when bad dreams threatened.

Then the news turned desperate. A Sioux cowboy passing through from North Platte to Pine Ridge told them Sitting Bull was murdered on December 15, by agency police at Standing Rock Reservation. The army feared he was urging his followers to join the Ghost Dancers and create an uprising. Buffalo Bill had come to Sitting Bull, his old friend, and tried to trick him into surrendering, but the ruse failed and Bill departed. The Indian ate sparingly though he was clearly hungry, and J.B. and Vera both urged more food on him. When he pushed away from the table he thanked them and J.B. let him sleep on the sofa so he'd have at least one warm night. In the morning, Vera gave him all the leftover beef, a chicken, and twenty biscuits she woke early to bake. Later, when Buffalo Bill was granted the use of the braves who held out in the Stronghold after Wounded Knee, J.B. wondered if the cowboy, Roy Dancing Spear, was among them. The men were allowed few choices: become part of Bill's show and travel to Europe, go to prison, or be relocated to Oklahoma, where the Lakota people were the most hated by all the other tribes.

CHAPTER TWENTY-NINE

In late December J.B. received a message from Father Hansen that urged him to return to Pine Ridge. J.B. was in a quandary. He didn't want to leave Hayward, and had no notion that he'd be of any help, yet the man asked and he still couldn't shake the images of those children. The priest said the military was poised to attack simply because it was winter, they were cold, and their patience had worn thin with a people who wouldn't stop dancing despite the lack of food and warmth. Families starved, and it made no difference. They danced with rags wrapped around their feet. Finally, a large contingent of Indians fled the encampment, but were followed by the army, found and taken to Wounded Knee Creek, and assured they'd be safe. One of their leaders, Big Foot, ill with pneumonia, was among them.

When he heard the news, J.B. decided to go, despite the frigid weather and the snow that would bury them any day now. He brought extra clothing, blankets, and food on a packhorse. Hayward was left in the care of Jorge and Willie Munday, since Vera and Higgs had taken the train to Denver. The hands wore grim expressions as he waved good-bye, and something in the pit of his stomach told him they were right. He had no business in the middle of this. He secretly hoped to see his wife, but he couldn't tell them that either.

When J.B. arrived at Wounded Knee Creek and met Father Hansen on the evening of December 28, the soldiers were drunk on whiskey a freighter sold out of the back of his wagon. Hardly anyone slept that night with the drunken yelling, singing, and fighting, and on the morning of the twenty-ninth the camp's mood was tense, soldiers prepared to shoot at any provocation, Indians wary despite the children playing around tipis, and the dancers and drummers organized at first light. As Father Hansen and J.B. drank their coffee and ate hard biscuits, they remarked on the sense of dread and hostility among the surly troops. "The army wants to attack," Father Hansen warned. "Their patience is gone. They'll attack. There's nothing else they can do."

"Then why am I here?" he asked in a bitter voice. The man had no right to drag him into this mess.

Father Hansen stared at him, then shrugged. "I couldn't think of anyone else who cared enough."

"To do what?" J.B. wanted to hit the priest.

"To bear witness. Someone has to know the true story. The army's already writing their version, the one that makes them heroes. I thought between us we could gather the facts. The truth." He shook his head. "Something terrible is about to happen, and there isn't a damn thing we can do about it but stand and watch." He clenched his fists and hit the ground, producing a crackling in his bones.

J.B. saw he was right, and wished he hadn't turned down the earlier offer of whiskey. As far as he could tell, there were no weapons in the camp except for the guards' Winchesters. He wondered where the young photographer was, where any photographer was when a fight could erupt at any moment. He saddled his horse as a precaution, pulled the rifle from the boot, confirmed it was loaded, and then checked the load in his revolver. He made sure he had extra ammunition in his saddlebags, took a handful of bullets and slid them into his buffalo coat pocket. He didn't question his actions. He knew how quickly things could change. In the back of his mind he wondered exactly who he was going to shoot. Shortly after, as the bystanders watched from what seemed a safe distance, Colonel Forsyth and Major Whitside demanded the Indians hand over their weapons.

The soldiers held their breath while the Indian leaders met and finally brought a handful of old, broken rifles and muskets to Forsyth and Whitside, dropped them on the ground before the two men, and refused to meet their eyes. Father Hansen drew a sharp breath and J.B. grabbed his arm to stop him from rushing into the confrontation. The officers indicated that the guards must hand over their rifles, too, and allow them to search the camp. A long, heated argument followed while four big Hotchkiss cannons were wheeled into place on the hillsides around the camp. J.B. looked at the soldiers lying or kneeling on the ground, guns at the ready, fingers on triggers, except when they took time to puke or gulp water to nurse their hangovers.

When the dancing was set to begin, a man hit the group drum once, twice, and the men and women in their ghost shirts moved into a ragged circle, oblivious to the guns trained on them. Beside him, J.B. heard Father Hansen take a deep breath as he pointed at the Indian who chanted and raised his arms in the air. "Stosa Yanka, Sits Up Straight," he said, "will signal the dance to begin." The man bent, grabbed a handful of dirt, and threw it at the sky, offering the road for the return of the buffalo —

Later the officers would testify that they thought the thrown dirt a signal to attack, despite the women and children in full view. And when a rifle was fired into the air by one of the Indians, the red-eyed, confused soldiers took it as their cue to begin.

J.B. threw up his arms and started to yell stop but Father Hansen grabbed his arm and pulled him backward as returning bullets cut close in the din of gunfire, men shouting, and horses and women and children screaming. Several Indians ran to their tipis to retrieve hidden weapons while camp animals and people scattered, running in all directions for cover. J.B. and the priest crawled to the end of the soldiers' line as the other white onlookers ran for their buggies and horses. J.B. did not draw a gun. He was afraid of what he might do, especially when he saw the men prepare to fire one of four big Hotchkiss guns on the rise nearby.

"There's no target," he muttered, then shouted, "There's no target!" as the gun roared, splashing through two women running away. After that, J.B. witnessed the sickening horror of superior weapons against an unarmed people, and the exhaustion of patience. The soldiers' fear surfaced in a kind of violence he had only heard about from earlier days. Some of the Seventh Cavalry from Custer's old command was part of the deployment, so there was a special vengeance at work, too. J.B. felt paralyzed to do more than witness as the soldiers rose from their positions to chase down stragglers, finish off children and crippled old people. It happened so quickly. Later he would learn that Big Foot, sick with pneumonia, was one of the fallen.

A cry went up among the ranks that people were escaping at the ravine on the opposite side of the camp, and a group of soldiers took after them. At that point J.B. rose and followed. His head swam in the terrible sounds and sights of the massacre, hoping he could stop the horror, despite Father Hansen's shout at him to stay. By the time he came to the ravine, the soldiers were already shooting down the fleeing women, children, and old people. A woman and child were felled by the same bullet as it passed through her back and took the top of the baby's skull. The men cheered. Two young sisters holding hands with their younger brother between them met a shower of gunfire that produced red roses on their legs and arms, torsos and faces, and they fell still linked, as if made of pasteboard. The elderly were the easiest targets, and the soldiers were methodical in cutting them down. A hunched old woman, her gray braids long enough to sweep the ground, tried to hobble past by creeping along the edge of the ravine. A soldier kept his rifle trained on the back of her neck, as if hunting a wounded deer. Finally, he squeezed the trigger and watched with satisfaction as she fell. Her head was severed from her shoulders and rolled a foot beyond the body as if it still inched toward escape. Often two or three soldiers fired on the same person and the body would fall, spurting blood from a dozen wounds.

The atmosphere was almost joyful, a kind of play at work as they took turns and pointed out the wounded who needed to be shot again until not even a foot twitched. J.B. looked at his hands and found he still held his pistol and rifle. He wanted to raise his weapons and kill every soldier in sight, but could not lift his arms, could only watch. As if in a dream, he saw two white men, not soldiers, chase a mother and young daughter. They passed out of sight where the ravine curved, narrowed and deepened. He hoped it was a trap for the white men, yet knew that it wasn't. He heard the men hooting as if chasing coyotes for the kill. It was too late to save them. He was too late.

When there were no more Indians to escape, the firing finally stopped, and there was only silence. The bodies in the ravine lay unmoving. The soldiers stepped back, and some collapsed and shook their heads as if to clear the terrible sight from their eyes. It was obvious now what they had done. They could embrace it, bury the corrosive memory to etch them like acid, killing them slowly, or they could shrink from it in horror and relive it for the rest of their lives as if the dead could rise like spirits looking for form.

The gorge rose in J.B.'s throat and he swallowed hard. He felt someone beside him, and heard Father Hansen praying in Latin, the monotone of the chant so discordant J.B. had to walk away. He should have used his guns against the soldiers. He couldn't use his guns against the soldiers. The snowy ground of the ravine was splotched pink and red and black with blood that looked like shadows of the fallen in the midwinter light of later photographs. Even as he made his way back to where his horses were tethered, the intermittent firing continued as soldiers chased people up to three miles to kill them. Though he tried not to look, he could not help himself.

The relic hunters and soldiers searching for souvenirs were already stripping the bodies, holding up their trophies: moccasins, beaded belts, hair ornaments, necklaces, and ghost shirts, especially with bullet holes and blood, the irony doubling the value in their minds. A group of schoolboys, caught in the midst of a game, lay in a row like a sad picket fence. Bodies everywhere. Later the military would underestimate the number by at least a hundred, a mistake made in part because the Indians retrieved as many of their wounded and dead as they could after nightfall. J.B.'s journey across the camp was a tortured winding path around the grotesque bodies twisted and contorted in every manner of agony with gaping wounds and sometimes worse: the top of a skull taken, the brain matter spilling and freezing pink and gray on the ground, the expression on the face peaceful, a hand resting on the chest as if the man were asleep. A woman with a missing lower jaw and her throat ripped open, her arms extending from her sides, eyes staring up as if she had fallen from the sky. A family whose mangled bodies seemed to exchange shards of bone and blood, faces shocked and outraged.

J.B. thought he heard a small cry, and stopped and knelt beside a woman whose body rested higher than the others. He hesitated, then carefully rolled her off her back and found that the cradleboard strapped there held an infant. The child silently scrutinized his face as he cut the straps off the mother's shoulders and lifted the board, then removed the baby and cradled it in his arms. A shadow rose behind him as he stood.

"You want I should get rid of that?" A soldier held his rifle so the butt was raised and ready to club the babe. His cartridge belt was hung with booty. He grinned, and J.B. could smell the liquor sweating from his skin.

J.B. shook his head and brushed past the man, prepared to shoot him if needed. He pulled the deerskin wrap over the baby's head and hurried on toward his horse without any idea what he was going to do. Several scavengers stopped work to stare after him, wondering what prize he'd managed to secure, wondering if it'd be worth it to follow him and take it.

He was untying his horses when Father Hansen found him. "You don't want that child," the priest assured him. "I can take care of it. We have room. Don't worry."

J.B. sighed, slid his rifle in the saddle boot, and drew his gun, pointed it at the priest, barely registering the other man's blood-streaked face and hands, the black robe bearing deeper black splashes. There was a bullet crease along his jaw and a knife wound on the back of his hand that the priest ignored as he held out his arms. "You need to leave. Go back to your ranch, your son. There's nothing here for you. I shouldn't have asked you to come." The priest looked around. "Nothing for anyone now."

Unable to mount his horse or move at all, J.B. stood and waited, heard the wind rustle the grass, the shouts of soldiers torn between their desire to kill the wounded enemy and their obligation to drag them back to the medics for care, and then the first wails of the survivors upon discovery of their dead. Finally his arms loosened, and Father Hansen took the baby, tucked it expertly on one shoulder as he gripped

J.B.'s arm. "Go home. Forget this."

J.B. stared at his retreating back until the priest disappeared into the crowd of gathering Indians searching for their kin.

He intended to ride straight through to the ranch, but snow and bitter cold forced him to stop in Rushville. He was able to find a bed in a large room crowded with twenty cots at the hotel despite the newspaper reporters and government officials and thrill seekers. When he went downstairs to the saloon crowded with soldiers and civilians, he stood at the end, head down over his whiskey glass, unable to avoid overhearing the noise of men celebrating their victory over a vanquished enemy.

He was on the verge of leaving when a man pushed his way into the narrow space beside him and called for whiskey. Turning to J.B., he raised his brow and nodded toward his empty glass. J.B. shrugged. The barkeep poured their glasses full and both men drank them half down.

"Percival Chance," the man said. He was tall, thin, and handsome in a varnished eastern kind of style, despite the rugged condition of his clothing. He had a thin nose and an angular face with elegant planes, a high forehead with longish blond hair. J.B. imagined he was the kind of man women appreciated. He still had decent teeth.

Chance raised his brow at him and J.B. remembered to introduce himself and thank him for the drink.

The high atmosphere of the saloon fit Chance. As he drank, the color mounted in his cheeks and his eyes seemed charged with electricity as if they held a secret. J.B. wondered if a touch would ignite his own clothing.

Finally Chance spoke. "That was something out there today, was it not?" His language and dialect was an unsettled mixture of sounds, as if he had lived in another country and forgotten how to speak his native tongue. Chance turned his back to the bar and leaned against it, propping his elbows and nodding toward the corner where the loudest group almost shouted in their efforts to out-tell each other's tales.

"That man in the middle there is my employer, Lord M. We were fortunate enough to take part in the skirmish with the red men today. He's thrilled and I received a very large bonus — in addition to other benefits." He pulled an eagle talon necklace from inside his shirt and worked it over his head. Laying it on the bar, he said, "An Indian has to earn this. Shows his prowess and bravery. I've always wanted one, though the talons are so sharp they dig into the skin. Indians are more disciplined to endure pain, I've found." He smiled and rubbed the back of his hand, which was raked with long scratches. When he turned his head, J.B. could see three long marks on his neck as well. J.B. pushed away from the bar, suddenly sickened by his suspicions. *Skirmish?* He couldn't dislodge the word now that he'd heard it.

"Oh don't go —" Chance straightened and lifted his glass in invitation.

J.B. pushed his way through the crowd, unable to tolerate another second of the man's company. When he met Chance ten years later, he still remembered his suspicions and regretted not beating the man to death right there in the saloon. For the rest of his life, J.B. was haunted by the execution of the Indians, and later the mass grave where soldiers dumped 146 bodies stripped of any possible relic or souvenir, half-naked and unwashed, their forms frozen in grotesque positions by the bitter cold, handled as if they were tainted firewood.

Father Hansen had wanted a witness, but it made no difference. The true story was unthinkable, unheroic, so it was changed by the newspapers, the military, and the government. Afterward, J.B. lived on his Sand Hills land as if he rented it. He felt like he was waiting for a landlord to evict him, no matter what his father believed. And the worst part was that he had traded Cullen for a ranch that could never rightfully be his own. The events of his life felt like a spool of thread he kept trying to trace back and back, never to reach the end.

CHAPTER THIRTY

Riding toward town, Cullen had just come from his father's ranch, sent away by his grandfather, called a bastard for the thousandth time. He believed it as he watched his mother fawn over his younger brother, making too much of him as if he were still the favored babe in arms. He used to spy on his father and brother, though he said not a word to anyone, when the loneliness swept him to the black chasm and he had to find a way to crawl back. He'd followed them to Pine Ridge Reservation during the Ghost Dance that ended so badly. His grandfather was up there, too, meddling old man, trying to secure another government beef contract since it seemed war was likely. Later, he watched his father fall to pieces as the soldiers slaughtered the people. Cullen followed two men who chased a woman and a child into the ravine. What they did to the woman made him sick, but he was still a boy and couldn't face the men. He almost froze to death waiting for them to leave the body, and then made his way back to the soldiers' camp, desperate to kill someone for what they'd done. The girl disappeared, he hoped escaped. Later still he would dream about her, and give her new lives much better than the one she lived. Sometimes he even dreamed she was his sister. It had infuriated him, so much so he planned to stick a knife in General Colby after he paid fifty dollars for a Sioux baby to bring home to his wife like a souvenir. Instead Cullen got drunk with a couple of soldiers who found it great fun to watch him stagger around and vomit. He woke two days later alone in an abandoned tent. Then made his way back to the ranch with a splitting head, throwing up every few miles. He never told anyone what he'd seen.

Now here he was again, unwanted by his mother and grandfather, hired hand and bastard to both. He wouldn't be pushed out this time, though. He had a plan, and the thought made him smile as he nudged his horse into a ground-eating lope.

"Cullen's too old for toys," Drum said the time his mother threw a party for his sixth birthday. The old man bent the silver flute over his knee, put his fist through the drum, and finally smashed the fiddle over the back of the kitchen chair. That set of music-playing instruments had been his favorite page in the wish book: the boys marching in a happy line filled all kinds of loneliness that dug itself a hole under his skin. There were picture books, too, and Drum pulled those apart between his ham-hock fists. Cullen thought his papa would explode, his face red as a frostbitten ear, but he stood by as Drum knew he would. Drum knew everything, Cullen realized that day. He hung the sky and cluttered the earth with cattle, and there wasn't anything the boy could do about it. He believed that for the longest time. Hayward didn't know anything, of course, except what Cullen told him — that his mother couldn't stand him, that's why she ran away. Came back with horses to bribe them. It was easy to play with Hayward's mind; he was still that little baby in his mama's lap, watching while Drum dragged Cullen away.

The time he was brought back he expected to feel the same, but Hayward was older, running around on his own two feet. Cullen stood and watched as his mother's eyes followed Hayward's every move, and his papa's face was a book of happiness — and he understood how it was like he had died. And slowly, the Cullen who had been their fair-haired boy did die, he disappeared like a shadow that couldn't be seen at noon, all that darkness driven inside a person, nothing splashed out, and that was him. He didn't go back again until he was ten and by then it was too late. She was gone, and Hayward wandered around like a bucket calf, bellering for his mama, and Papa looked like an empty pail.

When he turned thirteen he took off and stayed out at the line shack on the edge of the Lazy SK, some homesteader's place that didn't make a cent, on the banks of the Niobrara. When the old man found him, he gave him a good hiding, but it didn't make a damn difference. Go ahead, Cullen grinned, wicked and hard as the old bastard by then. It was Stubs stopped him that time, and another cowboy who quit the next day. Don't go on my account, Cullen told him. He ran away so often, it was like Drum's house was the one he was visiting and the shack his real home, fixed up the way he wanted it. Books he gathered or stole from J.B., old magazines men left as they traveled through, new ones when he could sell something in town. Drum didn't pay him more than his other hands, so there wasn't much money for extras. He had a wall where he hung stuff: buffalo skull he'd found in a blowout; arrowheads; part of a Sioux legging, fringed and beaded, so old it crackled; fiddle without strings he found in the corner of the shack under a pile of rags; photographic picture of a family standing in front of their house — not a smile to be found among them except for the fool kid laughing it up behind them; pair of ladies' white leather gloves, so soft he'd take them down just to hold them.

By the time he was fifteen Drum couldn't see why Cullen came back so often. The boy tried living in that shack through winter to learn the lesson Drum was teaching. Frost bit his toes, his fingers, his ears, and it felt like his eyelids would never come unswole. Ran out of kerosene middle of December, and cow chips were impossible to find after the early blizzards that year. He burned the chairs, the table, the bunk, and was starting on the walls of the shack, not an easy thing to pull down those boards, when Stubs rode in to check on him. He was weak as a kitten from having nothing to eat but canned peaches for the past two weeks, and his horse wasn't in much better shape. Stubs fed them both from the packhorse, loaded them up, and led them back. Drum didn't have much to say that time.

No beating, Cullen was too tall by then. Soon as the January thaw came, two more hands hit the trail. Guess they figured to take their chances in winter. There was the other thing that happened, of course, and to this day people around there didn't know for sure that Drum did it. They heard he did and no one would meet their eyes for a few years after that, then it was forgotten, and a pretty tale was spun and kept.

It was right after Cullen came back. He was lying around the house trying to get his strength up, because Stubs said he'd quit and take the rest of the men with him if the boy wasn't allowed time to recover. For once, Cullen didn't fight. He was too wrung out. It was one morning after the New Year, and there was a knock on the door. Drum was out with the men moving cattle closer since it looked like yet another storm was coming from the Dakotas: sky had that milky haze and the wind'd been blowing from the south melting snow, but every once in a while, there was a cold gust from the north that slid under the warm, and the birds were restless, circling and crying and grabbing what berries there were on the bushes, and the chickens ran up into their coop, then popped out again and ran down the ramp to scratch at the places where the snow'd blown clear. The dogs whined and were anxious about every little thing. The horses in the corral argued all morning, biting and kicking and turning their butts to the north wind. They could feel it coming. And the air had that peculiar charge to it, the one that made a person's skin feel like his shirt was cutting into his back where his arms came out, and the last thing Cullen was looking for was a knock at the door.

He shoved the cat aside; he wasn't about to let that thing out and have to go chasing after it in a snowstorm. Captain Jack was Drum's favorite, the only animal allowed in the house. Even the dogs had to sneak in after the old man'd shut his bedroom door for the final time. Two people stood on the porch. It took them coming inside and peeling off the layers of clothes for Cullen to realize they were a man and woman, and she'd got something in the brown-and-red carpet satchel she was being mighty careful about. Captain Jack came sniffing and scratching around the bag until it let out a squall that sent him scurrying half across the room, back humped, hair raised, hissing. The woman reached inside for a bundle that turned out to be a tiny baby, red-faced and sick-looking, its eyes never open, like a newborn kitten nuzzling the blind world.

They all looked about froze to death so Cullen gave them coffee. They had cream and sugar, and that made it easier to swallow. When he took Cullen, Drum had bought a cow for milk, and got to liking the cream skimmed off the top. More than once he caught Cullen drinking it straight from the pitcher and whipped his hide. Didn't stop him.

Another look at their faces, gaunt and burned by the wind, and he got out the biscuits from breakfast and a chunk of beef and a can of peaches, which he couldn't stomach anymore. At first they declined, and then they tucked into that food like they hadn't eaten in days. Cullen knew how that was. After a while, he realized the baby was too quiet, its breathing patchy, then hoarse, then snorting and silent. The woman ate with one hand while she rested her fingertips on the baby's skull and cheek.

When they'd eaten all the food, the man cleared his throat and said, "We'd be beholden for a place to sleep. Baby's too sick to travel and my wife's all in." He laid his big raw-looking hands flat on the table and shook his head once, trying not to glance over at the baby, who was mewling now, too sick for a proper cry. The man was about to the end of his rope and his eyes teared. He wiped them away like he got something caught in them.

His wife laid a hand on his arm but didn't take her eyes off the baby.

"What's wrong with it?" Cullen asked.

The couple looked at each other and something like guilt passed between, which made Cullen nervous. Finally the man heaved a big sigh and pushed away from the table. His long, angular face looked hand-built from scrap wood, a person could read the bones so clearly and they didn't exactly line up as they should. There were smallpox scars on his cheeks and the thick thatch of red-blond hair was cut in an uneven bowl around his face. He had yellow-brown eyes that offset everything else. Made Cullen wonder if the baby had the same eyes.

"Diphtheria, might be the diphtheria," the woman spoke for the first time in a soft voice filled with the kind of yearning that sent a shiver down the back. The boy stared at her and she stared right back. She had a plain oval face, the features set up so regular the eye passed right over them, but the longer he looked the more was revealed. Like the unremarkable nose turned up at the end, the medium brown eyes red-rimmed, and the cheekbones starting to show. A person could tell that when she lost the puppy fat she would have one of those high-toned faces except for the chin that hadn't decided yet whether to shove out or sink in, or maybe it was the way she didn't lift her face. She was always looking down at that baby, even when it wasn't there. She'd been chewing her cracked lips, there was a scab in the corner of her mouth, and her skin was blotched red and white. Cullen spent all that time noticing the details, like the fact there was no wedding band on her finger, and that her nails were rimed black with dirt, and that her clothes were actually ragged layers, men's and women's both, and her feet bound with rags to keep the man-sized boots on, as if they'd shared the contents of his wardrobe. Cullen tried not to think of that word she'd used.

"We took off soon as it hit the ranch," the man said with a sigh. "Thought we'd made it away safe." He looked at him with those yellow-brown eyes, like a dozy cat's almost, and Cullen couldn't look away.

"Don't mean to bring harm," he whispered. Cullen nodded and said they could stay. The baby mewled and coughed and its lungs grew thick and it couldn't seem to bear more than the touch of the woman's fingertips. When she tried to pick it up, it contorted weakly and bloody spit gurgled from its mouth and nose.

At noon Drum came stomping into the house, slammed the door against the wind, took one look at the couple, and jerked his thumb at the door. They silently gathered themselves. The woman picked up the satchel and held it against her chest as they shuffled out the door. Cullen wanted to send food along, at least a can of peaches, but Drum was there, removing his coat, impatient for them to leave. When the door shut behind them, he gestured toward the dish-strewn table. "Throw it all out." Later Drum made him scrub the table with salt and lye soap and burn the clothes he wore.

Deep in memory, Cullen didn't realize how close he was to the one-room church the Sand Hills families shared. He halted his horse and looked to the east where the church stood two hills over.

That spring he'd heard the couple had made it to another ranch and left the baby, which died, and nobody ever had a name for any of them. Cullen sat with them that whole morning and never thought to ask. A storm came up, and it was a miracle the baby lived long enough to die in a house. He hoped the couple didn't perish until they found safety again. Stubs later told him that Drum heard about the epidemic in town and was terrified when he saw the strange horses. Cullen didn't speak to him for six months after that.

When the owners of the ranch where the baby died built the church on their land and invited all their neighbors, he and Drum were the only ones who didn't show. Then they buried the baby, and again, Drum wouldn't go. Cullen went later. It was spring and the hills were dotted with brown-and-white cows and new calves, a pretty sight. After all that snow the wildflowers came busting out, and the wind was soft and warm without being hot. It was that kind of spring day when the sky didn't seem close enough to bother and the horse felt good but not too good. Cullen wished for a person to ride along with. It was a different feeling than being in the line shack, where his anger kept him company. Out in the hills, the land was so endless a person felt himself slipping away if he wasn't careful. There was so little to butt up against, to give a person shape, to stop or start him or make him turn away. A person in the hills could do just about anything he wanted. Besides that, there was so much to see, to point out to another person in a way that made it better to see it. That was what he remembered, before Drum took him, how his mother would show him a brown-and-yellow butterfly in the grass and stop him holding it too tight before he set it loose. Or a big yellow-and-black spider in a web drawn between the sunflowers she watered. Sometimes he'd say to his horse, Look at that, and point out the flock of red-winged blackbirds turning like a hand, palm up, palm down, then shaking loose over the hillside like pepper.

Drawing up to the church now, he was surprised by the mown grass and the newly painted white walls. Inside smelled of the fresh cedar beams and pews. There was a brand-new pump organ up front, and the brass-lined wood stops gleamed in the shadows. Cullen sat, placed his fingers on the keys, and pumped the pedals until he produced a wheezy squall that was hard on the ears. There was the same potbellied stove to take the chill off come winter and the kerosene lamps along the walls. He never understood how people could bow down to something like the huge rough-hewn cross that towered from the wall up front. The trees had to come from the reservation or were hauled all the way from Chadron, maybe. Cedar. It lasted. He ran his fingers over the axe-chipped surface, wondering that they had not bothered to plane it smooth. The wood felt warm to the touch, and he turned to see if the light streaming in the tall windows bathed the cross.

The little cemetery was out back. From the weathered markers, it was probably where some original settlers had buried their dead. The pink stone slab was larger than most and stood out so the eye couldn't stop seeking it, OUR BABY chiseled into its smooth surface. The grave itself was short and had sunk a few inches with the years. At least the kid got out before everything went to shit, he thought. But even as he rounded the side of the church, planning to ride the hell out of there for town, he felt drawn back. He tried pushing his legs forward but they slowed and stopped. Glancing at the church, he saw the tiny white skull of a bird, probably a blue jay judging from the hook-shaped beak, sitting on a windowsill. "Okay," he said, "all right, yes." He picked it up, careful not to crush it, for it was light and fragile as a locust shell, and placed it in his palm. When he reached the grave again, he turned his hand and let the skull edge onto the top of the pink headstone, and made sure it caught there before he patted the back of the stone and left. A breeze came up as he passed the church with a light sweet smell that stayed with him to the outskirts of town, where he thought, I will not live to tell this story.

Chapter Thirty-One

"You're my Telemachus, Hayward," his mother said, and the words rolled around in his head like marbles. What does that mean, he wondered, and she explained about a poet and a man named Odysseus gone for years to war and a woman named Penelope left at home, and he wanted to say, but he was the one left, and she the one gone, but her eyes were shiny and her face full of happiness of a kind he rarely saw so he let her keep talking though it was mainly nonsense. He wasn't fighting off suitors and she all but killed his father. Drove him to do what he did by leaving. He thought of that time his father dragged him to see the reservation, and then his father went again without him, and was never the same after that. If she'd been here, his father would have stayed home, not gotten sad. He thought about Star and wondered if she met his father at Wounded Knee, if that was why they were killed together.

"Your mother has a poetic nature," Father said one of the few times he ever spoke about her other than to assure him that she loved her son. Hayward pondered that for a moment, then asked, "What does that make us?"

He knew what he was. He was the one left behind, but he didn't feel sorry for himself. Soon as he found Cullen, he got over that. Cullen told him the truth — that Hayward was the one nobody wanted — grandfather, mother, and father by default, since they inhabited the same space and it was too much trouble to stake him out in the hills like a deformed calf to lure the coyotes.

Mother came into the parlor where he was reading a book of poetry Cullen gave him. She stood there like she was waiting for permission to speak. He glanced up from the book, which was about a bunch of weepy men who felt tender and sad all the time, according to Cullen, who preferred poetry to the adventure stories Hayward liked. When she realized what he was reading, she smiled.

"May I join you?" she asked in the overly polite voice that gritted his teeth.

"This poem, 'Ode to a Nightingale,' by Kates?" he said.

"Keats, with a long 'e,' " she said apologetically.

"He wants to kill himself, doesn't he?" He paused for effect and her lips parted slightly like she was about to say something. She nodded instead.

He continued, going line by line explaining the poem as Cullen had explained it to him. "But he hears the nightingale, its beautiful, sad song, and it helps him, doesn't it? So nature and her beauty, if we pay attention, can save our lives."

She nodded, the expression on her chiseled face almost afraid to show her astonished happiness. She reached out, patted his arm and nodded, believing she'd found her soul mate, the one the poets were always thinking about instead of the real live people around them. It was Cullen she needed for that, he should tell her.

Instead, he closed the book and tossed it on the table between them. "Pretty simpleminded, don't you think?"

He stood and pulled up the waist of his trousers and tucked in his shirt. "You didn't think I could read, did you?"

"I taught you to read, son." She wouldn't look at him and he felt a twinge of sadness. He'd made his point and hurt her, but it didn't feel as good as he'd thought.

Truth was, he didn't want her mooning around him all the time, trying to show him things, trying to make up for the years she wasn't there, trying to be a thing she gave up and thought she could just come back and reclaim like a hat from the attic. Besides, he could see it upset Cullen. Hayward had a gun, a horse, and a claim to the ranch. He said these things to himself, then his heart did that sick little trick and he wanted to drop to his knees, bury his head in her lap, and beg her not to leave him again. And that made him mad, too.

Then Graver knocked and entered without waiting for an answer. He removed his hat, J.B.'s, glanced at his mother, at him, and back to her.

"You wanted to see me?" he asked. Thing about the man was he didn't get nervous around his mother, didn't hem and haw like a raw hand, or duck his head and turn red when he spoke. He was confident, not like Drum, who couldn't even see another person unless he knocked into them, more like that lawyer Percival Chance or Judge Foote, men who knew their place in the world, like they'd taken hold and made it something. Hayward watched Graver and tried to square his shoulders and relax his hips and arms the way the older man did.

He lifted his chin, but not so high he'd end up strutting around like a rooster. Graver looked over, a smile pulled at the corners of his mouth, and he nodded to him, man to man. Better not be laughing at me, Hayward warned with his eyes narrowed like a gunfighter's. He dropped his hand to his side where the holstered gun should sit and remembered that he'd left it in the bunkhouse when he cleaned it.

Sympathy appeared in Graver's eyes, and Hayward wasn't prepared for it. He vowed then and there never to forget his gun again. And not to tell Cullen.

"You did a good job finding that orphan calf and bringing it in," Graver said, and despite himself, his chest swelled and he risked a glance at his mother. She smiled as if he'd just received good marks in school.

"Have the makings of a good hand, son," Graver said, and that tipped the whole thing over.

"I'm not your son." He did his best imitation of Cullen's snarl.

"Hayward!" His mother stood, fists at her sides, and the boy stepped back.

Graver raised his hand to calm the air, and Hayward studied the gesture at the same time he wanted to knock him down.

She turned her focus to Graver. "Please

get my horse ready, we're going hunting."

He looked startled, opening his eyes wide and raising his brow. "Not with that horse."

Her shoulders and back stiffened, and she lifted her chin and looked down her nose at him. "I see no reason."

"He's too valuable, ma'am. You have ranch horses trained to stand when there's gunfire and not spook at the smell of blood." Graver hurried his explanation and his mother cocked her head like one of the dogs when Hayward gave it a new order.

"We need meat. With all these people, I can't afford not to bring down a deer or antelope."

For the first time Hayward agreed with Graver and watched carefully as the man went to work persuading her. J.B. gave orders and kept his head down, so it was hard to learn anything from him. Instead of stepping into the fray, Graver seemed to slouch and lean back, as if the outcome wasn't as important to him as it was to her. The boy folded his arms across his chest to improve his stance.

"Stud's not gun trained, is he? Be a shame to lose him." He kept his voice low and even.

Her shoulders relaxed. "You're right. Go ahead and get the proper horses ready. We'll be out shortly."

Graver put on his hat and turned to leave, then stopped and glanced at him. "Can you help me?"

Hayward shrugged and tried to act as casual as Graver, but his heart pounded. The man had never asked for help before, and with Cullen gone wherever he got to after he shot off old Higgs's hat and acted rude at supper yesterday, he guessed it wouldn't hurt.

He climbed over the fence while Graver used the gate to the corral, and they stood eyeing the dozen heads that stared back and circled restlessly until the bay gelding Hayward liked stepped out of the crowd toward him. He always had to know what was going on, sticking his big nose in every kind of business. That was what Hayward liked about him and he usually carried a biscuit in his pocket as a reward. Graver watched as the bay ambled over and nuzzled him. Finally the horse took his shirt cuff in his teeth and tried to lift his hand. Hayward laughed and gave him the treat. As he chewed, he blew warm air on the side of the boy's neck.

"Got yourself a friend there," Graver said, and there was no criticism in his voice so Hayward nodded and smiled at the horse. "Which horses do you think we should use?" Graver gazed at him, and Hayward straightened his shoulders and scrubbed the gelding's face with his fist the way he liked.

"And let's not play any tricks on her guests. She's got enough on her plate as it is," Graver said as if they were just two cowboys doing a job, so it didn't rankle. It was good Cullen was gone.

It took him a few minutes to choose the horses and Graver didn't grow impatient, just folded his arms and leaned back against the fence rails. There was a lot to like there, Hayward realized.

"The gray with the striped legs for the judge. You could set off dynamite on her back and she'd mosey along. Take that tall sorrel for the lawyer, he's gun broke, and he'll give him a ride."

Graver turned to pick the lariat off the fence like he was working for Hayward now.

"And that little black for my mother, he's got a shuffling trot that's easy to sit. Are we going, too?"

Graver squinted at the house, then back at the horses, and finally let his eyes settle on him. "Be a good plan, don't you think?"

He took a minute to reply, like he was thinking it over the way Graver did, then gave a sharp nod and took another rope from the fence and dropped it over the bay's head. "You can use J.B.'s chestnut. He needs the experience."

They had the horses saddled, pack animals fitted, rifles in their scabbards, and were leading them to the house when Frank Higgs came out of his and asked them what the Sam Hill they were doing. Graver waited for the boy to answer.

"My mother wants to take her guests hunting," Hayward said, shoulders squared, chin up but not too high.

Frank glanced at Graver, the house, then back to the boy with a short nod.

"Hold the next two hands in for skinning and dressing the meat when we get back," Hayward said. Even Cullen wasn't able to give orders anybody would follow. Frank tipped his hat, a grin playing happily on his face.

As they mounted, Larson Dye from the Box LR came jogging up on a fat old spotted mare, bristling with guns.

"Good," he panted, "worried I'd be too late for the huntin' trip." The mare eyed them suspiciously, like they were the source of all her recent troubles, took a deep breath, ducked her head, and kicked out with her right hind. Larson grinned and patted her. "She loves a good chase." The mare reached around and tried to bite his leg,

451

but her teeth snapped harmlessly in the air.

Hayward made a note to stay out of her way, and Larson did the right thing bringing up the rear of their cavalcade as they departed. The lawyer stopped at the fork and said he had some business to attend to in town. Hayward was happy to see him go, but Graver frowned, and he wondered what that meant. Graver naturally took the lead, and Hayward fell in beside him, just as naturally, seized by a sudden sadness that his father was gone. The moment should have been them. Then he thought about Star, the Sioux girl he'd met on the reservation, who was gone, too. He wished he knew who killed them. He and Cullen talked about it all the time. Cullen thought it was the Indians they'd argued with on the rez last fall.

They'd been out about an hour, the sun high and distant as it headed into the afternoon, a light breeze on their faces, which was good since the game wouldn't smell them as they came down the tall hill. In the past, he and Cullen found antelope in the washout the other side of the next hill, so he pointed in that direction.

Behind them the judge muttered something to his mother. She replied with a single word as Graver waved for quiet and pulled out his rifle. Hayward did, too. He could hear the others do the same. His horse lifted its head, ears pricked, and filled its body, ready to whinny. He put a hand on its neck to check it, and the horse released the air in a long sigh as a turkey exploded into the air. Larson Dye's fat mare huffed up behind Hayward, and Dye pulled the trigger so close to the bay horse it lurched sideways and bucked. Guns went off all around him, and Hayward felt the air next to him singe his cheek.

"What the hell!" he shouted, regaining control of his horse and spinning to face the others. Graver jumped off his mount and picked up the turkey, so riddled with bullets the flesh and feathers hung off in strips. He threw it down with a disgusted noise in his throat.

Dulcinea's face was white and she clutched a rifle, while the two suitors checked their loads and avoided his eyes.

Graver looked at the ground, nodded as if he'd come to an agreement with himself, mounted, and turned his horse to face the group. Hayward thought he should be doing this, but knew he couldn't, and that brought back his bitterness.

"This boy here has a real future ahead of him," Graver said. "Hate to see it cut short by carelessness. Let's take turns. Mrs. J.B. first, then Foote, and Larson, you go after that. Hayward and I will back up the shooter. That meet with your approval?" He didn't wait for replies, just turned his horse and trotted on ahead with Hayward beside him. When they were several yards beyond the others, he asked, "You okay, son?"

Hayward didn't mind being that now. He wasn't low-rating him, and he was glad Cullen wasn't there to see Graver stand up for him.

"Let's head over to that washout to the right." Hayward was proud of the way he was handling himself as Graver eased his horse in the direction he'd indicated. The boy was glad he hadn't killed him, and he wondered if Graver knew it was him who'd shot him. It was on the tip of his tongue to tell him, but he couldn't yet.

Graver slowed his horse and stopped, sat absolutely still, as did the others. A tall, regal buck appeared, with a wide rack of antlers. He was packing good weight from the rich spring grass, his tan coat glossy in the sun. He sniffed the air, but the wind blew their scent away from him, and he lowered his head, pretending to eat as he observed them. They stood still. Then the buck grabbed a mouthful of grass and lifted his head to stare at them again and shifted his front feet as if ready to spin away.

"Mrs. J.B.?" Graver said softly, "Dulcinea?"

"He's so beautiful," she breathed, and Graver lifted his rifle in a fluid motion and fired. The deer raised up as if to leap, took a step, then collapsed.

"Oh," she sighed.

Immediately the suitors complained that they should have been given the shot. Graver ignored them and rode ahead to check on the deer. It was clean through the head. A good kill. After they dressed the deer and loaded it on the packhorse, the hunters pushed toward the wash.

All their shooting probably drove away every critter in the valley, but the buck was there, so maybe not. The judge and Larson Dye muttered complaints to one another, and Hayward smiled at the idea that they were finally getting together on something. Larson at least should have known better, but he wanted in on the thing, so he didn't much care how he cast his vote. At least that's what J.B. had always said about him. Another pang of regret made his stomach ache. Why didn't he pay more attention to his father? He should've been learning everything there was to know about running a ranch, getting the men to listen. Instead, his father treated him like an expensive hunting dog he let loose to roam and come to nothing. Why didn't he send him to live with his mother if he didn't want to raise him? Hayward didn't know who to be madder at, him or her. Or maybe himself.

He looked ahead at the wash, cut so deep they couldn't see what was in there until they were on top of it. Sweetgrass had to grow there since game was always hunkered down eating, resting. Last spring the boys found a couple of cows holed up with some deer after a late blizzard, all packed in safe and sound; they looked at the boys like they were ruining the party.

Suddenly Larson Dye's horse squealed and there was some general thrashing behind them, but when Hayward looked back, Dye was settling his hat and smiling. He suspected there was more to that man than they knew. He must have been a hand when he was younger. Maybe J.B. underestimated him. Maybe he used that when he talked J.B. into the deal for the road between their two ranches. Turned out they had the maintenance while he only had to build it, a loose term since all he did was drive his cattle up and down a path and then put in some old fence posts to mark it. That road had been a curse on them ever since. They were out there filling and scraping and no end of things since it was only two ruts of sand and weeds.

Hayward's mind was so taken with the injustice it took a moment to register the movement when a bullet thudded into the hill over his mother's head. Then a gun fired right behind them. They stopped and turned to see Larson Dye grinning happily.

"Got him," he announced. Dye pursed his mouth, glanced at the hill to his right, and shrugged. "Whoever it was, I think I got him." He smiled with less certainty.

Dulcinea stared at the hill the shot came from while Graver shook his head. The judge and Dye stood in their stirrups and scanned the grass. It was quiet. She started to speak, but Graver held up his hand. He was pretty coolheaded in light of being shot at a second time in the past two months. The boy's mouth was dry, and he wondered if it was Cullen wanting to add to his trophies after he shot up Higgs's hat. Graver held his rifle at his waist, finger on the trigger, ready to shoot as he moved behind them, stopping to whisper, "Stay here and protect your mother," and set off for the lowest hill, followed by the judge and Larson Dye. In a moment they were gone. It was like the shot had cleared the air and then it got busy again with birds swooping and arguing. Little goldfinches, swallows, and a killdeer complaining as usual.

"A silly prank," his mother said, hesitant.

His stomach sank at the idea of Cullen hurt out there. Maybe Graver would finish him like a broke-legged steer, or worse yet, drive away his horse and leave him to die. He lifted his reins to go find his brother.

"I'd feel better if you stayed with me." She kept her eyes down and it occurred to him that she was frightened.

"Guess we better head back," Hayward said. He couldn't imagine what Cullen was thinking. Who was he going to shoot? He was so mad at the world, maybe anyone would do. The realization made his hands shake and his bones feel light. Kill Drum, Hayward wanted to tell him, end your misery, but he noticed that most of the time a person looked away from what really bit hard on their mind. Animals were different, you bite them, they bite you, or they run away. His mother flashed in his head, her teary face the day she climbed into the buggy, arms empty of him, because he was hanging on to her skirt, legs, feet, anything he could grab. He ripped off the little watch on the chain around her neck, and tore the collar of her traveling coat, but it did no good. He ran after that buggy for a mile until his legs gave out and he lay there in the dirt, unable to find the breath to cry anymore. He wrapped her gold chain around his wrist so tight his hand turned purple and ached something fierce. It took Frank and his father both to hold him down and unwrap it. Damn her. His father told a different version of the story the time he asked about that day. Seemed like old people couldn't keep their memories straight.

They were half a mile from the ranch house when they came upon Cullen riding out to meet them. Hayward looked at his shoulder, but he didn't seem to be favoring it. He wore a fresh white shirt, was clean-shaven and bathed. Cullen glanced at the deer on the packhorse, smiled at his brother, and refused to look at or speak to their mother. "We got more company," he said.

"Someone shot at Mother!"

Cullen stared at him a long moment. "Why would anyone do that?"

"When did you get back?" Hayward asked.

"Hour ago. Had to check on things at our ranch. Without Drum around, the men think it's a holiday. Only half listen to Stubs, and Carter and Sergei the Russian gone missing again." He combed his horse's mane with his fingers. "Almost had to pistol-whip Faro Jack and Dance Smith to get them off their behinds to feed the stock. Drum will have some work to do when he gets back." He gave a mirthless laugh. "Old man's holding court in your parlor right now though, wait till you see it! I'm heading right back to get a front row seat. You better light a fire under you, don't want to miss this fun!" Cullen spurred his horse into a dead run, leaving them to eat his dust.

His mother's face was pale when Hayward glanced over, and it hit him: she was afraid of Cullen. His heart pounded. What if he lost her again? What if she got shot like J.B. and he didn't have anyone left? He felt the surge of fear and helplessness that made him cry himself to sleep as a child. He looked at her.

"You know I'll take care of you, don't you?"

She smiled gratefully, and that was enough.

CHAPTER THIRTY-TWO

"Didn't know whether you'd remember me, Dulcie."

Tookie Edson extended her thick, muscular arm and Dulcinea gazed up into the sunburned face that looked preserved rather than aged by ranch work. At six feet, Tookie towered over the other two women and most of the men crowding the parlor. She and her twin brother, Evan, bought their place twenty years ago and built the Crooked Post 8 into a ranch equal to the Bennett holdings. Tookie, as usual, came dressed in identical attire to her brother's: tan gabardine western trousers and jacket, white shirt, except where he wore a bolo tie with a silver slide, she tied a green silk kerchief around her thick, red, roughened neck. Her broad, honest face and watery-brown eyes peered so earnestly Dulcinea laughed and gave her a quick hug instead of shaking her hand. Her stout body pressed briefly, but long enough to experience the hard muscle-packed flesh as solid as a fence post except for the loose pillow of her breasts.

Dulcinea caught a glimpse of Evan, holding a glass of whiskey, deep in discussion with Drum seated beside him on the sofa. She was clearly at a disadvantage here. Tookie sensed her discomfort and said, "Drum invited us to supper. We was just coming back from town, ran into Rivers and his wife, Rachel, on the way here, riding in that big brougham with Stillhart from the bank. I think that other one is his niece or daughter or something. She was in the carriage behind them —" She raised her eyebrows and smiled mischievously. They glanced at the young woman, dressed in a brown velvet gown with a scoop neckline trimmed in seed pearls, which also lined the sleeve cuffs. The dress hung on her skinny figure as if it were made for a larger woman. She stood alone in the far corner and pondered the book of Keats's poetry Hayward had read from earlier.

"Looks like a dry cow in spring," Tookie drawled, crossing her arms across her broad chest and tugging on her earlobe.

Vera had enlisted Rose to serve drinks as she hurriedly prepared enough food for the additional guests, banging pot lids and slamming pans on the stove to let them know how she felt about it. Rose kept her head down as she brought the drinks. Following her, Lily carried a platter of fry bread cut into small pieces that she offered each guest.

"First time some of them have had Indian fry bread, I bet," Tookie said when Rose brought her a glass of sherry and Lily stepped from behind her mother's skirts to offer up the morsels. Tookie picked pieces one by one and placed them in the cup of her hand until she'd emptied half the plate. The little girl's eyes grew round until she couldn't stop from giggling and chancing a look at the giant woman. Tookie gave her a theatrical wink and Lily laughed out loud. Rose glanced between the two and smiled.

Cullen waved Rose off and gave the banker's young friend a glass of whiskey. He smiled, took the book from her, and opened it casually as if thoroughly acquainted with its contents. He stopped at a page and read lines to her, his eyes overly bright, until she retrieved it and placed it on the table. He leaned close, said something, then weaved his way toward J.B.'s study, and the young woman followed without a backward glance.

"Now what do you make of that?" Tookie

asked between pieces of fry bread. She chewed with her mouth slightly open, then drained the glass of sherry.

Dulcinea shook her head. "Did you catch her name?"

Tookie shrugged. "You know I ain't good at this social business, Dulcie. Evan might've. He has an eye on her, too. Young Cullen's getting to be quite a ladies' man, though. Have to give him that. Just like J.B." She glanced at Dulcinea's face and reddened. "Didn't mean —"

Dulcinea lifted her chin and smiled. "That's okay. I know J.B. could be very charming."

Tookie's eyes widened with sympathy and she awkwardly patted the other woman's arm with a hand as big as a draft horse hoof. "You're a good woman, Dulcinea, no matter what anyone around here thinks. I always liked you. J.B., he, well, he missed you every day of his life, well, you know."

Dulcie covered her hand with her own. Her arm was growing numb from the attentive patting, and she murmured, "Thank you," when what she wanted to do was yell at the top of her lungs, Then why didn't he stop me from leaving? Why didn't he go get our son? As if on cue, Drum limped over, his eyes bright with contention, the heated oak of whiskey rolling off him, which surprised her. He'd always been a man who could hold his liquor. Perhaps his recent injuries had caught up with him. When he spoke, his voice was the same old Drum with not a splinter of weakness.

"Miss Edson." He wiped his hand across the front of his worn but clean gray chambray shirt. "Mind if I have a word with my daughter-in-law? She's spending so much time entertaining her men guests these days, we don't get much opportunity to discuss the ranches."

Tookie glanced at her and went to join her brother, who was talking to Chance and Stillhart, the banker. Rose thrust the tray of drinks among them and they each took one, Tookie choosing whiskey instead of sherry and Chance choosing sherry instead of whiskey.

Drum cleared his throat to capture her attention again.

"What is it?" she asked. He continued to massage his chest as if his undershirt was too tight.

"You would, would you?" He kept his voice so low she could barely hear him above the din of the other conversations and whiskey-loosened laughter.

"Would what?"

He glared at her, digging his fingers into his chest. "Make this deal without even talking to me!" He stared as venomous as a snake in the blind. "After all this family has done for you, too!"

"Stop right there!" She kept her voice to a whisper. "I haven't any idea what you're talking about. And I don't need to hear any sanctimonious nonsense either, from you of all people!"

Apparently her anger got through to him because he stopped his chest kneading and rocked back on his boot heels and peered at her, cagey eyes half-squinted. "You swear?"

She started to turn, but he grabbed her upper arm and squeezed so hard she winced.

"You swear they haven't gotten to you yet?"

"I swear if you don't let go of my arm I'm going to punch you in the nose, Drum Bennett!" When he released her, she added, "And no, no one has spoken to me about anything other than the pleasantries of the day. What are you talking about?" It was no secret the old man was growing more suspicious with age, and for a person who started out that way, he didn't have far before plain crazy. Of course, Chance mentioned the oil business, but she wasn't about to share that.

Again, she wondered if Drum had killed his own son in a fit of suspicious rage.

Cullen interrupted them, striding in from the study with the young woman behind him, waving his arms and raising his voice. "It's all settled! This ranch is going to be the site of the first drilling in the Sand Hills, thanks to Western Oil and Gas." He looked toward them and grinned as if he'd won the prize money at the ranch rodeo. "Let's raise a toast to Markie Eastman and her father, who can't be here!" His voice rose and cracked at the end, but he was drunk enough not to care as he grabbed a tumbler from Rose's tray and hoisted it above his head, slopping whiskey onto his coat sleeve.

"No, damn you." Drum clenched his fists. Cullen grinned, his eyes dancing wildly at his grandfather. "I'll fix you, you little shit," Drum cursed under his breath.

The company stared at Cullen and a few hesitantly lifted their glasses, until Hayward interrupted the celebration from the doorway.

"That's all fine and dandy, Cullen" — Hayward paused and looked at Drum and his mother — "but you don't own this ranch. Mother does. And even if she doesn't, I do, and I won't have anything to do with Western Oil and Gas." He paused again and tilted his head as he stared at his brother. "But you knew that, didn't you? That's why you snuck off to town today."

Cullen grinned, slugged the whiskey and let the glass drop from his hand to the floor, where it rolled without breaking. "Little brother." He shook his head. "Little brother." His jaw tightened.

"Cullen, we have guests. Stop making a spectacle of yourself." Dulcinea kept her voice low and full of the motherly authority they both knew she lacked.

"Son . . ." Rivers stepped forward and placed a hand on Cullen's shoulder. The boy shrugged it off, and his face went from red to white, which meant he would explode any minute. The young woman grabbed his wrist and spoke into his ear, and that finally stopped him.

As he pushed his way through the guests, shouldering Drum aside as if he were a wisp of straw, Cullen gave his mother a look so filled with loathing it punched her breath away. She clutched her stomach and forced herself to breathe as he stormed out the door, cracking the glass when he slammed it. The sound would stay with her forever, so clearly did it mark the end of one part of her life and the beginning of another.

Drum was suddenly the congenial one,

murmuring apologies to one and all, coaxing them to the supper table while she stood alone watching, not quite able to grasp what had happened.

Finally Hayward offered her his arm and led her to the head of the table opposite Drum, who wouldn't look at her. The old man was always a surprise. In the years she'd known him, she never suspected he had a social bone in his body. Watching him tell a story to Rachel Rivers, she realized he had known about the deal Cullen made. He was probably most upset that she would authorize it without his say-so. Who else knew besides Rivers, Drum, Cullen — ah, yes, Judge Foote.

The dinner progressed with small talk and food she couldn't taste.

Hayward, seated on her right, leaned over and repeated his promise of that afternoon. "It'll be fine, Mother. Don't worry."

She dipped her head and peered at her son and managed a smile. "Of course it will, dear." What she couldn't say was that she would never rely on another man to take care of her.

He reached for the wine bottle and poured her glass too full, but she didn't correct him. She had to raise it with both hands to keep from spilling. As she drank, she caught

Judge Foote's eyes on her. She did nothing to acknowledge him and he turned to speak to Markie Eastman at his side, who seemed to have a way of flattering men without simpering or flirting, and the judge straightened and beamed at her remarks — becoming more of a man, just as Cullen had for that brief, jubilant moment.

While the men went outside to smoke and drink brandy, the women retired to the parlor. It was Dulcinea's first opportunity to speak with Rivers's wife, who appeared flustered by the economies of ranch life, or perhaps life in general. Rachel Rivers was a small woman with a big bosom who seemed to keep her shoulders back to avoid toppling over. Even as she sat on the sofa, she held her head high so her small brown eyes looked down at the world. She had the little round face, tiny upturned nose, and pointed chin of a pixie in a child's storybook, complete with plump little Cupid's bow lips that seemed on the verge of either kissing or spitting. When she spoke, her voice was higher than one might expect, and slightly singsong, as if she followed along with a melody in her head.

Tookie watched her with an astonished expression, almost slack jawed. Markie

Eastman paid little court, wearing a smile that could also be called a grimace if one looked closely. Markie herself was unremarkable, except for the extreme pallor and the features so regular and purposeful they lacked feeling. Mahogany-brown hair in soft waves caught with a bow at the back of her neck, unblinking brown eyes, perfectly straight nose, and well-formed mouth, the only defect being the slightly large ears she hid under her hair. Her lips and brows appeared painted. Dulcinea wondered that her son was so easily caught by this girl. As she examined her more closely, she realized the woman was older than she appeared, closer to thirty than the twenty she conveyed at first glance. She caught Dulcinea's stare and raised a glass of brandy to her lips, sipping while she returned the look, unblinking, as expressionless as a lizard.

"Tell me what you proposed to my son, Miss Eastman," Dulcinea said. In the background, Vera clattered pans for all she was worth, angry to be relegated to hired help in the presence of company. Dulcinea didn't blame her.

"Why, Miz Dulcinea — is it all right if I call you Dulcinea?" the other woman drawled in a Deep Southern accent.

"Mrs. Bennett will be fine," Dulcinea said.

Markie glanced at Rachel Rivers, who fluttered nervously.

"My son?"

" 'God handles the large actions, but the small he leaves to Fortune,' as the ancient Greeks used to say. Don't you agree? I've always found it so." Markie Eastman sipped the brandy she insisted on, though excluded from the men and their talk. Tookie and Dulcinea joined her.

"Ah." Dulcinea smiled and decided to play her game. "They also said, 'Fortune took the dearest thing I have as fee, and made me wise.' " She noted Tookie shaking her head while Rachel Rivers gazed about the room.

"I see." Markie stared into her brandy for a moment, then held up the snifter and sighted through it. Aside from sharing a classical education, Markie Eastman and Dulcinea were at opposite ends of the world. "There's money to be made out here, Mrs. Bennett. You, your neighbors" — she nodded toward Tookie — "or someone else, it doesn't matter. Your son was the first to come forward when he heard I was in town. Apparently he has an eye for the future." She raised her brow slightly as if she paid her a compliment, then lifted the glass and drank like a man, deep and long.

"He can't sell rights he doesn't own."

"I've always found that men have a better sense of business than women." She smiled at Rachel Rivers, who gave a tiny, obligatory nod. The harlequin dog plopped next to Markie's chair; she reached down and fingered its ears.

Dulcinea slapped the glass from her hand before she could stop herself. "You are no longer welcome," she hissed between her teeth. The dog cowered and whined.

Markie Eastman smiled at her folded hands and shook her head, her shoulders trembling until she could no longer control herself and she laughed out loud. "My Lord, woman," she gasped, "who do you think you are?" Then she rolled her shoulders forward and stood, brushed a lock of hair off her cheek. "It's been very entertaining, but I must be going. I'll have to contact my father in Denver and tell him to move forward on filing for a federal claim for oil and mineral rights." She glanced at Tookie. "I wonder how many of you will still be here when we're through."

She opened the door and glanced outside into the darkness, where the only sound was the jingle of the harness when the carriage horses stamped their feet against the mosquitoes. "I'll take that dog when you go broke, too," she said with the same infuriating smile and carefully closed the door. They heard the murmurs of the men on the porch quiet and rise again into farewells, then the jingling of the harness as the carriage began the long journey to town.

"A most unpleasant creature." Rachel Rivers yawned and patted her mouth with elfin fingers. Dulcinea smiled gratefully and offered her more coffee, but she pointed to the decanter instead.

Dulcinea poured three generous portions and, ignoring social graces, the women took long draughts of brandy to flush away the unpleasantness.

After they spent a moment with their thoughts, Dulcinea asked Tookie, "Does the government own the mineral and subsurface rights to our land?"

Tookie shrugged. "Evan says he thinks so."

Rachel Rivers nodded. "My husband says you're all in danger if you don't agree to let them drill. The government has been ignoring you for a long time, except of course for the open range and Homestead Act violations, but that could change if the right pockets are lined. And if there is any evidence of oil or gas out here. So far, nobody's been able to make that claim. It's all speculation."

Once again, she realized her hasty judgments had led her astray. Rachel Rivers was a good listener, apparently, with an accurate eye and ear. Dulcinea recalled the other day when she and Rose had spotted Chance digging in the hills.

"What does he think we should do?" Tookie asked, a worried expression on her face for the first time.

"Hire him to negotiate," she said, her eyes sharp and practical, very unlike those of the child's toy Dulcinea had imagined earlier. She wondered if her husband was working with the gas and oil company, too, but didn't ask.

"And you" — Rachel turned her gaze to her hostess — "might ask yourself who outside the family has had free access to your land of late." She gave her doll smile and returned her face to the pretty porcelain painted expression as the other two simply stared at her. Chance had said what he was doing, but not who he was working for. Was he trying to take her land? But how would murdering her husband and that girl help him do that? She'd have to speak to Rose.

"Well, missus, we is about done here." Vera had tied one of the plaid dish towels from Marshall Field's over her head like a Southern field hand and clasped her hands in front, head bowed in mock deference. Rose, behind her, looked uncomfortably toward the door while Lily tugged her arm, eager to escape.

"Wouldn't you-all like to sit with us and share this here brandy?" Dulcinea kept her face neutral as she lifted the decanter, even though there was a glint of hard amusement in Vera's eyes.

"Why thank ya, missus. You is too kind." Vera yanked the towel off her head and flung it over her shoulder, narrowly missing Rose and Lily as they sidled toward the door.

"Rose?" Dulcinea said. Rose glanced at Lily. The child was long past bedtime, and with lower lip outthrust, she scrubbed her eye with the heel of her hand as her mother pulled her out the door.

Vera lifted an empty glass, held it to the lamplight, frowned and rubbed a forefinger over a spot, then thrust it toward Dulcinea. When the glass was half-full, Vera raised her brows and drank. Watching her throat work as she swallowed, Dulcinea wondered if Frank knew more about this business with the gas and oil people than he let on.

"Good venison steaks tonight, Vera. You use butter or lard?" Tookie took another long gulp.

"Bacon grease. Add a little butter and a pinch of flour to the pan, make you a thin gravy, then pour it over the steaks." Vera drank again. "And if you have a bottle of J.B.'s brandy open, you can add a splash of that, too." She smiled.

"Mighty, mighty good," Tookie said. "Don't s'pose there's any extra bottles of that brandy laying around." Her glance at Dulcinea was earnest to hide the teasing. "The rate we're going these days, there won't be any brandy left in Cherry County." Dulcinea lifted her glass and drank, appreciating the smooth, smoky-sweet flavor on the back of her tongue. Honestly, that man had an unusually fine palate for a person raised without the niceties in life. Another pang of regret traveled the nerves of her arms and settled in her hands, made the bones ache, as if she struggled to hang on to something that tugged hard to get loose. She shook her hand like it had fallen asleep, and ignored Vera's inquiring gaze. Again, she had to wonder, who was her friend and who her enemy: Graver? Chance? Frank Higgs? Drum? Her boys? Judge Foote? Larson Dye? No, she didn't think the other ranchers were deeper into this than she was. Drum had shown the same shock. Cullen, well, he was an angry child, but surely, he was open about what he was doing. Hayward was much too young. Chance had admitted what he was doing. The ranch was big enough that all kinds of people could be wandering around unless one of the men came across them by accident. What about the men, now that J.B. was gone? Were they loyal? Drum's men? He was so hated, maybe one of them. She'd have to conjure a way to question Drum. She recognized that her worst enemy had to become an ally for the time being. But was he using the Eastmans to get his hands on her ranch? Maybe there was no threat, maybe she should just sell the damn ranch and move away. Drum would be furious. Someone was the betrayer, and she intended to find out who, and then they would discover her true nature, the one people kept underestimating.

CHAPTER THIRTY-THREE

It was early the next morning when Rose met Dulcinea in the kitchen. They eyed each other after a night troubled by dreams, muffled voices, and creaking saddles. The sun was nearly up, yet Vera was nowhere to be found. Rose quickly set about making coffee and frying bacon while Lily set the table. It wasn't until after breakfast that they found a moment to sit.

"We're not any closer to finding the killer, are we?" Dulcinea asked.

Rose turned the cup in her hands, tilted the coffee up one side, then the other until it was on the verge of spilling. Setting it down, she placed both hands flat on the table.

"Last night, while I was *serving* your guests" — she paused, showing her irritation — "this locket slipped out of my blouse." She pulled the chain over the neck of her dress and cradled the locket in her palm. "Hayward couldn't take his eyes off it."

Dulcinea frowned.

"Later, after the dishes, he tried to stop and talk to me, but Lily and I slipped away."

"What do you think he wanted?" Dulcinea's tone was flat.

Rose shrugged and opened the locket, revealing two faces. Dulcinea bent to examine it, then sat back stunned. Rose thought the man looked like a younger version of Drum. The woman was a stranger.

"You think my son's involved, that he killed his own father?"

Rose glanced away as she tucked the locket back in her dress, and the women sat there considering the implications. "Could be the boys. Or Drum."

Rose thought back to how Jerome had found Star's body. When he was a boy he could see the ghost herd that ran alongside their Indian ponies, all the animals slain in battle galloping stride for stride with the few half-starved animals left. When he described his vision, the tribe named him Some Horses, because he saw this world and the other, as Yellow Leg, an elder, promised years ago. Now, the ghost horses led him to find the missing. That night he let their horse loose and followed for hours until it led them to Star's body.

Last night she saw her husband watch from the barn as Vera slipped out of bed to meet someone and the oldest son rode off to town. A while later the youngest slipped out of the house, past his grandfather dozing on the porch, and followed his brother. Then the judge came down and sat with the elder on the porch talking for a long time. Jerome said three ghosts lingered around the men. J. B. Bennett, who never left the house, an Indian woman — a Mandan in traditional dress who stayed closest to the old man — and a limping white man in tattered clothes he didn't recognize. That was the angry one.

Sometimes she wondered if he imagined the spirits, as he did when he drank liquor and told people what they wanted to hear. "My name," he said, "means I was a rich chief until we lost the war. I had many wives," he lied, "and now only this poor one." He shook his head in mock grief and she wanted to knock his brains in and cure his hide with them. "Is this not the dress of a warrior chief?" He pulled on the headdress he bought at the trading post pawn in Rushville for two buffalo skulls, a cavalry saddle with a rusty iron seat and rotted leather, and a broken U.S. Cavalry pistol he found in the hills, and stood, sweeping his arms dramatically along his sides to show off the beaded, fringed white deerskin leggings and arm cuffs he'd won in a cutthroat game of stones last powwow. The bone and brass breastplate was actually given to Rose by her mother when her father died, and was older than any of them. The spear was a piece of crooked cottonwood tied with red felt, trade beads, and rotted deerskin. The stone point wouldn't scratch a dog, it was so clumsily shaped and blunt, but the whites didn't notice these details when they asked for the postcard or to take his picture. On good days he charged a nickel, on bad days he made them buy him a drink. He was a good man, better than most, and if she saw all those ghosts standing around she'd need a strong drink to blind her, too. It was hard enough with Star's tiny teeth chewing her flesh from the inside out. Rose had to send her spirit home before it ate their whole world.

Was it the locket that lured him to her, as he was now drawn to Rose? Before she died, Star told her she had set a trap for their mother's killer, and was selling him handmade goods. Rose told her to wait for Some Horses and their cousins before she went to meet him. Star said she would, then didn't.

The boys were too young to be part of the massacre, though, so Star must have arranged to meet an older man. This story was like a snake eating its own tail. Every time she thought she'd found the end, it led her back to the beginning. Tears filled her eyes.

Dulcinea placed her hand over Rose's. "I'm so sorry."

Rose shook her head and wiped her eyes with her arm.

"It comes down to three possibilities as far as I can see." Dulcinea stood and brought the coffeepot to the table and poured a splash in each cup. "Drum, Graver, or Chance." Rose picked a cold biscuit from the platter, broke it open, and covered it with Vera's mulberry jam. "Not my husband." She stole a glance at Rose. "And not my boys." She set the pot down on the table.

Rose shook her head. She knew Dulcinea would never consider her sons capable of murder, but on her own list she placed them pretty high. After last night, Hayward was at the top and maybe Cullen, too, despite their age. Drum Bennett she didn't know about.

"Maybe there's more than one killer," Rose said.

Dulcinea chewed thoughtfully and sipped her coffee. Her hands shook, and she steadied them on the table.

Higgs burst through the door, looked wildly around the kitchen and parlor. "Where is she? She's here, isn't she? You hiding her?" He spun and Graver, who followed, grabbed his arm to stop him. "She's not here!" His words almost an accusation. The two women looked at each other. Vera was gone.

"I'll go and look for her," Graver said. "Should I take anyone?"

"The Indian," Higgs said. Then his shoulders slumped and he remembered his hat, pulled it off his head, and held it in his hands as if he stood beside a gravesite. Dulcinea was about to offer him coffee and breakfast, half out of her chair when Rose put a hand on her arm to stop her.

"She's gone. Black Bill, too. They run off together," Rose said. Higgs ran a trembling hand up his forehead and the bald dome of his head.

"She hasn't been herself, I could see that, I knew she was unhappy." He glanced at the women at the table as if suddenly aware they listened. Without another word, he set his hat on his head, turned, and left.

"Do you think this has anything to do

with . . ." Dulcinea asked.

Rose thought for a moment, then shook her head. "Vera loved your husband like a brother."

"Why did she leave, then?"

Rose looked out the window and didn't answer.

Chance came down the stairs carrying his bag. He tipped his hat at Dulcinea and ignored Rose. His handsome face appeared hollow this morning with dark circles around his eyes as if he had not slept. A pallor like dusty fog clung to his skin. He had shaved, badly, nicking his chin and missing the dark stubble patches on his throat.

"Did you know about this business with the Eastmans?" Dulcinea asked, her voice harsh.

He gazed at her, rolled his lower lip under his teeth, looked at Rose, and then shook his head. "Last night's the first I heard of it."

"How can that be? You told me you were looking at my land, you must have someone who's paying you."

Rose wanted to add that he was too busy living off the fat of the land and pretending to prospect to do much work for anybody, but stopped herself.

"I haven't been in my office much of late. Miss Eastman arrived while I was out of town." He raised his brow. "Maybe Cullen can provide the information you seek." Rose could tell he was a person unused to questioning, especially from a female.

Dulcinea squared her shoulders. "Do we have a conflict of interest?" She poured herself more coffee without offering him any.

He looked startled, shook his head quickly, and tried to hide the anger in his eyes. "No, I'm working to gain clear title to the ranch for you. I told you I was looking for oil and gas. This new business with the Eastmans — are you wanting me to represent you in that, too?"

She paused, sipped her coffee without taking her eyes off him. "How can it be clear title if the rights are subverted? What led Cullen to imagine he could sell those, I wonder?"

He held up a hand, set down his bag, and stepped toward the table. "Mind if I sit and have a cup of coffee with you?"

She hesitated before giving a quick nod. Rose stood, took a dirty cup from the pile in the sink, placed it before him, and let him pour his own. He lifted a hand to reach for the sugar, glanced at Dulcinea, then

486

picked up the bowl. He looked around for a spoon, gave up, poured it in, and stirred with his finger. His eyes searched the table for the cream pitcher, but Rose had already put it away and made no move to retrieve it.

He drank from the cup, grimaced, and set it down. "In the matter of —"

Dulcinea jumped up. "Oh, stop it! I'll go to town today and contact my people in Chicago to discover the meaning of all this. I don't know who you think you're dealing with, Mr. Chance, but I am not the fool you have been taking me for!"

She gathered her skirts and marched to the stairs, where she stopped and turned again, saying, "Good day, sir." And then flew up the stairs to change into her riding costume.

Rose wondered how she could escape the lawyer, who always found an excuse to linger at the ranch. In some ways he reminded her of Crockett from the telegraph office. Lily skipped in and tugged on her skirt. Behind her three kittens followed, tails stiff as tiny lodge poles as they crossed the porch into the house to tumble at the child's feet. When Rose knelt to pet them, Lily whispered, "Mama, Mr. Higgs says his wife is gone, and Black Bill's with her. Mr. Higgs is so upset he wants to hurt someone, he says. Mr. Graver says don't act too quick, he'll find them." Lily gazed into her eyes, and her chin quivered. Rose gathered her in her arms and rocked her, crooning. She might be small, but she had to live among people who were not her own, and must learn vigilance, and how to guard herself by finding the secrets they carried. She felt the lawyer's eyes follow her every move.

"I'm leaving then." Chance stepped onto the porch. Rose kept her eyes on his tall black boots, their heels and soles worn to the thickness of a cottonwood leaf. He pulled a small leather pouch from his pocket and shook it. The sound of jingling coins caught Lily's attention. He loosened the drawstring and let a coin slip into his palm, then held it up to catch the light. Lily started to reach for it, but Rose drew her hand down with a shake of her head. The lawyer shrugged and slid the coin back in the pouch. With a tip of his hat, he left. Rose watched him all the way to his horse, already tied at the gate by one of the hands, who must have felt as she did about the man who never went home.

She held Lily on her lap as she nuzzled the gray kitten against her cheek, and was reminded of her sister. They were separated when Star was four years old by the priests who took Rose away to train as a servant at the mission school, but she had always kept Star close in her thoughts, especially after their mother was killed. She rarely thought about their father, who drank until he died on the road to Rosebud one winter night and wasn't found until spring melted the snow, revealing him on his back, one arm flung out in sleep, the other clutching the whiskey bottle he favored. His face gnawed some, the rest of him untouched, too old and sinewy, too pickled, people laughed, maybe he was onto something there. Ever know a drunk to get a mosquito bite?

As was the nature of her people, it was a good joke that grew until it was said that he'd died a happy death, smiling. Since his nose and cheeks were gnawed off, Rose didn't know how they could say that. She was still at school, almost trained, the whites said, enough for a dumb one, though what good it would do to write and read English and do sums when she would be scrubbing floors, washing dishes, and calling white people mister and missus, she couldn't say. They wouldn't let her go home for the funeral. Then her mother insisted she take the first job offered with the telegraph man because of the upheaval on the reservation.

After their mother was killed, Star was taken in by their aunt to live with her white husband and sprawling family on their rundown ranch. The white man was an indifferent rancher and left all the work to her cousins and other distant relatives, who knew enough to keep horses and cattle from starving and freezing, even if they couldn't hang on to their allotment of land. At least people wanted Star. After Rose left Crockett and the telegraph office, she fled to Pine Ridge with Dulcinea and stayed with those same relatives until she met Jerome Some Horses, who was already a man with a vision and a horse and a shack, where he lived with his grandmother.

Last spring, as they made their way north, through Babylon for a few supplies, and out to the Buffalo Grounds to set up summer camp, they met her mother's cousin, Byron. He shared a beer with Some Horses, and Rose gave him a bowl of rabbit stew, a poor meal, but it was a hard winter and the animals wore only thick coats over their bones. A few days before, Byron was drinking in town with the white man, Conway, married to her aunt, when Conway complained that Star was worse than useless, as he put it, and to top it all off, she'd run away. He suspected she'd gone to Rapid

City or even as far as Omaha to lift her skirts and earn her keep. Byron hit the man and was promptly beaten, then thrown in jail, but the sheriff released him two days later when a white boy charged with murdering his grandmother refused to share a cell with an Indian. Byron's long, pox-scarred face was still bruised and lumpy from the beating as he gummed the thin stew and swallowed.

Conway bothered Star, he said, and she had found two white boys to take her away. She trusted too much. Rose had tried to warn her, but it was already too late. She wondered which white boy it was, of the two of them, Cullen or Hayward. Which the lover and which the jealous one?

CHAPTER THIRTY-FOUR

Soon as Cullen stopped the rank dun horse in front of Drum's house, it was clear nobody had worked in the week since that stupid dinner. Cullen had spent the five days following in town with the Eastman woman trying to convince her not to return to Denver. This was the thanks for all his hard work. Geese and chickens wandered the porch, crapping everywhere. The old sow had rooted her way out of the pen and sprawled in his vegetable garden, wallowing in the mudhole she'd dug by butting the loose pipe he'd rigged for watering. She'd used her huge snout to plunder the lettuce and carrots, and the seedling tomato plants were tipped on their sides. When he rode closer, he saw wriggling around her and realized she'd given birth and was squashing half the babies. He climbed down, tied the horse to the rail, and ran into the garden to scare her up. She gazed at him with a lazy half-open eye, snorted, and flopped her head down on one of the babies. There were almost too many to count, and they mewled like newborn kittens. The sow snored.

He kicked her, but she couldn't feel it, so he got his rope, noosed it around her thick neck, and pulled. She had to weigh three hundred pounds. He tied it around her front legs, too, and wrapped the end around the saddle horn and made the dun back up, which it did like it'd been a cow pony its whole worthless life. It must hate that pig as much as I do, Cullen thought. He had a time stopping the horse, and they about pulled off the sow's hide. Once he untied the rope, she clambered to her feet, baby pigs crying and wobbling around her. The ones he'd thought she killed were up and at 'em, too. Still, he didn't want her killing the rest of his garden, so he looped the rope around her middle and drove her back to her dry pen, which would have plenty of mud once he refilled the water trough with its rusty bottom flaking in the heat.

"Those sons of bitches." Cullen cursed steady and low as he turned on the windmill and hand pumped the water. Soon as it was going good, he took up the boards and tied and nailed the pen back into some kind of shape, knowing it was hopeless if she decided to push her three hundred pounds of lard against it. She was down again, this time letting the babies nurse, packed in two layers lined up at her teats. Wouldn't you know it, he thought, there was an extra one, number thirteen, smallest, already runty-looking, and when it whimpered, sounded so damn pathetic, Cullen reached down and picked it up, snotty nose and all, and slipped it inside his shirt while he went to find some grain for the sow. The barn was a wreck inside. Drum would have a fit when he saw how the men had slung saddles, halters, blankets, pitchforks, and shovels every which way. Manure in the stalls looked a month old, and the grain was down to a sack the mice had started working on. When he grabbed a canful, corn slipped out the hole in the bottom. Then he realized the milk cow was missing. Lazy bastards must've turned her loose and let her dry up or stole her. How was he gonna feed the runt that squirmed and mewled against his stomach?

He poured the corn on the ground in front of the sow's snout so she could eat and feed the youngsters at the same time. There were no horses waiting for the noon change in the corral either. It was like the hands left the sow, geese, and chickens in charge. The cattle would be grazing the river pasture this time of year. Only trouble they'd be having was deerfly, mosquitoes, blackleg, pink eye, and other assorted diseases, with the rare snakebite and broken leg thrown in. He would have to ride out and check on the herd.

"I told you," he muttered. "I told you this would happen." He led the dun back to the house and tied him to the rail again. The horse heaved a sigh. Cullen loosened the girth and the animal only halfheartedly snapped his teeth.

"You never listen. Think you're God on earth, and now look at this mess we're in. Men gone. Place can't run itself. Animals every which way. I don't even want to know what the cattle are doing out there."

The door was ajar and he wasn't surprised by the wreckage within. They'd gone through, looking for what they could steal since they didn't dare ask for quitting wages. Drum was known to make a man fight him or Cullen for those. He couldn't go light either, or Drum would be next in line with his fists. Cullen didn't blame the men as he picked up the cans stripped of labels, a childish meanness, and righted the chairs around the table. They'd smashed Drum's big wooden chair with the arms that made it look like a crude throne. He grabbed the kindling it'd become. "This took some doing," he said, but the men had enough history here that they would spend the time. A nice breeze blew in the broken window, which accounted for the thick dust that coated all in sight. The stovepipe was askew. He reattached it, stuffed in the chair pieces, and lit the fire. The small saucepan was on the floor under the stove and rocked now with a big dent in its bottom. He picked up the cans and shook them to figure out which might hold evaporated milk. It took him several tries with his knife blade pounded into the top to find it. The others were canned peaches and pears and beans and corn. He figured he'd eat some and give the rest to the sow.

When the milk was heated, he fished one of Drum's leather work gloves from the pile in the wooden window seat the men hadn't discovered. There was also an extra rifle, an old Colt Peacemaker, several boxes of shells, a hatchet, and a bowie knife, the blade rimed with rust. He'd take those when he went after the hands, who wouldn't have made it much farther than town. Spending what they stole on liquor and those worn-out girls at Reddy's.

Meanwhile, he poured the warm milk into

Drum's glove, cut a hole in a finger, and held it to the runt's mouth. At first it squirmed and fretted until he squeezed out a bit of milk, smeared its lips, and stuck his finger in its mouth to get it to suck, then replaced his hand with the glove and it nursed so hard it had to stop, gulp and gasp for air, then went back, slower and more steady until its eyes drifted shut and its belly was a hard pink ball, and the milk dribbled down its chest onto Cullen's shirt. They sat for a bit, the sun warming the room, the pig pressed into his chest, its breath a steady little whistle against his shirt, and it seemed that maybe this was the best of times: without Drum, without the other men, without his mother and brother, just him and the animals and the Sand Hills breeze bearing the scent of tall fresh bluestem and wildflowers, sweet and green against the dust and greasy odor of bad food and old grudges. He pictured his mother's big gray stallion out in the corral, his sleek body dancing lightly around the pen, waiting for Cullen. He dozed for a few minutes, an unheard-of thing to do, until the dun snorted and stamped its feet, and gave a high questioning whinny, like he worried he was the last horse on earth.

Cullen carefully cradled the pig, laid it in

Drum's overstuffed chair by the hay-twist stove, and looked through the rest of the house, which didn't take but a minute. Drum's room was in pieces, literally, every bit of paper or cloth shredded with a special hatred. The room he used to sleep in was tossed around some but there was never anything worth having in it. He found an old shirt his mother sent him a few years ago wadded under the mattress where he had left it an hour after it arrived. Green silk. Hard to even guess what was in her mind that day. Buttoned up with sleeves tied together, it made a fine pouch to carry the pig.

As mad as he was, it didn't take him any time at all to make it to town. The pig rode peaceful until they slowed to a walk and stopped in front of Haven Smith's store. A couple of people walking by stopped and stared at the green silk bundle slung around his neck. He tipped his hat and they moved on. He didn't have a good reputation.

Haven Smith scooted out from behind the counter to head him off soon as he came through the door. He waved him away and headed for the canned milk and baby bottles.

"What ya got there, Cullen?" Pearl Stryker

swayed down the aisle and stopped so close he could smell the stale beer and sex on her. From the smeared lip color and black rubbed around her eyes, it was easy to see she'd come from work. She leaned in and pulled the silk off the small pink face. "Ooh, looks just like his daddy."

"You should know," Cullen said with a grin. She batted his arm hard enough that he felt it and smirked. Contrary to town gossip, he'd never been with Pearl or her sister. No reason not to, but that seemed reason enough.

"Give me a chance," she said and leaned over slightly and lifted her breasts from beneath so they bulged out of the low neck of the evening gown she wore even though it was noon. They were nice breasts, lightly freckled and soft-looking, made a person imagine the strawberry-red nipples almost visible at the edge of the heavy pink satin brocade.

"Have to work too hard for my money, Pearl."

She dipped her fingers in the top of her dress and nudged out a nipple. His breath caught. It wasn't strawberry red until she pinched it hard and giggled softly. "So do I."

The pig squirmed and nuzzled against

him and he noticed her nipple was chapped and leathery, like it'd been sucked too long. I know you do, he thought. She saw the shift in him and tucked it away, turned, marched down the aisle and out the door with Haven Smith running and yelling after her to pay for the bottle of medicine she'd taken.

As Cullen brought his purchases to the counter, Stubs hobbled in, spotted him right off, and hop-stepped toward him, one boot heel landing harder than the other on the wood floor. "Came to town to find ya," he panted, bracing himself against the counter and leaning over to cough. Least he didn't stink of liquor and whores. Maybe there was hope somewhere in this mess.

Then he caught sight of the pig poking its snout out of the sling.

"I knew it! Damn sow littered soon as I left yesterday, I bet. Any others make it?"

"Thirteen by my count. I moved them back to their pen, tied it up best I could, but it'll need rebuilding. What the hell's been going on out there?"

Stubs shook his head and toed the black crack between two unfinished pine floorboards. He removed his hat and rubbed the back of his head, working his way to the front, dry skin flaking as he went. "It was Carter and that Russian fella, Sergei,

500

claimed his cousin was a famous writer beheaded by the tsar or some such story? They sorta stopped working in dribs and drabs and the others seen so they did, too, until I couldn't get a one of them off their pockets to do a damn thing. I tried to tell them Drum would be home any day and they laughed, said he was too crippled to cause any trouble and you was out of the way, too." Stubs resettled his hat and spit on the floor, rubbed it in with the toe of his boot. "Yesterday they locked me in the feed room and ran through the house and took off with some horses. Tracked them here, spending Drum's money and making fools of themselves. Figured you'd show up sooner or later and we'd settle it with them."

Stubs's face was anchored with dark hollows under his eyes and deep creases in his cheeks. A slit from his upper lip to his chin had healed odd and puckered his mouth like he was drinking vinegar. He watched the boy with an expectant look in his eyes, as if he hadn't had enough fighting and killing in the War Between the States.

Cullen didn't want to ask, but he did. "What is it you think we should do?"

Haven Smith's quick steps interrupted them as he slid behind the counter, glanced at the pig, opened his mouth to protest, then closed it and toted up the prices of the milk, baby bottles, and the new shirt Cullen added to the pile.

Stubs raised his brows and nodded in the direction of the guns and ammunition. When Cullen shook his head, Smith waited to see if he produced some real money, then sighed and hauled out the red leather accounts book and opened it to their page. He tapped a finger on the bottom amount, started to say something, shook his head, and wrote the new amounts.

"Soon as he's on his feet," Cullen said.

"I didn't bring extra bullets," Stubs said in a low voice as the boy turned to leave.

"What is it you think we're doing?" Cullen asked once they were out of hearing. Smith had a big mouth and the boy didn't want that new peace officer leaving some poor soul in the dental chair to come and arrest them.

Stubs stopped outside the doorway and stared at him in disbelief. "What Drum would do, boy, what any right-thinking man would do."

"You want me to shoot those men dead?" The pig wriggled and tried to lunge out of the sling. Cullen set it down on the boardwalk where it promptly squatted and let loose, the stink enough to turn their faces.

The pig shook itself, wobbled a few steps, squatted again and scooted its butt, then tried a few more wobbly steps. Stubs and Cullen followed it down the walk, away from the mess they'd left for Haven.

"I get your point," Stubs finally said. "But we could take back the horses, ones wearing our brand, and get the dentist to arrest them for stealing." The excitement was in his eyes again.

"You have a list of what they took?" Cullen bent and picked up the pig, which seemed ready for another feed and nap, so he settled on the bench in front of Stillhart's Bank and broke out the supplies.

Stubs chewed his skewed lower lip with his stained brown front snaggletooth. "Got me there. What about the horses then?"

He nodded. "And the milk cow? What the hell did they do with her?" He held the bottle to the pig's lips. It grabbed the rubber nipple and sucked.

Stubs sat down beside them, ignoring, as the boy did, the stares of folks walking by. "You know, I can't rightly say. One morning I go out to milk her and she's gone. Guess that's enough to shoot a man over, ain't it? Cattle rustling."

Stubs was disturbing the peace and quiet Cullen had come to earlier. Why couldn't a person be left alone with his thoughts? Now he could feel needles starting in his head, striking his skull like tiny bursts of heat lightning, making the world go away a little, like he heard through a dense fog or wall of water, and he knew he was going to do something bad.

So there it was. He went back inside and added shells to the accounts book, for the Peacemaker he'd stuck in his saddlebag, and for the new shotgun Stubs insisted on, though it made the hair on his neck prickle with foregone conclusion. Oh, you would, a voice in his head mocked. He felt the suckling pig in the green silk cradled against his chest, warmer than the day's heat, the soft snoring contentment warring against the lightness that ballooned in his chest now that he was shoving shells in the revolver and breaking open the shotgun, careful not to nudge the baby awake.

You often see how things will go, he thought, and you are helpless to their untwining from your own desire. The flies buzzed on the pig shit tracked down the boards of the walk, tainting a town woman's long yellow skirt hem with a brown stain she wouldn't discover for minutes now, perhaps an hour, and would it be before or after the day went fatal? Already they walked on the plane of someone else's tragedy, and the details of the moment suffocated him: The brown dog with the long hair and limp, one ear cropped and cockeyed, lifting a leg against the wheel of a runabout from which stepped Percival Chance. The quarrelsomeness of the sparrows in the cornices of the hotel across the street as the judge and Drum and Rivers entered with the oil and gas woman, Markie Eastman. The politeness that flourished between them didn't bode well for Cullen. They would conduct business over a white tablecloth with wine in glasses and heavy silverware, tolling the boy's future against the china plates as they shared a meal too heavy for the heat of the day.

Somewhere above them in his room sat Mr. Eastman, who let his daughter's charms do the business he was too old or ill or negligent to conduct, and his coughing, which the boy could hear as he stood so completely in this moment, the guns heavy in his hands, pulling him to the earth, and others to follow in this small space of time, losing time breath by breath by breath.

It was as if he could peer into the small houses and shacks behind Main Street and see the lives lived into the future. There was Black Bill at Vera's side, packing for the journey to her family, finally right again in her preacher father's eyes. Frank would not know this until he received her letter, and he would never be the same, a man broken into pieces by the weight of a single piece of paper.

The boy was put to mind of all the lives around him, and how they toiled, until there was such an accumulation, they were knocked apart for simply being present.

The Peacemaker was heavier than he was used to, for he had never killed a man, not even shot at one. He lifted the silk cradle from his neck and looped it over the saddle horn, ignoring the dun's flat-eyed expression. The horse sank his shoulder away from the imaginary weight and warmth of the pig's body — and it struck the boy that none of us wanted to shoulder the life of another. Then the horse snorted and straightened, and relaxed hipshot where he was tied and commenced dozing, eyelids sinking, as close to benign as he'd ever been, hide rumpled with dried sweat, tail burr clumped, mud and ticks twisting his mane in a wild apotheosis; he was finally at peace. The boy almost reached out and patted him, but stopped so the horse's world would remain inviolate, circumscribed by its nature. There could be no breach. That was their fate, Cullen thought. Theirs and mine. So you're suddenly a man of words, the voice in his head mocked. No, that's the last of them, he answered, taking one final look around. He tipped his hat at the old men sitting in chairs along the hotel porch, glanced at Stubs, who bared his long yellow teeth, and waited like a shadow to walk into their time.

It took three places to find them, Sergei the Russian, Carter, Faro Jack, and Dance Smith, all laid out drunk and naked at Reddy's Shack, put up after the storm, where the girls now worked. Cullen stopped at the other bars, half hoping they'd gone, that he'd have time to consider whether to chase them or not, or hell, that they went back to the ranch to sleep it off. When he pushed open the door, there was a scurrying like mice when you go into a dark barn of a sudden. The first girl in her "room," divided off from the others by blankets, grabbed fistfuls of filthy sheet to hide, and gave them a dirty look and opened her mouth to protest until she noticed the gun swinging upward. He couldn't say he wanted to shoot them, but now that the blood rose in his head, the black howl, he couldn't say he wouldn't. It was Stubs pushed down the barrel of the shotgun and growled, "Wait a minute."

The man opened his eyes, took a moment to recognize them, and scrambled for clothes or guns or whatever, it made no never mind. The shotgun rose and there was a noise as it went off, splattering Sergei the Russian's head against the ample breasts of the whore, who howled as the buckshot punched holes in her arms. A tinny sound said, "Stop, damn it, stop!" as the boy let loose the second barrel. The left side of the Russian's face disappeared and the whore went quiet. A man crawled behind Cullen, who turned, took aim at the naked back, and this time used the Peacemaker. The body collapsed with a shiver on the bloody floor. He nudged it with the toe of his boot, and the sight of Carter's familiar weak chin and beak nose bent to one side evoked nothing. When the man opened his eyes, Cullen shot him in the face.

"That's enough." Stubs put his hand on his arm, not the one holding the pistol, and Cullen wondered where his shotgun had gone. He slipped on the bloody floor and Stubs held him up. "Them others is hiding back there. Let them go."

He looked at Stubs, who now seemed lost, tears in his eyes as if he hadn't urged this war, brought him to fight it. Cullen shook his head, let himself ride the clear even tide as he tore down the blanket and prepared to squeeze the trigger on a bed holding two young whores, naked bodies pressed together as if made whole, whimpering, then shook his head again and lowered the gun.

This was not what he meant — and then he heard a terrific roar and the room was suddenly red and black and he was on his back, watching the flies bump the low pine ceiling as the flood rose quickly up his legs, spread into his chest, filling him so he could not catch his breath to ask the man leaning over him, rifle barrel pressed to his throat, who would ride his mother's horse now?

Chapter Thirty-Five

Markie Eastman stood and smiled at the table of men she had just convinced to sell their mineral and subsurface rights when a ragged boy ran into the dining room and yelled, "Shootin' at Reddy's place!"

Judge Foote, Harney Rivers, and Percival Chance stood as Drum Bennett leaned back and drained the remaining inch in his brandy glass. He knew the Eastman woman was prepared to pay more, but the other men were greedy and couldn't wait. He hated doing business when others gummed it up.

"Aren't you coming?" the judge asked.

"None of my dogs in that fight." Drum reached for one of the cigars the lawyer had passed around so freely before they were interrupted. Rivers hesitated, glanced between the judge and Miss Eastman while Chance strode away.

"Go on," Drum urged. "Might meet a

man needful of your services." He laughed and twirled the cigar in his fingers. He shook his head. First he thought Dulcinea was going behind his back, now he had to figure out how to convince her to sign over those rights so he could make his deal and drive her out of the hills again. He and Rivers had lied about the deal, and he was thankful that damn grandson of his hadn't shown up to cause more trouble. Far as he knew Cullen was out in the hills running horses to pieces and tending cows like he was supposed to be doing. He'd make a decent hand he ever grew past those notions of his.

As he smoked he noticed the dining room had cleared, and he heard shouting in the street and voices like a crowd gathered. Maybe somebody got themselves killed, he thought, maybe it was their lucky day. He grimaced as his leg and arm picked up the staccato of the street voices with a steady jabbing ache in the healing bones, despite the whiskey he'd used to numb the pain. Must be weather moving in. Now he was going to be one of those old farts who sat around complaining and prognosticating, like that damn Stubs with his war wounds.

He gazed at the empty room, the tables covered in stained white cloths that'd seen too many days of service, the fireplace along the far wall with the pale green marble columns and mantel, over which hung a big oil painting of Indians chasing down buffalo. He never understood why people made such a thing of the past, as if white men hadn't come in and killed the buffalo and as many Indians as they could so they could take the land. It was warfare, and a person didn't sit around feeling sorry about all those Southern boys got themselves killed protecting a bunch of rich sons of bitches wanted their Negroes waiting on them, did they? Better to hang a painting of men working cattle. He'd mention that to Riley, the hotel owner, soon as he got the chance. He stretched his legs and stared at the dingy ceiling with its sooty plaster roses clustered in the center.

"Drum Bennett here?" someone yelled into the lobby, followed by the irregular thumping of Stubs, hobbling toward the table.

Drum looked up, ready to bless him out, but stopped once he saw the man's face, blood-smeared hands, and shirt. Suddenly he couldn't catch his breath, and his heart bumped hard enough to hurt.

Stubs shook his head and licked his cracked lips. "It's Cullen."

■ ■ ■ ■

It was to Dance Smith's credit he didn't pull the trigger that would have ruined Cullen's face. The thought circled Drum's mind during the long journey in the shambling livery stable wagon. A ruined ragbag of a man drove the spavined, broken-wind, rack-of-bones horses at a maddening walk or a shambling trot that almost bounced them out of the bed. Drum held his grandson's body in his arms and braced his own against the splintered side that creaked ominously at every hole the wheels found. And that was the other thought that circled Drum's mind, as relentless and stark as the rolling hills of grass, without relief of tree or rock or body. He wondered that he had ever loved this land. First his son, now his second son, his grandson who was to carry the Bennett name into the future, his legacy, but that wasn't a thought he allowed himself to entertain as the flies found the dried blood on Cullen's shirt, and overhead, the turkey vultures circled in a relentless arc, lowering themselves as they followed the wagon's poor progress.

Behind the wagon Stubs followed, leading the dun with the sobbing pig still tied to the saddle in its green silk sling, and Drum's horse. He wouldn't allow Stubs to ride in the wagon bed with Cullen. The old warrior had done enough. Since Cullen was dead, the dentist-sheriff had arrested Dance and Faro Jack, but Drum didn't care. It was too late. The men would be set loose tonight and told to leave town. It was good Dance hadn't pulled the trigger and blown his grandson's face to pieces, Drum thought. At least he could give his mother that comfort.

When they neared the ranch, Stubs rode ahead while the team increased their impossible gait to one that jerked the wagon so hard Drum grabbed the side and trapped Cullen's body with his own legs to keep him. It was strange how light the boy had become. In Drum's experience bodies grew heavier, heavy as stone, but Cullen was light, almost as if he were made of straw or feathers, while Drum's legs and arms must have weighed a hundred pounds apiece.

"It's for your own good," he murmured. "It always was, every last lick of it, son." He tested the sound of the word, *son,* found it foreign and hollow, his tongue too thick to shape it. As the wagon began its bone-cracking descent to the ranch house, Drum and Cullen were shoved against the broken seat back, and a splintered board gouged Drum's shoulder but he didn't move. Hair fell over the boy's eyes. Drum brushed it back and it flopped back down, and he remembered how mad he would get when the boy slunk around with his hair covering his face. There was nothing for it, he discovered, the hair had a will of its own, and he was thankful again Dance hadn't pulled that trigger. As the horses slowed to a plodding walk up the road to the ranch house, the cattle and horses raised their heads to stare at the spectacle. Drum knew he should hate Dance, want his heart carved out in old vengeance, but the truth was Cullen started it, he was always headed here, and nothing Drum could argue made things any different.

Dulcinea stood at the gate, clutching the posts as if to launch at him, while Hayward waited in the barnyard, legs slightly apart, hands resting on the butts of his pistols. Apparently someone from town had ridden out to break the news, and Drum was oddly relieved. Higgs took charge of the horses, and Graver came around to the wagon bed and lifted the boy out as if he were a child merely gone to sleep, leaving Drum to half drag himself to the tailgate and ease his legs to the ground. When they wouldn't hold him, he had to hang on to the wagon. Dulcinea lifted a hand to touch her son; Graver shook his head and carried him to the house, mounted the steps easily and entered without having to adjust his burden. Hayward stood his ground, continued to stare at his grandfather as if he intended to cause a ruckus. Drum dropped his eyes, found the steadiness in his legs and began the long trudge to the house. Higgs clucked to the horses and led them to the barn. The old driver didn't move, as if he were permanently fastened to the bench and bound to bring only the ill winds of poor fortune.

Inside the house the silence was so heavy it seemed to have always been there, resting in dusty vigilance against the windowsills and chairs, sparing nothing. Graver took Dulcinea by the shoulders and turned her away from the body laid on the table while Rose pulled the blood-stiffened shirt from the trousers. The buttons were sealed to their holes with blood and Graver sliced off the shirt with a knife, the sound of the material tearing like a saw across Drum's teeth as Dulcinea flinched. It should not be strangers who did these things, but he couldn't move as the bare chest with pale down between his breasts was revealed. When Graver peeled away the shirt, it stuck to the skin and the dark holes of the wounds seemed too small. He might still be alive — Drum stopped the thought and nearly reached out to Dulcinea, who started and took half a step forward before collapsing, arms wrapped around her body, silent but for her ragged breath.

They removed his pants and his worn undergarments and his patched boots and holey socks, revealing the toes bent and rubbed with calluses, and the shame rose inside like bitter bile to choke him. He could not catch his breath or swallow, it seared his lungs and burned his throat. Every scar, every untended wound, every bruise belonged to him. Dulcinea caught her breath and stared at him, her eyes full of dead reckoning, words over the contended boy unnecessary now.

Rose handed Dulcinea a pail of hot soapy water and she began to swab Cullen's body with long, tender strokes of a rag. She washed his hair, rinsed and toweled it carefully so it spread like a shiny brown shawl around his head. She patted his face clean, the blue shadows under his eyes, the slack muscles of his jaw, the cracked lips that had finally released their reckless sneer. Drum noticed how the sun had bleached the eyebrows and lashes to a gold-white against the deep tan of his face, and how there was a white line across his forehead from the hat that rested just so. He noticed the nose slightly off center from breaking. The white welt of a scar at the corner of his eye. Dulcinea's hands paused at the ear, stroked the lobe as if trying to remove some stubborn stain, until Graver touched her arm. She shook him off this time, took a deep breath, looked toward the door at her other son, and said, "Hayward, go and find clothing for your brother."

The sound of her voice startled the silence awake and Drum could hear Stubs shouting at someone outside and Higgs arguing and hoofbeats as someone else galloped into the barnyard. He was tempted not to move, but knew he would at the same moment he had the thought. Outside, Stubs and Higgs argued, the two men nearly at blows, though they should know better. Lawyer Chance walked to the house, his lathered horse tied at the gate, and a buggy came down the hill toward the ranch. The neighbors and the curious from town would pile on them now, professing all kinds of sympathy and useless words as if they ever cared one lick for that boy in there, as if they hadn't every one of them wished him the worst there was. Since they missed J.B.'s funeral, they felt they'd earned this one.

The rage stirred in Drum's belly like an old friend, and he opened himself to it. He grabbed Chance's arm, spun him away from the porch, and pushed him back.

"Dulcinea —" the lawyer said.

"Leave her alone," Drum said. "She has family in there."

Chance opened his mouth, gazed at the porch, thought better of it, shrugged, and turned back.

"Stubs, you take care of the lawyer's horse. Higgs, you make coffee. People are coming. We'll put them to your place for now." Drum tried to make his voice ring with the old authority, but his heart had gone out of it. Recognizing the truth, the men avoided his eye as they trudged off to their work. As if the news were carried by express rider across the hills, the cowboys returned early from their work. Hats in hand, Irish Jim and Willie Munday came to the gate, asked Drum what they should do. He sent them to help Higgs set up chairs and planks on sawhorses for the food and drink that would soon arrive.

The buggy pulled up and Judge Foote stepped down and offered a hand to Markie Eastman. Drum felt his belly stir again and it was all he could do not to horsewhip them both off the place, woman be damned. Somehow he felt it was their fault, this business distracted him when he should've been running cattle, his ranch, and that boy. Cullen had no business taking after those men like that, and Drum could only blame himself, and the others around him. He nodded curtly at the judge but wouldn't look at the Eastman woman or acknowledge her words of condolence. He pointed toward Higgs's small home, and with a brief glance at the house behind him, they turned away. They would want to see him, see the wounds, see his face in that final repose. It was a bitter thought. By heaven, he was the only one who cared for that boy all these years, he should be the last one to see his face, not these strangers, not even his mother — but there his thoughts hit a rough place, because he knew he was wrong.

In that moment Drum Bennett had his first real doubt, a luxury he had not afforded himself in years. His grandson had died a man's death, doing a man's job, though he was but half-grown, a job he was made to do because there was no other way. Drum had beaten it into him, and truth be known, if the boy weren't in there lying on the kitchen table, his grandfather would still be beating it into him, one way or the other, and for that, he was, by God, accountable. Drum felt his knees buckle, as if a two-hundred-pound bag of feed dropped on his shoulders, but he wouldn't allow that luxury either. He held the closed gate, blinked away the water in his eyes, and stood his ground, because he could go neither back toward the house, nor forward into the yard where people would want to talk.

The rest of the afternoon and into dark the yard continued to fill with wagons and buggies and horses. After a while, Graver came out of the house and for some reason, Drum yielded and allowed himself to be led inside to sit and wait in the parlor, stiff-backed, eyes cast to the figured carpet at his feet. Dulcinea would not leave Cullen's side, so they brought her a straight-backed chair and placed a glass of water in her hands, which she held like a chalice in her lap as she stared at her son's sleeping face. Drum took in the spectacle and wouldn't look at anyone after that. Hayward stood behind his mother for a while, became restless and began pacing the length of the house, finally expanding to the porch and then the walk, circling like a dog on alert. No one allowed in or out. Where was Graver? Drum looked up quickly and spied him in the barnyard pointing new arrivals to Higgs's place, telling them where to tie their horses, acting like he ran the place. He should go out there himself, but he couldn't move — he'd send Cullen instead, and in that breath, a tide of emptiness rushed in.

He looked over at the boy, willed him to rise, but the only movement was his mother reaching out to brush a fly from his cheek. Although she would not want it, Drum rose and walked into the other room, dragged a straight wooden chair from the wall to the opposite side of the table, and sat down, placing his hand on the boy's arm for the cold comfort of it. Later he would not remember his thoughts that long night, only his refusal of food and drink, and the annoyance at the least disruption of the short time he had left.

At dark someone lit candles around them, which guttered in the heat and filled the air with a greasy stink Drum could barely abide. Around midnight three white moths began battering themselves against the wavering shadows on the wall and hovering so close to the candle flames that they singed and dropped fluttering to the floor, leaving behind a silence all the more profound for being emptied of motion. A fly bumped lazily against the boy's face and staggered away drunkenly whenever Drum lifted his hand, but it was the buzzing that tolled loudly in his ear. He would remember it for the remaining days of his life.

In the morning they buried Cullen in a series of broken, awkward movements with no majesty or grace or meaning, as everything was undertaken with too much haste. The coffin lid didn't quite fit, so they bound it with rope, and the coffin itself was much too long, so the body slid back and forth with unseemly thumps that made it difficult to carry. When they set it in the ground, the hole was too shallow, so they dug deeper while the mourners waited. The body swelled in the heat and released a groan followed by a gagging stench. The grave-diggers, Irish Jim and Willie Munday, opened a snake hole and had to scramble out while Jorge shot the rattlesnakes. Hayward was back to pacing with his hands on his guns like he'd been hired to tame some outlaw boom town in the Black Hills.

Drum never moved a muscle and Graver stood beside Dulcinea, and seemed ready to catch her if she fainted. Drum was so angry he wanted to shoot them all. His hands kept reaching for something, an axe handle, a rifle, a pitchfork. Keep away from my boy! rang in his head as the terrible funeral stretched in an endless series of mistakes. The preacher got Cullen's name wrong, called him Cuthbert, and Drum started forward to beat him to the ground with his fists. Graver touched his arm and he stopped. Dulcinea's face twisted into hysterical laughter she forced down. When they finally lowered the coffin into the hole, it tilted and everyone could hear the body thump one last time against the end of the box and that about broke Drum's mind. A tide of red came over his eyes and he stopped seeing anyone, only the image of his grandson on that table.

The sun was setting in a slash of red-orange and purple when Larabee and Frank Higgs stepped back from filling the hole, wiped the sweat off their faces, and looked toward Higgs's house where the mourners had begun to laugh and talk loudly among heaps of food and drink.

"Think we're done here for now," Higgs said and stepped away without looking at Drum.

"We can bring in more dirt tomorrow," Larabee said. "Put some scrap iron in there to hold it."

"You would, would you!" Drum stood and grabbed the shovel from Larabee. "Get the hell outta here!" He began to drag dirt off

J.B.'s grave and throw it on Cullen's until Higgs sprang to his side and pulled the shovel from his grasp.

"That's enough. We'll see to it in the morning." He was Drum's size and when he looked the older man directly in the eye, it was Drum who dropped his gaze, then collapsed on the ground beside the grave. What he couldn't tell Higgs or anyone was that he had nowhere to go now. There wasn't one damn thing he could do. So he sat there, legs sprawled out before him, hands on his aching knees, and waited.

■ ■ ■ ■

PART FIVE:
PREPARE THE
HEAVENS

■ ■ ■ ■

Chapter Thirty-Six

It was all going to hell on a painted pony, Higgs thought. That son of a bitch Black Bill, he'd trusted him, trusted Vera for that matter. Now the two of them run off together. It was midmorning and nothing worth a wad of spit was happening. Drum still sat under the stunted mulberry in the cemetery where he'd been since they put the boy in the ground a month ago. Rose or Hayward hauled his meals out to him like he was bedridden again. Last week, Larabee and Willie strung up a tarp to cover him from the sun and wet if it ever rained again, then the other night the wind tore it down and Drum didn't lift a finger. Let the old bastard bake, then.

He raised his cup and gulped the rest of the whiskey coffee in one long continuous swallow, slammed it on the table next to his chair, and pushed up, staggering slightly until he caught his balance on the porch rail. When he looked to see if anyone had noticed, Graver was walking up to his house.

"Boss?"

Higgs waved off the concern in the man's eyes. He wanted to tell him to get the hell back to work, but couldn't remember if he'd given him any work lately.

"That stallion's going to pieces."

Higgs stumbled inside where the reek of rotting food on crusted dishes piled on the table and in the sink nearly made his eyes water. Goddamn it. Goddamn it. That son of a bitch Bill. Vera's note said only that she was going now and he shouldn't follow. She wasn't coming back. He believed her. He knew her to keep her word.

He opened the dresser drawer and pulled out the shirts she'd carefully folded, underwear, trousers, and carried them to the carpetbag he'd readied last week. He took the best horse he could find from the corral, figured he was owed, ignored Graver's questioning expression, tied the bag to the saddle, mounted, and rode away without uttering another word to another person. To hell with the Bennetts, he was going to Kansas.

CHAPTER THIRTY-SEVEN

Graver was the only person who seemed to notice that the foreman just quit. The men idled around the bunkhouse drinking, playing cards, and fighting or riding off to town to raise a ruckus. Hayward was primed for it. Graver knew he should follow Higgs down the road, but the stallion had kicked the corral to pieces, his hooves cracking the poles repeatedly as nobody paid him any mind. Graver looked to the house to see if Dulcinea was aware of her horse's actions, but there was nothing.

He sighed and pulled his hat lower on his forehead. He used a rope because he didn't trust the stud, and waited for the horse's natural curiosity to bring him around, hoping he'd read him right and that he wasn't about to tear a chunk out of his shoulder. It wasn't long before the horse was interested enough to follow him into the barn, where Graver brushed and saddled him with the same confident rhythm to hold the animal's attention. He was about to lead him out and mount him when he was interrupted.

"What are you doing?" Hayward stood in the doorway, his hands hung over the twin set of pistols. Although Graver couldn't see his face, he guessed it wore the rage that hid his grief.

"He needs to be ridden."

"That's my mother's horse and no one else rides him." Hayward stepped closer, his hands twitching nervously over the guns. If it weren't so ridiculous, Graver would be tempted to give the boy a good thrashing. Instead he shrugged and slapped the stallion's neck.

"Why don't you saddle your father's chestnut and we'll take them both for a run. Not good for blooded animals to be penned up like this, and your ma's still feeling poorly." Graver pushed a hunk of mane over to the right side and rubbed the stud's forehead while he straightened the forelock, watching the kid out of the corner of his eye as he circled him. Hayward's face was a torment of emotions. Eyes red rimmed from crying, mouth jittery like it couldn't decide whether to yell or pinch together in a sob. His skin was damp and greasy, like he'd drunk too much and it wasn't sitting well.

His hands trembled as they sought the gun belt with its extra holes punched to hold its heavy bulk on his narrow hips.

"Here, you hold him and I'll ready the chestnut. Won't take more than a minute or two. Just talk to him and pet on him like your mother does." Graver held out the reins. The boy was like an orphan calf coaxed to the bucket for the first time. The stud sniffed him as he approached and stepped back with a nervous swish of his tail.

"You can ride him on the way back if he settles." Graver placed the reins in the boy's hand.

As he saddled the chestnut, Graver shook his head. "Damn waste." He could feel the bitterness that had taken up permanent residence in his head since he lost his own family and witnessed the way these people tore each other to pieces. It made him mad. He stood for a moment, letting the horse settle as he watched Drum, who sat beside the grave as if it were a campfire. Half a dozen times he'd been tempted to march out to that cemetery and drag the old man to the house, force him to stand on his hind legs, and stop this nonsense. Now Frank Higgs was gone, things were getting worse. Wasn't nobody doing a thing out here but sitting around. Even Rose kept to herself now that Dulcinea wouldn't talk to her. One killing too many. Took the heart out of folks.

They rode out the back way, past the cemetery, hoping to get a rise out of the old man, and up into the hills beyond using the cattle trail. Graver glanced over his shoulder at the boy, who posted the chestnut's high trot with little effort, his long legs relaxed at its sides. Slowing the stallion to a walk, Graver waited for Hayward to ride up beside him, the stallion ready to shy and bolt. He rubbed its withers and crooned until the horse let out a long series of snorts and dropped his head, still chewing the bit like he could break the metal in two.

"Doing good with that chestnut." The boy's face reddened and he straightened his back without looking at Graver. "We'll have to use these two every day."

Hayward brushed a big green horsefly off the chestnut's neck, swatted it when it tried to circle back. "Cullen wanted to ride him." He nodded at the stallion. "Planned to sneak him out and run away." He shook his head, his mouth jittery again. "It was too late, though, we weren't kids anymore." He pulled down his hat and touched the horse with his spurs. When he leapt ahead, the stud fought to follow until Graver let him loose. The stallion was too big and out of shape to put in much of a run. He'd never catch the lighter cow ponies or the leaner horses like the lawyer rode or the chestnut that was at least a quarter mile ahead, but the sheer power of his mass thrilled none-theless.

When they came through the valley and stopped at the windmill and tank, the horses' sides heaved. "Best water the stud down slow," Graver said as he dismounted. "Cow horse like the chestnut has the smarts to take care of itself, but this horse prob-ably had someone watching out for it every day of its life."

Graver could feel Hayward study him, imitating his movements, so he put extra deliberation into each gesture. While the horses watered, he gazed around. This was where he'd been shot four months ago after he'd found the girl and J. B. Bennett mur-dered. He was surprised Hayward didn't remark on it.

"Come on over here." Graver led the stud away from the tank toward the ground that still bore the rumpled disturbance of a grave reopened. The pale sand gave underfoot as they trod its edges and sat on the firmer grass.

When the shadow of a huge bird coasted

overhead, cutting across the sun-bleached valley, then swam back again, giving a high-pitched scream, Graver and Hayward shaded their eyes and looked up.

"Golden eagle," Hayward whispered, and the bird screamed again, a commanding, almost angry cry that should have alerted any prey, but didn't. Then another joined, and another, and they swung in huge spiraling circles above the men, riding the drafts of air rising out of the valley before they rose higher and higher, almost into the sun itself, and disappeared.

"Never seen that before," Graver said.

Hayward turned shy, pulled a piece of grass and followed an ant with the end until it climbed on, then he flung it away and lay on his back. "Saw one up on the reservation a while ago when Cullen and me were there." Graver strained to hear him, the boy spoke so softly. "That's where the trouble all started."

Graver felt a chill. "That so?"

Hayward shifted to his side, then pulled his gun belt around so he wasn't lying on the pistol, his mouth working against itself the whole time. "Cullen and me met with these Indian kids at the rodeo in Babylon. Cousins. Two boys wanted to get drunk. Girl didn't. Cullen had some whiskey.

Didn't take much. They weren't used to it. Me neither. Cullen was."

Hayward scrubbed his face with his hands, knocked his hat into the grass. Squeezing his eyes shut, he continued, "We hung out after they closed the rodeo for the night. Then we snuck into the stock pens. Cullen and the Indians, Raymond and Little Knife, wanted to ride the bulls. I wasn't so drunk. Star, that was her name, tried to talk them out of it. They treated us like babies and it riled me up, but she asked me not to do it, so I didn't. We went off under the bleachers with the last of the bottle.

"Turns out the rodeo people had guards and they caught them soon as they opened the gate. Star and me ended up talking and holding hands. Her parents were dead, and I told her about my mother leaving and my father and brother. We weren't paying attention to time, except to notice the moon making its way across the sky. Around dawn Cullen and the other two found us and there were some ugly words. They'd got the crap kicked out of them by the guards and were plenty sore we hadn't stuck around to help. Raymond kept looking at Star like he wanted to accuse her of something and Little Knife was plain loaded for bear. Cullen stared at her and me like he knew a secret, with that grin on his face. Finally I said nothing happened and he looked happy. Her cousins didn't believe me. Little Knife walked up and whispered that he'd cut out my liver and eat it I ever come near Star again. Raymond pulled him off and they left."

Hayward sat up and picked his hat off the ground. Smoothing his hair back, he put it on and tugged it down so it shaded his face, which glistened with tears he didn't bother wiping away.

Graver had a feeling he knew what came next.

"I figured I'd never see her again, her being on the reservation and all, and J.B. and Drum telling us boys to stay away from there." He took a deep breath then let it out in a long sigh. "But Cullen said we had to go up and find her and kick the crap out of her cousins if we got the chance. I never knew which he wanted more. I don't think he ever, I mean, I don't think he was ever with a girl. They were afraid of him. They didn't understand.

"So one day we sneak up there and there's some kind of deal going on, Sun Dance, on the Buffalo Grounds, and we're the only white people and everyone's staring at us and nobody will talk to us. There's all this drumming, men sitting around a big drum the size of a cow tank, dancers in the middle of this ring surrounded by posts covered with cedar boughs, families sitting in the shade around the circle. A cry goes up, drumming gets louder and louder and everyone's watching this thing going on by this tall lodge pole in the middle of the circle with ropes and colored strips of cloth tied to it. The dancers are only wearing breechcloths and some of them are bleeding from cuts on their backs and chests. I grab Cullen's arm and tell him we better go, but he gets that weird light in his eyes and points at this cluster of men at the center pole. It was the cousins, Raymond and Little Knife. Little Knife was already attached to the pole by strips of deerskin pulled through cuts on his chest. He'd back up until the rope stretched tight, pulling the skin to the point of breaking, all the while chanting and dancing with the drums, then he'd move toward the pole again. I guess he was praying. Two old men worked on Raymond, getting him ready. One with a knife slashed twin lines in his chest and pushed a deerskin strip through, then knotted it to the rope while the other man held him still, chanting to him. There wasn't much blood, and I couldn't stop watching. Next thing I knew, Cullen was gone."

Hayward stood, then squatted. "Think we should get back?"

"Finish your story, son." Graver flicked the rein end at the stallion when it grazed too close. This might be his only chance to find out what happened the day that brought him to the Bennetts.

"He found Star with her family watching her cousins, so he stood beside her and grinned at the two boys. It was enough."

The silence filled with the sound of horses pulling grass and chewing.

"They claimed we ruined the Sun Dance and the coming year for their tribe. I guess they think one of us ruined Star, too. We met up a few times after that, and I wanted to give her something, but J.B. never thought I needed money. And I never had before. Cullen told me to do it, to run off with her, marry her. We'd catch sight of the cousins once in a while, but always managed to duck them in town. They had to be gone by dark so it wasn't hard. Town doesn't like Indians after dark. Saves wear and tear on the white folks, I guess. We didn't think they were serious. Star and I just wanted to get to know each other."

Something in his voice made him seem a boy again, and Graver reckoned that when a boy's mother leaves it takes him the rest of his life to fill the hole — if he ever could. He had a sudden vision of Hayward as the sort of man who would pursue women as other men followed dreams of gold or land. A cowbird landed on the edge of the churned sand by the tank and began pecking seeds out of a splash of cow manure, its silver beak stabbing quickly between moments when the brown head swiveled to keep an eye on the men and the horses. Finally the motion of the horses' tails flicking flies sent it soaring away, the dark body a glistening smear crossing out of sight.

"I didn't know half of what Cullen was doing, taunting the cousins, getting in fights with them, making them madder and madder, until something had to give. Little Knife wanted to marry Star, but she wouldn't. We came out here once and she liked it, said her ancestors used to camp here. Then she told me she had to meet somebody here, something about her mother. I told her I'd come and protect her, hide so he wouldn't see me. She wouldn't tell me who it was —" He choked and coughed and took a deep breath. "I was late." He paused again and wiped his face with his hand. "Maybe Little Knife followed her. I don't know what J.B. was doing here.

541

Saw two bodies but didn't realize it was my father until Frank told me the next morning. I was so upset I didn't notice it was J.B.'s horse either. Thought it was whoever Star went to meet. I asked you if he was dead . . . It's all my fault — I was too late —" He sobbed and his shoulders shook as he buried his face in his hands.

The boy dropped his hands. "Little Knife must have killed her. Then shot Pa, and —"

"Cullen was never here?"

The boy shook his head. "I thought you'd done it. Then I didn't know what to think until Cullen told me."

"What?"

"Raymond said Little Knife was gone to Canada or Montana or someplace, but he'd be back to finish the Bennett boys. That's when we started buying guns and practicing."

Graver sat up. "Is that who shot at me that day we went hunting?"

"Little Knife is still gone, far as I know. Guess it couldn't be him. It sure wasn't Cullen. Nobody understood my brother, Mr. Graver. He wasn't like the way he appeared. He never killed anything he could help it."

"It was you shot me here, then."

The boy nodded. "I'm sorry for it now."

They rode back in silence while Graver ruminated. It wasn't the boys. J.B. probably came upon the girl same as he did. It all came back to the girl.

CHAPTER THIRTY-EIGHT

Percival Chance neatly folded the *Omaha Herald,* laid it beside his breakfast plate, and picked up the china coffee cup. This was a splurge he couldn't afford, so he stretched out his morning by ignoring the waiter's increasing impatience, expressed through too much attention to his water glass. He glanced at his pocket watch, a heavy solid gold piece the young earl had carried. It was ten thirty and he'd met Harney Rivers at eight to plan their next step with the permits over breakfast, for which the older man paid. The trouble was Dulcinea hadn't been available for a month. The old man either. Chance tried to understand their grief, but the boy wasn't much of a go-getter. He could understand if Cullen were Frick or Carnegie, two men he read about in the paper, or J. J. Hill, now there was a man with destiny earned by his own two hands. It cheered him to read the life stories

544

of captains of industry who began as he had, grabbed opportunity and shook it until it rained cash. He was mixing his metaphors, the voice of his old teacher at boarding school warned him. So be it. He smiled.

Chance was sent away to school at five when his father, a merchant ship captain, took his mother and sailed to the Orient. His father had already made a small fortune in ivory and spices, and embarked on a longer journey to secure jewels, gold, and wild animals for the rising market in exotic species. They left funds for their son's schooling but failed to appear when the money ran out at age fourteen. Since leaving school, Chance lived by his wits, using his social polish and education wherever and whenever useful. For a time in his late teens, he clerked with a lawyer in New York City, until the man found him in bed with his wife. From there, he made his way into a circle of bankers always in need of a smart young man fast on his feet. He was twenty-two when he borrowed enough money from the bank to seek his fortune out West, without going through the formalities of signing papers. He was tired of the East anyway. The great fortunes to be made there were already taken and deposited in other people's accounts.

He met the young earl at twenty-five in Chicago and truth be told, he was in despair for his poor luck. He had tried commodities trading, but it was a closed world and he was an Easterner. He was actually considering work on a steamboat on the Great Lakes when he met the earl one night in a Gold Coast saloon. With his outlandish clothes and English accent, the earl was about to be spirited away and mugged when Chance greeted him with a hug like an old friend, and whispered the danger in his ear. He threw his arm over the young earl's shoulder and led him out the door into a horse cab.

It took three times around the lakeshore and park for the earl to spill his story and Chance to convince him that he needed a guide, a person who would protect and lead him through the wonders of the American West — Chance had never been farther west than Chicago, but he'd read a great deal. With the earl, Chance's life began an important new chapter that should have continued back to England, where he would remain a lifelong friend supported in the manner his parents had dreamed about.

Chance opened the paper, refolded it, and used the edge of his palm to sharpen its creases. He sipped the cold coffee, raised his finger, and pointed at the cup when the waiter arrived. The hopeful expression on his face slid away as he left for the silver pot.

What he had not foreseen, and what still troubled him, were the vagaries of the earl's taste — there was no other way to put it. His capacity for sexual adventure, nay, sexual experience, grew into a monstrous appetite for the strange, forbidden, and violent until it culminated ten years ago at the massacre known as Wounded Knee. It was as if all his vices were ingredients in a stew so vile the memory still turned Chance's stomach. Yes, they drank to the point of delirium in those days, a fever in the brain that burned away the edge of morality. Nothing was too outlandish. Chance lost himself, lost sight of who he was, what he wanted. The vanity of the old world became an acid on his soul.

"We can do whatever we want," the young earl said with a flourish of his hand — and he did. When Chance remembered the acts he participated in or simply watched, he felt beyond shame, he felt damned.

He felt frustrated, too, because he only wanted to make his way in the world, as the promoters advised: GO WEST! He imagined himself with a fortune in gold or land. He imagined his parents miraculously returned, praising him for becoming so prosperous. That's all he wanted in life. Was it too much? He was willing to work. He'd proven that, damn it.

When the waiter returned, he gestured toward the empty cream pitcher. The man brought a fresh one and set it down heavily so it slopped over and he had to wipe it with his fresh white apron.

Chance finally took mercy on him and said, "A few more minutes."

He would finish this damn business and be gone from this place. It was that girl, Star, who caused all the trouble. He was relieved the earl didn't discover her the night they killed her mother, Lord, that would have been a grisly scene — still, he tried to talk to her, to buy back the necklace, the last token of his mother and father, tried to use reason and deny his participation, but she would have none of it. He could not stop her. Maybe he should have told her how he took revenge on the earl, killed him and left his body to be eaten by wild animals, the bones scattered across the reservation the last time they went up there. But she saw the pouch and knew what it was. He saved it as a reminder of how vile he could be. He would never cross that line again, ever. She wouldn't listen to reason, though. He was only a relic hunter, a trades-man, the way her people were, he said. The whole world was a marketplace, and they were doing what people for thousands of years had done, trading goods. But she looked at him and drew her skinning blade. He had to stop her.

It was no use. He tried to be a good man. He was usually a *nice* man, polite and good-natured. But maybe he wasn't a good man after all. Maybe a person had to do good *after* he made his fortune, as Carnegie urged. He didn't know whether Star had told her sister about him, or if Rose found the necklace and knew it would lead to the killer. Honestly, he was tired of killing. The earl shot every living creature he came across. On days when big game was scarce he shot prairie dogs, rabbits, birds, cattle, and wild horses. For a while he employed a photographer to accompany them and capture the triumphant earl with his kill: rows and rows of snow geese left to rot after the picture was taken, five antelope also left because their horns were too small, and a dozen wild burros and horses trapped in a box canyon and slaughtered for joy. The man deserved to die. Chance did the world a service that day. He nodded to himself.

If he could explain that to Rose, maybe

549

she would understand. He knew it was wishful on his part. He had a fortune to be made here, and he could not allow a youthful misdeed to stand in the way. He was sorry. He was very sorry. Civilized people understood how it was in battle. The soldiers were awarded medals for the massacre. Why was he any different? The tension in his neck and shoulders relaxed. This was how he could explain himself. He was helping the army that day. And later, he was a relic and antiquities dealer — nothing illegal. He was a fair and just man. He was even a moral man in some circumstances. He definitely wasn't any worse than most.

That being said, he drank the last of his coffee, stood, put on his hat, brushed the crumbs from the front of his waistcoat, and left the hotel dining room. With a new energy in his step, he tipped his hat at the couple outside the hotel and went directly to his law office to draw up new papers for Mrs. Bennett to sign. And by Jesus, she would sign this time. Fortune smiles on those who force her hand.

Chapter Thirty-Nine

The cowboys argued beneath her bedroom window and the day was gray. Clouds massed on the horizon and pushed toward the ranch like an invading Old Testament army bringing submission and doom while the hands argued like sparrows, back and forth, building the nest of disagreement into which they would eventually settle.

Dulcinea went downstairs and pushed open the door, startling the men, who jumped to their feet. She clutched the shawl she carried as a chill worked its way down from her scalp and drenched her in cold as if she were caught in the rain.

Irish Jim's intense blue eyes with their bright glitter like semiprecious jewels took her in, then relaxed. "Just passin' the time, ma'am."

She looked at Larabee, second to Higgs.

"Nobody give us orders," he said and belatedly remembered to remove his hat, and the others snatched theirs off, too.

She turned to Willie, who looked over his shoulder at Higgs's house with the front door hanging open. "Higgs, he packed and scooted, ma'am."

Dulcinea took a deep breath, pulled together the last grains of strength, and stood straight, even though she became light-headed with the effort.

"Me and Willie will just mosey over there and clean up the place, then," Larabee said.

Irish Jim stood and fixed her in his gaze. "I guess that stallion's about broke out of the corral. I'll go fix it if that's okay with you." The men looked at each other, replaced their hats, and ambled off the porch like dogs reluctant to leave their comfort.

"You want I should send the Indians up to the house?" Larabee called over his shoulder. She nodded.

She waited until the men walked away before stumbling back into the house. The coffee Rose had made was warm on the stove, and although it tasted like the contents of a spit can, she still drank a cup. When a space yawned unexpectedly in a person's daily life, she often hastened to fill it, spreading chores to cover the place, as if it were an embarrassment, unseemly, and she must not be seen on its brink. Dulcinea had not spoken in a month for fear of what she might say.

She pushed away from the table, her hands unwilling to release the edge that had been rubbed smooth by men's bodies over the years. Four months ago her husband lay here. A month ago, her son. Yet they continued to pass the platters of meat, the plates of bread and bacon.

She had held Cullen's hand those final hours. *This living hand, now warm and capable of earnest grasping,* and the broken, dirt-lined nails, a boy's hand still, the tiny scar rising up the thumb, the knuckle that wouldn't bend on the index finger he'd broken, so young and already his skin grained with dirt, scarred and broken again and again. He was still a boy, palm narrow and delicate as a girl's, but with thick yellow calluses beneath each finger; another scar crossed his palm, bisecting the fate line. She caressed that hand all night, willing him back to a childhood when he stood at her skirt protected and loved.

This living hand, now warm and capable of earnest grasping, would, if it were cold and in the icy silence of the tomb, so haunt thy days and chill thy dreaming nights that thou wouldst wish thine own heart dry of blood . . . and thou be conscience-calmed. Oh son, when you read Keats to Markie Eastman, did you know he would write your epitaph?

And now cups sat where his hands had rested, knives and forks outlined his hips, his thighs, his thin boy legs. Was her place at the table where his bare battered feet waited to be bathed? It was scribed over and over, this story, these bodies, this place, this table where she sat those long hours all those years ago waiting for Drum to return and take her young son. Yes, she knew he would convince J.B., knew he would demand and receive the child she had waited so long for, loved so hard as she nursed him through the dangers of being alive, only to lose him. She thought if she put distance between them, if she stayed away as Drum demanded, then she could stand it, because she couldn't be within a day's ride without going after him — which she did until Drum laid down the law, and she had to leave. A disguised kindness, she later saw. Your firstborn was always the most loved. Hayward she loved, but he was an afterthought. She lost Cullen years ago, and now she lost him again, resurrected, reclaimed, and then just as she filled with hope once more, snatched away. If Drum Bennett were not out there in the cemetery waiting to die, she would kill him. She hurled her cup against the wall, satisfied by the brown streaks and gouge.

When she heard horses in the barnyard, she forced herself to the porch. Graver on J.B.'s chestnut and Hayward on the gray stallion, so relaxed it shambled like a cart horse, passed by. Graver looked over and touched his finger to the brim of his hat; Hayward ignored her. Fine. He was correct. An annoying hum stirred in her arms, she silenced it. So what if they rode her horse? What on earth good was he now? The person who wanted him was gone. In the old days, she might have slaughtered the stallion to honor her warrior son when he died. Cullen asked for the favor and she refused him. She saw it in his eyes, in the way he watched from the shadows of the barn. Now the stallion seemed a bright toy the boy was denied purely for the opportunity to deny him pleasure. She thought she had time. She thought she would teach him to ride the horse, that they would share him, though she never told him of her vague plans. What a simple, obvious gesture it was, yet she stepped around it like an inconvenient branch fallen in her path.

She watched Graver and Hayward dismount. The boy stroked the stallion's face and leaned his head against its jaw. She was too exhausted to open to the rush of love she should feel for *this* boy.

Irish Jim set down the hammer and followed the horses into the barn, where Dulcinea wouldn't go anymore. Graver reappeared, walked toward the house in her husband's hat, shirt, and boots. She imagined him wrapping his arms around her from behind, holding her despite herself. She closed her eyes for the briefest of moments and felt his lips touch behind her ear, the place only J.B. knew. How immense was her longing and her dread.

When she opened her eyes, Graver still walked with a stride that should cover the distance easily, yet he seemed suspended, moving toward her but never arriving. The coolness imprisoned her body, pulled her into it. J.B. had found her in the evenings, watching the gold light set the world afire, making the swallows glint like mica as they sailed in and out of the barn, the grass on the hills shining as if sewn with precious thread on an ancient tapestry, the cottonwood leaves rattling like pennies dropped in a collection box, and the horses' gilded manes and tails shimmering in the falling light. There could be nothing amiss in such a world as her young husband held her, his lips promising the caresses that would bring their naked bodies into one, bathed in the same golden light as it turned orange, then red, and the world burned down around them.

The cool released her and Graver arrived, hat in hand. She pressed her hand over her heart to steady it. Since Cullen, everywhere she looked was specific, as if she were scrubbed clean and free. Graver was unaware that he leaned slightly to the right as he continued to favor the wounded shoulder, and that he tilted his head slightly to the left for balance. His eyes were brighter after his ride into the hills, where they had caught the blue of the sky and lightened. He thought he was an unhandsome man, but his rawboned aspect gave him rugged strength, from the white creases at the corners of his eyes to the strong nose and deep grooves down his cheeks. There was a notch in his chin from an old cut, and his face, as battered as his hands, revealed a life of working to earn his keep. Sweat darkened the front of his shirt, and his jeans, mud-streaked, bore a small tear on the thigh where barbed wire caught the fabric and the white of his leg peered through. She was embarrassed to be caught staring. He banged his hat against his leg to loosen the dust and opened his mouth to speak. She held up her hand to stop him and turned to go inside with an incline of her head. He followed.

"Where is my dog?" She was shocked by how low and whispery her voice sounded after a month of silence, and by her banal question.

He gazed at her, and seemed surprised that this was the sole thing occupying her mind.

"Staying with Jerome and Rose in the tipi."

"Oh." She swayed and sat down again. "I want you to take this table and chop it up. Burn it right now!"

He stared at her. "Make it hard for the men to eat."

"Oh, they can sit on the porch or stand or something . . ."

"Can I get you anything?" he asked in a voice that was warm and cool and confusing.

"I want to thank you for taking Hayward to ride." She sounded insane.

"Maybe a glass of water?" he said.

"And the horses. Yes, that's kind of you." She meant the riding, but he pumped her a glass of water, then one for himself. She took it automatically and brought it to her lips. It was rare indeed, fresh and cool, with the crisp mineral taste of the hills. She had missed this water. They said it flowed beneath the hills in a great sea thousands of years old, and that was why it was pure blue when it came to the surface. Oh son, you will miss this world, won't you? She put her face in her hands but no tears would come. She should be out there with Drum Bennett, letting her tears water her son's grave. Why did she have to be so very alive when he was so very dead?

"Ma'am?" Graver was like a gnat that wouldn't let her alone.

"What? What do you want? Why are you still here? Higgs quit. The other men will quit. Go. Just go." She opened her eyes and found he sat at the end of the table in Higgs's place, and before him, J.B.'s. He studied her a minute, then gazed at the wall where pine shelves held her new blue dishes. Another bold, useless gesture.

"Now people have let you be for a good while, Mrs. Bennett. You've been in your grief and we let you be. Nobody asked a thing of you, and it has been hard. No denying it. But ma'am, it is time for you to stiffen your shoulders and start walking like you own this place again."

Graver scratched behind his head, and pushed his gray-streaked hair off his face. It had grown over his collar and he grabbed the damp curls and pulled them back. He rubbed his mouth, grimaced, and fixed her with a stare. "I'll tell you what I think, then you can do what you want — fire me or stand up."

She hesitated, wound her fingers together in her lap and forced herself to sit very still, the attitude of a child in the schoolroom. As he said, she could fire him.

"I am sick to death of the waste around here. You people act like there's nothing for it but to throw each other away, kill your animals off for the folly of it, and ruin every piece of land you can get your hands on. Those oil and gas people? Do you have any idea what it looks like when they're done? Your boys? They needed you and you ran off. Your husband, he didn't have the nerve to come take you back either. That old man out there? He should be running his own place — that's what killed Cullen, trying to do a man's job when the man was in town being played the fool so he could get his hands on more money." He stood so he towered over her.

She pushed back her chair, ready to slap him hard.

"Sit down, I'm not done yet!" His voice rose and he paced back and forth with his slightly irregular gait. "Speaking of money, the men haven't been paid and unless you have a trunk full of money upstairs or in the bank, we got nothing to run this place on without shipping cattle or selling off some land." He stopped, inspecting the room as if seeing her improvements for the first time. "You can't spend money on pretties when your men are hurting. We need to make the tally, cull the herds, get the hay in, reserve the stock cars with the railroad, contact the buyers and study the market figures. Ma'am, we have not done one thing, and unless we ship it'll be a mighty lean winter."

He looked at his hands, turning them over twice before they dropped to his sides. His voice lowered. "I'm not speaking for myself, you understand, I've put in the lean years. I'm used to it. It's you and the boy and what hands you can afford to winter over."

"I'm broke? How? My husband put money in my account every month. There was always plenty of money." As she said it, she realized that she hadn't ever asked how the ranch was doing, if cattle prices were holding, if he lost many head in the early or late blizzards. She just assumed —

Graver nodded and closed his eyes, something J.B. used to do, as if the ignorance of the other person was too embarrassing to witness.

She shivered. The repairs that weren't done, the state of the linens, for God's sake. Cullen and Hayward's poor clothing. Too few men to do all the work on a ranch this size. Oh Christ, what had she done?

"How long since we, since anyone has shipped?" Her voice quivered.

"Couple of years at least. Eighteen ninety-nine winter was coldest we've ever had. That and the drought, well, not a good time to be ranching. Some places have just turned the cattle loose, letting them fatten on open range or other people's land. Better than slaughtering them. Reservations buy some, but government gives bottom dollar, real bottom, and doesn't care what kind of cow gets sent, sick, skinny, old. Same price per head. According to Higgs, your husband wouldn't ship those and he couldn't lose prime stock. Drum didn't share his sentiments."

She got up and walked into the living room, jerked the curtain away from the window and peered outside. It was no use. She couldn't seem to find her dog anywhere.

Graver cleared his throat and when he spoke again, he sounded worn out. "You still have a son out there — a good boy who can grow to be a man in these hills. He'll do, if he has some backing. Don't throw him away. And don't throw away this ranch. You know how lucky you are? My wife and I — we would've given the world to have a place like this instead of what we settled for. You're going through hard times. It'll change. It always does if you have a place to ride it out. And you do." He rested his hands on the back of the straight chair at the end of the table and looked at her. "I'm done now."

She gathered herself, tried to force down the tide of anger and fear before it sheeted her eyes red and black. "You are never to mention my son Cullen again. In fact, you are not to interfere in my dealings with my other son either. Is that clear?"

He nodded and set his mouth in a tight line.

"But, since I am apparently without a foreman, I would appreciate it if you would stay and manage the men until I find a replacement. You may move your things into the foreman's house."

He nodded and a smile played at his lips until she held up her hand. "One more thing. You are to teach my son how to ride and care for my horses." He shrugged and nodded, not meeting her eyes.

"Finally, I want you to go out there, put Drum Bennett on his horse, and take him home. I'll expect you back in the morning. We'll discuss the cattle then."

He opened his mouth to speak, thought better of it, and shook his head.

She hadn't told the truth about why she had left her husband and children. She'd never told anyone, it was part of their bargain, for what good it did. She collapsed in the chair and gestured for him to sit. "I need you to understand something about Drum and me.

"It was the first break in the weather in mid-March when I tried again to take back Cullen. J.B. had left early to meet with the bank and cattle buyer in town and the hired girl had taken Hayward out to see the new calves in the barn. She'd moved in after Drum stole my boy and I went crazy. I had one of the men hook my half-blind mare to the runabout. I was determined not to fail this time.

"I found the old man at the smithy forge, naked to the waist, holding a red-hot horseshoe in pincers over the coals as he pumped the bellows. The gray horse being shod was tied to one side. My boy nowhere to be seen. I remember that Drum's skin was only a little loose for a man his age, and his muscles still looked hard as he pounded the shoe into shape, then plunged it into a waiting bucket of water and heated it again.

" 'What can I do you for?' he asked between ringing blows.

" 'I want my son.'

"Without pausing, he shook his head. 'You don't get it, do you?' He held up the shoe to check its shape, turned, raised the horse's front hoof, and set the shoe against it, releasing acrid smoke.

"I repeated my request and he began to nail the shoe on. When he was done, he reached into his back pocket and pulled out a piece of grimy folded paper. 'Read this. Tell me what it says.'

"I hesitated, and he waved it at me. I took it although I was filled with dread. I knew it was bad.

"The paper was a signed contract giving Cullen to be raised by his grandfather until he was eighteen in exchange for twenty thousand acres. At the bottom of the page, J.B.'s signature, the same he had signed his letters to me with, flowing and upright so there was no mistaking it. I crumpled the contract and threw it into the forge fire. Drum shook his head and uttered a small curse.

" 'He has a copy, too.'

"I was torn between betrayal and grief, unable to quite grasp how a man could do this. But Drum wasn't finished with me. He patted the horse, took another shoe from the bin, and began heating it.

" 'Now you and me are going to come to an agreement, missy.' He pounded the hot shoe into shape.

" 'These hills are a dangerous place, you know, all kinds of accidents happen to a person out here. Hunters shoot a man thinking he's a deer. Boy gets bit by poisonous snake and nobody there to suck it out. Person falls off and gets dragged by a horse or lost in a blizzard. I tell you, there's endless danger out here.' He stopped and held up the shoe, squinting at its form.

" 'Here's what I'm offering: You leave here and stay away, not a word to my son about it, and I'll keep your menfolk safe. Boys can grow up and J.B. won't have any accidents. Long as you skedaddle and keep your word.'

"He thrust the shoe back into the coals, heated it again, lifted it out, and put it on the horse's back hoof. For the rest of my life I will remember this scene every time I smell that unholy acrid smoke like the depths of hell.

"I couldn't find words to answer him. The proposal was so outrageous that I didn't doubt him. As I stumbled across the barn-yard and climbed into my runabout, he called after me: 'Best be gone come May. Dangerous time, branding season.' "

She hunched her shoulders and wrapped her arms around her body as if she felt the cold March wind again. "So you under-stand, I can't have that old man here. He was supposed to keep them safe." Her head jerked up and she felt her eyes blaze with a kind of madness that both frightened and made her glad. "He killed J.B.! I know he did! He wants the ranch — you've heard him —"

Graver waited a moment, then settled his hat on the table and sighed. "That's a hard tale, ma'am. It makes me sorry to hear it. You been through it all right. But —"

They heard Rose and Some Horses argu-ing as they stepped onto the porch and pulled open the door. Graver closed his mouth, stood, glanced at Dulcinea as if he wanted to say more, and then put on his hat, touched the brim, and slid out the door.

Jerome left almost immediately and Rose sat at the table with her head down like she'd lost the ability to speak. That hap-pened to everyone around her now. Only Graver — Did the men have noon dinner? Dulcinea had lost track of time. Was it morning or afternoon? She looked anxiously to the sky as clouds slid across the sun. A cool wind gusted and gathered and gusted again, driving the squawking chickens into the henhouse and scattering the horses in the corral. The trotting horse weathervane on the barn spun wildly one direction and then another. Dust and sand rose and swirled around and burst against the house as if flung by a giant fist.

"My sister says we're close to him now. He's going to reveal himself soon." Rose tapped her fingers on the table, pushed back the chair impatiently, and went to the parlor, where she picked up the hide scraper.

"Where did this come from?" she asked, turning.

Dulcinea shrugged. "Hayward collects Indian things."

Rose set down the scraper and picked up the red stone pipe. "Same?"

Dulcinea stared at her. "What're you saying?"

Rose put it down, made sure it was away from the shelf edge. "They belonged to our family." She stood at the end of the table staring at Dulcinea.

"I'll ask him, I will. But he didn't have anything to do with it, I swear."

Rose wouldn't look her in the eye. "Find

out tonight."

Dulcinea shivered. This wasn't her friend Rose — she sounded so cold. "You think Hayward killed your sister?" She was breathless even saying the words.

Rose stared at her. "Ask him where those things came from. Tonight."

After supper, which the two women cooked in silence, Dulcinea asked Graver and Hayward to stay. The boy was restless and wouldn't meet her eyes. Graver sat quietly meditating on his coffee while she went to the parlor and retrieved the items.

"Son, where did you get these?"

Hayward seemed rattled, folded his arms and stared at the table.

Graver cleared his throat. "Higgs brought them in." He paused. "From the windmill where — you know. J.B. was holding the scraper and the pipe was with the girl."

Hayward looked like he'd been slapped, his face red.

Dulcinea felt light-headed. Was he guilty?

Graver looked at the two of them and grimaced. "Boy, you need to tell your mother everything." He laid his hands flat on the table and made to stand, thought better of it, and leaned back in the chair.

When the tale was done, Hayward was

sobbing in his mother's arms. Dulcinea thought it lucky he didn't see the relief on her face at learning her sons weren't murderers. She knew J.B. wasn't either, and the two Indian boys weren't even around these days. Had to be an outsider. She never seriously considered Drum, despite what she said. He wouldn't kill his own son. Look how he was taking Cullen's — She couldn't think the word and willed herself back to the list of suspects. It had to be an outsider, then. Maybe someone who knew J.B. well enough to get close. That meant she and Hayward weren't safe. Drum was an old bastard on his own far as she was concerned, but she'd be damned if anyone was going to hurt this family again. She had to look harder, think about who stood to gain the most from their deaths. She needed to talk to Rose tonight.

CHAPTER FORTY

Since it was the middle of September and the men hadn't been paid in two months, Dulcinea forced herself into town to meet Chance and the banker. If she sold the ranch, she'd have the money to protect her remaining son. In her mind, she pushed aside the disappointment she was sure would show on Graver's face when he found out. Damn it, she did care what he thought of her and maybe he was right. To be honest, she couldn't imagine Hayward leaving these hills. She couldn't imagine herself leaving either.

Chance seated her at a scarred round oak table in the tiny office that used to hold his desk. The room was stripped bare as if he was moving, and when she raised her eyebrows he smiled and shrugged. He cleared his throat, but she ignored that, too, opened her purse and pulled out the papers he had sent.

The sweet scent of his Bay Rum cologne hung in the air, crowding the small space. Sooty lines framed the white spaces where his diplomas and pictures had hung. Was he leaving now, before the will was probated?

He sat across from her, elaborately crossing his legs to the side, his striped trousers pulled up to reveal the unpolished shaft of a black boot.

"Why have you sent me this contract, Mr. Chance? I told you I wanted nothing to do with those people."

"You must be feeling better, Dulcinea, you're looking lovely today." He leaned back with a smile and combed his hair from his temple with a forefinger.

"Your one job was to clear probate on the will. Do I need to find another attorney?"

He smiled. "If you will be patient for a few minutes —"

"I've been patient all summer and look at the results."

He took out a gold pocket watch embellished with an elaborate family crest, consulted it, and tucked it back in his waistcoat as if his time were more important than hers.

"That's it. Consider yourself fired." She stood, picked up her purse, and turned toward the door, which opened precipitously, forcing her to step back into the tiny space.

"Sorry, sorry we're late." The judge, Harney Rivers, a stranger, Stillhart the banker, and finally Drum Bennett came through the door, causing all to stand elbow to chin. "Town's filling up with rodeo crowd and it's hell getting anywhere. I don't know how they do it in those Eastern cities." The judge tipped his hat. "Mrs. Bennett, Dulcinea."

"What are you doing here?" Dulcinea asked Drum, who lingered behind the taller men.

The men removed their hats, put them back on, and then took them off again.

"Come in here, you can sit and I'll stand," Chance offered. "Dulcinea, you sit right there where you were before."

She almost protested, and then was overcome with curiosity. In her new state of mind, it was all she could do not to laugh them right out of their boots, as if they were caught in a ridiculous folly that any minute was going to split apart to show the awful, soul-grabbing horror beneath. She sat with a grimace. Across from her Drum kept his eyes on the flat-brimmed tan cowboy hat in his hands that he kept turning, stopping to brush off a fleck of lint every once in a while. His face, covered in greasy sweat, had aged twenty years, ravaged with wrinkles and hollows and sagging skin as if he were dying of a cancer or lung ailment. There was a slight tremor in his fingers. She looked away, unable to stop the stirrings of sympathy.

The stranger, an out-of-town lawyer who introduced himself as Joshua Kidd, possessed dark eyes that peered through dime-sized glasses perched on his nose. His jaw worked as if he chewed something not quite pleasant, something he could neither spit out nor swallow. Next to Chance's clothes, the man's appeared fresh, shelf-creased. He was too current, probably sold a bill of goods by some smart young clerk in Omaha whose job it was to get rid of fashions no one was buying. In contrast, the judge must have inherited his clothing from an older, deceased relative. The black wool coat was too thick, the cream linen shirt too heavy, and the silk cravat too boldly colored in yellow and blue swirls. Stillhart, the banker, wore a dove-gray Western suit with overstitching and a black leather string tie with a rough turquoise nugget the size of her fist holding it snug at his throat, like something straight out of a Denver catalogue. Harney Rivers wore his usual plain wool suit and black vest with a gold watch chain stretched across the front. Only his gold-and-green silk tie made him fit company for the others. She felt set upon by mannequins out of the Emporium window across the street.

"Dulcinea — May I call you Dulcinea?" the judge began, as if he hadn't sat at her table and drunk her husband's brandy of a night.

She waved her hand impatiently and concentrated on the wart on his chin in an attempt to still herself while her fingers worked J.B.'s ring on her thumb, twisting it back and forth until it began to saw her flesh.

"Let me say that we're all real sorry about what happened to your boy." He glanced over at Drum, who wouldn't meet his eyes, but the tremor in his fingers increased. "I know how broken up both you and his grandfather have been."

The ring sprang off and she felt around in her lap before it could drop to the floor. The room was warm and stuffy and her breath wouldn't quite come.

The judge snuck a look at the lawyers, carefully avoiding Drum, who still stared at his hat, although his face, burned from the days living outside, burnished to a deep red.

"Be that as it may" — the judge raised his finger in the air as if to punctuate his speech

575

from a campaign platform — "we in the hills have long-standing traditions," he began in a sonorous tone, and it was all she could do not to reach across the table and grab his lapels. "We, the founding families, like to keep things, our holdings, our business, among our families and friends. We don't need outsiders, folks who don't know or appreciate our ways — you understand."

She nodded, and remembered how long it was before anyone would do more than say a polite hello when she'd married J.B. — and when Drum took Cullen she couldn't find any lawyer interested in helping her get him back.

"We have business to conduct here, and it behooves you to listen. Please." He smiled to lighten the words and she clenched the ring in her fist.

"Just get to the point," Drum finally said, and she was grateful.

"All right. Your lawyer sent the gas and oil contracts to you, so you know what we need here. The deal only works if all of us in this room allow for the exploration and eventual bringing to the surface. Now" — he raised his hand to stop her interruption — "in return, Drum here drops the inquiry into the legitimacy of your husband's will. Yes, yes, I know it's valid, but I'm not acting as the court here and your father-in-law wields enough goodwill with the court to delay your possession for a long time."

She started to stand, and Chance came off the wall and put his hand none too gently on her shoulder, pushing her down. "It's best you listen." She slid the ring on her thumb and began twisting it so hard she felt it on the bone.

Drum startled awake. "No, damn it, that's not the way we talked about it." He glared at the other men, then fixed his half-mad expression on her. "Dulcinea, I know this is sitting hard, and what I'm about to say will sit even harder, but you need to consider Hayward and all J.B. worked for here more than your needs. You mean to sell the ranch, I know that, especially —" He brushed his hand as if to push recent history aside. "But I can't let that happen. Now I don't have the cash to buy you out, you know that, it's a cow business, not a bank. So here's what I figure, and it's only to keep the Bennett name alive, after J.B. and Cullen — well, I figure you might owe something here, too."

She pushed her fingers into her purse, and felt for anything sharp she could stab through his heart.

Drum put his hat flat on the table, took a deep breath, and leaned toward her. "I think we should get married."

The judge's and banker's heads jerked up from reading the papers on the table. Harney Rivers had to stop himself from laughing, she noticed. Chance, still behind her, placed a hand on her shoulder and squeezed. Since she didn't try to kill him, Drum continued.

"I've thought long and hard about our problems and it's the only thing for it. Merge our two places, make it one of the biggest spreads in the hills, and I can help finish raising Hayward and together he and I can run the ranches while you go off to Europe or wherever — that is, you'd be my wife in name only. You'll continue to be supported as you were when my son was alive." He leaned back and folded his arms across his chest.

She shuddered at the thought of Drum's proposal, the obscenity of it. The other men looked surprised and a little scared as they watched. They were probably wondering the same thing she was: Had he lost his mind?

"Marry the murderer of my husband?" She clenched the edge of the table, ready to leap at him. For his part, Drum's head snapped up and he stared at her in shock.

"No," he groaned, "I never —"

She leaned back in her chair, watching him.

Stillhart finally filled the awkward silence. "We're aware of your financial situation, Mrs. Bennett. J.B. was trying to ride out the poor markets like everyone else, and he would've made it if, well, if he hadn't been sending you such a generous allowance." Here the banker's eyes slid toward Drum and back, a move as quick as a lizard's tongue. "He wound up selling off that piece on the other side of the Dismal River, and I know for a fact he was facing having to sell a thousand-acre parcel this fall if he couldn't ship again." He held up his hand, and then let it slap the table to quiet Drum. "You need to sign the contract, Mrs. Bennett. It just doesn't make sense that you won't."

He had a kind face, one that was interested in the experiences of others, but his mouth was thin and set, and his eyes stared at her blank as a grasshopper's. Was she food or was she food? He reminded her of the traveling dentist who visited the ranch years ago, who sat each of them in a straight chair and tapped each tooth with a metal pick, asking, does that hurt, does that hurt? The dentist had some kind of sweet scent on his breath, a combination of licorice and clove, and when his tap produced a howling nerve, the smell made her want to vomit. She wanted to vomit now.

She gave J.B.'s ring a vicious turn on her thumb and felt her finger grow slick. "To tell you the truth, I guess I need to think about it." She gazed at the mannequin faces. "Just a day or two."

She pushed back her chair. This time Chance didn't attempt to stop her as she crossed the small distance to the door. She paused with a hand on the knob, glanced at the men, and left. They had her and they knew it. She wanted to sign, she wanted to, but something stronger told her no. Maybe it was Graver, who had reminded her that they would tear this land apart, J.B.'s land, their land, the fragile Sand Hills she loved as much as she hated for what they had cost her.

And Drum's offer was monstrous. Even if he didn't kill his son, he didn't protect him as he'd promised.

Underneath all of her protests, though, remained her desperation, pinching, gathering her corners and pulling them in so tight she could barely move or breathe, as if she would die of suffocation. What could she sell? The stallion and mares wouldn't bring money out here — people would laugh at her. Jewels? She never cared for jewelry.

How did J.B. have the cash to buy that telescope? She could sell that, except the image of Hayward fascinated by the possibility of the night sky intruded. Her parents? Never. She hadn't asked them for money since she left home to marry. She was a grown woman. Besides, her father had to borrow most of her money over the past few years. Then she remembered the men who worked for her, trusted that if she used their backs, she would uphold her end of the bargain and pay them. Graver said he would work without pay, he was used to starving, but she had seen the condition he was in when shot and she couldn't push him back to that. She'd have to sell a parcel of land, as J.B. had done, but the idea brought the memory she worked so hard to forget: the day she learned about the contract. No, she couldn't sell the land piece by piece, she couldn't even sell the ranch . . . then it would all mean nothing, her son's life, her husband's, her sacrifice, nothing.

CHAPTER FORTY-ONE

Graver found her standing in front of the bank, arm clutched around her stomach, face damp and pale. Was she fevered? He placed a hand under her elbow and led her down the street to the café, took a table against the back wall, where he could observe anyone who entered the otherwise empty room. He ordered tea, which he thought she'd appreciate, but she shook her head and asked for a glass of water. When the girl brought it, Dulcinea nodded to the counter where the headache powders and stomach relief medicines sat in a dusty glass case, and pressed her fingers to the side of her head and closed her eyes. The girl quickly brought the powders, which Dulcinea dissolved in her glass and drank with a grimace.

Graver kept his eyes on the front window, watched Drum Bennett limp past in more of a hurry than he should be, followed by the judge and Harney Rivers. Now what were they at? As he considered the possibilities, he noted that dust coated several tables along with the corners of the room, where the mop pushed the dark, greasy dirt. Not enough business these days with the stock market up and down. Took longer for things to recover out here. Folks couldn't afford to spend their dimes and dollars on extras like a meal or even a cup of coffee they didn't prepare themselves, especially during the fair and rodeo. That brought him back to Dulcinea and the ranch. He'd shouldered the burden of running the place, but how the hell was he supposed to do that with no money? He glanced at Dulcinea, who watched him with a slight smile on her face, and he felt the heat rise up his chest.

"I'm better now," she said.

He considered his next words, then decided to go for broke. "I was thinking we might could go to the festivities. Rodeo starting soon." He cleared his throat and straightened his shoulders. "I gave the men the day off. They're wanting to rodeo and, well, it sort of makes up for our being late with their wages." He paused and stared into the cold tea, the film forming in the cup he held between both hands. He'd paid their entry fees with the very last of his money but didn't tell her that.

"They're wanting to know about entering the horse race. They won't go through with it if, if it seems wrong to you." He watched her carefully as she pressed a trembling hand to her forehead.

She poured herself a cup of tea from the flowered pot in front of them. After a sip, she shook her head and pushed her tongue between her teeth as if to dislodge the taste.

"What does Hayward want to do?" she asked, listless.

Graver raised his brows, glanced out the window, and caught sight of Rose carrying Mrs. Bennett's satchel, followed at some distance by Percival Chance.

He shrugged. "Far as I know, he's entered. Don't know what he intends to ride, he and his brother —" There, he'd done it. He swallowed and picked up his cup and put it down again.

As if she'd been waiting for the words, she immediately announced, "He will ride my stallion." Her face hardened with decision.

Graver shook his head. "No, ma'am."

She tried to stiffen, and couldn't. Graver hated seeing her this way.

"He's at the livery stable." She gathered her string bag and prepared to rise. He put a hand on her arm. She looked down at it, and her expression softened.

He stumbled on the words. "If I may, I might could accompany you to the rodeo, Mrs. Bennett." He felt his face redden and tried to steady his hand, but something about her made him jumpy as a green colt.

She stared at him a moment. "Of course."

He removed his hand and picked up his hat. "I took the liberty of asking Rose to bring you more suitable clothes." He glanced at her dress. She always appeared so darn, what, he didn't know, but he liked it. He chastised himself, the woman was in mourning.

She picked up the skirt of her black dress and let it drop, then brushed at the front. "I suppose this would be a bit dampening on the festivities." She shrugged then as if she understood that wearing black couldn't do a damn thing to change the fates of her husband and son. She looked out the window. "I'll see if there's a room I can use at the hotel. They usually keep one for the Bennetts." She tilted her head and glanced at him with the slightest hint of flirtation in her eyes. "I can see myself to the hotel, if you'll come for me in half an hour?"

When he arrived, Graver was clean-shaven and wore a sky-blue shirt he'd bought from the peddler in July. The stiffness made him itch and he tugged on the cuffs of the too-short sleeves. It was the only shirt that fit his chest and shoulders once they filled to their former size with the extra food he'd eaten these past few months. The stiff collar creaked against his neck and he retied the dark-blue-and-black-figured scarf he wore underneath. He had half a mind to take the whole rig off and dump it in the water trough and start over, but he wanted to avoid shaming the boss. She was a handsome woman after all.

When Graver saw her standing with Drum Bennett without doing the old man any bodily harm, he grew uneasy, almost turned on his heel and left, then Drum saw him and lifted his chin and said something that made her turn.

What was she playing at? Graver nodded at Drum and waited until she'd concluded her conversation, then touched the old man's arm with her fingertips. If Graver hadn't seen the snakebit expression on her face when she turned her back to Drum, he would have suspected he was having the vapors. Drum gazed after them with the half smile of the snake that got the mouse.

"Ignore him," Dulcinea hissed as they headed for the door.

She wore a black buckskin divided riding skirt trimmed in fringe and a matching black vest beaded with red and yellow flowers over a white silk blouse with full sleeves gathered at the wrists. On her head was a black flat-brimmed hat to match her boots. She didn't wear her wedding band, he noticed, nor that wider one that had belonged to her husband on her thumb as she'd done since his death. As they walked toward the fairgrounds, he saw men turn to stare.

The entry parade at the rodeo was led by two trick riders dressed in white mounted on twin brown-and-white-spotted horses. Graver clapped enthusiastically and held his breath, but in the back of his mind the image of his own girls learning to sit the old horse dimmed the bright scene like a hand closing over a gold coin.

A group of seasoned cowboys came next, men who rode carelessly, shoulders rounded, legs stiff, rein hands raised as they clutched their hats and spurred their horses to a fast gallop past the crowd as if they had little time to waste. Graver could feel Dulcinea restless beside him on the splintered bench until three flag girls came trotting in, glancing anxiously at the snapping cloth over their heads and then at each other to keep their horses abreast and to not drop the flags. The crowd rose, placed their hands over their hearts, and the little band by the announcer's stand broke into "America the Beautiful," the tempo too slow and the piano off key.

After that it was a group of Sioux riders in full regalia. They pulled a travois and whole families walked alongside. The men were mounted on horses decorated with war paint and feathers. Some Horses and Rose walked in the middle of the group, with Lily leading Dulcinea's dog painted with a circle around his eye and a feather tied to the rope around his neck. Graver hoped she wouldn't notice, but she gave a sharp intake of breath and pointed her chin at the ring.

"That's my dog."

"Yes, ma'am," Graver said.

"Looks happy, doesn't he? And what horse is that?"

Graver squinted. "Must be their pony." He was puzzled at Rose's miserable expression. Some Horses beside her, determined and grim in his long war bonnet and the beaded outfit from his picture, led the horse.

"Hayward's on my stallion," Dulcinea murmured. "Sits him well."

The rest of the parade was rodeo clowns pushing each other in wheelbarrows, a line of local cowboys in wooly chaps and bright scarves, and girls in flowered shirts and pants.

"I thought he was supposed to ride him in the race." Dulcinea stared at him until he turned to face her.

"He's warming him up?" Graver tried to still his face. She tightened her lips and frowned.

He was saved by a series of firecrackers set off by one of the town boys, which startled some horses to rear and buck and spin. Graver noted that Hayward sat forward, pushed his feet down in the stirrups and grabbed the horn while the stud stood on his hind legs and teetered, on the verge of going over backward, then came down again.

Dulcinea grabbed hard onto his arm but didn't utter a word as her son spurred the horse into a gallop and guided it safely around the motley circus and out the gate.

"Boy has good instincts on a horse," Graver said, and she nodded, face pale.

As soon as the ring cleared, the rodeo commenced with saddle bronc riding, followed by steer wrestling, then bareback riding. Willie Munday rode his saddle bronc to a standstill but scored low because it hadn't bucked very hard. Larabee tried steer wrestling but jumped too late and missed the steer entirely, his horse coming to a stop and staring at him balefully. Then they worked the chutes and encouraged the other men. When the calf roping came, Jorge and Irish Jim tied for the fastest time and had a runoff that resulted in Jorge winning when Irish Jim's pigging string came untied and the calf jumped up and trotted away. Jorge rode around the ring at a dead run, whirling his lariat over his head like a trick rider, while the crowd hooted and clapped. Dulcinea's cheeks glowed pink and Graver was happy to see her laugh. When she sat down, she put her hand on his arm.

"That was wonderful, wasn't it!"

Graver nodded and returned her smile, then a peculiar thing happened — their gaze held a moment too long and he felt the flush rise up his neck into his face, and he couldn't drop his eyes. He wondered about the freckle below her eye, and the bump in her nose, did she always have them? When he put his hand over hers, he couldn't have stopped himself if someone held him at gunpoint.

"Oh," she said and tried to change the way her lips parted in a smile, but she couldn't make them stop.

He watched her struggle to compose an

expression and rubbed his fingers softly over hers, the way he'd gentle a startled horse.

There was a break in the action and Larabee came up the stands to collect them for the race. The scent of spit-roasting beef in preparation of the night's supper made their mouths water, and Graver searched for something to feed her, settling on fried chicken sold by the piece. He had just enough for one each, and felt again the pangs of being a man without money to treat a woman right. Larabee hung around them, giving Graver the eye until Dulcinea waved them away.

As soon as the men were out of earshot, Larabee said, "You can't put that stud in this race. He's too old. I could outrun that horse on one leg."

Graver nodded. "Where's the boy?"

"Brushing it. Got him shined up like Fourth of July and Christmas both."

Graver raised his hand. "I'll take care of it."

By the time they reached the horse preparation area to the west of the stands, Hayward was settling his saddle on the stallion, which pawed the ground and arched his neck in anticipation, already splotched with dark patches of sweat.

"Bring the chestnut." Graver nodded to

the horse tied to the rope stretched across the bare lot for the racers.

"Son." Graver put his hand on the boy's shoulder, who immediately dipped and twisted away. "You can't ride this horse."

Hayward's eyes blazed and his body turned rigid. "Like hell! My mother wants her horse in this race."

Graver patted the air between them. "It's not that."

Larabee stopped the chestnut beside them, careful to stay out of the stud's reach. "That horse of your mother's will still be trying to make it home come supper. Remember how much slower he is than Red here." He spit to the side and gave a quick chew on the wad in his jaw. "Now this horse, your pa bought him for this race. You know that?" He grinned, exposing blackened teeth and brown juice that threatened to drip down his shirtfront.

Graver nodded. "He'd want you to ride him. Give the men something to feel good about."

Hayward looked at the horse, then his boots, then the stallion. For a long minute Graver thought the boy wouldn't bite, then he nodded. Larabee handed him the reins.

"Go light on his mouth, hold him to the pack till you round the last turn, then set him loose and hang on. And don't whip him. He'll get you there." Graver patted the horse's neck and watched the boy mount, settling lightly in his mother's flat saddle. He'd do.

Hayward gave them a curt nod, bit his lip, and shrugged to loosen his shoulders as the chestnut danced and tossed its head.

"Your pa'd be proud of you," Larabee called and spit again. Then he turned his head to the side and muttered, "Hope he stays on."

They found the other hands waiting for the race, exchanging bets. Graver looked over the gathering crowd for Dulcinea and was relieved to find her occupied with Tookie and Evan Edson from the Crooked Post 8. She was drinking lemonade and smiling at something the other woman said as her son rode by on his father's horse, and missed his anxious search for her.

There were more than twenty riders and horses, including Percival Chance's long-legged Thoroughbred mare, Rose on their Indian pony, as well as other locals and several cowboys who traveled on the rodeo circuit. At the end of the ragged line, Graver spotted Irish Jim bareback on a rough-looking bay horse he'd never seen before. The horses pranced and shook their heads and pawed in response to the noise and rising tension of the onlookers until finally the announcer read the rules and fired a pistol in the air.

Two horses bolted, and a couple spun and tried to run the other direction. By then the dust rose in clouds and someone with a spyglass shouted, "They're off and running, a bay and chestnut in the lead." Chance's Thoroughbred was behind the leaders, and two others paced behind them with the main bunch back a ways.

Graver saw the boy had listened and held the chestnut in check. Let the others run the legs off their horses. The distance was too far for a front-runner to win. As the swirling dust settled, he removed his hat and waved the air in front of his face, then wiped his mouth with his hand and spit. The horses were spread out now, a long dark string pulled by the small bunch in front, like a child's toy. Squinting against the dust, Graver could make out the figure of Irish Jim hunched low on the rough bay's neck, and what looked like Hayward at his side while a big gray paced Chance's Thoroughbred in front. Behind, a horse in the middle of the pack stumbled and nearly fell, scattering those that followed and driving several up against Irish Jim's bay, who held on, switching leads as it absorbed the bump and leapt forward.

Then suddenly they were there, the wall of horseflesh pounding, shaking the ground, foam and dirt flung against the spectators, great lungs heaving for air, a rhythmic roar rising over the crowd's shouts, absorbing and annihilating, and it wasn't until the front-runners were well beyond that it was possible to sort their order again. Half the horses slowed after the first mile, chests labored, legs wooden, clumsy, heads flung, eyes wide, nostrils flared red, teeth bared against the bit, riders foam flecked, faces masked with dirt, already rising upright as their beasts faltered beneath them, broke into a trot, and pulled up in front of the spectators. Jumping down, the riders quickly dragged their horses off the raceway as the leaders neared the far turn.

Graver noticed Rose's spotted pony maintained a steady pace the whole time and now passed those in front, picking them off one by one as more slowed. A white horse staggered to a walk, then halted while the rider kicked uselessly. Graver started out there at a fast walk, but a man on horseback passed him, saying, "I got it." He hurried back before he was caught as the horses headed into the last quarter mile.

The gray, Hayward, Irish Jim, and Rose were neck and neck, thundering down on the people that pressed back at the vision: Would they make the final turn or simply run headlong into the crowd?

That was when Hayward made a young man's mistake. In his eagerness to win he flailed the horse with the end of his reins. The animal, already full out, slowed, which drove Hayward to slash him again and the horse stopped, tossed his head and humped his back. If he weren't exhausted, he would've bucked at the injustice. Instead he whipped his head around and bit the boy's leg, hard enough that he yelped in surprise and stopped flailing, sat back, and rubbed the spot. The chestnut, satisfied, picked up a trot, then a lope, and joined the stragglers.

The gray slowed and dropped into a choppy lope, head burrowing toward the ground, and the race came down to Irish Jim and Rose. The bay Jim rode was still game, but it foamed pink from its mouth and blood streamed from its nose. The lean spotted horse that had maintained the same rhythmic pace, unaltered for nearly two miles, surged ahead and swept over the finish line to a stunned silence. The Indians grouped to the side glanced nervously at the white crowd, nodded to each other and smiled, then quickly dispersed. The paint pony passed Graver with enough energy left to cast a malevolent eye and snap its teeth at the silent mass. Graver and Larabee laughed and the noise that followed was like a giant's breath, expelled in guffaws and hoots and applause. For a time it looked as if the temperature of the day had suddenly cooled.

Dulcinea pushed through the crowd as Hayward led the horse to where they stood. Grinning, the boy shook his head and rubbed the chestnut's neck. Graver stepped forward and patted him on the back. Lesson learned. Hayward looked at him, eyes shining with pride and newfound humility. This boy would do. Graver touched the brim of his hat.

"Son . . ." Dulcinea stepped closer, and Hayward stepped back.

"Have to see to the horse," he mumbled and walked on.

Dulcinea spun on Graver. "You simply must obey my orders!" She was all drawn up, like a dog on point, almost quivering in anticipation of the explosion.

"No, ma'am, I cannot obey orders that go against good sense."

She stared at him for a good long minute, then something shifted in her eyes. "You were right. He rode a wonderful race, didn't he?" She reached out for his arm. "I have to go congratulate my son."

Graver watched her ease through the crowd, and smiled despite himself.

"Guess we been skunked," Larabee drawled. "Never guessed that spotted pony had bottom. A woman riding it, too. Put us all to shame." A tall, white-haired stranger on the other side of Larabee spat and looked them over before he turned his bland face away and shouldered through the crowd. Graver searched for Hayward among the horses with heaving sides walking in circles, their backers disputing what went wrong in loud voices.

Irish Jim, next to the water trough, poured buckets over his little bay, which stood spraddle-legged and shaking. Jim stopped, took off his shirt, soaked it in a bucket, and then covered the animal's head with it. The horse groaned and Jim removed it, squeezed water between its ears so it ran down its face, and gently sponged the nostrils, crooning and murmuring to it the whole while, "There's a stout lad." He dipped the shirt-sleeve in the bucket and dribbled water in the horse's mouth.

"Need help?" Graver asked. When Irish Jim looked up, there were tears in his eyes.

The horse sighed and slowly collapsed, sat down like a dog for a moment before folding his front legs and rolling to its side, eyes closed.

"No!" Jim knelt, panicked. The horse answered with a deep rattling snore and smack of its lips.

"Believe he's tuckered out." Larabee walked up and spit not an inch beyond his own boots. "Unusual, but in his place, I believe I'd do the same. Might could use a beer when he wakes up."

Jim looked up at Graver as the horse snored with a regular rhythm.

"He'll be fine. Seen a few take this approach to no harm. Let him be." Graver looked at the people avoiding the animal as they walked past.

Larabee cleared his throat and stuck his hands in the back pockets of his trousers, his eyes focused on the racetrack. "You need to see this."

Graver's heart sank. Was the boy giving the horse grief?

Chance was still on the raceway, his tall boots coated with dust while his mare stood with its right front leg hanging limply from the knee, unwilling to place weight on it. The horse's breath came in short, staccato rushes, and shivering waves rolled over her body, some so strong she tried to shift her weight back on the injured leg and had to be steadied by the lawyer.

"Your chestnut cut us off! That boy's dangerous!" Chance shouted as soon as Graver and Larabee came in earshot. "This is a valuable horse! She's won every race she ever entered." The horse tossed her head, tried to lurch back and away.

"She's so dear, I'm surprised you put her in a two-mile race over rough country." Larabee lifted and resettled his hat so it shaded his eyes. "Hot out, ain't it."

Graver approached the horse, laid his hand on her right shoulder, and spoke to her quietly as he ran his other down the injured leg. She calmed, snorted, and dropped her head when Graver stood, stroking her long neck where the pain made the muscles stand rigid until they, too, began to release in quick ripples.

"Broken?" The lawyer looked at Graver, the horse, and back at Graver, who pinched the mare's skin between his fingers and released, noting how long it took to relax.

"Needs water pretty bad."

Chance threw up his arms, dropping the reins. "What's the point?"

Graver stepped into the punch, and hit the lawyer so hard his head snapped back and he staggered to his hands and knees. Behind him, Larabee picked up the reins to stop the horse from panicking and running away.

The lawyer struggled to his feet, and felt to see if his jaw was broken.

Larabee unfastened the cinch and set the saddle and blanket in the dust.

"You think so much of her, take her," Chance said, his voice muffled by the bulb starting to swell on the right side of his jaw.

"Don't forget your saddle!" Larabee spat a long brown stream at it as Dulcinea arrived, followed by Willie Munday, who struggled with two full buckets of water.

"How's — Oh no!" Dulcinea glanced between the two men and the horse. "I'm so sorry —" She touched the lawyer's arm. He shrugged her off and stepped around her to pick up his saddle.

"My own damn fault," he muttered, then shouldered the saddle and limped away. Graver stared after him a moment, thinking the man might have some grit after all.

CHAPTER FORTY-TWO

It began at dark when the prize money was passed out in the tent beside the grandstand. The group of Indians waited patiently at the end of the line for their race winnings, as if they knew that was where they were expected to be. It wasn't the whole group, only six young men, plus three of the older men, and Rose and Some Horses. The race organizers had passed out cheap bottles of whiskey freely after the win, and the older people wondered about the tactic. A couple of the young men had so much to drink they had to be supported by their Sioux brothers, those who saw the ruse for what it was. Now the little group wavered unsteadily as if an ill wind built its ire against them. Irish Jim stood with the Bennett Ranch cowboys while Jorge counted his money. Men from other ranches stood in similar knots inside and outside the tent. As darkness fell an electrical tension had spread among the crowd. Now left with little to do but drink, they focused their attention on the Indians, who had finally made it to the pay table.

"What can I do you for?" the bland-faced, white-haired man asked as his fingers flashed through a stack of bills, fanned them like cards, then shuffled and squared them. When he looked up he had an oval, fleshy, boneless face that reminded one of a mask as much as anything. The impulse was to dig a finger where the cheekbones should be to see if anything firm lay behind it or if his face could be peeled off like a rubber mask. A cigarette resting in the corner of his mouth bounced as he spoke, barely parting his thick lips. "Chief?"

Rose strode through the little group and placed her blue ribbon and cheap tin loving cup on the table, not slamming it down but making such a definitive move there was no question about her feelings.

"Won you a trophy and a ribbon, I see, well good for you," said the bland-faced man with the bloodless smile.

"I want the prize money goes with it," Rose said. Jerome and the other Indians murmured behind her. The cowboys enjoying the scene either nodded or shook their heads. Then one enterprising man removed his hat and offered odds on the Indians getting their money, and the men with fresh dollars in their jean pockets stepped up to bet on whether the man would successfully fleece the Indians.

"I gave your braves all the whiskey they could swallow right after the race. Now let me get back to my figuring." He made the dollars between his fingers disappear and began to stack the coins, then they vanished, too, like he was some kind of illusionist.

Rose stepped closer and rested her hands on the table. He merely eyed her fists and continued counting. When he'd made another stack of coins and bills disappear, he reached under the table, lifted a Colt revolver, and placed it next to his last stack of money.

The Indians behind Rose were silent as knives slipped into the hands of the younger men. They pressed forward. Irish Jim slid outside while Jorge stayed and reached for the knife he hid in his boot. Some cowboys left while others inched forward to back the man at the table.

"I won the race," Rose said in a low firm voice. "I want my hundred dollars."

The bland-faced man made the last of the money disappear, placed his hands palm down on the table and rose, the pistol sliding smoothly into his hand as if it had a will of its own. "And that was a hundred dollars' worth of whiskey. You people don't even know what money is." When he smiled it was a boyish grin that likely disarmed most. Jorge slipped around to the other side, halfway between Rose and the man behind the table. He held the knife low, the blade up in gutting position.

Rose stared at the man so long she seemed mesmerized, until her face slowly relaxed, shifted, and she leapt at him so quickly he didn't have time to shoot or move before she'd yanked the gun from his hand and pressed her skinning knife to his throat. The struggle was nearly over before the other men joined the action, swarming the fighters, and then taking on the Sioux and each other. Jorge swiped his knife at the barrel-chested steer wrestler, sliced his red shirt in half, and the man spun away, wiping the bloody scratch with one hand and holding the other up in surrender. Jorge stepped back and looked for another way to defend Rose as a crowd rushed the tent; so many piled in, the ropes squeaked and pulled the stakes from the ground, collapsing one side and pushing the fighting men outside to spread like wildfire through bunchgrass. In a matter of minutes, half the town was embroiled in the melee. What began as standing for the Bennett brand was now well beyond that as men burst noses and broke fingers and arms and teeth with abandon.

The Indians quickly dispersed, and with them the strongbox that held their prize money in addition to the rodeo proceeds. No one saw them except Irish Jim, who laughed and punched the man standing beside him in the ear. Jorge straddled the bland-faced man's back, whipping and spurring him like a bull as the man tried to buck him off. Hayward traded punches with a town boy who always seemed to mock him, mimicking his every move when he brought the ranch list to the store or went to church. They'd eyed each other since they were eight and now was the time. The other boy outsized him by forty pounds and three inches, but his body wasn't as lean and quick. Hayward hit him repeatedly in the kidneys with short jabs that built deep bruises and took his breath until the boy finally dropped to one knee and held his head. Hayward looked around to see if anyone had witnessed his victory, and since no one had, he shrugged and wandered toward the hotel where his mother was staying. He had been hit enough that the world was fuzzy and tilted. He put his eye on the open doors of the livery stable and staggered inside.

As if he were the ringleader, the fighting mob followed, men staggering in and out of contact, trading blows and sometimes just hugging each other, refusing to give up the battle as they collapsed from the beating and were later found in each other's arms like drowned lovers. Hayward was dimly aware of the commotion at his back as he entered the stable and walked down the long line of cheap straight stalls toward the back, where four box stalls held his mother's stallion and the chestnut, the lawyer's mare and the stable owner's personal animal, an ancient gelding he'd had since a young man.

At first Hayward thought he was still groggy from the fight, wiped his face with his hand, shook his head to clear it, and then accepted it as true — his mother and Graver were in each other's arms, kissing.

"What the hell," he murmured, took a step toward them and stopped. Graver stepped back first and glanced at the lawyer's mare dozing in the corner of the stall. His mother pressed her fingers against her lips. Hayward almost rushed to her then, thinking Graver's kiss unwanted, but stopped when he saw her tiny smile. She spoke in a low voice he couldn't quite hear and Graver lifted his gaze to her. She spoke again and the man shook his head, paused, half turned to leave, then turned back and swept her into his arms. It was like a scene from one of the dime novels the hands traded in the bunkhouse.

He couldn't interrupt them now, Hayward realized. A funny ache gripped his gut and spread its fingers up his spine until his shoulders and neck stiffened and hurt from holding his head upright. His father hadn't made her stay, and the blame had grown into hate until he was almost relieved when his father died and his mother returned. He wasn't sure how he felt now, things had changed. He heard the brawl move slowly down Main Street, away from the sound of broken glass, and the shouts of fighters and onlookers. That would be the store, where Haven Smith ruled their lives like petty cash, and would now discover the mob looting each freed bag of flour or pair of socks with the kind of malicious glee reserved for tyrants and bankers. One by one, Hayward heard the windows shatter along the street, followed by triumphant cries from the rioters. His brother would have joined them, no doubt, but he didn't feel the same enthusiasm for destruction. Truth be told, as he watched his mother and Graver embrace, he felt only one thing, the familiar sense of longing for comforting arms he'd had his entire life.

A gunshot rang out, followed by the explosion of a shotgun, more breaking glass, screaming and yelling and people running. A saddled horse galloped by the open door of the stable, eyes flashing, broken reins flapping in the air while the stirrups banged its sides, urging it to go faster, faster, faster. The joyfulness of the crowd changed into panic, and then to outrage as they spun and hurried back toward the source of the shots. Hayward half turned to watch through the open doors as the last building at the far end of the street burst into flames. The fire quickly dissolved into thick gray-white smoke more like heavy fog than burning as it billowed along the street, briefly blanketing the crowd, then passed beyond, leaving the figures shrouded in what seemed a mist as they coughed and straggled away. He knew the horses would panic if the cloud of smoke entered the stables, but if he moved, his mother and Graver would know that he watched. The horses in the straight stalls shifted and sniffed the air. Ironclad hooves banged against the wood sides and a horse sent a high questioning call into the darkness, to be answered by several low, reassuring nickers.

The stallion sensed Hayward's presence, and recognized his scent. He had been watching the melee, too. He recognized the smoke as from a smothered fire, and stood calmly as wisps entered the stable and disappeared into the blanketing darkness.

It was calmer now, business owners were tidying up, and the sound of tinkling glass could be heard in concert with the swishing of broom bristles against sidewalk boards. Here and there, men staggered together down the street toward one of the bars, arms across shoulders or hands locked like children struggling to reach home in a storm.

The dentist-sheriff, mysteriously absent during the riot, appeared with his hat slightly askew and his shirttail, untucked, hung over a large gun belt slung much lower than usual, as if he'd dressed in a hurry. His gait as he patrolled the sidewalk had a slight hitch and weave to the side that he struggled to straighten. It would be two hours before he was discovered in his office, near death with a knife wound in his back, the victim of an angry husband or dental patient, it was never determined which.

It would not have surprised Hayward that

Dulcinea's skirt brushed his leg as she walked past on Graver's arm, oblivious of her sleeping son or the fray that had swept through town, or of the figure who watched them from the dark alley as they crossed the street and made their way to the hotel.

CHAPTER FORTY-THREE

They hurried up the stairs, without noticing the sleeping desk clerk, down the second-floor hall to the large room at the end that was always saved for a Bennett, a courtesy passed from one year to the next, one generation to another. If Dulcinea felt any hesitation as she turned the filigreed brass knob, if she noted the floral design under her palm, it was impossible to tell, there was such confidence, such certainty in her movements. Standing to one side, Graver removed her dead husband's hat and scuffed the toe of her dead husband's boot across the cabbage rose carpet, as if smudging away a recent stain or clot of mud.

Inside the room, he shut the door as she assessed the chaos of clothing she'd abandoned in her haste. The mauve satin bed-cover she ordered all those years ago was faded and bore dark holes from cigarette ash and stains from careless eating and drinking in bed. She remembered only the exhilaration of the first night she'd slept here with her husband, newlyweds even after three months. Then she felt Graver's hands on her hips as he lifted and placed her on his lap. She buried her face in the matted hair of his chest, her fingers finding the new ridge of scar over the bullet hole in his shoulder. She thought she smelled the green sunlight of the hills as she held her breath, then felt the brush of his lips at her ear. "J.B.," she whispered.

She didn't realize she'd closed her eyes until she felt the empty cooling space and heard the door click shut behind him. When she reopened her eyes, she saw the shabbiness of the room, the glow of J.B. had dissolved, and Graver was gone. Maybe it wasn't possible to recover the past, she thought, or to find a true present. She could only live in this shadow version of both, without love and purpose.

With her cheek against the cover, Dulcinea imagined her breath was like a breeze caressing silk drapes at an open window, creating a strange music like someone running their fingers across satin. When she held it, she swore she could still hear it, and began to breathe in tandem with the sound, unsure whether she created it or it created itself. Whether she imagined J.B. or Graver with her that night, she could not say, for it seemed they were one. She felt the terrific weight of her husband alive outside this small vial of present time, and she also felt Graver breaking into her world, shattering every window and flinging the door off its hinges each time he was near, until the more drawn she was to him, the more alive J.B. became.

Everything was silent and black when she rose sometime during the night and knelt at the window. She looked down at the two figures in the shadows, struggling, cursing, and saw the taller one stab the shorter, thicker man. He wrenched the knife upward and lost his grip when the victim staggered and fell. The attacker looked down the alley each way, drew his pistol, nudged the body on the ground, seemed to decide against the noise it would make, and put it away. He searched the victim's pockets, withdrew a packet of papers and money before sliding into darkness. When she awoke in the morning, she was convinced it was a nightmare.

When Drum Bennett was found, barely alive, the next morning, the sun was well up, and the day promised to be the hottest of fall, the air filled with the pounding of nails into boards to replace broken windows and voices calling up and down Main Street reporting damage. Drum lay in a narrow alley between the hotel and the boot maker. He was discovered by a gang of boys searching the debris of the night's revelries for anything they could find, which thus far had produced only a pocket knife with a broken blade, a couple of whiskey bottles with a drop or two in the bottom, and a silver dollar they fought over.

CHAPTER FORTY-FOUR

It was Dun Riggins, owner of the livery stable, who woke Hayward with the news of his grandfather's injuries and the demise of Percival Chance from a collision with a runaway wagon. Hayward sat, blinking in the dusty light, unclear where he was. Then the fight flooded back, followed by other confusing images, and he stood, confirmed the Bennett horses were still in their stalls, and lurched toward the almost unbearable light beyond the big double stable doors.

He was horribly thirsty and unsteady on his feet, and some part of him knew his presence was required at Drum's bedside. When thoughts of his mother came, he found it easy to push them behind the pain that sat like a skullcap behind his eyes, crushing his head as it moved to the back of his neck. He was halfway to Doc's when he thought he heard someone call his name. He didn't slow. Then he heard it again, along with a thumping, irregular boot step. He stopped and turned to face Stubs, Drum's ranch hand.

The man tilted his head for them to continue without speaking, and they were almost there before Stubs paused and turned toward the street, watching as the riders from the Box LR, led by Larson Dye looking worse for the wear, walked past. Across the street, Stillhart the banker spoke with Harney Rivers, both staring and nodding toward Doc's place.

"Gonna be a lot of that," Stubs said. "Smart man sticks to his relations, keeps his mouth shut till he know the lay of the land."

Hayward felt an old anger rise in chest. "Like Cullen did?"

Stubs shook his head and rubbed the knee that always ached. "Not saying do what he did. Sometimes he knew enough to sit quiet and wait to see how the game played out." He glanced at Hayward, took in the bruises, cuts, and blood, and nodded with satisfaction. "You're carrying the name now. It's up to you."

Hayward opened his mouth, about to ask the old cowboy what he was talking about, when the sudden weight of the words caught in his throat so dry he couldn't even cough.

He shook his head and walked on until he reached the door to the clinic built onto the side of a tidy brown house. The small rooms housed the doctor, his old-maid daughter, and a strange young girl from Ireland whose passage was to be paid as an indentured servant. She puzzled Hayward even now as she pulled open the door before he had a chance to knock. Standing slightly behind him, Stubs whispered, "Them crows are circling, boy, better make tracks."

Hayward jerked as if stung by a wasp, then explained who he was. She led them through the entryway, down a hall, into the kitchen, and through another door to a room large enough for six beds with a wooden chair beside each; a tall cabinet with glass doors and shelves that held jars, bottles, and stacks of cloth for bandages; and a narrow harvest table littered with scraps of paper and a ledger book. Although every bed held a patient, including the dentist-sheriff, the last bed against the back wall drew their attention.

Graver stood at the foot, hat held at waist, while Dulcinea sat beside Drum, holding his hand — a sight so strange Hayward almost took a step back. As he approached, he saw that his grandfather's face was white and drained. "Cullen?" the old man whispered in a weak voice. "You fighting again? Soon as I'm up and around, I'll see to you —"

Hayward snatched off his cowboy hat and shook his head.

His mother was focused on Drum, and brushed the hair off his forehead with a light touch. "I decided you're right. You'll be better soon, and we can combine our two ranches, live in my house, rent out the other or let the men use it. Hayward will take over in a few years."

"I'll build a new house for us, and the boys." Drum gazed at her and smiled, his eyes filled with tears. "I never meant harm to any of you — J.B. — wasn't me —" His voice slid away as he struggled to breathe against a wave of pain.

Dulcinea glanced over her shoulder and didn't seem to notice the condition of her son's face and clothes. Without dropping Drum's hand, she tilted her head to beckon him over. Hayward leaned back like an unbroken colt tied to a post, then stepped forward as soon as Graver put a hand on his shoulder. The old man lifted his free hand as if to wave them closer.

The confusion on the wounded man's face rendered him harmless, even childlike, something no living person had ever seen.

It unnerved him.

"We're glad you're here." Dulcinea patted Drum's hand.

Hayward was about to bolt. Graver stepped back to give him room to breathe, then eased over and took the chair beside the dentist's bed as Hayward sat at his grandfather's side.

"How's he doing?" Hayward asked. The harsh glare that usually shone from Drum's eyes was gone, replaced by benign confusion. Brain stroke? He had seen cowboys fall off their horses and wake with this expression, but he'd never expected to see it on Drum Bennett.

Dulcinea released Drum's hand, placed it on his chest. He hesitated to touch his grandfather. When Judge Foote walked through the doorway, Dulcinea's lips parted and Drum's breathing became labored.

The judge glanced at the family, paused at the foot of the dentist's bed, and nodded to the room. He cleared his throat, then reached out, grabbed the dentist's foot, and gave it a good shake. Receiving no response, he cleared his throat loudly as Doc entered the room.

"Here now, stop that!" Doc pulled the judge away from the bed, then dropped his voice. "He's sleeping, for Christ's sake."

"Dying?" The judge squinted with a near-sighted expression and lifted his chin at the patient.

"You keep bothering him." Doc shook his head and moved to the far side of Drum's bed with the judge fast on his heels.

"Drum Bennett going to make it?" The judge's voice seemed to bang against the walls like a gunshot, making the family jump.

"What's wrong with you?" Doc shook his head and peered over his glasses at Drum's face as he checked the old man's wrist for a pulse. He shook his head again and released the hand while Drum watched without interest.

"How you doing, sir?" The judge's booming voice ratcheted around the room again. The other patients muttered and tossed in their sleep.

"Heard Lawyer Chance didn't make it. You have his body here?" The judge looked at the doctor, who shook his head and moved to the next patient. "That's a hard way to go, trampled by a runaway team, especially your own. Too late to appreciate your own irony." His bright eyes swept the group around Drum's bed. Dulcinea's face paled at the news and she glanced at her son. Hayward didn't respond. He'd never had any use for the lawyer. He reckoned she'd have to hire Rivers now. It had nothing to do with him. She hesitated, then stood and motioned the judge to follow as she swept past Graver and Hayward, across the room and out the door. Hayward gazed after her until they were out of the room, then he slipped into her chair and peered closely at the old man, his last living Bennett relative.

Hesitantly, he reached for his hand, touched it with trembling fingers, and jerked away when the back of it twitched like a horse ridding itself of a fly. "Grandfather? Drum? Sir?"

Drum moved his head and fixed him with his stare. Hayward cleared his throat and inched closer, opened his mouth, closed it, and opened it again, licking his lips. His hair fell forward across his cheek and he brushed it back impatiently. The small moment of order strengthened him and this time he squared his shoulders and spoke.

"I know you got no use for me, sir. That's as it may be. I wanted to say something." He looked at the crack where the whitewashed wall met the raw cedar ceiling. "I miss my brother, sir, much as you." He paused and swiped his eyes with the back of his hand. "But I ain't a baby. I'm grown enough to run the ranches and that's what I'm fixing to do, sir!" His voice rose on the last words and Drum gave a deep guttural groan that made him leap to his feet and eye his grandfather with horror.

"Need gold," the old man struggled to say.

"No, sir. I can make them pay on their own. You always low-rated Cullen and me, and I'm gonna show you."

Drum shook his head and coughed so long it seemed he wouldn't stop. Hayward reached to lift his head, and the old man said it again, "Gold."

Dulcinea rushed in and placed a hand on her son's chest. "Stop it!" she commanded in a harsh whisper. Hayward spread his arms and shook his head before stepping back against the wall.

"I didn't do anything!" He pouted as the adults did an elaborate dance, trading places around the bedside until Graver was back where he started at the foot.

Dulcinea looked at the judge on the other side of the bed. "Are you ready?" She picked up Drum's hand.

"Ma'am?" The man was balking like a calf on a rope. Hayward couldn't figure it out.

"Do it now." When the judge merely raised his brow, she continued. "You're to marry us, remember?" She used the clasped hands to point to Drum and herself while Graver took a step back and Hayward a step forward as if to stop her.

The judge looked at the old man to make sure his eyes were open, and then at Hayward, who fingered the felt brim of his hat. With a deep sigh, the judge lifted his chest, ran his fingertips lightly over the top of his head as if smoothing a baby's downy hair, and began the ceremony, which after five brief sentences concluded with: "I pronounce you married."

Dulcinea nodded and pressed the battered old hand against her lips, with her head bowed and eyes fixed on Drum's face, over which spread the slightest glow of pleasure, as if he had waited an entire lifetime for this moment. When he muttered "Geneva," the name of his first wife, J.B.'s mother, everyone pretended not to hear. Hayward felt the sting of her deceit deep inside his chest.

"I'll get the papers now," the judge said. His face wore a peculiar expression like he struggled not to laugh, as if he'd just seen the mouse swallow the cat whole.

"Please hurry," Dulcinea said.

Hayward straightened off the wall and seemed to grow several inches in his outrage. "What the hell is this, Mother?" He grabbed her shoulder, yanked her to face him.

She looked at him but held her tongue until he released her. "Go run the ranches. This marriage means we have a clear title, son, don't you see? Your father wanted you to have the land." Her cheeks burned pink under his glare. "We can talk later."

"No. No, we won't." Hayward's mouth twisted and white foam appeared in the corners. He merely stared at the tableau of the widow bride, the hired man, and the old tyrant who finally closed his eyes.

He looked at his mother. He hadn't seen this coming and didn't have a name for it. If the old man pulled through — He grimaced. Didn't have a name for that either. He looked at the woman he'd recently vowed to protect and realized he didn't understand her at all and had completely underestimated her. He wouldn't be surprised if she lay down on the bed right there and then and took the old man in her arms. The hated old bastard, her new husband.

Hayward pulled on his hat and walked away, and didn't turn when she called him back. Cullen had been right about her the whole time.

CHAPTER FORTY-FIVE

Drum died at dawn after their wedding night, as if mocking all marriage for all time, except no, that was her. Dulcinea sat by his side, held his hand, and restrained him when he tried to rise at the end, reaching with his other hand as if to stop some vision. He cried out a name, Wilke, and a horrified expression crossed his face. He tried to speak, his throat clogged with blood, and still she held on, refusing to let him flee. "You're mine now," she whispered so Graver and the doctor standing at the foot of the bed could not hear. "I've got it all now."

Drum shook his head and slapped the bed with his other hand as if to signal, but it meant nothing. He began to choke, then finally drowned in his own bright blood. When Dulcinea left, clutching the marriage certificate, instead of the triumph she'd expected, she felt burdened by a terrible sense of waste. Graver was right. This dreaming land had killed them all. It didn't stop her, though. After sitting with the dead man until midmorning, she sent word to the judge, Stillhart, and Rivers to meet her at the hotel. She had made up her mind about the oil and gas leases.

She turned to Graver, who lingered in the corner of the room, a watchful expression in his eyes, and motioned him outside, leaving Drum Bennett without a backward glance. The old bastard had finally given her family a future.

"I know what you're thinking," she said as soon as the door to the doctor's house closed on them.

Graver put on his hat and crossed his arms, staring at the dusty toes of his boots.

"I did it for my son. Drum would have taken it all and corrupted Hayward in the process. You know what he was like." When she met with silence, she put a hand on his arm. "I couldn't give him another son. I couldn't let him take everything J.B. and I worked for, and he would have. You know he would have. He was going to sell us out, too. Everything can go back to the way it was now . . ." Her voice fell and she dropped her hand. "What passed between us, what we did in the stable, I — It's too soon. I want, I hope —" She stopped when he

627

shrugged and turned to walk away.

"I'm not finished!" She almost stamped her foot she was so tired.

"I need to round up the hands and get back to work, ma'am." There was no inflection in his tone. Neither he nor her son understood or forgave her. She bit her lip to keep from crying out and begging him to stay. Across the street she saw the judge and Rivers enter the hotel. She had to take care of business now. She'd finish this later.

She knew what they thought, it was written on their faces, the bright, expectant eyes and smiles despite Drum's passing. She let them sit, hands folded like expectant schoolchildren anticipating cookies, and looked down at her white silk shirt, dotted with Drum's blood, noting the dark constellations like a reversed sky.

"I've made up my mind," she announced. They nodded, and Stillhart pushed the contract toward her while Rivers uncapped his pen and laid it next to the papers, in charge now that Chance was dead. The men seemed to have little reaction to his passing. She realized that he had no allies or friends among them. It was just as he'd described when they first met: no one in town wanted to know him. Thinking back, she'd always felt Chance had other irons in the fire, plans she might not like or approve of, as if he were steering her in his own secret direction. She never trusted him, and she sensed these men didn't either. He was a stranger passing through. No past and no future. It was likely that in a few years, no one would remember he was ever here. She looked at the men before her, men she would spend the rest of her life dealing with in one way or another. They needed to understand each other.

"You know J.B. loved the Sand Hills." The men nodded eagerly, as if anything she said now would sound perfect to their ears. "I've grown to love them, too. Yet I know how terribly difficult it is to live here. I've lost my husband and son, and now Drum —" They murmured their condolences, and it sent a small tremble through her clenched jaw because truth be told, she *had* lost something with his passing.

She picked up the contract, pretended to read, then dropped it on the table and stood. "I'm not signing anything. J.B. wouldn't want this, and before he died Drum told me he no longer agreed with it."

"We'll sue!" Rivers said, and Stillhart swore under his breath.

"Oh, I think my father still has enough

connections to stop you in court, don't you? Besides, I'm a widow and I've lost a son and two husbands. You're going to steal my land, too?"

As she left, she patted each man on the shoulder to reassure him of her continued goodwill.

Dulcinea didn't allow the tears until after dark, halfway to the ranch with Rose, who was waiting for her in the stable when she left the hotel. The soft thudding rhythm of the loping horses muffled her sobs and Rose kept her eyes on the road in front of them. In her heart, she knew she could only give in to the overwhelming sadness this one time. The ranch and her son required too much from her now. As they approached the valley, the two women halted on the last hill as they had four months before when she had rushed home following J.B.'s death. She shook her head at how ignorant she'd been. She'd had no idea how great her losses could become. She turned to Rose.

"You know why I married Drum?" she asked.

Rose patted her horse and gave it rein to graze. "Figured it was to hold the land in your name."

Dulcinea felt a pang at her words. What

could she do, give it back to the Sioux? She and J.B. had talked about who owned the hills, and they'd never solved it either.

"We aren't any closer to finding the murderer," she said. The stallion pulled at the reins and tried to grab a mouthful of grass. She let out more slack.

"Maybe he's already dead."

Dulcinea glanced at her friend. Did she mean Drum or Cullen? "Percival Chance?"

Rose shrugged.

Chapter Forty-Six

Nearly a month had passed since the rodeo and Drum's death. During that time, Dulcinea gave Hayward the running of his grandfather's ranch and Graver the running of J.B.'s. Late September was the first time the cattle would run together without splitting them afterward. With such a huge herd, it meant dark-to-dark days for everyone on the two ranches as they collected and pastured them for winter near the two houses.

Dulcinea fed the branding fires for late calves and yearlings they'd missed and handled the chuck wagon and water. She was bone tired and relieved it was the last day. They only had ten head to go, but the hands had to change horses and eat. The break would help settle the herd, though. Right now, they were dangerously close to stampeding, and any little thing could set them off. The men withdrew carefully, skirting the edges, avoiding those cows searching for their calves. Dulcinea admired the natural rhythm between Rose and Some Horses as they worked the cattle.

She watched Graver, too, a man whose body moved with the horse as he roped a yearling and dragged it unwillingly to the cowboys waiting by the fire with hot branding irons. The stench of burning hide rode the dust churned under hooves and drifted to the chuck wagon. Dulcinea tried to breathe through her mouth, but it sat on her tongue, so she gave up and let it soak her clothes, hair, and skin. If she was to stay here, she'd better get used to every inconvenience. A horse loped by with an empty saddle, stirrups banging wildly at its sides. She shaded her eyes with her hand and squinted in search of its rider. Sure enough, a figure trudged toward the camp. She felt relief at recognizing Hayward, still so angry he barely spoke, and God only knew when he'd forgive her. But she did it for him, she protested during the daily argument in her head. It was all for her son. She never questioned the rationale, though she felt the hairline cracks in it.

When Hayward caught the dun gelding that had once been Cullen's, Graver and the other hands clapped and cheered him on. Hayward bowed and shook his head. She wanted to join them, but thought he would misinterpret her intentions. She turned her back and stirred the beans and beef in the big pot on the fire.

"Some damn prospector spooked him," Hayward said as she handed him a plate.

"Prospector?" Her hands stilled. She gazed at the top of his head as he sat on the ground and tucked into his food.

He looked up and nodded behind her. "That's him."

The stranger wore khaki-colored trousers and shirt, and a wide-brimmed plantation hat over a nondescript face. Dismounting, he gazed at the camp and loosened the saddle girth. A pick and shovel and metal sample box hung from his saddle. He slipped a halter and rope over the bridle and let the horse drop its head to graze.

"Ma'am." He touched his hat brim and eyed the hot food.

Dulcinea wanted to drive him off her land, but knew the hospitality laws of the West demanded she offer him a meal first.

After he'd eaten two platefuls, he pushed back his hat and gazed at her. "You'd be Dulcinea Bennett." Without waiting for a reply, he continued, "Name's Pittcairn, from Western Oil and Gas."

"I know who you are, and the answer is still no," she said. Folding her arms across her chest, she pushed back her shoulders and lifted her chin.

"You sure? Last opportunity. All this sand, usually find something. Can't say there's oil for sure, but what do you have to lose? Get money for exploration, much more if we find something." He paused and watched a calf struggle against the branding iron, then it kicked a cowboy's thigh so hard the man fell down. "Beats this." He spread his hand to include the roiling cattle and distant hills.

"My mother said no. As co-owner, I back her." Hayward stood over him. "You've had your fill, now ride." He stepped back. "Don't let me catch you here again." He hooked his thumbs on the twin holsters he still wore.

The man shrugged. "Missing an opportunity. Were me, I'd much rather see derricks pumping black gold than cattle slopping up the place with green crap. You folks will die poor. What about your children? Don't you owe them something?"

Hayward shook his head. "Ride three hours north, you'll get to a railroad." He moved to Dulcinea's side and put his arm around her. She nearly broke down with relief, but knew better and stood straight, biting her lip to keep the tears from springing to her eyes. It didn't matter that he dropped his arm the moment the man was out of sight.

"Have to keep them off the land. More coming and we can't tolerate it. I'll march them off at gunpoint if I have to." He sounded so grown, she smiled.

"That's good, son," she said and bent to stir the beans and beef again as the cowhands drifted in for their meal.

Without Chance to advise her, Dulcinea realized she wasn't sure of her legal rights to deny the exploration of her land. She hoped the other ranchers would lend their support. Tookie would. They had spoken briefly at Drum's burial in the graveyard next to J.B. and Cullen. No one had much to say about the old man, and most were too embarrassed by the quickie wedding to stick around and talk to Dulcinea or Hayward. Tookie did mention the lawyer's face was so battered by the runaway horses that he had to be identified by his clothes and the papers in his pocket.

They were down to the last five calves and despite the odd haziness of the sky, Dulcinea thought the weather would hold long enough for her to ride to the line shack that had been Cullen's while the others finished the work. The boundary between the two ranches was nearby, and she could follow the barbed wire fence to the cabin. Over the past few weeks she'd started to piece together the fragments of his life after he was taken by Drum. Everything she found made her feel closer to her son. When she reached the windmill, she stopped to allow the stallion a drink. Soon she would have her men tear down the fence dividing the land. A breeze from the north pushed the windmill blades around with an uneven squeal that ground in her ears like she was chewing sand. She and J.B. had always laughed about this one. The memory brought tears to her eyes, and she vowed never to replace it no matter how much it irritated.

She thought back to the moment she finally understood what the ranch meant to J.B. and what it had cost them all.

It was early spring after Drum took Cullen, and before she left. She couldn't eat or sleep, paced days and nights, searching for the reason J.B. allowed this to happen, and why he wouldn't do a thing to bring back her son. She took to getting up in the night once she heard his light snoring, and thought nothing could allow her to sleep as naturally as he did. One night she hoped a glass of brandy would help close her eyes, and went to his office. She never sat in his chair, it hadn't seemed right, but she did that night. She sat too low to command the desk the way he did, and poured a glass of their wedding brandy. The thick, sweet bite threatened to turn her stomach. She clenched her teeth, drank until her throat grew numb, her head light, and her body unsteady. She decided that night that she would leave in two weeks as Drum had ordered.

She had married Drum to secure the ranches for Hayward, but she also did it to save herself, to save something for herself — these hills, this dream, when for a short, lovely time she believed that her life, their life, meant this place and what they did here, what they learned by living and loving each other. It was because she still felt him here, J.B., he touched her, and nothing could change this place, this land, lest he and Cullen were left alone in their separate graves.

It was how she understood the Indians like Rose and Some Horses who mourned the land, not as wealth but as the place where all was alive, all living, in one form or another. The whites took it but the dead still walked it, the spirits, whatever they were. Her faith had removed God, dispersed him like seed or gravel. It was not that God didn't exist. It was that he wasn't alone, but in pieces, parts, always whole, sufficient, always multiple. So like the ancient Greeks she trod lightly, carefully, tried to give no offense to the land, the sacred grass her feet crushed, the ants hurriedly preparing caverns for the winter, pushing tiny yellow boulders out of a hole the size of a bee's leg. Oh the offense, to walk so clumsily through the world, to crush and bring havoc, that they couldn't help. But to give no recognition to the cost of their being alive, to the price paid for their dreams by everything else? J.B., Cullen, now Drum.

She turned the stallion back toward the dim path that led to the line shack and thought of Hayward. He was seeing Pearl Stryker now. She was too old and experienced for him. He was also seeing the new schoolteacher from Ohio. And a girl from Rosebud Reservation. And several others. In a dream J.B. told her he would love many women, unable to resist them, but he'd marry and live a long life, have a son and send him to military school in Missouri, position him to inherit the Bennett fortunes, and though she would not live to see it, a long line of children followed. There was a red smear on the white tile wall of the future. People couldn't help the pain that rode them like overbroke ponies and tired them too soon for the length of a life.

Lost in her thoughts, she didn't notice the weather change until the cold breeze made her shiver and she realized the hazy sunlight had thinned and the air turned gray-blue. She put her heels to the stallion to hurry him. Overhead heavy gray-white clouds eased back and forth, casting dark shapes across the valley. To the north a wall of gray-white, a mile away and several miles wide, rolled toward them, sent by the sudden gusty wind that lifted the stallion's mane and scattered it, breaking the sky to pieces. He stopped and danced sideways, swinging his haunches into the wind, and called long and loud into the empty hills, ears pricked, waiting for a reply that didn't come. She looked at the empty horizon and saw she was the only vertical thing for miles. The wind, filled with bits of sand, stung the skin and threatened to fill their eyes. They'd never make it home; she'd have to try for the line shack though it meant riding straight into the storm. She turned the stallion and slapped him with the reins.

The sun disappeared and the wind became a roaring whirlwind and she couldn't tell direction anymore. After a while, she understood that it was snow and ice that pelted her bare skin, not sand. Her chest hurt as she held her breath against the cold that encased her in her soaked clothes, and trembling waves rose up her legs into her arms and teeth that she clenched to keep from chattering. Don't stop, she urged the stallion, keep moving. They were in one of those early blizzards that came sweeping across the hills without notice, stranding cattle and killing people. She looked into the white walls of whirling snow and called for help, but the wind whipped her words away with a loud roar. Her eyes were heavy with ice, and she decided it was better to close them than have them freeze open. She pulled her hair from the bun and tried to wrap it around her neck, but the wind caught it, filled it with snow and ice and flung it back like a club beating against her shoulders and head. She buried her hands in the stallion's snow-filled mane, fought to keep her fingers tight on the reins. She should knot them around her hands, she thought, she should knot the reins so they didn't slide over his head, she should knot them, and put the end in her mouth, or under her thigh, she should stop, remove the saddle, wrap herself in the blanket and ride bareback so his body would keep her warm, but how to remount, he was too tall, so she lay on his neck for protection. The stallion lifted his head to push her back, and she was forced to open her eyes. When he whinnied, the sound started deep in his belly and shook his body, again no answer. Dulcinea became aware of parts she rarely thought about, the tops of her thighs that burned and then grew numb, her knees that felt as if she knelt on a frozen lake, her elbows so sharp with cold they rubbed raw where the frozen cloth of her shirt touched.

In her delirium, she saw a picture of J.B. and herself and their old dog Jesse James, named after a distant relative in Missouri, caught in a blur of motion in front of their half-finished house. They were so young and handsome and the snow turned the world white around them. She saw J.B. reflected in the window of their completed house, fingerprints from his hand on the glass as he called to her. She startled awake. "I'm here! Help!" The wind snatched her words.

She saw him gather his old buffalo hide coat, hat and scarf, and horsehide mittens lined in rabbit fur, and pull out the bag he kept at the ready for winter mishaps when stranded cattle and folks on the road needed rescuing. She was trapped between alternating wind shears and storms, and felt snow crisscrossing in front of her face. "Keep moving," she heard J.B. say. "Don't stop."

Then she was sure he was there beside her, reaching for the ice-encased rein, pulling the stumbling horse along, rubbing the horse's shoulder and speaking low words of praise, telling the stallion he was brave and strong, calling him his night horse, blowing his own breath into his nostrils dripping with ice, stroking his nose and heating the ice until his face dripped and his large eyes gained brightness and he fought fiercely onward, lifting his legs high above the gathering drifts, marching to the music of his words. She felt him rest his hand on her small boot. The leather warmed and a sigh escaped her lips. He moved his hand up her ankle, calf, knee, and thigh, and his extraordinary heat relieved the numbness of her muscles, the bitter cold that had begun to settle in her bones. His heat pushed beneath her skin, deep into her flesh. She imagined he could feel her blood as he swam up onto the horse's back, settled behind her, wrapped his coat and arms around her, and held her in the saddle. All he wanted was her forgiveness, she realized. The horse stumbled to a stop, nose pressed against the door of the old line shack. When the door unlatched, the animal stepped inside to the warmth of a small fire and a candle flickered in the sudden gust of blown snow.

Dulcinea slid down, pushed the door closed, and stumbled to the fire to warm her hands as snow dropped off the horse and puddled on the hard-packed dirt floor. When she was warm, she stood, shook the last of the melting snow off her clothes, and glanced at the walls of the shack, surprisingly tight, the cracks filled with animal hair, grassy mud, and paper. A candle guttered on the table among several pieces of scattered paper and a dirty plate and cup, as if someone had just left the room. Who was living here? Her heart leapt. Cullen! She calmed herself. Of course not, but someone.

Curious, she lifted a page from the table and saw it was a deed for Drum's ranch, with a shaky signature at the bottom that bore little resemblance to his firm block letters. She quickly scanned the other pages, which included the deed to J.B.'s and what appeared to be someone practicing Hayward's and her signatures. Even though they were poor efforts, their intent was clear. She sank into one of the two straight-backed chairs. Who could this be? Whoever it was, it meant she and her son would have to disappear. A deeper chill came over her, and she began to shiver uncontrollably.

The stallion lifted his head and gave a deep guttural whinny as the door opened.

Chapter Forty-Seven

Graver fought against the image of Dulcinea frozen beneath a ten-foot snowdrift that wouldn't melt for another two weeks when one of those warm trade winds rode through the hills, melted everything in a day, and delivered the dead as casually as flowers in spring: cattle caught in fence corners, crowding each other, trapped by their own panic and blindness in the storm, people caught unawares when the winds shifted and the sun fled behind a wall of snow and ice. Sometimes a horse and rider were found together like lovers, belly to belly in a last frantic arrival at the end. Once, a whole family in their buckboard on the way home when it struck, somehow too blind and exhausted to move once the horses mired in a six-foot drift, and the family froze to death where they sat, as polite and still as worshippers on the splintered boards, reins still gripped in the father's hands, his mouth open as if calling his last benediction upon the sleeping heads of his little ones.

At least he knew where she was headed, unless the stallion had lost its instinct for survival. He patted the chestnut, shouted encouragement, and kept his eye on the fence line as best he could in the whiteout. It couldn't be much farther.

The chestnut nearly rammed the wall of the lean-to behind the shack. Graver had to turn him aside as he dismounted, then feel his way into the dark shelter. He unsaddled the horse, tossed some hay off the mound in back, and hooked the wire gate. With the saddle in his arms, he pushed a shoulder against the shack door and shoved it open. At least it wasn't latched. He was surprised when the stallion greeted him like an old friend. Dulcinea stared at him in disbelief.

"It's *you*?"

Graver looked at her. "You expecting somebody else?" He dropped the saddle by the fire.

She eyed him, loathing on her face. "I trusted you. My son trusted you."

Graver was confused. He'd followed her through a blizzard and this was how she greeted him? It didn't make sense. "You want me to put your horse in the lean-to with mine?"

She gazed at the cabin walls as if searching for something, and he had a bad feeling it was a weapon. What had he ever done to her?

She picked up a paper from the table and waved it at him. "You think I don't know what you're doing? How long have you been living here?"

He shook his head and grabbed the stallion's reins. "You know where I live. Think about it. How would I get back and forth without you noticing I was gone all the time? The men would say something. Your son would know. Rose and Jerome, too." He lifted the reins and started to turn.

"I don't know what to think." She set the paper on the table, gathered the others into a neat stack, squaring the sides, and placed the ink bottle and pen on top.

"Try trusting me. I never did a damn thing but work to earn my keep. I'm beginning to think you want me gone." As he unsaddled the stallion he felt the exhaustion he'd fought for months now. He was tired of this life he'd been leading since he came to Nebraska. It was no good, his trying with her. He should know better. "I'll put him in the lean-to. Wait out the storm, be gone soon as it quits. I can stay out there with the horses if it suits you."

"Don't be ridiculous," she said.

Graver led the horse outside, gathered more hay, and warned him not to fight with the chestnut gelding or he'd be standing out in the storm. He was fastening the gate when a tall black horse appeared out of the snow with a rider slumped on its back. He reached for the reins, pulled them from the man's hand, and led the animal into the shelter. The horse nuzzled the chestnut and ignored the stallion as it grabbed hungrily at the hay after Graver pulled the bridle over its head. He wondered if the rider was alive; he appeared frozen, bent over the saddle horn the way he was. He shook the man's leg, pressed his chest against the horse's side, and eased him down as best he could. Gradually, the man slid off and Graver released his boot from the stirrup. Once on the ground, the man leaned on the horse and took several deep breaths before pushing off and nodding. Graver rested him against the fence while he unsaddled the animal. Then he fought the storm and drifts to the shack door with the saddle in one hand and the man's arm in the other. Inside, he sat him beside the fire to warm. When he turned, Dulcinea stood glaring at them both with a rusty muzzle loader in her arms.

"Who is that?" she demanded. "Does he live here?"

Her questions struck Graver as odd. He ignored her and found a pot, filled it with snow and began to heat it over the fire.

The stranger sat with legs stretched out and shoulders slumped, hiding his face. He was dressed in a motley array of coats and pants, and his dirty blond hair hung in greasy strands. His new beard had grown in red and brown.

As soon as the water steamed, Graver poured a cup and handed it to him. When the man looked up and smiled, Graver was shocked.

"Chance. Thought you were dead."

"Almost. Went out hunting and got caught by the storm. Same as you folks, I'd say." He lifted the cup, drained it, and held it out for more.

Dulcinea edged forward, aiming the gun at the two men.

"Doesn't fire," Chance said. "Already tried it."

Her eyes sharpened. "You live here?"

He nodded. "Not a bad place for a retreat. Cullen was right."

She flinched at the mention of his name. Graver stepped toward her, and she swung the musket in his direction.

650

Chance laughed. "She doesn't trust you either."

Ignoring the drama, he unlaced his wet boots, slid them off, and a sweet stink oozed into the little room. "I'm afraid" — Chance looked apologetically at his feet — "they're frostbit. Third time it's happened. Slightest chill they split and bleed." He shook his head.

"Let me see." Graver knelt on the hearth and eased off the white silk dress socks stuck to the toes with dried blood. Chance looked on the verge of fainting. Graver poured warm water in a pail and eased his foot into it. As the cracks opened and released the material, he whimpered. Graver searched the room for bandages and finally settled on a mouse-chewed shirt from a box of clothes on the shelf.

As they thawed, the toes swelled and broke open, oozing yellow fluid Graver sponged away.

"Whiskey in my saddlebag by the bed," the lawyer whispered.

Graver dragged the bag to the middle of the room. He put a hand inside and his fingers touched a smooth glass surface. He was about to remove it when he heard a whisper of cloth behind him, and Dulcinea cried out, "No!" as a blow to the back of his head drove him to the floor and another to the side dropped him into darkness.

Graver peered up at the man's face from the floor. It had an odd glow in the candlelight. His handsome features transformed, as if they were melting in the heat of a brain fever or in madness. His mouth twisted and puckered, his eyes shrank and gleamed as they darted from one side of the room to the other, his high, flat brow rose and fell as if in argument with voices other than those in the room. For almost the first time, Graver was afraid. He was woozy from the blows and had to squint to focus. He tried to move, and discovered his hands and feet were bound with strips of blanket. Dulcinea was tied to a chair. Blood on her mouth indicated she'd been hit. Graver thought something must have broken in Chance's mind, and he was getting into the heat of it. The knife on the table worried him.

At first Chance limped around the small room, stopping to examine the walls here and there. Suddenly, he stopped and leaned close until his nose nearly touched the wall, then tapped it with a long, elegant forefinger.

"Ah, we've come to an intersection, a crossroads if you will. I knew there was a reason we met in this godforsaken place. A force of the universe has drawn us together in one of life's storms." As he mused, his face relaxed and softened, and instead of melting, it seemed to stage itself. His pale eyelashes sparkled with the flickering light from the candles he'd placed around the room.

"Perhaps you're wondering what I'm speaking about, Mrs. Bennett?" When Dulcinea didn't acknowledge him, he hobbled to the table and picked up the knife. Graver tensed and tried to wrench his hands apart, to stretch and tear the cloth that held him. The lawyer grabbed Dulcinea's hair from behind and yanked her head back. Placing the point of the blade at her cheek, he drew a drop of blood. Her eyes went wild and a low moan rose in her throat. Graver kicked and tried to tear the strips of old blanket that held his feet. It gave only slightly, so he worked on his hands, brought them to his mouth and chewed at the fibers. He could taste the must of mice and years of use in the wool, and it held like iron against his grinding teeth.

The lawyer leaned over, stroked her cheek and neck with the flat of the blade, and pushed his hand down her shirtfront and rubbed her breasts. Dulcinea couldn't suppress the gasp, and stared straight ahead with hatred in her eyes. Graver gritted his teeth and tried to move the strips down to his ankles, where maybe he could slide them off his feet. Chance seemed to sense the motion, and his head jerked around. He frowned. Graver closed his eyes and lay still. Chance sat in the other chair beside the table. "It's a long night out here, isn't it? Don't worry" — he glanced at Graver — "I'm not going to kill you. I thought we'd talk first, then we'll get to what I need. A certain set of papers to be signed. I tried, but I'm terrible at forgery." He tapped the blade on the stack of pages, then paused as if deep in thought, spread his arms, and bowed slightly. "I apologize for the sparseness of my rooms, but I haven't been myself of late, and these reduced circumstances are, well, merely transitory. You understand. Great fortunes take time and one must go through trials and deprivations and —" He glanced at Dulcinea with the trail of blood on her cheek. Graver stared at the fire, considered rolling over and thrusting his feet in the flames to burn off the bonds but worried his clothes would catch fire, too. He couldn't risk leaving Dulcinea alone with this man.

"Let me tell you a story. It all began at

Wounded Knee." He softly stroked the side of his jaw with the flat of the blade as if petting a cat. His eyes softened with nostalgia, his jaw relaxed, and his face took on the creaseless countenance of boyhood.

"It was my first time to the West, 1890. I was in the employ of the Earl of Manset, the first son of the Duke of Sullywood, meaning he would succeed to the title and ownership of the estate, which would make him the second-largest landowner in Britain after the Crown. You can see why every measure was taken to ensure his safety on his safari through the West. We may have won the War of Independence, but we still have to accommodate royalty whenever it pokes its head into the provinces. At least that was his belief, and I wasn't about to dissuade him. At the time I was rather at the end of a certain rope. My parents had sailed away to find a fortune and soon enough I was an orphan casting about for opportunity, and he presented himself one evening. Fortune shines on her favored children, I say."

He stopped and stared into the fire, rubbing the knife blade with his thumb. Graver thought if he freed his feet he could jump him, bring him down.

"I didn't know anything about the West,

so I read the dime novels and true-life stories and decided it would be perfect. Few laws and fewer authorities to get in my way. With luck, we would find gold, too. Off we went. We shot every living thing. The young earl killing, skinning, beheading, stuffing, and sending his bounty home to decorate the great houses that would soon be his. Imagine the horror that awaited his relations once he filled their walls with his kills. Finally, there was nothing left that we hadn't shot, eaten, mounted, or cast aside. Still, there was a certain restlessness about the young man. A small, slender figure, he seemed determined to force his personality upon every person or creature he encountered, and that's a delicate way of saying it."

The lawyer stood before them, waving his gun. "I don't think I've enjoyed myself so much in a long time. I'll tell you about it, a tale to pass the time on a cold winter's eve, a story that begins, 'Once upon a time' and ends with 'All the king's horses and all the king's men couldn't put her back together again.' "

His eyes reflected the flames of the fire as it took a new log and hungrily ate it.

"I was doing what men do in war." Chance shrugged and opened his palms to declare his innocence. "I certainly didn't see the child or I never — Well, I'm not a monster, am I?" He turned to Dulcinea, and the irony of her bound and bloody form seemed to dawn on him. "Point taken," he said with a sigh.

"The young earl proved an increasingly difficult person after that encounter with the Indians, and nothing could satisfy him unless he, well, I don't need to go into more details and make you uncomfortable, Dulcinea."

Chance limped back and forth, his hands thrust in his pockets, head up, eyes darting as if he reenacted the battle in the small cabin space. Graver hoped the man would weave closer so he could trip him or use his tied legs to push him into the fireplace.

"Something had to be done. There were too many bodies, too many damaged women, young girls even, he didn't discriminate. It was all his fault!" Chance scrubbed his face with his hands.

"He expected me to participate, begged me, then ordered me, threatening to cut off the funds we shared equally by that time. I couldn't have that!" He looked at them, eyes searching for sympathy. A piece of burning pine in the fire suddenly cracked and hissed and the sound jerked him around. When he turned back, his expression had darkened, and Graver took a quick breath.

"Turn us loose, Chance. There's no reason to do this." He spoke calmly to not provoke him.

"You don't know me very well, Mr. Graver, or you wouldn't point out the obvious. I need something from Mrs. Bennett, and I need to convince her of the seriousness of my intent." He gazed around the cabin, then picked up his chair and brought it to the fire so he could sit in the warmth facing them.

Dulcinea sighed. Both men startled and looked at her. "Is this all a plan to convince me to sign with the gas and oil people?"

Chance smiled and shook his head. "That was my original thought. But you decided to take matters into your hands. You had your cowboy here and the deeds to the ranches with Drum dead. I had to come up with another. How do you like it so far?"

"Things can go back to the way they were," she said. Graver heard the desperation in her voice. "You can represent my interests. I'll even put you on retainer."

"I will tell you the rest of the story now so you understand." He smiled, congenial now, eyes light.

"You see, I dropped a most precious keepsake that night at Wounded Knee." He

658

looked at Graver. "I met you after the massacre, remember? Your husband, too, Dulcinea. I guess none of us have the high ground here, do we?" He poked Graver in the ribs with his foot.

"I hadn't known exactly where I'd lost it, the locket with the pictures of my beloved parents, not until I was at the trading post on Rosebud last spring, and there was a certain Indian girl there, well, not a girl, rather a young lady named Star, and I happened to spy it around her neck." He pivoted in the chair, crossed his legs, leaned his elbow on his knee, and propped his chin in his hand like a schoolboy studying the fire.

"I was surprised, of course, and curious as to how she came by it, but I didn't want to scare her, so I agreed to meet and discuss it. It took three meetings before I was able to ascertain the story — what a relief! She hadn't told a soul. She had been there that night, with the earl and me — witnessed the whole tragic event. Though I wondered at her lack of feeling. I could hardly have worn the keepsake of my mother's murderer, but then, Indians are Indians the world over. In that the earl was correct. Too bad." Chance shook his head. "Too bad he didn't live to meet her."

Dulcinea struggled in her chair. "It was you! You killed them!"

He held up a hand. "Please, allow me to finish my story. I've never had the opportunity to share it with anyone, and I'm receiving a certain pleasure from the telling."

CHAPTER FORTY-EIGHT

Graver knew Chance was going to kill them when he was done. He brought his hands to rest under his chin and gnawed again at the edge of the cloth. Even a small tear would weaken it.

"I lured her into the hills, well, took her to a place we could conduct our discussion in private. Can you believe my luck, though? I'd only begun burying her when my horse whinnied and I hid, just as your husband trotted up. Down he swings, walks right over to the girl's body, leaving me no choice at all — I had to shoot him." He scrubbed his face again with a low moan. "I was ready to convince him to join the oil and gas venture, too. Terrible luck.

"My quiet place turns out to be more like a county fair. Before I can bury the girl and J.B., I see *another* rider coming over the hill in the distance, so I decide there's only so many people a man can kill in one morning before someone hears the shots and brings a bigger gun. I slip away. Then I'm guessing it's you who comes up, Mr. Graver, followed by one of the Bennett boys — Cullen or Hayward? My money's on Hayward, am I right?" He peered at Graver and nodded. "Thought so. Cullen hated his father too much to shoot a man he suspected of killing him."

Chance stood, pulled out his revolver. "Rose found the necklace. Star's sister. Again, my unbelievable luck." He paused and waved the gun in the air. "It doesn't really matter. I'll be dealing with her when the time comes. You understand, Graver. A man has experiences in war like no other. You fall through the world and then bang, you're back again!"

He aimed the gun at Graver and shot him in the thigh. Graver's leg went numb first, followed by a stabbing pain, and he gritted his teeth against it.

Dulcinea yelled and jerked against the strips of cloth that held her to the chair. His body was tense with shock and pain as blood pooled on the floor beneath him.

"Now let's chat. You can see the problem with me acting as your lawyer when I'm supposed to be dead. No, I'm afraid it's not going to work. But don't worry, I have another plan."

"It was you stabbed Drum," Dulcinea said, her tone flat.

"I tried to persuade him to work with me, but we couldn't come to an agreement, so he had to go. Lucky you.

"I need you to sign your mineral and surface rights over to me, Dulcinea. You won't need them. I've decided to let you keep the land, but I need those rights so we can drill this whole region. Oil and gas. Can you imagine how rich I'll be? If you choose, we'll be married, and I can keep my name clear of any scandal from recent episodes. That's how we'll think of them in years to come, isn't it, my darling?"

Dulcinea struggled to reply, and Graver swung his legs at Chance's chair with the intent to tip it over. Chance sensed the motion and kicked his wounded leg. Graver fought to remain conscious. "Try that again, I'll gut shoot you."

He turned back to Dulcinea and stroked her bloody cheek with the back of his hand. "You were separated from your husband for so long, I doubt there's any feelings left to be awkward between us, are there?"

She shook her head. "I thought you were dead. I was going to contact you to sell the rights, but you died." She looked puzzled.

"Who did they bury?"

Chance laughed and shook his head. "Damned if I know. Man stood in front of my buggy as I was leaving after taking care of Drum in the alley, so I ran him down. I'll tell you, getting him out of his clothes, into mine, well, it was no Sunday picnic. I did a fair job, though. Fools buried him as me. And that, my dear, is the luck that always saves me." He bowed.

"You surprise me," she said. "How are you going to explain coming back from the dead?"

"Mistakes were made. They buried the wrong man. I need a few weeks unhampered to put all the pieces together. I could disappear for a time, let everyone forget me, then take the signed papers to Denver and work directly with the company from there. No one here the wiser, especially if the last two heirs meet with the kind of violent accidents that seem to plague your family." Chance cocked his head and raised his brows. "I should be insulted that you imagined this cowboy" — he nodded at Graver — "had the wit to accomplish what I have."

There was a timid knock on the door, then it pushed open in a burst of wind-driven snow. As if someone was still deciding whether or not to enter, the snow swirled into the room and the candles fluttered.

"Hello?" a timid voice called.

"Come in, for heaven's sake!" Chance shouted.

It was too much coincidence that Rose appeared, snow crusted as Chance shut the door behind her. She must have followed him, Graver thought. Did she think he murdered her sister? He was so light-headed from the blood loss, nothing made much sense.

He struggled, and felt a slight give in the strips around his feet, pulled his legs again and felt the cloth give another few inches. He tried his hands and heard a tiny tear.

"Mr. Graver's uncomfortable, and you need to sit by the fire, Rose, so why don't you drag him out of the way." Graver understood that the man was clearing a killing floor.

"He's too heavy," Rose said. "Help me."

Chance laughed. "Unlikely. Leave him there. Be careful you don't sit in his blood, though."

Rose squatted with her back to the fire.

"But first, Rose, I know you've been curious as to what happened to your mother. Just like your sister. It's not enough to survive with you people. You won't let a thing die, will you?"

"You killed my sister," Rose said, no inflection in her voice, her eyes on the fresh blood that pooled around her.

"It was you people and your Ghost Dance. I'm not going through that whole story again, so yes, I strangled her. Happy?"

He stood over her, hands on his hips. "I never understand why people want every last detail. She's gone. *Finie.* Done." He chopped at the air with his hands. "Now let me get on with my tale. Please." He took a deep breath and brushed back his hair. When he began again, his tone was one of exaggerated patience.

"First, you find the locket with the photos of my parents. Yes, I saw Hayward looking at it. Your sister Star paraded it around. I had to put a stop to it. It doesn't want to stay put, though. You have it now?"

Rose clutched the front of her shirt.

"Good. When we've completed our transaction, I'll have it back. There aren't any more of you, are there? I trust Lily will never know what happened to her mother, aunt, and grandmother. I'd hate to have dealings with another of your family. Three's enough."

His eyes twinkled as he reached into his pocket and brought out a little tanned leather drawstring pouch with what appeared to be a brown button at the bottom. Upon closer inspection, Graver realized with horror that it was a nipple, withered hard as bone. "Do I need a new change purse?" He dangled it in front of Rose, who kept her eyes down.

"Now where's my necklace?" He reached in her calico blouse, but it wasn't around her neck. "Where is it?"

"We have to trade," she said, her eyes on the pouch now.

Chance pretended to toss it into the fire, and then revealed it was still in his hand. "Just playing with you. I know how much Indians love a trade. Okay, my family for yours."

She stood and opened her hand to reveal the chain and locket.

He snatched it, and then tossed the pouch in the fire. Rose's shoulders slumped as she watched the flames take the last of her mother's flesh.

"You bastard," Dulcinea growled.

He frowned. "Not very polite, Mrs. Bennett."

He opened the locket, clicked it closed, and held the chain up to the light. "You Indians don't like gold, do you? I'm beginning to see your point." He rubbed his chin. "So much would've been different if I hadn't dropped this twice. Almost as if Mama and Papa wanted me to be punished for what I did." He slipped the locket in his vest.

Graver heard Chance's voice drop, bemused. He glanced at Dulcinea.

Chance turned to face the others. "It's always an interesting problem, what to do with hostages. You see, you're held by them as much as you hold them. The question is who can let go first. Because that person wins." He smiled and limped across the room and back, appraising each of them.

"You didn't really think I could marry you, did you?" He stopped beside Dulcinea and lifted her chin with a finger. "I was indulging myself. I do that, especially when I spend too much time alone, as I have of late. If the earl were here, we'd concoct an entertainment with you, but I'm afraid I'm growing weary of this business. As soon as the storm abates, I need to be off. You understand that I can't leave you alive." He made another circuit of the room, took the time to peer out the window and place an ear to the wall. "Still blowing," he announced.

Dulcinea said, "I'll sign. If you let us live." Chance grabbed the knife from the table, sliced through the rags holding her arms, and dragged the chair so she sat before the papers. He uncapped the bottle of ink and handed her the pen, keeping his eye on the other two. Dulcinea dipped the pen, scratched at the edge of the paper he'd used to practice their signatures, dipped and tried again, this time producing ink. He tapped his forefinger, indicating where she should sign, and she leaned over the paper. Despite the wind and crackling fire, the slow scratch of her signature whispered along the cabin walls.

As she finished, and he leaned down to inspect it, Rose sprang to her feet, pounced on his back, and pressed her skinning knife against his throat. They staggered and fell, breaking Dulcinea's chair into pieces. Chance grabbed at Rose's arms, and she steadied the tip of the blade with her left hand, hacking and sawing at his throat as if castrating a bull. Dulcinea flew at him and struck him in the chest to no effect, while his arms flailed and dropped and his struggle against the knife slowed. Then with one last burst, he yanked at Rose's arms, pried one away and loosened the other. Dulcinea hit him in the face with the chair's leg, which only enraged him more. Graver slid closer, drew back his legs, and kicked him in the knee, dropping him, his shirt an apron of blood from the deepening cut as Rose rode his back.

"You can't kill me!" he rasped, a bright bubble at the corner of his mouth.

Rose leaned close and whispered in his ear, "Why not? You're already dead." Her right hand on the hilt, her left, gloved in red, wrapped around the blade's point, she hauled hard on the knife. There was a pop and a bright hissing spray. "Hestovatohkeo'o," she murmured as he fell forward into the blooming pool of his own blood.

CHAPTER FORTY-NINE

Dulcinea sat on the porch with a cup of coffee and her first attempt at doughnuts. The pastry was so heavy it thunked against the saucer after she took a bite.

J.B. was gone, she knew from the shifting gravity of the air, a missing weight, as it was when someone left a room, like a veil torn for an instant, and a sharpness appeared around the objects and people, then slowly dissolved again.

Despite the early blizzard, the winter had been mild with the right amount of snow and then spring rains brought the hills alive again with wildflowers and new grass. She woke early on these fine May mornings to watch her two mares graze with their foals in the pasture. One of the old cottonwoods behind the barn fell when the rains softened the ground in spring and settled across the creek, forming a natural bench at the far end that Hayward would lie on late afternoons when the work was done. The small purple knobs on the mulberry trees offered a fine harvest and a sparrow hopped down a branch a few feet, tested one, then another, and let them drop to the ground where more trees would sprout. In years to come a large grove of mulberry trees would provide pleasure to children and grandchildren, who would take handfuls of ripe berries and smear their faces and arms and run to show the adults. There would be Bennetts, as well as the families of the men who worked among them. J.B. always said they would prosper, and as she watched her son and Graver work horses that evening, she believed him.

Rose sat beside her on the porch while, in the corral, Graver showed Hayward how to halterbreak a filly without roughness. Her son let Graver rest an arm across his shoulders as they watched the long-legged bay filly gambol about wearing her new halter. When she had finally explained to her son about his grandfather's bargains with both J.B. and her, he took a few days then decided to try to forgive.

Some Horses lifted Lily onto the spotted pony's back and led her up and down the barnyard while Rose smiled at her daughter's cajoling to be turned loose.

"She needs her own horse," Dulcinea said.

"I'm sure she'll have it, too, with all these men spoiling her," she said with a laugh. Rose was her friend, the bravest woman she knew. They never spoke of it, what happened at the line shack. Rose's family lived in the foreman's house in the winter, and spent summer in the tipi behind the house.

Rose placed her fingertips on Dulcinea's arm. "I have to go home," she said. "It's my sister. It's time for her to go home, too." Her eyes filled, and she bit her lip and looked out across the ranch yard to the hills beyond. "Jerome will come if Lily can stay with you. It won't be long."

Dulcinea reached over and squeezed her hand. "She'll be so spoiled you'll be sorry," she said. Then she hesitated, not wanting to make a mistake because she didn't fully understand the Sioux ways, and said, "I hope your sister finds peace on the red road with Wakan Tanka."

Rose nodded. "She already has."

They sat in silence as the men finished with the horses, and the hands drifted to their bunkhouse. Rose went to meet her husband and daughter, and Dulcinea stood on the porch, watched as Graver and Hayward started for the house with the gait of tired, satisfied men who've worked a hard, long day.

Graver had moved into the main house, and slept in the extra room upstairs for now. The past months brought her the strength that was in him, his firm hand under her arm, his back broad enough for the work that lay ahead. He would not replace J.B., but she felt sure he would stand beside him someday.

Dulcinea could not leave this land. She finally understood how the wind out here made a place for itself in your ear, in your mind, and in your heart, stilling your thoughts, making everything you see one vast wholeness: the swan gliding across the silent marsh, the mossy turtles climbing like ancient men out of the water, their claws gripping the soil with great effort to drag themselves despite the tangled water plants that dragged their yellow-scaled legs back, their ragged beaks parted with effort. She couldn't think without the Sand Hills wind hushing the great world around her as she pushed herself into its embrace. Maybe a bad thing never died, as the men were fond of saying, and good lived but for a moment. This was a thing she could accept.

In early November, she had been able to ship cattle and pay the men some of what she owed. They'd made it through the winter, though money was short. She watched as Hayward led J.B.'s chestnut out of the barn. They were teaching the horse to work cattle, and Graver showed her son how to ride in concert with the animal, not against it. She saw that was the way a person must move through the world, while across the hills, the evening fog drifted like an exhaled breath and the peepers began their rhythmic chirring music as the night horses pulled the dark curtain across the sky until they slept and awakened once more, rising like dreamers out of the mist to claim the world again.

REFERENCES

Jensen, Richard E., R. Eli Paul, and John E. Carter. *Eyewitness at Wounded Knee.* Lincoln: University of Nebraska Press, 1991.

Lavin, Stephen J., Fred M. Shelley, and J. Clark Archer. *Atlas of the Great Plains.* Lincoln: University of Nebraska Press, 2011.

Peavy, Linda, and Ursula Smith. *Pioneer Women: The Lives of Women on the Frontier.* Rowayton, CT: Saraband, 1996.

ABOUT THE AUTHOR

Jonis Agee has been praised by the *New York Times Book Review* as "a gifted poet of that dark lushness in the heart of the American landscape." She is the award-winning author of twelve books, including the *New York Times* Notable Books of the Year *Sweet Eyes* and *Strange Angels*. Her awards include the John Gardner Fiction Award, the George Garrett Award, a National Endowment for the Arts grant in fiction, a Loft-McKnight Award, a Loft-McKnight Award of Distinction, and two Nebraska Book Awards. A native of Nebraska, Agee teaches at the University of Nebraska–Lincoln.